MW01001217

GODDAMNED FREAKY MONSTERS

The Tome of Bill

Part 5

RICK GUALTIERI

Copyright © 2014 Rick Gualtieri

No part of this book may be reproduced or transmitted in any
form or by any means, electronic or mechanical, including
photocopying, recording, or any information storage and retrieval
system, without prior written permission of the author. Your
support of author's rights is greatly appreciated.

All characters in this novel are fictitious. Any resemblance to actual
persons, living or dead, is purely coincidental. The use of any real
company and/or product names is for literary effect only. All other
trademarks and copyrights are the property of their respective
owners..

Edited by Megan Harris at www.mharriseditor.com
Cover by Mallory Rock at www.malloryrock.com
Proofread by BZ Hercules at: www.bzhercules.com

Published by Freewill press
Freewill Press
PO Box 175
Dunellen, NJ, 08812
www.freewill-press.com

ISBN: 978-1-940415-21-5

Contents

For Mom, even though I know she really doesn't like the title of this book.

* * *

Special thanks to: Alissa, Solace, James, Jonathan, Simon, Jason, & Sheila. Thank you all so much for helping me polish this story. I appreciate you more than I can express in mere words.

Me, Myself, and I

ARISE, FREEWILL!!
Ugh. There are few things that can fuck up a good night's sleep quite like the goddamned alarm clock going off.

I stretched and sat up, feeling as if I'd slept for weeks. A yawn escaped my lips and I blinked several times as my body continued *booting up*. Once my head was clear, I put my glasses on - snapping things into focus.

Before it could go off again, I smacked the button on the clock - giving it a good whack to drive the point home. Jeez, what a stupid alarm. Who the hell would program something like that into a clock, anyway? It had to have been my roommates fucking with me...*again*. The dickheads seemed to have a hard-on for doing so.

Oh well, it was probably time to get my ass moving. It's not like the work day was going to start without me.

I hopped right into my morning routine, pausing only momentarily as I tried to think of what was on the docket for the day. Surely there was some fire to be put out - a project due that was probably giving Jim, my manager at Hopskotchgames.com, a near aneurysm. It was the same thing week after week. Sure, it could get annoying, but there was a certain comfort in the routine of it all.

The only problem was that I had no idea which project needed tending to. Was it *Farm Fury*? No, we launched that already. Maybe *Birds of War*? Could be *Doctor Dexter's Daring Dash* - that one was coming soon...I think.

Odd. Usually, I was pretty spot on for my schedule, but for the life of me, I had no clue what I was supposed to be working on. Hell, come to think of it, I had no idea what *day* it even was. It could have been the freaking weekend for all I knew.

But then, why the alarm clock? Oh well. It would probably sort itself out as the morning progressed.

Trying to ignore the concern that nagged at me, I grabbed my clothes and headed toward the bathroom. Hopefully, it would be unoccupied and there would still be some hot water left. Surely a shower would help clear my head.

* * *

Just as I sat on the couch, a bowl of Cap'n Crunch in hand, a sense of déjà vu hit me. That was stupid. I mean, *of course* I'd done this before. I lived in this place, for Christ's sake. I'd probably eaten hundreds of bowls of tooth-rotting cereal sitting right in this spot.

I shook it off as part of the general paranoia that had become a part of my existence ever since dying and rising from the proverbial grave as a vampire. The supernatural world was a fucked-up place, and it seemed that I couldn't take a dump without some entity deciding that I needed to be vaporized. Such things tended to mess with one's outlook on life after a while.

Well, fuck that shit. The worries of the underworld could wait until after I'd had my breakfast.

I flipped on the TV, enjoying the rare moment of normalcy. Well, that wasn't entirely true. Hell, a disturbing amount of my life remained mundane. There was my job, for starters - believe me, becoming one of the undead hadn't been an instant lottery ticket to riches. There were also my roommates...

Speaking of which, where the hell were they?

I guess it made sense that Tom had either left early for his job in Manhattan or maybe slept over at his girlfriend's place, but Ed worked from home like me. There wasn't anything requiring him to be in the office today, at least that I could remember, and last night was...

I paused, a spoonful of cereal halfway to my mouth. Last night was what? That was a blank too. It couldn't have been too memorable. I mean, heck, the apartment wasn't even close to being trashed. At the very least, I should've had some remembrance of what show I'd watched or video game I'd played, but there was nothing.

Don't get me wrong. I didn't seem to be suffering from amnesia or any bullshit like that. The important stuff was all there: who I was, my job, where I lived -

that kind of shit. It was just the recent past that eluded me for some reason.

I had to admit - it was starting to get odd.

Maybe we had all gone...

Come to think of it, when was the last time I had even *seen* my roommates?

No, that was stupid. We were the best of friends. We hung out all the time...even when the forces of evil were trying to collectively ass-fuck us.

Weird. Maybe I drank a few bottles of overly skunked beer last night and it was screwing with my brain. That didn't sound so farfetched. If so, my vampire metabolism would take care of it as the day went on, hopefully allowing the fog to lift from my head.

Yeah, I'd let things sort themselves out. There was probably no point in worrying.

I bit down with a satisfying crunch, then began scanning through the channels, hoping to find something worth watching.

Not wanting to burden my soul with *Good Morning America* or similar insipid morning shit, I quickly skipped to the cable channels - finally stopping on what looked to be some sort of action flick.

There was a battle taking place on a rooftop. Multi-colored lightning flashed in the background as the combatants recklessly tore into each other - gotta love low-budget sci-fi. Yeah, this had promise.

A glowing blonde angel was trashing the bad guys in the middle of it all. Damn, she was hot. Hopefully, this flick had some nudity in it. That wouldn't exactly be a horrible way to start the day.

Another character, this one decked out in a SpongeBob backpack of all things, hopped onto the screen and began similarly kicking ass. She looked to be of roughly schoolgirl age. Maybe this was a Japanese fetish flick. Talk about a country that was seriously fucked in the head when it came to entertainment.

I was about to change the channel and see what else was playing when my hand paused on the remote. The walking Nickelodeon advertisement was tackled from the side and dragged screaming off the edge. It should have been hilarious. I mean, seriously, I've never seen a Wilhelm scream scene that didn't crack me up. Something about this bothered me, though.

That déjà vu feeling hit me again like a brick to the forehead.

No idea why, but the whole thing felt oddly familiar, and not in a good way. Sadness filled me at the poor little character's demise. As the rest of the scene unfolded before me, I actually had to reach up and wipe a few tears from my eyes.

I quickly glanced around, making sure neither of my roommates was present to see my sensitive side coming out to play. I'd never hear the end of that. After a few moments - satisfied that I was still alone - I turned back to see how things played out.

The battle seemed to be over. The angel stood there, victorious. She was still wearing too much clothing for my personal gratification, but nevertheless, I was tempted to stand up and cheer for her. Then I noticed one of the bad guys was still alive and approaching from her blind side.

I actually shouted, "No!" at the screen as he pulled out a ridiculously large gun and pointed it at the blonde Xena's head. A bullet to her face ended the showdown.

I stared transfixed, wondering how the director could allow such a downer of an ending. Asshole should've been fired. Things weren't quite over yet, though. Apparently in need of a fucked-up finale to finish things off with, a bad CGI monster - some kind of Hulk rip-off - jumped into frame from out of nowhere and began tearing shit up.

Okay, this was getting a little too *out there,* even for me - which was strange in and of itself. Normally, I enjoyed fucked-up foreign movies, but this one had left a bad taste in my mouth for some reason.

I clicked off the television and placed my bowl down, my appetite gone too.

Standing up, I turned my thoughts toward work. Heck, after watching that shit, I was actually looking forward to it. Maybe a few hours of coding would slap me out of my funk. I still had no idea exactly what I was supposed to be programming, but maybe that didn't matter. Hell, worst-case scenario was I would wing it - maybe take a stab at creating something from scratch. It's not like Jim would say no to some extra...

A knock at the door interrupted my train of thought.

I waited for a moment, making sure I hadn't imagined it, but then it came again. Hmm, kind of early for visitors.

Not thinking too much of it, I stood up and walked over - assuming one of my wayward roommates had locked himself out again. In the back of my head, thoughts of wizards, vampire assassins, and angry Sasquatches played out, but I dismissed them all. Most of those, especially that last group, probably wouldn't have bothered knocking. Besides, I lived in the middle of Brooklyn - not exactly prime Bigfoot country.

Chuckling at my own paranoia, I reached for the knob. As the door opened, though, the sound instantly died in my throat. For a moment, I could do nothing but gape in stunned silence.

The person who stood there was quite familiar to me. I'd have known him anywhere, even with the black eyes and razor sharp fangs.

How could I not? It was me.

Yeah, my day had just gotten a wee bit stranger.

Conversation with a Madman

Alternate-me elbowed his way past. "Get the fuck out of my way."

Maybe it was the shock of being told off by myself, but I obeyed and stepped aside. I mean, he...err I...obviously lived here.

"Make yourself at home," I muttered. Yeah, this day was definitely ratcheting up the weirdness points.

My duplicate sat down on the couch and picked up the remote. "Grab me a beer."

To my great surprise, I actually walked to the kitchen and opened the fridge. It was there that I paused to consider things. Ignoring that the other me was obviously a pushy bastard, I didn't have a single clue as to who or what he really was. Obviously, I was me. I'd been Bill Ryder my entire life and beyond. Maybe this guy was a...

"I'm not a doppelganger," he said from the couch. That was a bit creepy. Couldn't those alien pods from...

"*Invasion of the Body Snatchers* was just a movie, numb-nuts. Now hurry the fuck up with that beer before I kick your ass."

Well, that was just rude. This fucker obviously didn't know who I was. I'd stood toe to toe with some freaky monsters in the past...much scarier shit than, well, *me*. There was no way I was going to be intimated by a dorky looking...uh, make that *devilishly handsome* opponent such as him.

I pulled a Samuel Smith from the fridge - wondering for just a moment when we'd started stocking the good stuff - and popped the cap. I raised it to my lips. Fuck this guy if he thought...

"Don't even think of backwashing into that."

Goddamn, was this guy Uri Geller wearing a Bill mask or something? This was getting odder by the moment. Rather than further antagonizing either of us, I walked over and handed him the beer - resisting the urge to spit in it.

"Do you mind?" I asked sarcastically, indicating the chair.

"It's a free country." He took a long pull, then clicked the remote. The exact same scene from earlier - the end of that disturbing movie - played on the TV. "All right. This part always makes me laugh."

I sat down, making sure I was out of arm's reach. Just because I wasn't all that afraid of him didn't mean I was going to be stupid about it. The act wasn't lost on my other self, who grinned - showing off his fangs.

"I don't suppose you could put those things away."

"You suppose correct."

"Fine. Be that way. Listen, *Bill*, I don't know what kind of bullshit this..."

His eyes flashed dangerously for a moment - pretty impressive stuff, considering his lack of pupils. "Don't call me that."

"But if you're supposed..."

"That's your name, not mine."

"Then what the fuck should I call you?"

"Think about it real hard. I'm sure it'll come to you."

What the hell was that supposed to mean? Did he want to be called William? Perhaps *Mr. Ryder?* Fuck that shit. I couldn't even get my bank to call me that. There's no way I was going to refer to this asshole as mister just because he thought he had some rad evil look going on.

Wait...*evil?*

Oh, fuck.

Some days I am a goddamned moron.

"I can see the light of comprehension dawning in your eyes," he said, chuckling.

"Dr. Death?"

"And Bingo was his name-o."

* * *

"So you're really that...uh...*thing* inside of me?"

"The world lost a great poet when you decided to go into programming."

"I expected you to be a bit scarier."

"And I expected you to be less of a dim bulb."

This was going nowhere fast. Talking smack at each other had its amusement value, but wasn't the most useful tactic for figuring out why the beast inside of me...wasn't. If he was who he claimed - and I wasn't quite ready to buy into his crap just yet - then he was my uber-scary half, the side effect of being the vampire Freewill. He was the thing that reared its ugly head when I got majorly pissed and turned me into something akin to the more monstrous versions of the Dr. Jekyll and Mister Hyde retellings.

That made no sense, though. It wasn't like he was someone who stepped out of my closet when I got angry. When I was in the midst of unbearable rage - or pain, let's not forget that - my body somehow transformed. My power would increase umpteen times, but my conscious mind would completely blank out. When I finally woke back up, there was usually blood, a lot of it. Needless to say, I tried to keep my temper in check around my friends.

In the comics, the Hulk had guys like Thor to smack him down if he got too uppity. As far as I was aware, though, the only thing that could stop me was...

"The Icon?" he asked. "Yeah, that didn't work out so well."

"Stop doing that. It's fucking creepy." I paused for a moment to consider things. "How exactly *are* you doing that? I didn't realize mind reader was on my resume."

"It isn't."

"So then how..."

"Come on, you can do it."

"If you can't..."

"Right on the tip of your tongue, isn't it?"

Holy shit. Nah, it couldn't be. That only happened on...

"Lousy television shows when they want to show the abstract concept of thought?" he asked idly.

"We're in my mind, aren't we?"

"Technically *our* mind, but yep. Give the man a cigar!"

* * *

"So..." I was unsure of where to start. If we were in my mind, a dubious concept at best, then who was manning the store, so to speak?

"Why don't you just try asking, genius?" evil alternate me offered. "Christ, in the time you spend thinking rather than doing, whole civilizations could rise and fall. I mean, fuck, you couldn't even ask one girl out on a date."

"I was going to..."

"No, you weren't. Let's not bullshit ourselves here. You'd have pined for her until such time that she married some other dude. Then you'd have spent the next ten years being fucking miserable and wondering where it all went wrong when the answer was blindingly..."

"Shouldn't you have a goatee?"

"Huh?"

I smirked, having finally caught my asshole inner-self by surprise. "I thought all evil duplicates were supposed to have goatees."

"Remember that mustache you tried to grow in high school...certain that the chicks would dig your manly facial hair?"

"Yeah, it wound up looking really fucking stupid."

"Same principle applies. Now, do you have anything real to ask, or should I just kick your ass out of here and get back to my show?"

"You're kicking me out of my own apartment?"

"Technically this is *my* apartment. No, that's not true. It's more my cage. You've just been keeping it warm for me."

"Cage?"

"Yeah. It's where you keep me chained most of the time while you're busy fucking everything up."

I looked around, doubtful.

"What?" He shrugged. "Just because I'm a prisoner doesn't mean I have to suffer for it."

"So if this is your cage, then what am I doing here?"

"You don't know?"

"No idea."

Parallel universe Bill put his feet up and took another long pull on his beer, draining it. He let out a loud belch. "I guess that's not too much of a surprise. That much adrenaline coursing through a brain for that long is sure to fuck up one's short-term memory. Don't worry; I'm sure it'll all come screaming back to you in excruciating clarity...probably at a time when it's least convenient."

"You do realize I have no clue what you're talking about, right?"

"That makes it even more fun. Bottom line is this: we switched places. You willingly gave up control and retreated here. That left me free to take over."

Oh shit, that didn't sound particularly reassuring. The person sitting in front of me wore my face, but if he truly represented what I'd come to call my Dr. Death persona, that meant on the outside, I had become a rampaging hell-beast. Who knew what atrocities I'd committed while he was in charge?

"Yes."

"Yes, what?" I asked.

"We killed a shitload of people."

"Oh, fuck..."

"Although not in the way you think...or that I'd have preferred."

"I'm not following you."

He put the empty bottle down and raised a hand to scratch the back of his head. "You're too much of a pussy to share. I knew there could never be a compromise between us, so I longed for the day you'd willingly give up control. I made a promise to myself that once I became the dominant personality, I wouldn't come back here ever again - no matter what."

"Okay. So why are you?"

"Turns out that old saying about being careful what you wish for is more apt than I would've suspected."

I raised a bemused eyebrow at that.

"What?" he asked, his tone surly.

"It's just funny to hear you waxing philosophical. I thought you were supposed to be a mindless rampaging monster."

"When you're cooped up in solitary, with only limited time for recess, you tend not to waste much breath with the small talk. It's more fun that way too. Speaking of which..." My doppelganger stood and stepped over to me. "It's been a blast chatting, but you really need to get the fuck out of here now." He grabbed my arm and pulled me to my feet.

"Hold on," I protested. "What the hell do you mean?"

"It's simple." He dragged me toward the door. I tried to put on the brakes, but he was a lot stronger than he looked. "That fucker has been torturing me nonstop for months now. I'm tired, plain and simple - not to mention bored out of my fucking skull. I need a break."

"What fucker...and what torture?"

"You'll see...in fact, considering the time, I think you'll see far more than you want to." He chuckled again. "Hell, I might stay awake just long enough to see the expression on our face."

Dr. Death pulled the door open, and I saw that there wasn't a hallway beyond as expected - just a bunch of dark nothingness. What the fuck? I put out my hands and grabbed both sides of the frame to halt my progress. I didn't want to go. It was safe here, familiar. I had no idea what was waiting for me outside. I wasn't sure why I was here to begin with, but there must've been something out there that had caused me to retreat deep inside of myself.

"Have fun, Bill. Oh, and try not to need me too much. As of right now, I am officially on vacation, and I tend to be a sound sleeper."

"Wait..."

But I was too little, too late with my final protest. He gave one last shove and I was propelled forward into the void. The faint sound of a door being slammed shut accompanied me into the darkness.

* * *

"Freewill, it is time."

I opened my eyes and sat up with a start. What the fuck?! The nothingness I'd been floating in immediately receded. What was left in its place wasn't much of an improvement, though.

I was sitting upon what felt like a pile of broken rocks poking me in all sorts of unpleasant ways. Having shards of granite stuck in my ass was all the motivation I needed to clamber to my feet. Looking around, I didn't see much. Everything around me was basically just formless blobs of fuzziness. Where the hell were my glasses?

I reached down to check my pockets, but didn't find them - nor anything else, for that matter.

Not quite willing to believe what my hands were telling me, I looked down at myself. Forget my glasses - where the fuck were my clothes? I was standing there buck-ass naked.

"Ahem."

And I was apparently not alone.

A figure stood about ten feet away, little more than a semi-fuzzy shape against a colorless background. Crossing my fingers that it was friendly, I shuffled forward - stopping dead in my tracks the moment his mismatched eyes came into focus.

Oh, shit.

Standing before me was Alexander the Great, conqueror of the ancient world and leader of the First Coven - the vampire ruling body. His presence was only part of my shock, though. He was naked, too - his muscular form glistening with oil.

What the fuck had I gotten myself into?

A Shock to the System

"Well, this is most disappointing." Alex sighed, standing there as if having his dick out was the most natural thing in the world for him.

"Uh, listen," I stammered, holding my hands up and backing away. "I'm...err...glad to see you, but not *that* glad, if you know what I mean."

"I see our weekly wrestling match will need to be postponed."

Wrestling match? In the nude?

Before I could ask what the fuck was going on, he made an about face and walked away from me - quickly fading out of focus again. I heard the squeal of hinges and then a slam as something heavy was shut. "The Freewill has reverted *again*. Make sure he is made presentable." His voice was heavily muffled, but my sensitive vampire ears made out the annoyed inflection behind his words. "We have a very important guest arriving soon, and I will not tolerate being embarrassed in front of him."

Presentable? Hopefully, that meant they'd at least be giving me a pair of pants. There was something about standing around with my wang swinging in the wind that threw me off my game a bit.

Of course, while clothes would be nice, they still wouldn't begin to answer the all-important question of where the fuck I was.

As I pondered this, that sound of squealing metal came again. Wherever I was, there seemed to be a really heavy door leading into it. Somehow, I had the feeling that it wasn't there for ornamental purposes.

The sound of footsteps reached my ears as the glow of a flickering light approached - damn my nearsightedness. One of these days, I really needed to invest in LASIK.

The leader was holding a torch to light the way. I was able to make out four of them, whoever they were. They finally approached close enough for me to tell they were all wearing black robes with matching hoods. That didn't bode well. Typically, one didn't find room service clad in such attire.

"Uh, hey, guys," I said as they spread out to surround me. "I don't suppose you have a spare pair of boxer shorts."

"Your glorious form is requested, Freewill," one of them replied in a German accent.

Before I could ask what that meant, the four of them produced long metallic rods from out of their robes. Electricity arced at the ends of them.

Oh, crap. I had a feeling that whatever shock I'd felt at waking up here was going to be nothing compared to what they had in mind.

* * *

As far as leisure activities were concerned, being tazed was about one of the least fun things I could imagine. Go figure, though. Being tazed *while naked* was even less enjoyable.

I immediately crumpled into a little ball of crispy-fried pain as all four of them assaulted me in unison. Opening my mouth to scream did nothing, save provide one of them with the opportunity to stick his cattle prod into it, leaving me with the wonderful taste of burning tongue.

They moved in and continued in their zapping, convincing me once and for all to never date anyone with an electric dildo fetish. There was no way for me to cover my exposed flesh from their attacks mainly because I was currently nothing *but* exposed flesh.

Again and again they hit me, each time picking a new spot to charbroil. My consciousness, reclaimed only moments earlier, was reduced to nothing but pain and the smell of my own cooked skin. Why was this happening? Was this some sort of punishment? Had my past transgressions against the vampire nation been found out?

After a few more moments of electrocution, none of it mattered because I could no longer form coherent thoughts. My waking mind ebbed as I once more began to retreat into myself. A red haze of pain and rage descended over my blurry vision.

I knew what it meant.

In the past, I'd fought against it - managed to fend off the beast - but then something had changed. I'd given up for some reason, allowing the creature inside free rein. Now it seemed as if my time back in the real world would be a short one. I was about to hand over the keys to the castle again. Without knowing the hows or whys of my torture, I had nothing to grasp onto to keep me fighting against it.

Long moments passed, and I continued to have the shit shocked out of me. Nothing changed, though, except maybe my body receiving several new and interesting burn marks.

What the fuck?

Where was my Mr. Hyde?

I was in pain, massively pissed off, and continuing to be turned into a French fry...in short, all the right ingredients for a Dr. Death sandwich with a side of ass-kicking. Yet, for some reason, I was still me. It didn't make any sense.

I tend to be a sound sleeper.

Oh shit.

I'd no idea what my evil alternate-self had meant when he'd said that, but now it was beginning to become painfully obvious.

I was on my own.

* * *

"Why does he not honor us with his glorious power?" one of the robed assholes asked.

The attacks against me momentarily ceased. They were probably as confused as I was. Unfortunately, I doubted it would last. I was barely in control of my muscles - twitching in a little ball on the floor. There was also the fact that I was outnumbered four to one by foes I knew nothing about.

Thankfully, beast-mode or not, I wasn't without a few tricks up my sleeve. Pity I didn't have any sleeves at the moment.

Regaining just enough control of my limbs to take a wild shot, I sat up and swung my arm clumsily at the nearest of them.

Bingo! My blow connected solidly into his crotch with a disturbingly loud crunch - hard enough so that somewhere in the future any unborn children this guy had were screaming as they were erased from history.

He went down with a cry of pain, distracting his buddies just enough for me to leap at another of them. Before he or his friends could drag me off, I bit down into his neck through the robe.

Short of Kevlar, there aren't too many fabrics that are gonna withstand vampire fangs, and thankfully these guys didn't rate high enough on the pay scale to warrant that. I tore through it and into him with no problem.

Blood flowed from the wound, and I quickly sucked it down. It was my only chance to even the odds. The ability to turn into a rampaging hell-beast was just one of the extra powers I possessed as the Freewill of vampire legend. I could resist compulsion, the vampire equivalent of mind-control - which was pretty awesome. Better yet, I could do what no other vamps could...drink the blood of the undead without retching my guts out. Doing so temporarily added their strength to my own - pumping me up like I was on supernatural PCP.

The hooded douche flailed against me, putting up a much weaker struggle than I'd have guessed - the pussy. I took a long swallow and gave him a shove, sending him flying back past the edge of my clear vision.

Now I was gonna show these fuckers exactly what I was made of. Any second now and his blood would power me up; increasing my strength and healing all my wounds.

Yep, any second...

And, of course, nothing happened.

Jesus fucking Christ, was that power burnt out too? I just couldn't catch a fucking break. I mean, what was next? Was Alex going to return and compel me to bend over so he could finish whatever he'd had in mind when I woke up? That would be just my luck. Ever since I'd been turned, the vampire nation had continually fucked me over, figuratively. I guess it was only fitting that they'd eventually decide to go all the way with that analogy.

I sighed and licked my lips. At least the blood had been refreshing. I wouldn't have to die thirsty.

Hold on...there was something slightly different about the taste that I hadn't noticed earlier. Then it hit me.

"Are you guys humans?"

Well, this was a bit awkward. I'd been expecting a bunch of seasoned vamps. Instead, I got a foursome of regular people, making me feel ever so slightly insulted. I mean, I'm not the most terrifying monster in the pack, but my track record wasn't *that* bad.

My hurt feelings would have to wait, though. With one down cradling his crushed nut-sack and another holding his gushing neck, that still left two high-voltage cattle-prod wielding foes.

For all I knew, they might've been ninjas. At the very least, I expected them to be heavily trained mercenaries.

Either way, I was in for a fight.

* * *

Or not.

Their advantage of surprise taken away, the two remaining humans turned out to be surprisingly inept. They pretty much just came straight at me, holding their shock rods out in front of them. With vampire strength and speed at my disposal, not to mention having been in my fair share of scraps, they were both down and out within seconds.

I actually stood there with my mouth agape in surprise for longer than it took to beat them. I'd faced down so many badass enemies - ones whose power made mine look like nothing in comparison - that I barely knew what it was like to administer a beat down.

But you know what? It felt pretty goddamned good.

I allowed myself a moment to raise my hands victoriously in the air, Rocky Balboa style - at least before those last two movies - before remembering that I was doing so with my dick flapping free in the breeze.

Fortunately, I had my gaming experience to fall back upon. What's the first thing a party of adventurers does upon beating a group of enemies? Why, steal all of their shit, of course.

A part of me felt bad for taking out a group of regular people, especially the one I'd put the bite on - but that was heavily offset by the fact that they'd worked my ass over with stun guns. Fuck it. The assholes were lucky I was a lot less of a prick about these things than other vamps.

I pulled the robe from the nearest of my attackers, revealing he was as naked as I underneath it. Jesus Christ, had I been kidnapped by some sort of fucking supernatural nudist colony?

The hell with that. I did my best thinking when I wasn't in danger of slapping dicks with people who were trying to kick my ass. I pulled the garment over my head, immediately feeling a bit better, then moved on to the others.

The next one was as scantily equipped as the first. Fuck me. If Dave, my group's dungeon master, had ever given my party such shitty amounts of treasure, he'd have had a riot on his hands at the game table.

Jackpot! The third guy, the one whose balls I smashed into paste, was wearing a pair of wireframe glasses. Not daring to hope for much, I placed them upon my face and was delighted to find I was able to see where the fuck I was. It wasn't a perfect match, probably ensuring me a headache in short order, but was close enough to my prescription that I wouldn't be stumbling around completely blind.

I was in what looked to be some sort of dungeon created out of a natural cavern. Rather than smooth carved stone, jagged outcroppings lined the walls, as well as parts of the floor and ceiling. The place was pretty spacious, at least twice the size of my whole apartment back in New York - albeit considerably less cozy.

The walls were covered in gouges and rocky debris littered the floor. It wasn't too hard to guess that my Dr. Death persona had been none too happy with the accommodations. Go figure - must've been the shitty room service or something.

It was only then that the underlying stench of the place registered with my nose. It absolutely reeked. A part of me hoped that I wasn't the source. After all, I didn't exactly see shower facilities in the immediate vicinity...or a toilet, for that matter.

That wasn't entirely the case, though. I recognized dried blood amongst the rank odors. Following my nose, I stepped around a grouping of stalagmites and found the source - immediately understanding what Dr. Death had meant when he mentioned the people we'd killed.

Oh my God.

A pile of desiccated corpses, in various states of decay, lay before me. The bodies were mostly nude with a few wearing the remnants of the same robes as my attackers. From the look of things, they'd all had their throats torn out to varying degrees.

Since being turned into a vampire, I'd made it a point to keep humans off the menu. I stuck strictly to the bottled stuff...which, technically, still came from people, but at least spared me from hearing them scream while I drank it. It was the little things that sometimes helped me sleep at night.

Apparently, Dr. Death had been making up for lost time.

I could've stood and stared for hours, imagining what had happened - the final moments of these people - but that wasn't going to help any of them. Pushing aside thoughts that I'd turned into the very monster I had feared becoming, I decided it would be best to concentrate on getting the fuck out of wherever I was. I could always torture my psyche later.

Backing away from Dr. Death's breakfast nook, I turned toward where I'd heard the four stooges enter from. There! Embedded in a section of particularly hard looking rock was a dull grey metal door.

I walked over and gave it a push. When in doubt, always try the obvious. Unsurprisingly, it didn't budge in the slightest - locked up tight.

"Hello!" I shouted, trying to put on an accent - learned from countless hours of watching Indiana Jones outwit Nazis. "Ze Freewill is transformed. You can let me...err, us out now."

No response.

Oh fuck this shit. I cocked my fist - putting all of my vampiric strength behind it - and hammered it into the door.

The next few minutes found me cradling my broken hand, waiting for my healing to kick in. I hadn't even put a tiny dent into the metal. Hell, my blow had barely resulted in a small thud of sound. How the fuck thick was that thing?

That's when I remembered it would have to be pretty damn strong to keep my alternate form contained. Stupid memory. Couldn't have thought of that before I turned my knuckles into jelly, could I?

That escape plan was obviously a dud. The walls were out too. From the look of things, I'd need a couple tons of high explosives to make any sort of progress there. About the only other options that came to mind were saying "Open sesame" or clicking my heels together.

I found a nice uncomfortable spot and sat down to think things over - occasionally interrupted by the need to punch the humans out, lest they start getting all zappy again.

Speaking of which, how the fuck were these four yahoos supposed to escape once they'd succeeded in bringing out the beast in me?

Wait...hadn't a few of the corpses been similarly attired? Maybe they weren't supposed to get out.

Maybe they'd been sacrificial lambs of a sort, sent to stir the monster inside of me and then serve as his refreshments. They were both the wake-up call *and* in-room meal.

Whoa.

Jumping Jesus Christ on a hand grenade - what the fuck was this place?

Almost as if in answer, a clanking sound came from the door, followed by the squeal of hinges.

Apparently, I was about to find out.

The Devil You Know

The heavy door of my cell - for that's what it seemingly was - opened, revealing that it was probably better suited for a bank vault. The fucking thing had to be about a foot thick. No wonder I hadn't so much as even dinged it. Forget Dr. Death, I'd need a cruise missile to knock that thing down.

As interesting as that was, my attention was quickly diverted away from the finer points of heavily armored egresses as the door was unlocked from the outside with a heavy click. I had visitors.

"I have little doubt you will be impressed by the Freewill's battle prow..." Alex paused mid-sentence as he stepped through and laid eyes upon me. A brief grimace passed over his face before a mask of neutrality replaced it. Oh well, at least he was dressed this time.

I had a moment to consider his words, specifically the part about *battle*. My short-term memory might've been scrambled, but I definitely remembered him and that he was the cause of all of this. It had been through his manipulations that I'd ended up inadvertently starting a war that threatened to burn the world to ash. What a fucking...

A high-pitched noise buzzed in my head, and I winced as it resolved into a voice of sorts. *What is the delay, vampire? I am not known for my patience.*

There was something else waiting outside the door. Whatever it was, it was big...and scaly. What the...?

Alex stepped aside and gestured for it to enter. "Of course, mighty Druaga. Please forgive the delay, however slight."

Druaga? Why did that name sound familiar?

Oh fuck.

My tenth-level adventuring group had gone up against him years ago and we'd gotten the ever-living shit kicked out of us. Dave had been in rare form that day, enjoying the total-party-kill far more than he normally would - the asshole.

Well, okay, that had all been part of my weekly D&D game, but still. Didn't a lot of myths - and game stats, for that matter - mostly have their basis in reality? If so, that didn't bode well. And here Alex was, showing me off to this guy like I was a panda at the Bronx Zoo.

I subconsciously backed up a step as what I presumed to be Druaga entered. Whoa. His *Monster Manual* portrait definitely hadn't done him justice. Think some bizarre combination of a monitor lizard, centaur, and one of those overly tattooed dudes that used to headline at freak shows. Over eight feet tall, he almost had to kneel to step through the door. He had four long legs, each ending in claws that would have made a velociraptor weep with envy. Multi-colored scales covered its body and glinted despite the lack of light in the room. He crossed two muscular arms over his chest, which was covered in various sigils. One looked an awful lot like the Cobra symbol from G.I. Joe - Tom would've definitely had a dipshit remark at seeing that. A reptilian head full of teeth, horns, and two sets of angry red eyes sat atop a short, muscular neck.

What is this? His voice reverberated in my head, despite the fact that the creature hadn't moved its mouth - except maybe to drool a bit.

"May I present to you, the Freewill," Alex said before turning toward me. "You should be honored. You stand in the presence of Druaga, one of the seven esteemed lords of the dead." He inclined his head in the direction of the ugly fucker standing next to him.

What is an ugly fucker?

Oh shit.

The corner of Alex's mouth raised ever so slightly. "You will have to forgive his errant thoughts, oh merciless one. He is not used to conversing psychically, and I have found his mental processes to be somewhat...convoluted. In some ways, though, it is a refreshing breath of air compared to the usual idolatry afforded those of station."

I see, Druaga thought...I guess...turning his creepy eyes my way. *Show me.*

Show him? What, my convoluted thought processes? Fine. You asked for it, asshole.

I imagined a female version of him - basically a lizard monster with tits - and then visualized myself railing it from behind. *Yeah, that's what I did to your mother last night. How do you like that?*

After a moment, Alex said, "I'm sure the Freewill is just conserving his vast power at this time."

That's what he wanted me to show him? Oh, crap.

Druaga stared at me for a moment, his four eyes blinking at different intervals. Then he glanced toward Alex. *The Freewill wishes to copulate with my kind. Such offspring would be potentially useful in the coming conflict. I shall consider this request.*

What?!

"Hold on, dude. I didn't..."

"We can most certainly discuss such accommodations should our alliance be formalized." Alex stepped in front of the big gecko, cutting me off. He turned and fixed me with a glare before I could utter a peep. Guess he didn't need to be psychic to figure out I might have something negative to add. "We will do *whatever* is necessary for the good of our people. Is that not correct?" His tone for that last part was pure iron.

He was a vampire over two millennia in age, possessing power enough to pound me into paste with no effort whatsoever. Hell, assuming what he said earlier was true and not just some homoerotic pillow talk, he was strong enough to engage in recreational sparring with my nigh-undefeatable alternate mode.

That wasn't even counting the presence of Druaga, a creature that at least in game terms was considered a god - a lesser one, but I was pretty sure that would prove to be an unimportant detail should he decide to eat my face.

Needless to say, I'm not a complete fucking idiot. I clammed up and put on my best polite smile.

I still require a demonstration of his power before committing my forces to such an alliance. A forked tongue darted out of Druaga's mouth and reached up to clean one of its eyeballs - freaky.

I insist that you immediately commence with... He cocked his head to the side, looking like the world's ugliest stupid dog. A buzzing sound filled my ears as if I'd stuck my head into an angry beehive.

If Alex heard it too, he gave no indication. He stood there between me and Reptilicus as if this was the most natural thing in the world for him. Goddamn, sometimes the supernatural world was just plain weird.

After a few moments, the buzzing ceased and Druaga raised his head again. *My attention is needed elsewhere. I will return at my convenience. The Freewill shall show me his power then.*

Pushy fucker, wasn't he? I was almost tempted to tell him such, but then - without even so much as a goodbye - Druaga was gone. His body appeared to fold in on itself, imploding into nothingness. A soft pop of air rushed to fill the spot where he'd been.

The relief I felt at not having to test my hit-points against his was short-lived, however. I was now alone with Alex, the madman who was currently plotting the end of the world.

I just hoped he didn't want to resume his nude wrestling match.

* * *

"That was most fortunate for us," Alex said after a moment. "Our guest is not known for his tolerance of disappointment."

He strolled over to the human I'd bitten and raised his boot. "But then, neither am I."

Crunch. He crushed the man's head into paste.

Ewww.

"I suppose the fault is mine for sending thralls to attend this task at such an important juncture. You should know, you picked a poor moment to revert again."

I had trouble prying my eyes away from the person he'd just snuffed like a bug, but somehow forced myself to focus. "Again? What do you mean by that?"

"You have reverted twice in as many months, as I am sure you remember. Those episodes were short lived, of course. Your more impressive form has been quite easy to coax out prior to today."

I had no clue what he was talking about. If I'd woken up before in this place, I didn't remember dick about it. Of course, if I had opened my eyes, only to have the shit immediately zapped out of me by hooded zealots, then perhaps that wasn't too surprising. Horrific trauma had a way of doing things like that.

"Alas, as amusing as it might be to have your more loquacious half back for the time being, I must insist that you allow yourself to change. I cannot allow the opportunity at hand to pass."

I backed up a step. "What opportunity?"

"The war to cleanse this planet, of course. Druaga commands an impressive force of fell creatures. Though he has traditionally remained neutral with regards to the signatories of the Humbaba Accord, he has recently reconsidered committing to our cause."

"Um, any reason why?"

"Those are matters for the First Coven and the First alone, Freewill, as I'm sure you can understand. Now I do apologize, but..."

"I can't! I mean, it won't work."

"What will not work?"

"I can't change. Something is...broken about it. Your guys did their job, but it didn't do anything. Believe me, I wanted it to. I like getting ass-raped by cattle prods about as much as the next guy."

Yeah, I was rambling. Kinda pathetic, but I figured I was due some slack. I mean, I'd woken up naked in a dank dungeon, been assaulted by a bunch of maniacs, and met the equivalent of a demon lord. Talk about a stressful day. I wouldn't be the least bit surprised to learn that it was a Monday.

Sadly, my pleas fell upon uncaring ears.

Alex made the subtlest of movements and appeared immediately in front of me, covering the distance between us far faster than my eyes could follow.

"Once again, I apologize for what must be done. Know that I do not take any pleasure in this."

Why did I not find that statement particularly comforting?

Blood Bath

"I see you spoke the truth, Freewill." Alex casually wrung his hands, sending drops of blood - mine - flying. "This is most concerning."

I would've replied with a great big "Duh!" but my jaw hadn't healed enough yet. At least I was no longer in pain. At some point in the pummeling that ensued, my nerve endings simply gave out, leaving me uncomfortably numb.

I was pretty sure every single bone in my body was now a fine white powder. I'll give him credit, though. He was a master at his craft. He spilled very little blood, and at no point did I lose consciousness. His ability to take a person apart, leaving them as little more than human Jell-O, was damn near an art form. I just wished it was art I had observed on the wall of a museum, not lived through.

I thought back fondly to nearly being incinerated at Sheila's touch as she hung from the edge of...

Wait, when had *that* happened? The memory scattered just as quickly as it came. But then, hadn't my less than personable half mentioned that my memories would probably return at inconvenient times?

Speaking of which, I sure as shit hoped he was enjoying his little nap because if we ever met up again in my head, I was going to beat the ever-living fuck out of him with every abstract piece of mental furniture I could grab.

"I must consult with our seers on this." I got the sense that Alex was more talking to himself than the puddle of goo that was me. He turned back toward the exit. "I will send more thralls..."

Oh fuck. No more electrocutions. For Christ's sake...

"...to make you more comfortable, as well as presentable. It would be regrettable for Druaga to return and find you in this state."

I was tempted to tell him not to do me any favors, but thankfully, my tongue was still dislocated. The truth was I actually wouldn't have minded a few favors right at that moment.

* * *

Thankfully, the next batch of robed humans that appeared in my cell seemed much less inclined to turn me into a tater tot. They carried in what looked to be an oversized cooler and set it down beside me. Before I could ask whether they were throwing me an undead kegger, they proceeded to scrape me off the floor and dump me into it.

Whatever pithy remark might've been on the tip of my tongue was drowned as I immediately submerged beneath the surface of the viscous red liquid within.

Blood!

And not just any blood. Within a minute, I felt better as my bones began knitting themselves back together. The casket - for lack of a better word - was filled with vampire blood. It jumpstarted my own healing and then augmented it further. It wasn't a huge boost, but it was a lot more juice than I normally had in me.

As I let it work its magic, I tried not to think about the unlucky donor. Judging by the strength of the blood, I'd guess some minor underling had been unfortunate enough to have crossed paths with Alex on his way out of my cell. This day had certainly sucked for him every bit as much as it did for me, with the exception that I'd get a chance to do it all over again. Joy.

And it was just at that point that my overloaded nerve endings began working again.

Fuck me.

* * *

After spending the next several minutes alternating between screaming, crying, and trying not to wet myself, my body finally pulled itself back together. I climbed out of the blood and found myself alone again. However, before vacating the premises - and no doubt locking the door behind them - the thralls had been good enough to leave me a fresh change of clothing, including a new pair of glasses. I put them on and the room finally snapped into crystal clear focus. The vampire nation supposedly had detailed files on all of their minions. Normally, I wasn't too fond of that concept, but considering mine apparently included my prescription, I was willing to overlook the gross invasion of my privacy just this once.

I quickly toweled off and got dressed - feeling considerably less insecure once I had a pair of underwear and jeans standing between *Titanosaurus* and the rest of the world. I finally felt human again, the irony of that statement not lost upon me.

The massive door of my cell opened again about ten minutes later and, once more, Alex stepped through. I'd be lying if I claimed that I didn't come close to shitting myself at the sight of him - fearing he planned a repeat performance.

He must've sensed my tension, for he held up a hand in a placating manner. "Be at peace, Freewill. If you did not change earlier, I have no reason to believe further persuasion will trigger it."

"Well, that's good to know."

"Druaga will be returning shortly, but I thought you might care for a chance to stretch your legs until then. Think of it as my way of...making amends for my earlier actions. After all, you are the one the legends speak of. It would be rude of us to treat you as a mere animal, especially now that you have regained a mindset that does not favor attacking everything in your sight."

I kept any flippant remarks to myself. I needed to remember that I'd been locked up here for God-knows how long, and it was well within Alex's power to just turn around and leave me to rot. Telling him to go fuck himself would be satisfying, but it wouldn't do much toward helping me get out of this asylum.

Taking my silence as affirmation, he turned back toward the door. "Come walk with me, Freewill. Fret not, for we will be duly informed when Druaga returns."

That wasn't exactly in my top ten things to *fret* about, but once more, I figured it best to keep my opinions to myself. For a moment, I was hesitant to follow, fearful of venturing too close to him, but then I realized how stupid that was. The guy could move at speeds that basically made him a character straight out of *Dragonball Z*. It wouldn't matter much if I was a foot away from him or a mile. If he wanted to be all over me like a new suit, I would never see it coming.

Fuck it, fortune favors the bold...sometimes. I caught up to him and stepped through the doorway, eager to learn exactly where the hell I was.

* * *

Wherever we were, it was big. A cut stone hallway ran in either direction from outside my door, leading off farther into the darkness than my vampire-enhanced eyes could see. The ceiling was about fifteen feet high, tall enough to accommodate guests Druaga's size or larger. I found myself wishing for a magic sword, or maybe some plus-five plate mail - for surely this was the real-life equivalent to the dungeons me and my friends had explored every week in our imaginations. Much like in those adventures, I was also forced to wonder what else lurked here, waiting to spring upon us.

Alex began walking and I followed.

"Right hand rule," I muttered, noting our direction.

"Excuse me?"

"Sorry, gaming terminology. We use it for dungeon crawls."

"We?"

"I guess you had to be there. So, where exactly is this place?"

"You are in the stronghold of the vampire nation. It is from here that all of our actions worldwide and beyond are planned and carried out." His voice echoed off the solid walls around us. The faint rhythm of dripping water sounded somewhere off in the distance.

"This is a lot different than Boston."

"You are far from that city, Freewill."

"How far?" A sinking feeling hit my gut. I had the disturbing notion that whatever he said next, it wouldn't be good. I seriously doubted it was only a quick train ride from home.

"You are deep under Lake Geneva in one of the many secret catacombs we keep..."

I racked my brain...Lake Geneva? Was that one of the Great Lakes? Fuck, geography had always been one of my weak subjects. I mean, I knew where Geneva itself was located, but there was no way..."

"...deep beneath Château de Chillon."

"Just chillin in Chillon," I quipped rather unhelpfully, still with no clue as to where I was.

"Pardon?"

"Um, I meant where..."

"Western Switzerland."

"Western..." Oh, fuck me.

I was definitely *not* in Kansas anymore.

The Accidental Tourist

"I'm in Switzerland?"

"Yes, Freewill." Alex turned left down another corridor, this one leading toward a stone staircase.

"As in Europe?"

"There are many locales that share in that name, but since I assume you are referring to the country, then once more, the answer is in the affirmative."

I followed him up the stairs, my mind racing to process things. What the fuck had happened? Had I stowed away in a cargo ship or something? How in hell had I ended up here? "So, I'm actually *in* Switzerland?"

"We have already established that."

"In this...err...castle?"

"Deep beneath the crypt, to be exact."

"And this place is the vampire headquarters?"

"In a word, yes."

"The whole castle?"

"The entire country."

I stopped mid-step, letting that one sink in. Nah, I couldn't have heard him correctly. That was just insane. "What exactly do you mean by that?"

"Exactly as I said, Freewill." He looked over his shoulder at me, bemusedly raising the brow over one of his mismatched eyes. "Did you expect less of our kind?"

"Well...not to sound insulting, but yeah. I mean, the whole country? That sounds pretty damn farfetched."

"It only seems as such because we wish it to be so. We have been entrenched here since the very beginning. Our influence extends to all aspects of life, from the mundane to the profound."

"Why this place?"

"Because it is perfect for us."

Unhelpful answer or not, my mind reeled at the concept. I'd heard that our seat of power was in Europe, but much like anyone raised on a diet of Hollywood tripe, my imagination automatically turned toward crumbling castles in Romania surrounded by ignorant peasants who locked their shutters at night to ward off evil.

I thought back to what I knew of Switzerland, which wasn't much. I mean, there were busty blondes...that was kind of cool, but probably not entirely relevant to my predicament. I remembered from history class this place was historically neutral in wars, partially because the entire nation was a natural fortress backed by a heavily armed populace.

Holy crap. In short...as Alex had said...perfect.

Then there was the rest: Swiss watches, banks, um...cheese. No wonder it always seemed like vamps were flush with cash. It was because they were. Hell, even my own coven always seemed to have plenty of scratch to go around. I mean, sure, I'd never gotten my hands on any of it, but that was thanks to Sally keeping the bankcards all to herself and...

Sally!

Fuck, I hadn't even considered her since waking. Did she know where I was? Hell, was she even aware I was still alive? Could she have had anything to do with my being here? She'd done it before, shipping my ass off to China. But that had been a goof on her part, her way of fucking with me. Somehow, I didn't believe she'd just hand me over to Alex - or perhaps I didn't want to believe it.

No. She and I were cool...at least when we weren't busy pissing each other off. I'd give her the benefit of the doubt until such time as I learned different. She couldn't have had anything to do with my being here.

Which then still left the question: how exactly *did* I get here?

* * *

We reached the top of the stairs where another heavily fortified door awaited - this one ajar. We stepped through, at which point two vamps on either side snapped to attention - guards, obviously. It wasn't a stretch to guess they stood straighter due to Alex's presence rather than mine.

This next level was much less dank. The finely worked stone gave the appearance of royalty. Electricity was also apparently one of the perks for those who moved upstairs. It was actually fairly well lit by vampire standards.

"You should feel honored, Freewill. You enter the heart of the First Coven."

An interesting use of words, considering that vampires traditionally didn't get along well with things that were unexpectedly introduced into their hearts.

I considered that analogy as we walked. Alex had been the one responsible for manipulating us - *me* - into starting this war in the first place. He was hell-bent on finishing what he'd started over two thousand years ago - conquering the planet. Unfortunately, he wasn't overly concerned if most of it burned to the ground while he was accomplishing his goals.

In an interesting twist, many were under the impression that it had been me who'd started things. Our allies used my name as a rallying cry, while our enemies were no doubt putting me at the top of their to-kill lists.

Alex either didn't know, or care, that I was opposed to the entire thing - and I wasn't the only one. My friends were behind me in our plans to thwart...

The image of Gan, the crazed Mongolian pre-teen who'd become a constant pain in the ass, unexpectedly flashed in my head. I remembered how she'd told me of her plans to overthrow Alex. Her desires weren't entirely altruistic, though. She wanted him dead for no other reason than she desired the crown herself - with me by her side. What a fucking nutcase.

Well, you don't have to worry about her anymore. She's dead.

The thought...no, the memory...slammed into me like a freight train. Dead? When? Sure, I would've been more than happy to keep half a world between us for the rest of eternity, but I never wanted to see her killed. That was...

The movie I'd been watching in my brain apartment! Had that really happened?

"Are you unwell, Freewill?" Alex asked from beside me. He'd stopped walking and was now staring at me quizzically, no doubt due to my silence. Unfortunately, I'd tuned out his voice during my moment of introspection - stupid of me, since what he'd been yammering about was potentially useful information. "Did you, perhaps, need more time to recover?"

Asshole. Like he really needed to rub it in. "I'm fine...this is just a lot to take in."

That answer seemed to mollify him. Brilliant as a strategist as he was, he was still susceptible to a little ego stroking. "As I can imagine. Most are introduced to our inner circle gradually. For one so young, I would think it would be overwhelming."

Overwhelming? Seriously? I hadn't expected to learn that we basically owned one of the most prosperous nations on the planet, but it wasn't quite pants-pissing news either.

* * *

Alex continued his tour, blathering on as he took me through more passages and tunnels. Sometimes we went up, sometimes down. I really should have paid better attention, at the very least for when it was time to bug the fuck out of here, but after a while, all I could hear were my own thoughts screaming *shut the fuck up already* over and over again. Goddamn! Apparently, two thousand years of life hadn't taught this narcissistic clown the value of brevity.

Finally, we entered a passage where, once more, there were no light sources - a non-issue for vamps. At first, I only noticed an odd scent in the air - like someone was burning dirty dog fur - but as we continued on, it became thicker. Eventually, we were walking through a smoky haze that continued to grow heavier.

I coughed, interrupting whatever historical factoid Alex had been droning on about. "Someone needs to cut down on the hookah."

"It is a special incense, first cultivated by pre-Aztec mystics," he explained, apparently unbothered by the stench. "It is said to expand the mind."

"I know a few mind-expanding herbs. None of them smell like this." My eyes began to tear up. "What is this place, anyway?"

"As I was saying," he continued, a slight hint of annoyance in his voice, "we are paying a visit to our elder seers. I have sent word ahead that I wished for them to...*consider* your current condition."

Oh, fuck, that didn't sound good. I hoped that didn't mean I'd now have a lot of vampires testing out new and interesting ways to kick the shit out of me in a futile attempt to get Dr. Death out of his metaphysical bed.

Voices came from up ahead. I couldn't see the owners through the haze, but they sounded irritated. Unfortunately, I had no idea what they were annoyed about. Whatever they were speaking, it definitely wasn't English. Was it the native language of the land? Beat the shit out of me. I had no idea what they spoke in Switzerland. Oh well, a U.N. translator I was not.

If the argument up ahead perturbed Alex, he gave no indication of it. That figured. When one was the high muckety-muck, one didn't need to concern oneself with the fretting of the peons - asshole.

The hallway abruptly ended in an arched doorway, which Alex stepped through. I followed him and stopped to take a look around.

Despite everything, I couldn't help but smile. "It's about fucking time."

* * *

My short tenure as a vampire had been filled with many disappointing revelations. For example, the regional headquarters that my coven reported to was little more than an underground corporate park. Talk about mundane. Where I stood now, though, was more like what I'd originally envisioned. Finally some epically dark shit that was worthy of the vampire name.

The chamber I entered was circular in shape with a domed ceiling about twenty feet above our heads. It was still smoky, but the space was large enough so that the haze thinned out and gave me a better view than in the hall. About forty feet in diameter, the walls were some sort of smooth stone, maybe marble, polished to the point where they were almost mirror-like. They reflected the lone source of light in the room, casting bizarre shadows that the owners of any haunted house in America would have sacrificed their children to reproduce.

A fire pit, about five feet across, dominated the center. Low flames and the noxious smoke I was trying not to breathe emanated from it.

And it just kept getting better from there.

Robed figures sat in a circle facing the center, spaced evenly apart. Before each was an iron rod, one end of which hung in the fire pit.

What caught my eye most, however, was their lack of that very thing. Having heard my little utterance upon entering, they were all turned toward me. Various faces, some bearded, others clean shaven, stared back...sorta. Empty sockets, blackened and scarred, stared sightlessly back from where their eyes should have been. Whoa, kinda creepy.

At the far end of their circle, three more beings stood. One was dressed like the other weirdos. A long, white beard fell from his chin, nearly to the floor. The rest of his face bore the same wounds as his fellows. The other two, a man and a woman, were dressed in more contemporary garb. The woman wore a black gown - accentuating her milky white skin - that flowed around her shapely form...oh yeah. I could dig that. The dude had darker skin; Middle-Eastern in complexion would be my guess. He had longish hair, a neatly trimmed beard, and wore khaki-colored clothes in stark contrast to his hottie of an acquaintance. Their differences were further punctuated from the rest by the fact that they had eyes in their heads with which to stare at me.

"Welcome to the chamber of seers, Freewill," Alex said from beside me. "Here our elder prophets gaze out across the planes so as to divine the mysteries they hold."

"Doesn't look like they see much of anything to me."

"In that, you are quite mistaken."

The couple across the way each flashed a set of fangs at us. Whoever they were, they didn't seem all that pleased at our entrance.

They took a step toward us when a deep bass rumbled in the chamber as if someone had struck a massive gong somewhere.

The bearded seer immediately disengaged from the two he'd been huddled with and walked over to an empty spot within the circle.

As the old guy sat down, Alex's hand fell upon my shoulder and he gently guided me back a step. The two others across from us likewise backed up, seemingly respectful in how they did so.

"What..."

"Shhh," Alex quietly shushed me. From his tone, I gathered it would probably be unwise to interrupt, especially since I was well within pummeling reach.

Silence returned to the room as the seated figures placed their hands upon the iron rods in front of them.

Smoke rose from their skin where the hot metal touched. Ouch.

But that was nothing compared to what came next.

The bearded one muttered something unintelligible, at which point the rest answered in kind. They lifted the rods, ends glowing red hot, and proceeded to jam the near molten metal into their already ruined eye-sockets.

"Holy shit!"

All eyes - and lack thereof - in the room immediately trained upon me. Uh oh.

The leader of the gouging cult pointed a finger in my direction and screeched something that I couldn't make out. Call me cynical, but I had a feeling it wasn't "Hello."

A moment later, he followed up with a compulsion to his buddies. His words were still indecipherable, but the meaning translated in my brain. *KILL THE BLASPHEMER!!*"

That didn't exactly sound promising.

The Eyes Have It

Almost as one, the weirdos sitting around the pit plucked the burning rods from their skulls and stood, brandishing them as weapons. Great. Not only was I about to get my ass killed, but it was going to be with red-hot pokers coated in burnt eye-juice.

The couple that had been conversing with the elder whack-job stepped back, smirks on their faces. They'd come for the conversation, but were apparently staying for the floorshow. How wonderful.

Oh well, I might've been outnumbered, but they were just a bunch of blind nutjobs. I was debating how best to handle things when Alex stepped in front of me.

"*Desino!*" he commanded, whatever the fuck that meant. For all I knew, he was encouraging them.

I stepped to the side to get a better view of what they'd do, only to find their heads all turning to track me - definitely creepy. Just what I needed - a fight against a group of Daredevil wannabes.

Alex turned his head and directed his words at the couple, who still stood there smirking like douche-nozzles. The woman threw a dirty look back his way in response, but nothing more.

The nearest of the eyeless monks was almost within reach to clonk me with his crowbar of doom when Alex said something else to the couple, a distinctly angry tone in his voice.

The woman let out a disgusted sigh, then she and her companion joined in shouting foreign phrases at the blind lynch mob. More words followed until, finally, the angry snarl left the old guy's face and he held up a hand. His fellows immediately stopped in their tracks. Neat trick.

A moment later, the eyeless minions shuffled back to their spots around the circle. Phew! Before joining them, though, their leader turned toward me and bared his teeth - showing his gnarled fangs. He hissed in my direction, then spat on the floor.

I kept my mouth shut at the implied insult, not wanting to agitate the old fuck any further. I'd seen enough kung-fu movies to know that never turned out well.

I did, however, flip him the finger.

Alex stepped once more to stand at my side. "That is really not helping your situation, Freewill."

"They're the ones who overreacted."

"Overreacted?" The woman's tone was one of outrage, but at least she spoke English. "You were the one fool enough to interrupt."

"Sorry. I didn't realize that there were rules to an eye-gouging circle jer...*urk*!"

She was across the room before I could finish the sentence, lifting me from the floor by the throat. Okay, perhaps I needed to rethink my attitude.

"Theodora, please," Alex said, almost sounding bored. "Kindly release our guest."

"He is an insolent lout. Need I remind you that we do not tolerate..."

"You need remind me of *nothing*. That is the Freewill you are holding. What I suggest is for your own benefit, not his."

"*This* is the Freewill? Hah! He looks nothing like the magnificent beast your men captured."

Magnificent beast? I would've replied to that, but my windpipe was currently being crushed...although considering my assailant's appearance, I might've categorized it more as autoerotic asphyxiation.

"Go right ahead and see for yourself, though I would caution you to release him before doing so. He is more than your equal should you anger him."

Well, that was a load of bullshit if ever I'd heard one. Right then, my best defense would have consisted of wheezing and passing out.

To my amazement, though, the angry hottie lowered me to the floor and let up on the pressure ever so slightly. "Very well, Alexander."

She turned to face me, eyes becoming as black as her dress. "*ON YOUR KNEES!! LAP THE BOTTOM OF MY BOOT CLEAN LIKE THE DOG YOU ARE!!*"

The compulsion felt like a good solid kick to the head. My eyes rolled back for a moment from the force of it. Whoever this chick might be, she wasn't anyone to mess with.

Even so, the most powerful of compulsions might be able to knock me on my ass, but they still did shit in the way of making me obey.

I meant to say something moderately respectful with regards to her inability to control me, but at the last second opted to be a bit more direct.

"Fuck you, Cinderella."

* * *

Impressed or not by my ability to resist her, Theodora hadn't been particularly keen on my sass. She flung me across the chamber like a human Frisbee and I slammed into the far wall hard enough to mar its polished sheen.

Laughter echoed through the room. At first, I thought it might be the blind assholes, but they were still busy sitting around their campfire circle. Theodora's companion had been the one laughing. Glad to know I could be so entertaining.

"I believe you have made a grim mistake, dear Thea," Alex remarked, backing up a step.

What the fuck? He knew I was no match for her.

But maybe she didn't.

Trying my best to conceal just how rubbery my legs were, I stood up and casually dusted myself off. My eyes darkened and I extended my fangs, hoping that they hadn't been knocked out by the impact.

"My turn, bitch."

* * *

It was all a bluff. Thankfully, it was one that didn't give me cause to embarrass myself. Turns out, I didn't have to do anything but stand there menacingly.

The look on Theodora's face changed ever so slightly and her eyes opened just a wee bit wider. It wasn't quite the look of fearful shock I might've hoped for, but if she was as old as her power suggested, then it was probably the equivalent of pissing herself and then shivering in the corner like a little rat dog.

The problem with some dogs, though, is that when they're cornered, they'll turn and bite.

Fortunately, I didn't have to find out if that was the case. Alex stepped between us and held up his hand. "Peace, Freewill. Know that though they have angered you, Theodora and Yehoshua are both of the First and worthy of your respect. They are one with the hands that guide you."

I had no idea what the fuck he meant, aside from the revelation that the bitch who'd choked me out and her laughing hyena of a boyfriend were both members of the Draculas - aka the First Coven. That was enough for me to stop and consider. I'd sooner tangle with an angry Sasquatch than any of that bunch, especially since they were well known for their mercy - as in lack thereof. On paper, I might be important to Alex's cause, but that didn't mean any of them wouldn't put their egos first and shit-stomp me into my component parts.

Trying my best to play it tough, while still waiting for my bruises to heal, I put my hands in my pockets and said, "It's cool." Yeah, I know. It's amazing they didn't all drop to their knees and proclaim me king right there.

The ensuing silence stretched out a bit too long for my comfort, prompting me to tempt fate once more. "So, assuming nobody else is going to freak out, what were these guys doing?"

"The oracles see clearest when their eyes are blackened," Laughing Boy replied in accented English.

"As elder vampires," Alex explained, noticing my flummoxed look, "the seers' abilities to heal are unmatched by most. Thus, once every hour, they ensure their visions will not be compromised. It is their sacrifice for us all, their sacred act of devotion to me."

"Us," Theodora said.

"Of course," he replied smarmily. "Their loyalty lies with the entirety of the First." One could practically hear the "fuck you" in his tone. Trouble in paradise, perhaps? "But do tell, dear Thea, why are you and Yehoshua here?"

"The same reason as you, Alexander. To seek wisdom. The northern offensive begins in a fortnight. If indeed we are to secure a foothold deep within the Siberian Taiga, we must secure every advantage at our disposal - as I'm sure you realize."

"Of course." His response was covered in frost. What, did this chick give him a case of the blue balls a thousand years ago or something?

"And you, Alexander?" Yeho...whatever the fuck his name was...asked. "What wisdom do you seek?"

"Wisdom requiring the discretion of the seers."

"The First hold no secrets from one-another," Theodora said. "Or is that yet another edict which you have chosen to ignore?"

"Your tone wounds me, dear sister. Alas, this is a personal matter. The Freewill seeks direction as the end times near. He requested that only I be present so as to help him interpret the guidance provided him."

I did?

Thea and Yahoo's eyes narrowed. They no doubt smelled a rat, and were smart to. By Alex's own admission, however long ago in Northern Canada - the site of the war's beginnings - he wasn't averse to going against the other members of the Draculas. Personally, I had little doubt he'd gladly fuck them all up the ass with a wooden stake if it meant getting what he wanted.

"Is this true, Freewill?" Thea directed to me. "No offense to you, *Lord* Alexander."

"I take no offense from my honored fellows," he replied evenly before half turning to face me, his brown eye meeting both of mine. "Answer true to their question if you will, Freewill."

Although part of me wanted to scream out what a filthy fucking liar he was, I considered that potentially unwise. He'd already proven his capability to fuck up my day with no effort. It was also evident that he was the leader of the Draculas. That meant that as strong as Thea and her friend were, they might not be enough to take him down. Hell, there was no reason to expect them to even try. They might just shrug and walk away, leaving me to get several new assholes torn. Vampires can be dicks that way.

Fuck it. Sometimes the right thing to do is also the most stupid. "Yep, that's why we're here. Hoping I can pick up some strategy, maybe a few lottery numbers, too. That sort of thing."

Alex sighed heavily, indicating that perhaps I'd gone a bit overboard with my answer. Oh well, I blame it on corporate America. If my time spent working for the middle management of Hopskotchgames had taught me anything, it was never say with one word what you could with a thousand.

"There you have it," Alex said brusquely. "Now, if your own business is concluded, I would ask you to give our guest his time with the seers."

The two other Draculas shared a quick glance before heading toward the door. Thea stopped long enough to fix me with a glare, then she turned to Alex. "He is still too insolent for my tastes."

Despite her comment practically begging for a response, I somehow managed to keep my mouth shut as they left. Their footsteps echoed for several seconds before fading away, leaving us in silence.

Standing there in the smoky gloom, the world I remembered might as well have been a million miles away. I wasn't sure what would happen next in the chamber of blind psychos, but I had a bad feeling it wasn't going to be fun.

While You Were Sleeping...

Yeah, it definitely wasn't fun. Boring was more like it.

Alex pulled the head seer up from where he sat and dragged him off to a corner, where they conversed in hushed whispers. To add insult to injury, they did so in yet another language I couldn't understand.

The fuck? When I got home, the first thing I was gonna do was invest in a phone with a good battery and Google Translate loaded on it. Either that or hit up Sally for the funds to hire my own translator fluent in ancient Hittite or whatever the fuck they were blathering.

Speaking of Sally, I needed to get back to her. She wasn't that much older than me, yet somehow, she always seemed to have a clue as to what was going on. She'd be able to tell me what had happened and how long I'd been gone for. I mean, sure, a calendar could also do that last job, but I didn't know of any that had as sweet of an ass to look at.

At the very least, I needed to get back to people I could trust. That certainly didn't include my present company.

I resolved to pay better attention...at least until I was home and could go back to vegging in front of *Eve Online.*

Eventually, that gong sounded again and the old seer disengaged from Alex, mid-sentence from the looks of it. He returned to his buddies so they could all make sure they were masters at Blind-man's Bluff.

This time, I made it a point to zip it as they proceeded to cauterize their eye-sockets. Goddamn, what a bunch of weirdos. Once they were finished, Alex stepped over and directed me back toward the chamber door.

"That was most disturbing," he said as we left, once more stepping into the thick smoke of the hallway.

"You're telling me. I'm sorry, but you couldn't pay me enough to sit there all day poking out my eyes, no matter how stoned that burning shit got me."

"You should speak not of that which you do not understand. The elder seers are a priceless treasure to our people. They see much, and their honor dictates they keep the secrets they are told, even from others of my circle."

"And what secret are they keeping, if I may be so bold to ask?"

"That is an interesting choice of words, Freewill. Outside of the First, you are indeed perhaps the boldest of our kind I have met in some time, at least in your speech."

I opted for silence rather than acknowledging the dig. Besides, I had no interest in being the bravest of them all. Leave that shit to the heroes. I just wanted to get back to my life, my friends, and...

The thought trailed off. I'm sure I meant to add Sheila to that list, but a memory stirred within me again, reminding me that there were pieces of the puzzle that I was still missing...potentially dark pieces.

"The seers are at a loss to explain what has happened to you, other than to confirm your claims."

"You mean that I can't go all murderous demon-beast?"

"Precisely. It is unprecedented in our history. None of the Freewills of days past were ever known to have suffered from..."

"The Mr. Hyde equivalent of erectile dysfunction?" I silently thanked fate that my roommates weren't present to hear that.

"This is no laughing matter." He quickened his pace down the long subterranean hallway.

"Did they say anything else?"

"Nothing that made any sense..." His tone seemed to waver a bit, but he quickly covered it up. "That is not uncommon, though. The mists of time are not always clear. What matters most at the moment is that all of my efforts to hone you to a fine edge may be in jeopardy."

"Does that have anything to do with me waking up to find you standing there naked?"

He merely chuckled in response - which was highly preferable to putting me through a wall. "Know that I have never once in over two millennia shied away from testing my own mettle, Freewill - not against you, and not against others of your kind."

"Um, okay. So that whole honing me to a sharp edge thing..."

"Yes?"

"Well, what's been going on? How did I get here? *When* did I get here?"

"You really do not remember much when you are in that state?"

"Not a thing."

"Very well." He continued to retrace our steps through the bowels of wherever we were. Various vamps along the way snapped to attention as we passed, but he paid them not the slightest heed. "I suppose it would not hurt to tell you. You were tracked to the marshes south of your coven some three months ago."

"Three months?"

"Yes."

"Oh, I am so fired."

"Excuse me?"

"Uh, never mind." It's not like my paycheck meant a whole lot in this hell of endless catacombs. "Marshes...do you mean close to the Meadowlands?"

"I believe that is what they call the arenas there, yes."

"So how did you find me?"

"Remington, of course."

Colin had sent that douchebag to assist in tracking down and killing Sheila. I specifically remembered him being a massive dick, more or less trying to take charge the second he walked in. Then there was that fight up in Westchester where Gan had made her sudden, and unwanted, reappearance. I had a vague memory of a battle atop a building too, but its conclusion was all fuzzy in my mind. Judging by Alex's remarks, though, I was forced to assume I had lost that one. "So he found me?"

"Remington is dead. He and his men were slain by the Icon, or so we were told."

Way to go, Sheila!

"A pity," I lied.

"Indeed. He would have potentially been a great asset to our war effort."

"So then how does he play into my being found?"

"His blood, of course."

My reply to that was to stare at him in utter confusion.

"Before going out into the field, it is standard protocol for strike teams such as his to consume a radioactive isotope. It allows them to be tracked in case their retrieval becomes necessary."

Interesting and far more high-tech than I expected. For all of their traditional bullshit, I needed to remember that there were some parts of the vampire nation that were up to snuff with technology.

Alex grinned smugly as he spoke. "My fellows were at a loss as to how to track you. Our intelligence suggested that even your scent had changed along with your physical appearance. I, however, was willing to make the assumption that perhaps some of his team's blood had made its way to your person."

Uh oh. Sally and I had worked against Remington from the very start. We had operated under the assumption that his ego wouldn't allow him to call in backup. It had seemed a safe bet - assuming we were able to kill each and every one of his team. From the sound of things, we'd succeeded, but apparently Alex had been smart enough to consider that some underhanded shit might have gone down.

"How so?" I stammered, losing yet another opportunity to play it cool.

"Considering the Icon's power, I would think it logical to assume you would have partaken of their blood to increase your own strength in the conflict."

"Oh...okay. I mean, yeah, that's what happened."

He glanced at me sidelong with his mismatched eyes. "As I had surmised, the isotope signature led my recovery team straight to your location - as it did the second and third teams sent to secure you."

"*Second and Third* teams?"

"Your alternate appearance can be marvelously uncooperative."

Translation: I fucked them up. Maybe I needed to cut Dr. Death a little slack after all.

"Finally, you were sedated and I had you secretly airlifted back here. We've been training you ever since."

"Training?"

"A constantly changing regimen designed to add a modicum of discipline. If you are to lead our forces in the coming conflict, it will be a necessity to have control."

"And how successful were you?"

"Needless to say, that is another aspect where you are unique compared to..."

Another vamp rounded a corner and raced up to us. "Lord Alexander, sir!" He skidded to a halt and stood at attention. Although the newcomer's face was unreadable, annoyance clearly shown on Alex's.

"And your reason for disturbing me?"

"You wished to be informed once Druaga had returned."

Alex's expression softened to one of neutrality again. I guessed that the underling's excuse was good enough to let him live to see another night. "I am afraid we shall have to cut our tour short, Freewill. Druaga will be expecting a demonstration of your powers."

"But, I can't..."

"Oh yes, you can." His odd eyes twinkled as he spoke and he laid a hand on my shoulder. "Trust me. I always plan for contingencies."

That's what I was afraid of.

Escape from Alcatraz

Alex descended a hidden stairwell - one that I made a note to remember. Sadly, our destination was my holding cell. Rampaging monster or not, it seemed I was still expected to call this place home.

Of course, that was assuming there was still a me left after whatever demonstration he had planned.

Two vampire guards waited outside the open door of my rocky prison. One breathed a noticeable sigh of relief once we were in sight. They must've been unlucky enough to have been assigned as Druaga's minders. One could only imagine what they'd be forced to do if he demanded a night out on the town.

Waiting just inside, impatiently tapping several claws on a rocky outcropping, stood Druaga's monstrous form - looking even uglier than before, if that was possible.

You were not here when I returned. Why is this?

"I needed to be taken for a walk and a belly rub," I replied without thinking. Goddamnit, I really needed to stop doing that.

Druaga cocked his head to the side, momentarily looking ridiculously idiotic for a reptilian demon-god.

"Our apologies, mighty one," Alex said, stepping in. "These are trying times, requiring my attention. No offense was intended."

"Uh yeah, what he said," I added.

Alex guided me past Godzuki and then we turned to face him.

So be it. You will now proceed to show me the Freewill's power.

"Of course, oh Lord of the Festering Pit. Behold the Freewill as he is now. What would you say if you encountered him upon the battlefield?"

I raised an eyebrow at that. What the fuck?

I would say he was unworthy to feed to even my lowliest dretch-hound.

"And you would be correct in thinking so." I hadn't realized Alex's contingency plan included using me as comedy relief. If so, I'd have requested a pair of clown shoes to round out my ensemble. "Strike me, Freewill."

"Huh?"

"I said strike me - full on. Use all the might at your disposal."

Was Alex actually asking me to hit him? Tempting. Heck, once I started, I might not want to stop. Unfortunately, there was always the chance he'd hit back...

No. Strike me, instead. I wish to know your power.

"Um..." An ancient vampire warlord was one thing, but now a freaking *god* wanted to go punch-for-punch? That didn't sound like a winning battle to me.

Alex crossed his arms and looked at me expectantly. "Do as you are bidden, Freewill."

I so hated being the low man on the totem pole. It's like this at work whenever I'm in a meeting with my manager and some director from another department. You could always count on shit sliding downhill right into my lap. The difference was that the worst that could happen there was getting fired. Here... well, I didn't even want to think about it. The supernatural world seemed to specialize in messy endings.

The silence stretched for another second. Oh well, I had the feeling there was no way around it. On the upside - considering the many ways people die every day, there was one advantage to doing this: not many folks could honestly put on their tombstone they'd gotten a chance to punch it out with the dude who signs the Grim Reaper's paycheck.

"Here it comes," I said in my best tough-guy voice. The reject from the reptile house held his arms out to the side. Gut shot it was, then.

I stepped up and let loose with a haymaker powerful enough so that this fucker's second cousin would feel it.

Or so I told myself.

There's some truth to the old saying of *this is going to hurt me more than it does you.* Druaga didn't even flinch. Hitting the scales on his midsection was like punching a pile of sand. There was the tiniest of give, but I might as well have slapped him with a feather for all the damage I did.

The brows over his two rightmost eyes raised questioningly and he inclined his head ever so slightly toward Alex - his lack of awe painfully clear.

This is the reason you called me forth from my realm? I am close to being insulted, vampire. Know that I have unleashed my wrath for far less.

Oh, crapola.

* * *

I backed up a step, hoping Dru's main beef was with Alex. Safe to say, I wouldn't take offense if he considered me unworthy of smiting.

Instead, Alex laughed. The death god and I turned toward the leader of the Draculas, no doubt wondering why he'd chosen this moment to go batshit insane.

"Do you not see how perfect he is, oh mighty one?"

Explain yourself.

"Our enemies will view him the same way - as no threat whatsoever. This makes him the perfect weapon. The Grendel and their allies will seek out the strongest warriors on the battlefield, failing to realize what they have foolishly turned their backs upon."

Yeah, me, the guy who'd get the fuck out of Dodge the second they ignored me. I wasn't too proud to admit that running away was a strategy I hadn't quite ruled out.

And they would be correct. The disgust practically dripped off Druaga - along with some drool. *Tell me, Alexander of the First, does your grand plan involve our enemies pissing themselves to death with laughter? This creature represents no threat.*

"Yet."

"Yet?" I mimicked, unsure where this was going.

"The Freewill's appearance is deceptive with regards to the true power that lies inside of him."

I grow tired of this...

"Power that I will now show you."

I almost blurted out, "How?" but managed to bite my tongue. Had he already forgotten that I couldn't change, that the beast inside of me was taking a time out? Hell, even that pack of crazy blind assholes couldn't help him out. Was he planning to bluff the scaly freak?

Alex held up an index finger. His nail immediately thickened and elongated into a wicked talon three inches long.

Uh oh.

Raising his other arm, he slashed his wrist open in one fluid motion.

No. He couldn't be serious.

But he was. Moving with that same lightning-fast speed as before, he grabbed me and clutched the back of my neck, forcing my mouth onto the spurting wound.

"Now you will see, Mighty Druaga, just how easily the prey becomes the predator."

* * *

A small part of me was tempted to clamp my mouth shut. Hell, maybe if I did it long enough, Alex would just save us all the trouble and bleed to death. Wouldn't that be nice? It'd definitely save everyone a lot of trouble to come.

The truth was that I was terrified of drinking his blood. The last time I'd done so, when he'd secretly slipped it to me back when we were in Canada, it had been far too powerful. The result had caused...

Was that his plan? If he couldn't beat Dr. Death out of me, he'd force him out with an overdose of his blood?

Would that even work? And if it didn't, what would happen? They could probably try to...

Goddamn, what a fucking moron I could be.

If it worked, then I'd change and give Druaga whatever demonstration he was looking for. Alex would probably be happy enough to go grease himself up for another nude cage match. In short, I wouldn't be in any worse shape than I was.

But if I didn't change...

Fuck it, it was worth a chance.

I opened my mouth and bit down upon Alex's arm, letting the lifeblood of quite possibly the most powerful vampire in the world pour down my throat.

* * *

The effect was nearly instantaneous. It was like drinking a gallon of rocket fuel, followed by a lit match as a chaser. It spread to my extremities, sending tingles of energy coursing through them. All at once, I felt like a million bucks, as if there were no force on this planet that I couldn't stand against. My body felt light and springy, ready to bound over rooftops with the barest of effort.

In short, I felt like a supercharged engine, the RPMs pushed into the red as the gas pedal hit the floor. The blood wasn't done affecting me, though.

"ARGH!" I backed away from them and doubled over, feeling as if I were on fire. This was it. I opened my eyes, holding my hands in front of them and expecting my claws to elongate as my body enlarged. My thoughts would become cloudy as the desire for carnage began to take over, until at last my vision would turn red and I would remember nothing.

Except that didn't happen.

Physically, I remained unchanged as the spasms brought on by Alex's blood subsided. Holy shit, talk about riding out a high. I'm not exactly what you'd call a hardcore pothead, but was known to indulge from time to time. Smoking even the really good shit was nothing compared to this, though.

I stood up straight, feeling the difference in the world around me. As intense as my senses normally were, they were even more jacked up. I could smell the faintest of scents - something Druaga really didn't benefit from. I could hear the shallowest of breaths by the guards still standing watch outside my cell. I could...holy fuck. I glanced over the rim of my glasses and realized everything was still in focus. Freaking awesome! That alone was incentive for living two thousand more years.

It probably wouldn't last, but maybe I could still use that to my advantage.

First things first, though.

"Behold, oh glorious one," Alex said. "The Freewill who stands before us now is not the same man he was mere seconds ago." If he was disappointed that I hadn't changed, he didn't show it. He was one cool cucumber.

Pity that I was about to play the part of the paring knife.

* * *

"Now, Freewill, show the mighty Druaga..."

"My pleasure." I used my amped-up speed to move to Alex's side in less time than it took to think it.

Quickly, before I could psych myself out of what was surely a suicidal move on my part, I grabbed him by the shirt. He barely had time to raise a questioning eyebrow when I spun and flung him toward the far end of my cell with everything I had.

It turned out I had even more power than I thought. He flew like he'd been shot out of a missile launcher, crashing into the wall and sending out a shower of debris. Yeah, that was probably gonna piss him off a little.

I had no delusions about my chances. I might've temporarily possessed equal power, but he had centuries of experience on his side. This was a battle I had little chance of winning. Thus, a change in locale was dictated, pronto.

Impressive, Freew...

I didn't let the oversized Sleestak finish the thought. Bringing all of my stolen strength and speed to bear, I rushed toward him shoulder first.

Ugh! Even with Alex's power, it was still like trying to tackle a tractor trailer, but fortunately I'd caught him by surprise. I knocked the god of the underworld off his feet, which left me a clear route to the door. Heh, how many people could make that claim?

There was no time to waste gloating, though.

I raced to the entrance, paused in the doorway, and turned around. "So sorry, Dru, but I must bid you adieu. P.S. Fuck you."

Well, maybe there was a *little* time to gloat.

Or not.

Hands fell upon my shoulders. Shit, I'd forgotten about the guards.

Pity for them I hadn't *also* forgotten the part about having enough strength to arm-wrestle Spider-man and win. However old they were, they were still no match for a vamp of Alex's power.

I stepped out into the hall and grabbed hold of them on either side of me. Bringing my arms together, I slammed the two of them face-first into each other with a satisfying crunch of bone.

My newly sharpened eyes caught movement on the far end of the cavern. Time was up.

I shoved the semi-conscious guards inside and slammed the heavy door shut just as a massive impact hit it from the other side.

I jumped back, worried that it would give under Alex's assault, but then remembered it had been designed to handle me in my Dr. Death form. Judging by the minimal damage I'd managed to inflict upon it, it was a safe bet that it was built to exceed specs.

The outside of the door included an airlock-like crank as well as an old-fashioned keyhole - conveniently occupied by a thick metal key.

Oops, make that occupied by the *broken* end of a thick metal key.

None of that would stop Druaga, who'd already shown a talent for teleporting, but hopefully he'd be too preoccupied with bitching out Alex to come after me.

Another impact sounded from inside. The stonework around the door rattled from the force of it. Oh yeah, definitely time to go.

I removed my glasses and put them in my back pocket. My eyes would serve as the test for when Alex's power was beginning to falter. It was a fuck-load better than jumping into a fight before realizing I was back down to normal levels. Also, it was nice just not to wear them. I'd never been a big fan of contacts...dry eyes and all that crap.

I turned right and sped off down the corridor, not really sure which way to go other than to keep heading up toward the surface. Even if the door held, I wasn't sure if the thick walls would block any compulsions for help Alex might send out. I had to assume the worst - that it was only going to be a matter of time before he escaped.

I needed to be as far away as possible when that happened.

Head Cheese

Goddamn, what a fucking rat maze. Even using my stolen speed, it was still a pain in the ass of tunnels, stairs, and dead ends. Christ, I could barely find my way around an amusement park without a map. This was near hopeless.

I only slowed when I sensed other vamps near, which happened pretty frequently considering this was their base of operations. Fortunately, barely any of them batted their eyes in my direction. Thank goodness for vampire arrogance. For the past three months, anyone who'd had any contact with me had only seen whatever the fuck it was I turned into. I, as just myself, was just a lowly child to them - hardly worthy of their attention.

Bunch of pricks.

After several long minutes of making shit progress in my bid to escape, I slowed down and tried to use some strategy - falling back on my gaming expertise. After all, my elven battle-mage, Kelvin Lightblade, was an experienced dungeon crawler. He'd made it into and out of worse places than this - usually burdened with gold and glorious tales to tell. As the brains behind him, could I do any less? Fuck no.

That was it - I had to imagine myself in the game. Forget the vampire nation; I was on a quest, sent from a far off kingdom ruled by the beautiful Princess Sheila...

She's dead.

No! That wasn't helping. It was just distracting. Forget the princess too; I was on a mission to find a powerful artifact that would save...oh, screw it. I was looking for some fucking treasure. Yeah, that was the ticket.

Using that mindset, I was able to start making some real progress.

Well, okay, it also helped that I happened to stick my head in what looked like a storage room. Inside, a bored-looking zombie was performing inventory of some boxes. He looked up expectantly at my presence.

"Chillon Castle?" I asked, hoping for the best. Man, vampire, or other, one should never be too proud to ask for directions.

To my surprise, he hooked a desiccated thumb in one direction, sending me on my way.

At long last, I saw it. Barely an arrow slit up above - near the top of yet another flight of stone steps - I finally glimpsed a sliver of sky. Even better, it was dark out. If I could find a door or window, I could make a run for it. I had no idea what would come next, but I'd figure it out...hopefully.

All I knew for certain was that my opportunity was rapidly drying up. I'd been out for too long. It was only a matter of time before an alarm klaxon sounded and every vamp in the place was ordered to hunt me down.

I followed the hall I'd just emerged into, hoping it would lead somewhere useful. Continuing on, I came to a four-way intersection, but heard voices coming from the left and right. Figuring I'd pressed my luck enough for one day, I kept going straight until the hallway turned to the left and... yet another dead end.

Fuck!

All that stood before me were some candle sconces and a few paintings. Who the fuck had designed this place?

In frustration, I let loose and punched the wall - smacking the fine wood inlay with a hollow *thunk*.

Wait...hollow?

Once more, my finely tuned gaming senses tingled. Was it possible?

I lifted the paintings - nothing. Twisted the sconces - *nada*. Lifted the candles from them...yes! Something made a clunking noise, and a section of the wall slid open to reveal an ornately carved wooden door. If Dave had been there at the moment, I'd have kissed him.

The door was probably locked - which would have been a problem had I not possessed the augmented strength of the undead.

I grasped the handle, intent on turning it until the tumbler inside shattered. Typically, I wasn't really gung-ho on destroying antiques, but this was owned by vampires, and they could mostly go fuck themselves. To my surprise, though, it opened with a click - unlocked. Odd.

Waiting a moment to see if it exploded or shot poison darts at me - as any good adventurer would do - I finally opened it up and stepped inside, praying it was the way out.

It wasn't.

* * *

Whoa. It was another hall...no, screw that. It was more like a full luxury apartment - one made for a king.

A hallway led forward. There were open doorways on both sides leading to rooms, each putting my humble abode back in Brooklyn to shame. There was a small library with rich mahogany shelves stacked with ancient-looking books and scrolls. Another room appeared to be an office that would have made any corporate executive weep with joy. It practically exuded authority, with walls covered in expensive-looking paintings - most of them depicting scenes of a black horse charging into battle. Jeez. Someone must have a *My Little Pony* fetish.

It wasn't all old, mind you. There was a living room, dominated by expensive leather chairs with a huge flat-screen TV hanging from one wall over a fireplace. Whoever lived here certainly wasn't suffering from want.

I stepped through the doorway at the end and entered into a massive bedroom. It was like stepping into some sort of sultan's fantasy. A huge bed, covered in satin sheets and pillows, dominated one side. There was an in-floor bath, a steam room, changing area, another TV...you name it. There was no way one could own a bachelor pad like this and not be swimming in pussy.

I was beginning to get an inkling as to who might call this place home, when all doubt was erased. Of all the places in this dump I could've stumbled, it had to be his.

Towering over the center of the room - standing out like a sore thumb - was a marble statue, nine feet tall and obviously carved by a master craftsman. Every inch was well defined in painful detail. Even the veins on the muscles were plainly visible. It was blindingly white in color, so the mismatched eyes weren't apparent, but the resemblance was uncanny nevertheless - Alexander.

I took it in, head to toe, noting it was quite anatomically correct, although I had to question whether certain aspects were more a result of his overinflated ego than reality. Talk about being full of yourself. Vampires as a whole tended to be egomaniacal, but this guy put them all to shame. He made Vanity Smurf look humble in comparison.

Oh well, this was all fine and good, but it wasn't helping me find a way out.

I began looking for another egress when I stopped and considered the possibilities. Oh, fuck it. It's not like he could end up more pissed off than he probably already was. I made a fist, intent on defacing his effigy. Crumbling his man bits to dust wasn't much, but it would give me some satisfaction. Yeah, it was petty, but then so was keeping me locked up naked in a fucking dungeon for three months.

I stopped myself short, though. Doing so would make it hard to miss that I'd been in here. There was probably no point in making my escape route that obvious.

Regaining my focus, I stopped dicking around and noticed a couple additional doors in the master bedroom. Maybe I'd finally get lucky and one would lead to a balcony or something. By that point, I wasn't averse to trying my luck swan diving into the moat. I began opening them.

There was a closet full of robes and other finery. Fucking thing was bigger than my entire bedroom back home. Goddamn, it was good to be king.

Next was a sparkling white bathroom. At least now I knew where Alex pinched his princely loaves.

A set of double sliding doors stood at the far end of the room. It was my last choice left. That *had* to be it.

Ugh! They were locked and much heavier than I would have guessed. If this was an exit, it sure as shit wasn't a convenient one.

Thankfully, I still had some extra zing to my step. I applied pressure, trying to pry the doors apart. Holy crap, talk about sturdy. Had I been at my normal strength, I wouldn't have been able to budge them. Thankfully, that wasn't the case. I put my back into it and metal squealed as the lock snapped and the doors finally parted.

They slid open and I immediately bit down on my tongue to stifle the scream that wanted to come rushing out. I hadn't expected the sight of so many faces greeting me.

* * *

Three rows of shelves stood before me. Each held multiple glass cylinders stacked side by side. These cylinders were full of a red-tinted liquid, transparent enough so that the preserved head contained within each was clearly visible.

My first thought was the head museum from *Futurama*. Alas, the resemblance ended there as I didn't see Richard Nixon or any other smiling celebrities.

Their expressions reflected the tortured pain of their last moments, as if they'd died in excruciating agony - which was probably not too far from the truth. Staring at them all, a strange feeling entered the pit of my stomach - almost like mild indigestion. That was weird. Maybe Alex had eaten something earlier that was disagreeing with me. Regardless, I pushed it aside for the moment.

While I stood there looking at a collection far more macabre than anything my roommate, Tom, had on display, lights turned on and illuminated the scene. Hmm, maybe the doors opening activated it.

A low buzzing noise reached my ears, seeming to originate from within the containers. Sure enough, the liquid in each moved slightly and there seemed to be small bits of debris being thrown up from the bottoms.

I leaned in closer to look, nearly touching one of them. An odd swirling began at the base of it. What the...?

Just then, the buzzing ceased and the motion stopped - affording me a clearer view. There was a blade in the bottom, like something you'd see in a food processor. Squinting, I saw that the flotsam it had disturbed was actually bits of flesh from the ragged remains of the neck upon which this container's resident noggin sat.

What the hell? Was this Alex's fucked-up version of a personal wet bar? Jesus Christ, what a...

A slight wave of vertigo swam over me as my eyes defocused. The room's appearance became all fuzzy, and I put a hand onto the container I'd been examining to steady myself. The power of Alex's blood was starting to wear off. A pity. I'd begun to get used to it.

With my free hand, I reached into my back pocket to retrieve my glasses. It had been nice to visit the land of twenty-twenty vision, but all vacations must come to an end. As I put them on, the world swam back into focus - including the now-open eyes of the jarred head in front of me...eyes that were staring directly into mine.

"Holy shit!"

I staggered back a step. Unfortunately, in my panic, I brushed against the jar I'd been studying, causing it to teeter. Oh crap.

For a moment I thought I was screwed, but then it resettled itself.

That's when the impossible happened.

* * *

Somehow, the head within jerked forward, coming into contact with the glass. The container overbalanced and fell. All of this happened within the space of a second. Had I not been completely freaked, I might've still caught it. Sadly, would've could've and should've were all taking a siesta right then. As I stood there dumbfounded, it landed on the floor and shattered - drenching my lower half in the reddish liquid inside.

Even with my diminishing senses, there was no mistaking the scent of blood - albeit very diluted.

The head within, now freed of its glass prison, rolled to a stop next to my foot. Before I could punt the creepy thing away, the eyes again focused on me and the mouth opened, revealing the fangs within. These weren't the severed remains of human victims. They were vampires.

My friend on the floor wasn't alone, either. I looked up to see that all of the heads now had their eyes trained on me. Talk about fucking weird.

Back when Gan had first visited New York, in a deluded attempt to win my heart, she'd explained it. When vamps of significant rank wanted you dead, there usually wasn't much you could do except obligingly die a horrific death. Sometimes, though, that wasn't enough for the merciless fuckers. Occasionally, they'd opt for that whole fate worse than death thing.

In such cases, a vampire could be decapitated via a silver blade coated with a specific poison. Under normal circumstances when that happened, you'd be left with nothing but a pile of dust. The poison would retard that process, however. The head would still be living - or whatever we vampires do - and could be kept that way indefinitely if placed in blood.

Diluted blood was apparently good enough, and also seemingly served the dual purpose of letting the captor see the submerged head in question - presumably to gloat at it.

How long had they been here? And what had they done to piss off Alex so badly that he kept them around in his fucking closet like trophies? It wasn't hard to imagine, judging by the strength of the door, that they were for his eyes only. I imagined that most vamps, especially the Draculas, wouldn't be shy about displaying such things to their peers. So what was the story here?

I shook my head. Why the fuck did I even care? This was most definitely not my problem, at least outside of the fact that I'd probably just made room for myself in the collection. I easily envisioned Alex being pissed off enough to do something like this to me, prophecy be damned. Most of the elder vamps I'd met weren't shy about putting their own egos ahead of the greater good. Even worse, I was standing there like a doofus as the last of his power left me. If even a lowly guard happened by, I was toast.

That being said, I considered that possibility low. If this was indeed Alex's abode, I doubted anyone would be insane enough to trespass. It hadn't been particularly difficult to break in, leading me to think that theory had merit. Regardless, it wasn't like I could just move in and hope nobody noticed. I'd outstayed my welcome, and it was time to do something about that.

I hesitated, though, my eyes surveying the mess I'd made - including the severed noggin lying there. There was little chance of me cleaning things up, what with me lacking a mop, dustpan, and a shit-ton of glue. Even so, I needed at least to try covering my tracks.

I used my foot to slide the glass shards under the shelving, then glanced down at the head, still alive and staring at me. Fucking thing was definitely giving me the heebie-jeebies.

Whoever he'd been, he had a strong chin and long dark hair - ending where his neck did, obviously a result of the makeshift Cuisinart he'd called home. There was no telling what the rest of him had been like, but his face could have almost passed as a stunt double for Arnold Schwarzenegger during his Conan days. Oh well, I had no time for "I'll be back" jokes. I reached down to pick him up, intent on putting him back onto the shelf where he belonged.

But wait. Whoever this was, he'd obviously done something to get on Alex's bad side. Wasn't there that saying about the enemy of my enemy being my friend? Wasn't it possible he might have some information that could be useful? I mean, sure, he was just a head, but maybe Sally or James could read his lips or something.

There was also the fact that...well, I'm not a total dick like Alex and most of his buddies. It seemed like an asshole move to just leave this guy there to rot after he had spent God knows how long living in a margarita blender.

That settled it. I'd been doing my damnedest since waking up undead to avoid being a prick like my fellow vamps. In the end, that could very well be the difference between winning and losing in my bid to save the world. How? I had no fucking idea. I was pretty much grasping at straws.

The glass out of the way, I pulled the double doors shut - putting my back into it, now that Alex's strength had fled me. One hernia later and they were closed again, the busted lock thankfully unseen from the outside. Aside from Captain Cranium, there was still plenty of diluted blood on the floor, but I got an idea that would possibly solve that.

Make that solve *both* problems. Outside of his personal aquarium, the head wasn't much different than a fish that had leaped from its tank. He wasn't looking too good - I mean, even worse than a decapitated head should look. His eyes, formerly focused on me, were starting to roll up into his...well, y'know.

"Hang in there, buddy," I muttered and then got to work.

Sightseeing

Five minutes later, I stepped back out of Alex's room. His other closet had contained everything the doctor ordered, and I helped myself to as much as I dared without making it look completely ransacked.

I'd grabbed a few of his robes and used them to clean up the blood - saturating them in the process. They'd need a bit more than a good bleaching before they'd be wearable again, but fuck it. I was fairly sure the puppet-master of Switzerland could afford some new terrycloth.

After cleaning up my mess, I'd wrapped Max Headroom in the bloody robes, hoping they'd keep him hydrated enough until I could think of something better. The shoulder pack I'd swiped to stuff him into appeared to be weatherproof. Hopefully, it would keep anything from dripping out. It wasn't the best of plans, but it was all I had at the moment.

I closed the door behind me and then replaced the candle that had revealed the secret door. As expected, the action caused it to close up again. Ah, so cliché. Oh, Alex, you really need to read some new material. That crap wouldn't have fooled a first-level rogue and it sure as shit hadn't fooled me...mostly.

I wasn't out of the woods yet. Sure, I was above ground, but that was the extent of what I knew. I still needed to find a way out of this medieval rat maze.

Going down again wasn't an option, so I decided to follow the side corridors that I'd passed upon reaching this level. I just needed for luck to be on my side for a little bit longer.

* * *

I went down a few hallways before finally finding another locked door. This one, though, was latched from my side. Considering that a promising sign, I unlocked it and stepped through into some sort of sitting room.

A fat man stood there for a moment, staring at me while he continued eating his sandwich. He regarded me with bored disdain, munching away as he did so, before reaching into a pocket with his free hand.

His stubby fingers emerged, holding a smartphone. He pressed a button on the screen and I immediately went into panic mode. I was too close to be caught now. There was no fucking way I was going back, especially since I had a feeling I'd be joining the guy in my knapsack on a shelf somewhere - destined to be at Alex's mercy for all of eternity whenever he decided a good Freewill skull-fucking was just the thing to curb his boredom. No thank you.

I was pretty much back to my normal strength, but my nose was telling me that this guy was just a human -

one for whom hygiene wasn't apparently a top concern. Unless he was a Shaolin monk in disguise - and that would've been a hell of a disguise - I could take this fucker before he sounded the alarm.

The guy barely had time to open his jowly mouth in surprise before I was on him, driving my fist into his meaty face. He went down with a thud. Oh yeah, I still had it.

I bent down and pried the phone from his greasy fingers, holding it up to see what was on the screen. It was the...the camera app? What, was he looking to take a photo of me? Maybe share it on Facebook so he could prove to his masters that he'd found the escaped Freewill?

"Deiter," a shrill voice called from somewhere outside of the room. "Deiter!"

I stepped to the opposite doorway and peeked out. An equally large woman, with her hair done up in a sloppy bun, was looking about curiously. Her eyes fell upon me and immediately passed over as she continued calling what I assumed to be the man's name. What the...?

Beyond her, I could see more people. They were milling about in a group, following a man who was speaking in what sounded like German and pointing at various knickknacks in the room. Most of the group held cameras, which were clicking away at whatever the guy pointed at.

I ducked back into the sitting room and looked down at the dude I'd just decked. Now that I had a moment, I realized he didn't look even remotely like a guard.

Oh, fuck - I'd just mugged a tourist.

* * *

Panicking, I dragged the fat guy through the door I'd entered from. I turned to leave, hoping maybe to lose myself amongst the tour group, then stopped. At this point, I'd already committed felony assault. It wasn't like I could be in much deeper shit. When life hands you lemons...you go through their pockets and steal what you can. At least that's what I did. I grabbed the guy's phone and wallet. If I was going to be a fugitive, I might as well go all the way.

Propping Chubs up against the wall, I stepped back out, trying to look touristy. Yeah, I was making it up as I went.

I couldn't have planned what happened next better had I tried. Apparently, the guides didn't take kindly to people wandering off. I'd no more than walked ten paces before an angry, red-faced man came marching up to me, speaking sternly in words that I couldn't understand.

I held up my hands to let him know I had no idea what he was saying, causing him to shut up and glare at me expectantly.

"Um...Americano?"

The guide sighed painfully. My guess was he'd done this before. "Can you not read?" he asked in heavily accented English. "Wandering off is strictly forbidden on night tours."

"Sorry, I was just exploring a little. This place is quite...fascinating."

"Be that as it may, do so again and I will have to ask you to leave."

"Leave?" I asked, not believing my luck.

"Yes, and I am afraid that no refunds are given."

"Oh, well in that case, did I mention how good your mother is at sucking dicks?"

"What?"

"Yep. Last night, that bitch gobbled down my bratwurst like it was Oktoberfest."

The man's face turned even redder. "That is it. Your disrespect will not be tolerated!" He turned and beckoned me to follow. "Hopefully, this will teach you to respect the rules."

I thought back to my adventures from the past several hours. "I highly doubt it."

* * *

The true beauty of a stolen smartphone is, without a doubt, Google Maps. It took me a few seconds to force the English version of the site to load, but finally, I was no longer flying blind...and flying was my goal.

I kept walking, making sure to put as much distance between myself and the castle as possible, despite knowing it wouldn't help if they decided to track me down. They knew my scent, and I probably likewise reeked of blood - not to mention decapitated cranium.

Regardless, I wasn't about to give up. They might still catch me, but I sure as fuck was going to make them work for it.

Walking along the shores of what I assumed to be Lake Geneva, I hit pay-dirt on the phone. There was a major airport nearby. Even better, it was just on the opposite side of the lake. Unfortunately, it was a big fucking lake.

There was also the fact that I had limited money, no passport, no ID, and was carrying a severed head. Yeah, this was gonna be a tad tricky.

* * *

Thank goodness for petty larceny. My escape plan was greatly accelerated once I realized that, regardless of being on the opposite side of the planet, any airport of note was going to have buses going to and from it. I sincerely doubted the wallet I'd swiped had enough money to pay for a ticket back home, but there was certainly enough to cover bus fare. Once on board, a quick sniff of the air confirmed that the rest of the passengers were all human. Thus, I slipped into a seat - just another tourist looking to go home.

The vampire choice of strongholds was smart. They controlled a ridiculously rich country that was situated in perhaps the world's most perfect natural fortress - a fact attested to once I was able to relax and enjoy the view out the window. Mountainous peaks could be seen in every direction, silhouetted against the stars shining in the night sky.

There was just one small mistake in picking such a place, as opposed to a foreboding fortress deep within the mountains of Transylvania: a massive tourist trade. There was no way - not even with the end of the world nigh - that the vampires could put the entire nation on lockdown to search for little ole me. The international community would probably notice such things. I just had to stick with the crowd and get to the airport.

From there - okay, I had no fucking idea. I still somehow had to figure out which plane was the correct one, get myself a ticket, then make it past security without them x-raying my bag and noticing the gruesome contents within, all in a place that I had absolutely no knowledge about, save what I could pull up on a phone that only had thirty percent battery life left.

It was a piece of cake...had I been Jason Bourne. For me, well, there was always the hope for a minor miracle.

Regardless, my spirits perked up as the lights from the airport came into view. A plane took off and I imagined myself safely aboard it. It was destined for parts unknown, but who cared? The truth was, finding the right flight was a wish-list item at best. Any plane headed out of this godforsaken country would be an improvement. Yeah, first priority was finding myself on soil that wasn't owned by the undead. Once that happened, I'd have some time to plan out my next steps.

The bus pulled into the drop-off lane and slowed. I stood and grabbed my bag - hoping my traveling companion was faring well. Unfortunately, I had a feeling that opening up to check on him might cause a bit of a scene. Oh well, we had to rely on the resiliency of his vampire physiology. If he was going to make it, he was going to make it. If not, there probably wasn't much I could do about it. If he died, I could at least take comfort in knowing he died free - minus maybe the part about him being stuck in a backpack.

I got in line and stepped toward the exit, anticipating blending in with the crowd beyond - heading to whatever destinations called to them. A smile crossed my lips as my feet touched the ground.

It disappeared just as quickly as a female voice reached my ears. "Greetings, Freewill."

Theodora and Yehoshua stood there on the curb no more than ten feet away, flanked by a small contingent of airport security.

Stowing aboard the correct flight suddenly seemed like the easiest thing in the world compared to getting away from this bunch.

A Problem with Customs

I stood there gaping, hoping for a brainstorm that wasn't currently forecast. As I did, the remaining passengers disembarked from the bus. The doors closed behind me and I heard it pull away.

I quickly glanced around, considering making a run for it, but it was a fool's errand. Things would be problematic enough with just the guards, all of whom registered as vamps via my senses, but I was facing off against not one, but two members of the Draculas. My chances of escape were somewhat less than finding a winning lottery ticket in my pocket, followed by a supermodel pulling up and offering me a complimentary blowjob.

There was only one possible chance: bullshitting my way out of this.

Putting on my best arrogant sneer, I looked at them both, as if seeing them there was the most natural thing in the world. "You guys are late."

Theodora faced me down smirk for smirk. "Are we?"

"Yep, I figured I'd have seen some resistance by now. You do realize it's all futile, though."

"Oh?"

"In case you haven't heard, I'm the Freewill. I'm prepared to face down the worst the world has to offer. Do yourselves a favor - step aside and this doesn't have to get ugly."

Yehoshua smiled and turned to the guards, saying something to them that I couldn't understand. They all snapped to attention for a moment, then turned and headed off into the terminal.

He and his gal pal stepped up to me, the amusement never leaving their faces.

"Your friends were smart. Maybe you should follow them." I said, hoping that sweat wasn't currently beading on my forehead.

Theodora lifted a finger and trailed the nail gently down my chest. Under normal circumstances, it would have been hot, but knowing who she was just made it extra creepy. "Or what? You'll continue trying to unconvincingly bluff your way out of this?"

Oh, crap. "You probably don't want to tick me off. That tends to end bad..."

"Please, child," she said, sounding unimpressed. "I was present when Rome fell. I bore witness as the last Caesar arrogantly threatened reinforcements that weren't coming. He was far more convincing than you, yet his blood still painted the walls before the sun rose the next day."

"I don't need reinforcements. I'm the reborn..."

"By all means, continue to insult my intelligence with your lies..."

Yehoshua interrupted our foreplay. "Please, time is short."

Theodora sighed, then turned to him. "You are always one to spoil the fun, Joshua."

He smiled broadly at her before addressing me. "Kindly follow us, Freewill."

He hooked an arm around mine and guided me in a direction parallel to the terminal. He was gentle about it, but at the same time, there was the implied power behind his actions. We both knew damn well he could've just dragged my ass, regardless of my protests.

I debated making a scene, but then realized the only ones who would respond would probably be vampires - and they weren't likely to be all that helpful. Thus, I followed his lead with Theodora keeping step on my other side.

"How'd you guys find me?" There wasn't much I could do against them, but maybe some small talk would give me a bit of insight.

"Find you?" Thea huffed. "You came straight to the airport. You could not have been more obvious had you left a note explaining your intentions. Next time, I would suggest making for the Alps. At least the terrain is vast enough that it might buy you a few hours."

"I'll keep that in mind. I assume you're taking me back."

"You assume incorrectly."

Uh oh. I got a bad feeling in my gut. Either she was still ticked from our little standoff earlier, or they were here to make an example out of me. Hell, maybe both. "Let me guess. Alex is pissed."

"Quite the contrary," Yehoshua, or whatever his name was, replied. Unfortunately, if I was hoping to be further enlightened as to his meaning, I was in for disappointment. This guy seemed to be a man of few words. Thea, on the other hand, was typical of the vamps I'd met - full of herself. I figured I'd have better luck with her as they continued leading me onward.

I tried to keep the surprise out of my voice. "That's a bit unexpected."

"I will admit that your escape was somewhat amusing," she said. "Locking up Alexander with Druaga...an inspired concept. Suicidal for most, but amusing nevertheless."

"Well, I'm not most." We turned a corner. A heavy gate stood about a hundred yards ahead of us, guarded. Beyond it, another plane took off. Freedom was so close, yet at the same time, impossibly far away.

"Don't forget, that I'm..."

"Powerless?" Thea offered.

"Uh..."

"The grand seer told us everything," Yehoshua explained. "We know that you can no longer access the power inside of you."

They did? "But Alex said they..."

"The seers are known for their absolute loyalty and discretion," Thea said. "They are the keepers of secrets from time unmeasured. For them to do otherwise is a great dishonor to their station."

"But?"

One side of her lips raised in a half smile. "But they are not stupid."

"What Theodora is trying to say is that the keepers of knowledge are not so blind as to ignore the threat to us all." He smiled again. There was something disarming about it. Had I not known what he was, I'd have been tempted to take him at his word. He just had one of those faces. But I wasn't stupid, either. I wasn't about to be so easily won over by a friendly smile...at least on a guy.

"And how do you know Alex didn't specifically tell the seers to spread that rumor?"

The air around us seemed to drop twenty degrees as Thea's eyes practically bored a hole through me. "I could tear your arms off if that would help verify their story."

Oh boy. I needed to remind myself that these guys were not known for their tolerance of mouthy underlings. "Um...maybe we can just assume, for argument's sake, of course, that perhaps they were on to something."

Yehoshua placed a hand onto my shoulder. I was half expecting it to tighten into a crushing grip, but thankfully, it didn't. "The reality, Freewill, is that your condition is only one of several disturbing factors at play right now...perhaps the least of them."

Way to stroke a guy's ego. Oh, fuck it. These guys weren't buying my bullshit, so there was no point in continuing to try hawking it.

"Fine. Let's cut the crap." I took a step and turned so that I was facing both of them. If a serious ass-beating was incoming, I at least wanted to be aware of it. It would also serve to, hopefully, keep me from staring at Thea.

She, much like many other female vamps I'd known, was a fine piece of ass. Considering her supposed age, though, I had a feeling a slap across the face from her would knock my head clean off.

"One part of my power seems to be...broken, if you will. I'm pretty sure it's temporary, but regardless, the usual methods of bringing it out don't seem to be working. So no, there isn't much I'm going to be able to do if you guys are here to drag me back."

"To which we have already told you, we are not," Yehoshua replied.

"I know, which makes me curious as to why you're really here."

"Child," he said, his tone oddly tolerant, "know that the First need not answer to any but our own. Sadly, we find ourselves in strange days indeed. Thus, I see no reason to not speak freely just this once, especially being that our kind holds you in such high regard. To answer your question, we are here because Alexander has ordered you to be returned."

"So he sent you..."

"Do not misunderstand," Thea interrupted. "We are of the First and not at his beck and call. Such missions are for lesser beings."

"We came of our own accord," Yehoshua clarified.

I opened my mouth to reply, but found it hanging agape as he finished his sentence.

"...to ensure that Alexander's edicts were not successful."

* * *

"Wait, did you just say you were here to fuck up Alex's plans?"

"I do not believe I phrased it so crudely, but that is essentially correct."

"Why?"

Thea sniffed impatiently at that. "Our motivations..."

"It is quite all right. I believe he can be trusted." He turned back toward me and said, "Long ago, when I was still able to enjoy the sun on my face, I spoke of peace to my fellow man."

I raised an eyebrow and he chuckled. "I will admit to being a very different person back then. That man is long dead, put to death by those who claimed him an insurrectionist then reborn in darkness - turned by those who wished to make a mockery of my teachings. Despite that, I survived. Though I do not live up to the naïve ideals I once upheld, I have never forgotten them. I have always advocated that we live alongside mankind peacefully."

"Peacefully?"

"We are wolves amongst the flock, true, but does not the pack only take what they must to survive? A wolf may consume the rabbit, but he holds no ill will toward its kind. Once sated, he will be content to let the rest go about their lives. Such has been my philosophy."

"And the same goes for you?" I asked Thea.

A sly grin appeared on her face as she momentarily eyed him. I wouldn't have doubted that he was slipping her the old blood sausage. "Joshua can be quite persuasive. Though I am cut from different cloth, I too enjoy the status quo we have shared with the humans."

"So how do you know I won't rat you both out? I mean, it's not like you can compel me to keep my mouth shut."

"True enough," Yeho...Joshua said. "But then, one does not typically attempt to escape from their confidants."

"We have also heard rumors, Freewill."

"Rumors?"

"Yes. The eyes of our people see far indeed. There are those who question the veracity of the events relayed to us from the Woods of Mourning. Indeed, there are whispers that indicate a distinct lack of enthusiasm for Alexander's war on your part."

Talk about the understatement of the century. That I was apparently being sold to the masses as the poster boy for world domination was a particular sore spot for me. Fuck that. I was no hero. Hell, I wasn't even a passable foot soldier. All I wanted out of life was to spend some good times with my friends and maybe eventually settle down with...well, the girl who could potentially disintegrate me with a touch.

Regardless of that, though, I most certainly had no interest in watching the world burn around me. If there was anything I could do to stop it from happening, I would - providing, of course, it didn't get me horribly killed. Did I mention that I'm no martyr either?

Unfortunately, I had no way of knowing if these two clowns were playing me or not. Their actions would suggest that they weren't, but that didn't mean shit. Vampires that old would no doubt be masters at manipulating others to believe what they wanted. That being said, vamps also tended to be massive suck-ups to those who outranked them. Alex was at the very top of the food chain. He was a cult of personality all unto himself. Showing him anything other than sycophantic worship was practically unheard of for most of our kind.

That was a possibility...one that could potentially get me beaten to a pulp. Oh well, it was all I had to try.

"Those rumors would be correct," I said. "This entire war is because Alex is a giant egomaniacal douchebag. As far as I'm concerned, he can go fuck himself sideways with one of the seers' hot pokers."

I braced myself, first for the shock on their faces, and then for the bigger shock of myself being torn limb from limb. Thankfully, neither came.

Instead, the slightest look of amusement crossed over Thea's face. "The rumors also mention that you've quite the unique way of expressing yourself."

"What can I say? I have a colorful vocabulary." I was just making small talk, trying to process it all. By rights,

I should have been put into chains, then tossed into the back of a truck headed for Chillon Castle - my destination being an even danker dungeon than my previous one. "So where's that all leave us?"

"In an ideal world, I would wish to see us return to our former status quo," Joshua said. "Alas, I fear that the time to avert this war has passed. We are going to battle our ancient enemies whether we wish to or not. The outcome is still undecided, though."

"The prophecy," Thea offered.

"How are we to know if it means anything?" he countered. "Who is to say the prophecy hasn't been massaged by Alexander to suit his needs? You heard the seers today. We are sailing upon unknown waters - the Freewill's powers, the forbidden name, and then their proclamation that the so-called sun walker would be the catalyst..." He trailed off, shaking his head. "Mad ramblings, all of it. At this point, I fear they are making little more than guesses."

"Huh?"

"Nothing more than prattle," he replied. "The seers are able to see the distant shores of time, but I suspect, with destiny looming, they can peer through the immediate mists no better than the rest of us."

I was tempted to comment about the general dumbassery of sitting around, making shit up, with the only consolation prize being burning your eyes out every hour, but Joshua wasn't finished. Considering Thea had already nearly kicked my ass once that day, I opted to keep my opinions to myself.

"Defeat at our enemies' hands is an outcome none of us want. However, the victory that Alexander desires is a dark one as well. He was once an emperor. He has tasted unlimited power. Though he claims to do everything with our people's best interest in mind, I can foresee a time when he craves that title once more. There would be no need for the First, as he would seek to become the One."

"Whoa, so you're thinking he's gonna pull a Palpatine on you guys?" Their confused looks were, once more, confirmation that elder vamps really needed to turn on the TV once in a fucking blue moon. "I mean, he's gonna snuff you all?"

"I would not doubt that."

"Then why not take him down first?"

Something passed through both of their faces. It was quick, barely noticeable, but as someone who'd gotten his ass kicked in high school, I knew it well - fear.

"Alexander is too powerful," Thea said. "The bulk of our people are too loyal to him."

Her tone faltered and I was tempted to offer a counter-argument. After all, Gan sure as shit hadn't been bothered by the idea of putting Alex on ice. Then again, she was batshit crazy, so perhaps using her as an example wasn't the best of ideas.

"Theodora is correct. Our best bet is to weaken his position. If we can end this war in a stalemate, or perhaps diminish the glory of his victory, then he would have no choice but to stay his hand - accept the wisdom of the First."

"So where do I play in all of this drama?"

"Is it not obvious?" Thea asked.

Goddamn, I so hated when people asked that. Made me want to slug them in the face. Of course, most couldn't put you through a cinderblock wall as way of response. "Pretend I'm an idiot."

"You are Alexander's great prize. He has been using you to strengthen his position - even more so since you came to join us."

Hmprh, they'd either been fed a plate of bullshit regarding my capture or they had a very loose definition of the word "join." Even so, I sorta liked where they were going with this. "And if I escaped?"

"If you were instantly recaptured, nothing. But if you were to return to your coven, make our people aware of your reemergence, he would either be forced to admit to your escape - a great embarrassment for one who holds us all to such a high standard - or proclaim it was meant to be by the seers."

"So he couldn't touch me?"

"Not openly. Our people are uncertain. If they were to view our leadership as desperate, it would potentially compromise us."

"More importantly," Joshua added, "you would be free to continue along whatever path destiny has in store for you."

"You have to be aware that I've been trying my damnedest to shit on my destiny since day one."

"Exactly!" He beamed at my response. "Your reputation for being *unorthodox* has spread. Now that

Theodora and I are certain that you are not Alexander's willing pawn, we know that you will work in your own way to avoid the cataclysm at hand. Though we must all tread carefully in the coming days, perhaps our combined efforts can shift the winds of fate enough so as to not bring us all to ruin."

He kept droning on, but I tuned the rest out. It was all just a lot of fate-related bullshit with no real direction. Despite their bluster, I got the distinct impression that neither of these two would truly put their ass on the line if push came to shove. Still, who cared? The main thing that was of interest to me had already been implied.

I was going home.

Upgraded Seating

We approached the gate, beyond which lay the airport's tarmac. Two guards walked forward to greet us. There could still be trouble if they managed to sound an alarm or...

Out of the corner of my eye, Thea flashed her fangs. I thought she might be readying to attack, but the two guards immediately snapped to attention, shouted some greeting I couldn't understand, and then bowed deeply.

We continued to approach until I was close enough to smell that they were both human. Interesting. Did these guys work for the First, or were they just used to vampires bossing them around?

One of them produced a printout with a picture of me on it - a wanted poster. Well, that explained it.

The two guards began to question us...or more precisely, my companions. All I could do was stand there and nod like an idiot, trying to pick up the occasional word or phrase I might understand. Their tone remained respectful, but the tension began to build.

At last, one of them pulled a walkie-talkie out and raised it to his mouth.

"*THAT WILL BE ENOUGH!!*" Joshua compelled them.

Their eyes glazed over as they awaited whatever came next. Joshua, for his part, looked unfazed. The extra oomph needed to compel humans apparently wasn't an issue for vamps his age.

"*YOU WILL GIVE US THE INFORMATION WE SEEK, THEN LET US PASS!! NOTHING OUT OF THE ORDINARY HAS OCCURRED HERE!! ONCE THE FLIGHT WE SEEK HAS DEPARTED, YOU WILL BOTH COMPLAIN OF ILLNESS AND RETURN TO YOUR HOMES!!*"

Thea stepped up to him and Joshua turned to her questioningly. She smiled back. "Loose ends, my friend."

He bowed his head slightly and bade her to continue.

"*YOU ARE BOTH DEPRESSED!!*" she commanded. "*YOU ARE UNHAPPY WITH THE DIRECTION YOUR LIVES HAVE TAKEN!!* She turned to the first. "*YOU WILL HANG YOURSELF!!*"

Holy shit! What the fuck was she doing?

"*AND YOU WILL TAKE YOUR FIREARM AND USE IT TO PUT A BULLET INTO YOUR BRAIN!!*"

I opened my mouth to protest, but realized there wasn't much I could do. A compulsion by a master vampire was nearly impossible for someone like me to undo. I'd have needed to put the bite on one of them first, absorb their power, and then try it. And that all assumed they would let me...probably a losing proposition.

Holy fuck, talk about a lousy way to go. I'd have almost sooner seen these two assholes just snap the guards' necks and be done with it.

It just served as a reminder that, regardless of what they claimed, we weren't even close to being on the same side. It was something to keep in mind. I had a nasty habit of getting comfortable with people. Fuckers like these, well, I'd be wise not to turn my back on them too readily.

Joshua consulted with one of the guards - still glassy eyed - at their station, then walked back while the other unlocked the gate.

"We are in luck," he said. "There is a flight leaving shortly, bound for your home country. We have just enough time to get you aboard."

"Well..."

"Yes, Freewill?"

"There's the little problem of me not having a passport."

He smiled broadly at that, letting out a small chuckle. "Trust me. That will not be an issue."

* * *

Rather than reenter the terminal, we walked across the tarmac. Once inside, nobody paid us any mind. I had to assume the vamps did this sort of thing often. I briefly turned back toward the gate as we walked. How many humans had been casually tossed to the side like garbage, all because they happened to be at an inconvenient place at the wrong time?

"There is a problem, Freewill?" Thea asked. "You seem pensive."

"It's just those guards..."

"My apologies. I should have offered them to you first."

"Huh?"

"I assumed you were sated."

"What?"

She stopped and sniffed. Oh crap. The severed head in my pack could be a difficult one to explain if it was found out.

"You reek of blood, after all." She raised an eyebrow. "Your bag, in particular, is heavy with its scent."

I'd forgotten about that. Diluted as it was, it was still blood, and I'd gotten pretty doused with it. There was also the fact that the head was wrapped in material soaked through with it. I needed to think fast if I had any hope of covering my ass.

"Um...I killed a tourist on the way over. Stuffed his liver in here just in case I...got hungry during the flight."

"Planning ahead, I see." The barest tone of admiration entered her voice. "Perhaps your escape was not as amateurish as I had assumed."

It was, but there was no need to let her know that. I was too close to take any chances. I'd only breathe a sigh of relief when I was safely buckled into my seat. Now, to only hope that they weren't stuffing me into coach. There was also the issue of what to do once I got back to the States. I doubted customs back home would be quite as forgiving as that of this bloodsucker paradise.

Fuck it. I'd worry about that bridge when it came time to cross it. Hell, living in an airport like in that stupid Tom Hanks movie would be preferable to hanging out in the dungeons of Castle Douchula for all eternity.

"There, Freewill." Joshua pointed toward a massive 747 with the *United* logo on it. "We must be quick. They will be loading the storage hold soon."

"Wait...storage hold?"

* * *

Goddamnit! What is it with other vampires constantly shipping me like I was a fucking piece of luggage? Christ! Sure, I didn't often buy into the hype, but even so, I was the Freewill their legends spoke of. You'd think that would at least rate a seat in fucking business class. Oh well, at least I wasn't nailed into a box this time.

Thea and Joshua used their compulsion voodoo to fuck with the minds of the humans loading the luggage. I tried real hard to not listen, but even so, I had the feeling that the next day would bring with it news of a string of unexplained suicides.

I understood why they were doing so. Despite the unlikelihood of Alex getting his own hands dirty, there still existed the possibility he would interrogate people to find out my whereabouts. They obviously knew he was strong enough to overcome their own compulsions. It was the ultimate act of covering their tracks. Much like a black ops mission, the only way to ensure there were no dissenting viewpoints was if there were no witnesses.

Even so, it made me sick. I had little doubt that many lives would be lost in the coming war. As sad as that made me, I couldn't allow myself to become burdened by the guilt of them all. I mean, shit happened. Still, those people today had been thrown away needlessly just so a few vamps could cover their bloody asses.

Oh well, I would have plenty of time in the hours ahead to torture myself - assuming, of course, I didn't freeze or pass out from oxygen deprivation during the flight. Hell, with my luck, we'd suffer a midair collision with some primal god and they'd end up sifting my ashes from the wreckage.

That kind of *positive* thinking wasn't exactly going to make this trip any shorter. I needed to stow it and worry about more important shit - like what the fuck I was going to do if I needed to catch a connecting flight to actually get back home. Hell, even assuming that wasn't an issue, there was still the problem of slipping out unnoticed once I was back on the ground.

Pressed with the need to think through my next steps strategically, I opted to pass the time by opening up the luggage around me and going through the other passengers' shit.

* * *

To help pass the time, I busied myself by pretending a twelve inch pink dildo was a lightsaber - noting with amazement how many I'd found in the surrounding suitcases. After the plane took off, it had been child's play to snap those sad little luggage locks people use in a futile attempt to keep folks like me out of their stuff. I then settled into a little nest I'd made out of coats and sweaters - keeping myself relatively comfortable in the coolness of the cargo hold.

With that all done, the boredom of the long flight ahead set in. I rapidly grew tired of fighting off an imaginary Darth Vader with my Jedi vibrator. With nothing better to do, I pulled out my misappropriated phone to see if maybe there were any games loaded. Even if it was in German, Angry Birds still wasn't all that hard to figure out.

Oh nasty! Upon opening the photo app, I realized my fat friend and his unattractive wife had made a sex tape. Jeez, it was like watching two hippos fuck.

On the flipside, it wasn't like I had much else to do. Screw it. Even shitty porn still had entertainment value.

* * *

The snow that fell around us began to mix with the blood and ash of the battle, leaving the rooftop covered in a vile slush. Remington and his men had crashed through our meager fortifications and engaged us. The numbers were on their side, but we'd managed to hold our own for a time. Sadly, it hadn't lasted.

I looked around and took in the bleakness of our situation. Ed was down, possibly dying. Christy stood over him defensively. Sally was doing her damnedest to inflict as many casualties as she could, but was slowly being forced back.

Things got worse from there. Gan was waylaid and driven over the edge. I cried out for her, not believing she was gone. I then watched as Christy collapsed from the strain of the constant battle. That was two of our number down. Surely defeat was near.

Then I saw her. A glowing white angel clad in armor, she cut through Remington's men like butter. Ashes flew wherever she touched them - the fires of faith empowering her. She was marvelous to behold. Sheila, the reborn Icon of Faith, foretold as the last defense of humanity against the coming darkness. Even had she not been the Icon, she was still the girl I was hopelessly in love with. Pity that a part of the prophecy entailed a final fight to the death between us - the world going to the victor.

I didn't believe it, though. The hell with seers and their mystic bullshit. We'd make it to the end of this war, but we'd do it together - hopefully as more than friends, but I'd take what I could get.

Except that wasn't to be.

The battle moved on seemingly in fast forward. Tom pulled a gun on us, his mind pushed to the breaking point. He was fairly easy to subdue, although I hated myself for having to do it. Unfortunately, Remington proved to be a much harder foe to dispatch.

Before I could stop him, he pulled the trigger - shooting Sheila point blank in the head with the heavy caliber weapon. Her - our - destiny was erased in one terrible moment. Mankind's defender was felled, but I couldn't have cared less. Without her, it didn't matter if the world burned or not. All I wanted in that moment was my revenge...

* * *

I awoke with a start, a cry escaping my lips. Despite the coolness of the cargo hold, I was covered in sweat. Awake or not, the dream refused to leave me - continuing to play out in my mind. After several minutes, I began to understand why. It was exactly the same as that stupid movie I'd watched in my brain - the same outcomes my subconscious had been insisting were real every time I thought back upon the participants.

There was only one conclusion - it hadn't been a dream.

Whatever block had been in my mind shattered upon that realization. I remembered it all - at least up to the point where I descended upon Remington. I had no idea what happened after that, but considering what I'd heard, it was a fair bet that he hadn't survived.

The only question was whether anyone else had. I'd succumbed to the beast inside, gladly giving up any pretense of control. Once released, had he fallen upon my friends as he had Remington? That was a possibility too horrible to consider.

Even so, the story I'd been given was somewhat different from those events. If there'd been no survivors, it was still possible that a vampire cleanup crew could've come to those conclusions. Still, it sounded a little too tidy. There didn't seem to be any speculation as to the betrayal I'd made against the vampire nation. No, it was definitely too neat, as if someone had spun it that way, someone with a vested interest in covering their own actions in the whole fucked-up endeavor. This practically reeked of Sally's involvement.

If she had made it, wasn't it possible that the others had, too?

Not all of them, though. Gan and Sheila hadn't. I'd seen enough to know that. That first one stung - my heart going out to the little psycho. That other, however, was utterly devastating.

Or at least it should have been.

It had been the event that pushed me over the edge, throwing me into the equivalent of a subconscious prison for three months. Hell, if Dr. Death hadn't decided that he'd had enough of the constant poking and prodding, I'd still be there, blissfully unaware of anything except my daily routine.

Even knowing all of that, I couldn't seem to quite grasp the same pit of despair that I had. I wasn't happy about it, don't get me wrong, but I felt - I don't know - hollow inside. It was as if whatever grief I had in me had been completely burned out.

That wasn't too surprising. Running on nothing but pure rage for months would probably be a bit much for most anyone. The truth was, I wasn't entirely upset about that. Despite wanting to crawl up into a little ball, a sense of clarity came over me. Whatever future had been ahead for Sheila and me- whether real or just imagined by me - was gone, but it didn't have to be for nothing.

Thea and Josh were hoping that I'd work against Alex's plans, but I was going to make sure to do one better. The Icon was foretold to be humanity's last defense against the coming darkness, but the prophecies weren't worth shit - I knew that now. Alex might as well just use them all to wipe his ass. All of it was a lie. So why not work with that?

The others could believe what they wanted, but I would be forging ahead with my own destiny. Sheila was gone, but she would not be so easily forgotten. Not only would I refuse to be the spearhead of evil I was expected to be, I would step into her shoes - figuratively, of course.

Humanity needed a defender, and I just so happened to have an updated resume, so to speak. I vowed to honor her memory and make her proud - wherever she might be looking down from.

I would stand tall in the face of ultimate evil.

I would...

The plane shuddered and I fell off the suitcases I'd been sitting upon, landing on my ass. Whoa! I would need to survive this flight first.

The jostling continued as the massive plane passed through what I hoped was only some nasty turbulence. It would be really fucking difficult to defend humanity if I wound up smeared across a mile of wreckage.

The cabin tilted forward and the whine of the engine indicated we were descending. I'd never been overly afraid of flying, but I'll admit I tried to mentally calculate our downward angle - my plan being to shit myself once it got past sixty degrees.

The shuddering got worse, and another sound roared over that made by the aircraft's engine - thunder. Oh, fuck. Before my little rage nap, a weird-ass storm had rolled into town. Multi-colored lightning, unseasonal temperatures, and the like followed in its wake. Gan had been of the opinion that it was supernatural in nature - a showing of strength by whatever entities were about to burst through into our world and fuck it up. After everything I'd seen, I was inclined to believe her.

While it was possible that we were just flying through a regular storm, I sincerely doubted fate would let me off that easily. I seemed to be a beacon for weird shit. It would be just my luck for Thor, God of Thunder, to check up on things and inadvertently blow me out of the sky at the same time.

The plane jolted again and once more knocked me from my feet. I clonked my head a good one against the fuselage just as the whine of wheels braking sounded all around me.

Holy shit, we'd made it.

That final jostling had been the plane landing. I was back - hopefully. That meant I could return home, maybe take a breather and plan my next step. It would be so awesome to see my friends...

Oh no.

I replayed the newly regained memories of that final battle. What a goddamned selfish asshole I was. I'd been so busy focusing on Sheila that I'd overlooked Tom and Ed. What a piece of shit I was. They were my two best friends in this world, and I hadn't given them a second thought.

Christy's errant magic had brainwashed Tom into despising me. I'd snapped him out of it, but how was I to know what had happened next? I was hopeful he'd survived, but there was a good chance he'd done so continuing to hate me.

I couldn't even say that much about Ed. He'd been in the process of turning when we'd saved him. Even Sheila, with her magical healing touch, hadn't been sure of his survival. It was possible he hadn't...

No!

I couldn't torture myself with that. There was no point. I needed to know for sure - *then* I could torture myself.

As the plane slowed, I remembered what was in my pocket, then smacked myself in the forehead. What an idiot I could be. I still had that fat dude's cell phone. Sure, he'd probably get fucked with roaming charges, but that wasn't exactly my problem.

I pulled it out and immediately realized I had a completely different problem - it was dead.

Guess I shouldn't have spent so much time staring at his homemade *Deep Throat* remake. Go figure.

Pit Stop

If my knowledge of airlines was still valid, then I didn't have much time before the cargo doors were opened. I needed to get my shit together.

The first order of business was to make sure my glorious return wasn't a short-lived one. I had no clue what time of day it was. It could've been high noon for all I knew. The storm continued to rage outside, but that didn't mean shit. With my luck, it would quickly clear up and leave me standing around in broad daylight for all of the thirty seconds it would take for me to vaporize.

There was also the fact that I wasn't too big on getting soaked if it was raining. Hey, being an undead monster didn't mean I liked walking around wet and miserable. Squishy sneakers weren't cool no matter how dead you might be.

Fortunately, I had an entire cargo hold at my disposal. Sure, some of the passengers might be pissed to find their stuff missing, but maybe next time they'd know better than to take a flight with a stowaway in the luggage hold.

I tore through the bags until I found a hoodie, coat, and gloves. I also found a new pair of expensive-looking Nike high tops in my size. I already was wearing a pair of shoes, but what the fuck? It's not like I wasn't already committing a felony.

Once suitably attired for whatever weather awaited me, I grabbed my bag and...

Oh crap, my bag. I had completely forgotten about my traveling companion - what with worrying about my roommates, mourning Sheila, and watching homemade porn. Hopefully, those blood-soaked towels had kept Richard Cranium properly...err...bloodified.

I quickly unzipped the bag to check, moving aside the now dry and crusty towels.

Oh, that wasn't good.

In the space of however long the flight took, my bodiless friend appeared to have aged a couple of centuries. He'd had a rugged jaw and dark hair when I packed him away, but now, he kinda looked like he drank from the wrong grail from *Indiana Jones and the Last Crusade*. His skin was wrinkled, cracked, and sickly grey in color. His formerly black hair was now dull and shriveled. His eyes had rolled up into his head and the parts I could see were all dried out. Worst of all, his mouth was locked open in what appeared to be a silent scream, as if he'd tried crying out for help, only to be ignored.

"Um...hello?"

There was no response, not that I expected there to be any. Sad to say, but he didn't appear to have survived the trip.

How wonderful. I was now the proud owner of a mummified vampire head - quite the souvenir. It would probably look dandy on a shelf next to Tom's action figures.

I was tempted to just toss the sack back amongst the rest of the luggage. That ought to give some poor shmuck a start when he picked it up. The look on their face alone would probably have made this entire ordeal worthwhile. On the other hand, leaving around evidence of vampire existence was probably not an overly smart thing - especially since it would undoubtedly be traced back to me. Oh well, I could figure out how to get rid of it later. Maybe toss it in a dumpster or something once I was out of there.

And out of there I would soon be, for that's when the door to the cargo hold was cracked open.

* * *

I considered standing there and letting them see me, maybe saying something awesome like, "Declare *this*, bitches." Instead, I hid like a pussy - realizing my triumphant return would be spoiled if it began with a dozen TSA agents tackling me.

A man stepped into the hold. A conveyer belt led downward behind him. Beyond that, the storm raged in full force, the rain coming down in sheets. It wasn't quite perfect cover, but it would hopefully be enough to let me get off the tarmac and get lost in a crowd somewhere.

The man bent down, still unaware of my presence, and began grabbing luggage. Thinking quickly, I hefted an oversized bag and threw it at him. He went down with an "oof!" amongst the sea of suitcases and I made my move.

I raced to the exit and took a look around. Sure enough, there were others working below, but thankfully, they were all heads-down - shielding themselves from the weather. I wasn't going to get a better chance at this.

The drop to the ground wasn't too bad, especially for one with vampire powers. I slipped out, landed, and immediately put all of my speed to bear - running full out so as not to be noticed. The weather was absolutely awful - rain pelting me sideways with barely any visibility at all, even with my enhanced senses. Regardless, I was happy to have it as I made my way past parked airport vehicles, trying to be careful not to wander out onto the runway.

Lightning flashed across the sky. Unsurprisingly, it blazed a color other than the normal white. The sky was heavily overcast, yet I could tell by the light it was daytime. That was probably good. It would give me a better chance of finding a crowd to disappear amongst.

I kept dodging and weaving, making it a point to keep my head down in case anyone saw me, which was also practical with the weather.

Finally, I vaulted a chain link fence with a running start and found myself in what looked to be long-term parking. Yes!

Not wanting to press my luck, I kept moving and finally spotted an entrance to the terminal, one that was in heavy use. A few more moments found me inside and lost amongst the crowd of people either commuting or going on vacation.

I kept expecting a hand to fall upon my shoulder and turn to find a small army of angry security guards, but for the moment, I seemed to be anonymous - just one more wet, annoyed traveler amongst the pack.

I allowed myself a small sigh of relief as I passed a Dunkin Donuts. Oh yeah, I was definitely back in the States. I even briefly considered stopping in for a cruller. Sadly, all I had on me were a few German krugerrands or whatever the fuck I'd stolen off that guy in the castle. I had a feeling those wouldn't be accepted and it wasn't important enough for me to waste the effort looking for a place to exchange them.

No, it was time to figure out exactly where I was and how to get back home. If luck was with me, this was either La Guardia or JFK. If so I could...

It wasn't.

I spotted a sign that told me exactly where I was - Newark Liberty International Airport.

It wasn't quite Hell, but close enough.

Of all the places to be, I was in fucking New Jersey.

* * *

My plight wasn't ideal, but it wasn't terrible, either. I knew where I was and, best of all, had a friend in town. I wasn't sure what his thoughts would be upon seeing me, considering my absence had caused me to inadvertently blow off his game for the past three months. Dave was nothing if not an angry god when acting as dungeon master for my gaming group. There was also the fact that when last I'd seen him, he was busy cultivating a small colony of vampire mice - courtesy of him being amongst the few humans who knew my secret and the only one gleefully conducting crimes against nature by way of said knowledge.

Oh well, that didn't matter to me right then. What did was that Dave was still a friend, even if he did insist on occasionally doing questionable things like snipping off my toes for his research.

* * *

With no American currency and being forced to move at normal human speeds, it took me longer than I'd have liked to reach his apartment. Newark, even in the middle of a biblical torrent, was never an empty place. By the time I got there, I was soaked to the bone despite my purloined coverings.

It was with no small amount of relief when I finally knocked on his door. My only hope was that he was actually home - a rarity some days. Dave was a medical resident and tended to keep odd hours. Breaking into the apartment of the guy who could smite my character with any of a thousand different curses wasn't my ideal reunion tactic, but I would still do so rather than stand out in this storm like a...

"Who the fuck is it? I'm trying to take a nap."

Gotta love Dave. His *pleasant* bedside manner extended to all parts of his life. It was a small wonder he hadn't chosen some other altruistic profession such as priest, grief counselor, or Guantanamo Bay torturer.

"Open up, it's the police!" What can I say? I was in no mood to fuck around. It wasn't like I was having a good time prancing around in a warm summer shower.

Needless to say, the sound of footsteps approaching reached my ears in due order.

The door opened a sliver - as I'd taken the liberty of putting my finger over the peephole - and I was met with a pair of angry, questioning eyes.

"Show me a badge."

"I can do one better." I whipped off the sopping wet hood and grinned.

Dave blinked in surprise, his eyes opening wide. "Holy shit. Bill?"

"No, it's Mother Nature. Now open the goddamned door and let me in before I drown out here."

He backed up a step and opened up the door, giving me a look at him standing there in a t-shirt and boxers. Not exactly the sight I'd hoped to find greeting me upon my triumphant return.

I stepped past him, glad to be out of the weather. He shut and locked the door behind me before turning to my still dripping form.

"You know, they have these wonderful new inventions called umbrellas."

"I'll try to remember that the next time I stow away on a flight back from Switzerland." I dropped the bag containing the desiccated head onto the floor with a *thunk*. Oh well, it wasn't like he was going to be feeling much. I then proceeded to peel off my purloined coat - making a mental note that next time I'd steal something a bit more weatherproof.

"Switzerland?" he asked. "So that's where you've been all this time?"

"Apparently." I took a seat on his couch, not caring much if I got it wet. It's not like his furnishings were exactly top of the line.

"So all this time that you've been blowing off our game, screwing up my experiments, and worrying everybody sick, you've just been on some fucking vampire vacation?"

I couldn't help but notice the priority he'd given to his accusations, albeit it wasn't all that surprising, considering the source. Still, I decided it would be best to save that topic for another time. "Not quite. What your people call a vacation, I call an incarceration."

"I couldn't have called it anything." He walked over to his bathroom. "Nobody would tell me shit. The only thing I got out of Tom was that you were busy with vampire business. Not exactly the most useful thing to go on." He emerged holding a towel and tossed it to me. I caught it, but only barely registered that it wasn't exactly the cleanest thing I'd ever touched. His mention of my roommate had definitely not gone unnoticed.

"Thanks."

He probably assumed it was for the towel, but it was really for letting me know my best friend was still alive. It was the first real piece of good news I'd gotten in what felt like far too long. I opened my mouth to say more, but he beat me to the punch.

"I have some bad news for you, my friend," he said as he sat down opposite me. His face had grown somber. A sinking feeling hit my gut as he stared me in the eye.

Whatever small moment of good cheer I had been allowed was about to be erased.

A Hell of a Souvenir

"Seriously?" I cried. "You couldn't have just sent Kelvin off on some nebulous adventure or maybe retired him to a life of luxury?"

"What did you expect? I was a little ticked off at first and the Elemental Plane of Broken Glass just happened to be convenient. Sorry about the rape-trolls, but they *are* native to that dimension."

Son of a bitch. There were some days when I really hated Dave and his fucking house rules. As if things weren't shitty enough, now I'd learned that my favorite character had been imprisoned as a sex slave. "And all of his stuff?"

"Pawned to the merchants in the City of Doors."

"Well, that's just great."

"It's not all bad."

"Oh?" I asked, pacing - my stolen sneakers squelching on his floor.

"Gonar the Brave got engaged to Princess Sheila. They bonded while everyone was mourning your capture."

What? Leave it to my gaming buddies to fuck me over the second my back was turned. "Well, congratu-fucking-lations to the happy couple. You can tell Adam I am so gonna kick his ass as a wedding present."

"Oh relax. Now that you're back, I'm sure we can think of something. Hell, if you help me get my experiments back on track, maybe we can arrange for a last minute stoppage to their wedding - like in *The Graduate*."

I knew it was only a matter of time before we got back to that. Dave seemingly had only three interests in life: our game, hating all of his patients, and trying to use my blood to concoct some miracle drug. "Not going well, I assume?"

He sighed. "Not going at all."

"What happened?"

He stood and stretched, walking over to the window and glancing out at the storm beyond. It finally seemed to be petering off a bit. "It's been one disaster after another. Hell, the only thing that's saved my ass is all the weird-ass shit that's been going on."

"Oh?"

"Yep. First my experiment with the mice went up in smoke, thanks to my asshole landlord. The fuckhead let himself in when I wasn't here to fix some plumbing and opened up the wrong set of shades. The poor little guys never stood a chance."

I had a feeling that "poor little guys" wasn't a particularly apt description for a tank full of ravenous vampire mice, but refrained from saying so. If anything,

I felt a bit of relief. I had been certain that one day I'd arrive for my weekly game only to find the city of Newark besieged like in some horrific sequel to *Willard*.

"That wasn't the worst, though. The guy was understandably freaked - threatened to call the cops on me."

"So what did you do?"

"Fortunately, he's an ex-meth head - or not so ex anymore."

"Dave, what did you do?"

"Needless to say, it's amazing the silence that can be bought with enough prescription drugs."

"Nice to see you living up to that whole Hippocratic Oath thing."

He waved his hand in dismissal. "I tried to get things back on track, use what samples I still had left, but then the hospital caught me *borrowing* some of their lab equipment." He sat down and laughed. "The administration wanted to put me on leave, based on what they called 'questionable ethical choices.'"

A chuckle threatened to escape my lips, but I once more managed to keep my mouth shut. My character was in dire straits as it was. I didn't need Dave throwing more shit at him.

"Thankfully, there's all of *this*," he proclaimed, gesturing toward the window where the sky was starting to lighten. "You won't believe the strange crap that's been going down."

"Oh, I might."

"We're getting weird-ass cases left and right - victims with odd burns, cuts, and even bites. The hospital is short-staffed as it is, so they pretty much had no choice but to let me off with a warning."

Well, I guess it was nice to see some good - sorta - had come from the evils I'd inadvertently unleashed upon the world. I stopped short of telling Dave that, though. He knew more than enough as it was - even if taking credit for the horrors that had saved his job might be enough to earn my character back his gear and then some.

I was tempted to ask if I could use the phone since my purloined cell was dead, but hesitated. I didn't know what was waiting for me back home, but I got the feeling that it might be best to take it all in face-to-face. If there was bad news to be had, and I had little doubt there was, it was probably not a great idea to hear about it over the phone. These people were my life - as it was. At the very least, I owed them a chance to personally throw it all back in my face. I'd had three months of taking the coward's way out. That was long enough.

"I don't suppose you have any cash you could lend me?"

"Huh?" he sputtered, caught off guard by my change of topic.

"I really need to get home, but all I have is some foreign currency. For all I know, it's probably worth ten cents American."

He arched an eyebrow. "So you just stopped by to bum bus fare off me?"

"Well...no. I really did want to know what had happened to Kelvin. Even so, it's been a while and I..."

Dave sighed and got up. He walked over to a nearby desk, pulled out two twenties from his wallet, and handed them over to me. "You might as well grab some lunch while you're doing so. It's a long trip."

I gratefully accepted them. "I've had longer."

"I'll expect your help in getting me started again, though," he said. "Seriously, I was starting to make some progress with the cell regeneration."

"Really?"

"Well, not much. Some of it really does..." he trailed off, mumbling the rest in a voice low enough so that even my ears couldn't make it out.

"What was that?"

"I said that some of it really does seem like magic," he snapped, earning a smug grin from me. "Now get the fuck out of here before I think twice about loaning cash to a loser like you."

I thanked him and went to shake his hand, but at the last second pulled him in for a hug. He was an asshole, but he was one of *my* assholes. I was glad to have him.

After releasing him, I grabbed my pack and turned toward the door. I'd taken no more than a step when an inspired thought stopped me in my tracks.

Why not kill two birds with one stone?

"There a problem, Bill?"

"What say I pay you back right now - in triplicate even?"

He arched a questioning eyebrow, but the gleam in his eye told me he was open to hearing what I had to say.

"Check it out." I plopped the bag onto the back of his couch and unzipped it. Pushing the crusty towels aside, I revealed to him the most gruesome of souvenirs.

Most would have questioned its authenticity, being that it now looked like a dried out Halloween prop, but Dave had a slightly better trained eye than the average person. "Why do you have a severed head with you?"

"Long story, trust me. Needless to say, I do."

"Is it..."

"A vamp? Well, it was at one point."

"I thought you said that dead vampires turned to dust. Hell, I can attest to that from the tank of mouse ashes I had to vacuum up."

"That's mostly true," I replied, "but I've been told there are ways to preserve body parts if need be. Some sort of poison that vampire enforcers use when they really want to fuck up somebody's day. I don't know the exact details. Bottom line, though, is that it's the real deal."

"How old is it? Looks like it really did come from Dracula's crypt."

"Don't know and don't care. Look, do you want it? If not, I'm just gonna toss the thing into the nearest dumpster I can find and..."

He immediately put his hands on the bag. "Are you kidding? Of course I want it. Even desiccated as it is, I can learn a shitload - unless you've changed your mind and are now willing to let me perform that brain biopsy..."

"Have fun." I handed it over and turned toward the door.

Walking away, I felt pretty good at having rid myself of two potential burdens: being in Dave's debt and carrying with me an item that would surely set off the alarm bells of even the most slow-witted cop on the force.

The rain had let up, but the sky was still overcast - a near perfect daytime scenario for me. Best of all, though, I was finally heading home.

I had no idea what was waiting for me there, but honestly felt that I could handle it, no matter what. Just being back where I belonged was empowering.

It was like a metaphorical beam of sunlight shined down from above. The worst was undoubtedly behind me.

Homecoming

The sky was clearing up by the time I arrived back in Brooklyn, but thankfully, it was starting to get dark. Even if the clouds parted, I was no longer in any real danger of combusting.

Unfortunately, the closer I came to home, the more my hopeful mood evaporated. I knew Tom had survived, but that was it. I didn't know what shape he was in or what his demeanor toward me might be. For all I knew, I'd walk in and he'd immediately spit upon me and send me on my way. He wouldn't entirely be in the wrong to do so, either.

I stepped out of the subway platform and had to suppress a grim chuckle. The last time I'd felt this way was when I'd returned home upon being turned into a vampire. Although I had only been gone a day, it had felt like a lifetime. Back then, I'd had similar thoughts of walking in to find my friends taking up the mantel of slayers.

It had all been a bunch of bullshit then, but now I wondered if those feelings had been a foreshadowing of this day. I was returning home following months of unexplained absence and my friends, assuming they were okay, might now have actual cause to take up arms against me.

I swear, if I knew then what I knew now, I might have just slunk off into the night, never to be seen again. I could have become a mysterious stranger, drifting aimlessly from town to town, never staying in one place for long. Sadly, it was too late for that. Too many vamps knew my name, face, or scent. It would be impossible to hide from the bloodhounds forever.

Even if I tried, the world didn't have forever to wait. It might have just been me, but as I walked the few blocks to my apartment building, I could have sworn things felt different - stranger - almost as if something were leaking into our world that didn't belong. It was hard to quantify, but the air felt thicker and the shadows seemed longer.

Of course, I could have just been imagining it all - my subconscious doing its best, as usual, to psyche me out from an encounter that it assured me would be unpleasant.

I stopped at the foot of the stairs leading to my building. When no howling wraiths leapt from the gloom to rend my flesh, I decided that maybe I was just looking for excuses to not head in.

The hilarious part was that I actually had one really valid excuse - my keys were missing. They were no doubt long gone, lying wherever my brutish alter-ego had left them - assuming he didn't just eat them. Ugh, there was a thought. I can only imagine the joy of trying to shit those out.

There I was again, indulging in daydreams rather than facing reality.

Enough of this crap. I was Bill Ryder - Dr. Death to some, the legendary Freewill to others. If I couldn't even knock on my own fucking door, how the hell was I going to fool myself into believing that I could save the world?

I walked up, put on a brave front, and pushed the doorbell for my apartment.

* * *

Okay, so maybe pressing a doorbell wasn't quite the same as an epic showdown with the forces of evil. Give me a break; I had to start somewhere.

What happened next was certainly equally anticlimactic. The door unlocked with a quick buzz. Oh well, at least someone was home.

I walked up to the top floor, my knees shaking with each step. So much for all of my bullshit bravado down at the door. I felt more like the legendary pussy of the vampire race.

I reached my floor, stepped over to the door, and raised my hand. I needn't have bothered, though. It swung open as I approached.

My roommate and oldest friend, Tom, stood there.

"Bill?" he asked cautiously, his eyes opening wide with surprise. I was filled with hope for a fleeting moment, but then I saw his face droop with disappointment.

I was right to worry - my fears were about to become a reality.

* * *

"You didn't happen to run into a guy with Chinese food on the way up, did you?"

"Huh?"

"He's late and I'm hungry. I thought you were him."

"Uh, no."

"Oh. Well, then..." He eyed me skeptically for a second. "You're not, like, some kind of doppelganger, are you?"

"No, it's definitely me. I'm..."

Tom stepped forward and threw his arms around me in an embrace. "Good, just checking. Everyone keeps telling me we can't be too careful these days."

I didn't return the hug immediately. The whole delivery question had left me a bit gobsmacked. I stood there and blinked uncomprehendingly for a few seconds, letting things sink in. "So..." I stammered, "we're cool?"

He pulled back from the hug and looked at me like I had two heads. "Of course. I mean, you're still an asshole for punching me in the face like you did, but Christy told me that wasn't really your fault, so I guess it's okay." He turned around and walked back into the apartment. "Still sucks that I couldn't find that Megatron figure again when I woke up," he muttered.

I remained where I was a second longer. "Can I come in?"

He glanced over his shoulder, giving me a look that said he thought I'd gone soft in the head. "Why not? Are you waiting for an engraved invitation?"

I breathed a sigh of relief and took a step forward, tentative at first - afraid that I might be dreaming. My foot hit the floor and I was inside. I was home.

My eyes grew misty and I had to blink back tears. Who would have thought our crummy apartment in this shitty old building would have such an emotional hold over me?

"You okay, Bill?"

"Uh, yeah...just forgot how dusty this place is." I turned and wiped my eyes, but then realized that maybe I should hold off on that for a moment. I'd still only seen one of my roommates, and I'd already known from Dave that he was okay.

I steeled myself and got right to the point. "Ed, is he..."

"Gone," Tom said solemnly.

"Oh." I sank onto our couch and put my head in my hands. I'd been afraid of that. Sheila, for all her holy power, hadn't been strong enough to...

"Yeah, dude's been putting in some crazy hours at his new gig. It's fucking weird, if you ask me. Now where the hell is that food?"

"What?" I asked, sitting up.

"I ordered like an hour ago."

"Not that! What about Ed?"

"Well, it's just that I don't think I ever saw him even put in his basic forty hours a week when he was working for Jim..."

"No, stupid. You mean he's alive?" I stood and grabbed him by the shoulders. "He's okay?"

"Well, yeah. I mean, where have you been?"

I wasn't sure whether to kiss him on the lips or punch his fucking lights out. So I opted for somewhere in between - smacking him upside the head. "Obviously not here."

"Oh yeah. So what's up with that? Christy said you hulked out and ran off. What have you been doing all this time?"

"The usual. Been locked up in a castle dungeon in Switzerland."

"Meet any hot Swiss chicks?"

"No idea. I might've eaten a few, though."

* * *

Tom's food finally arrived, sparing me the horror of listening to him whine about how he was starving to death. It gave me a moment to reflect on things. A few short days ago, I would have sold my organs for a chance to be back home. Now I was only back for a few minutes and was already ready to scream at him to shut the fuck up already. It's all relative, I guess. Go figure.

While he ate - and after I snagged an eggroll just on principle's sake - I brought him up to speed on what I knew, which wasn't much. At least it was a good story. He especially got a kick out of the part about me locking Alex in a room with an ancient, and probably pissed off, demigod.

"You should call Sally and tell her that shit."

"Village Coven has survived without me for more than three months. I'm sure it can handle one more night. Maybe I'll head in tomorrow and see what damage she's done in my absence."

"You might need to travel a bit farther than that," he said in between mouthfuls of fried rice.

That caught my attention. "Why?"

"Well, I don't think she's there."

That same sinking feeling hit my gut again. "What happened to Sally? Is she all right?"

"Last I heard. I mean, I haven't really seen her. She popped by once, right after you disappeared, to threaten to beat the shit out of me for some reason, but that was it."

I raised an eyebrow. "Then how do you know she's not there?"

"Christy. She ran into her a few weeks back. Said something about her maybe leaving town for a while."

"Leaving? Where?"

"No idea. She was kinda vague about the whole thing, but I think she might have mentioned something about a stopover in Vegas."

All worry evaporated in an instant. That bitch! There I was, being Alex's personal gimp in the deepest, darkest dungeon in all of Europe, and she was off on a fucking vacation - probably spending the coven's money like it was going out of style. "Did she say when she'd be back?"

Tom just eyed me over his meal. "Do I look like her secretary?"

He might not have been, but Starlight was - despite any misgivings I had about it. She'd undoubtedly know what was up on the off chance Tom was right and Sally was off gallivanting somewhere. Jeez, turn your back for a few months and people just take the fuck off.

Oh well, maybe that was a good thing. If she was on an undead party cruise, that probably meant nothing too important was going on. Perhaps the world wasn't quite as close to the brink of madness as I'd assumed. Sally had her annoying quirks, but I couldn't believe she'd take a powder if things were truly getting that bad.

Yeah, that cemented it. I could wait one more day to announce my glorious return. Tonight was for spending with my bros and enjoying a few hours at home. Speaking of which...

"Um, so..."

"Yeah, Bill?"

"My room?"

"Have a little faith, man. We left it just like it was."

"Really?"

"Yep, although I hope you don't mind, I kind of forged your name on your checkbook. Your share of the rent wasn't exactly paying for itself."

I was tempted to comment on that, but let it drop. Hell, they could have thrown out, sold, or just outright burned my shit. They would have been within their rights to have done so, too, after the first month of my absence. That they hadn't said a lot about their faith that I would return...

Or that nobody else really wanted to live with either of them, but I chose to believe the former.

I will admit to perhaps a tear in my eye as I got up and walked to my room, *my room*. A big smile upon my face, I opened the door and felt it slam into something that kept it from swinging in all of the way.

What the?

"Almost forgot," Tom said, "we didn't change anything, but I figured you wouldn't mind if I stored some shit in there. Been buying a lot of stuff for the baby and didn't have any place else to put it."

Oh yeah - I was definitely home again.

No Rest for the Wicked

I took some time to move Tom's boxes out of the way, noting that a good chunk of his "baby" supplies consisted of old, semi-broken action figures that he'd probably gotten off eBay.

After that, I finally changed into some of my own clothes. They smelled a bit musty - apparently, nobody had bothered to wash them in my absence - but I didn't really care. They were a shitload better than the damp mishmash of clothes I'd been wearing, but best of all, they were mine.

Or at least I thought they were. I cinched up my pants and they almost fell off me. I tried another pair and noticed the same thing. A quick trip in front of the bathroom mirror and my eyebrows rose up in surprise. I'd somehow lost almost a pants size. It wasn't much, nothing quite as dramatic as Tobey Maguire going to bed as skinny old Peter Parker and waking up a buff Spider-Man.

Even so, it was definitely not expected. I'd thought that physical change wasn't possible for a vamp. Guess I was wrong. If it didn't involve killing so many people, I might've almost been tempted to see what else the Dr. Death diet could do.

That could wait, though. For now, clad in my favorite Doctor Who shirt, I felt like me again, even if my belt was cinched extra tight.

I stepped out of my room and sat down to let Tom fill me in some more while we waited for Ed to get home. Christy's pregnancy had kept him pretty busy, although luckily, it sounded like she'd taken some precautions to ensure she didn't turn his brain into sludge again.

"That's good to hear."

"Tell me about it. You hit really hard for such a big pussy." He rubbed his jaw for effect.

"Sorry."

"It's all good. I'd have done the same. The whole thing was fucked up. I figured it would be at least a couple of years before I went all Darth Vader over a kid. Oh, speaking of which, you might want to check in with your parents at some point."

My parents? Oh, fuck. I hadn't even considered them, with everything that was going on. I knew how my mom was with these things. When I was a kid, she was the type to call the cops if I was even five minutes late for dinner. I could only imagine what...

"Relax," he said, obviously seeing my panic. "They're cool. Fortunately for you, I am the master of making excuses. You've just been busy every time they've called. They do probably think you're a dick for not calling back, though."

I sighed in relief. "I can live with that. Thanks. That's another one I owe you."

"Who's counting?" he replied with a sly grin that told me *he* was - the ass.

I was about to respond when I heard footsteps approaching the front door. If you live with a person long enough, you learn to identify them in any number of ways - including how they walked. One didn't need vampire senses for that. My super-sensitive ears were useful for hearing it from further away than a regular person, though.

Had my heart still been beating, it would have probably sped up in joy at the anticipated reunion. Even so, I figured it wouldn't hurt to have a little fun with things.

"Play it cool," I said to Tom before getting up and walking into our kitchen nook. I opened the fridge, noting with a bit of regret the lack of blood. Oh well, I couldn't really blame them. Keeping the refrigerator full of O-negative when nobody was around to drink it would just be fucking weird. For the moment, I grabbed a cup out of our dish drain and poured myself a glass of Pepsi.

The front door opened and the familiar voice of my other roommate followed. "Goddamn, what a fucking day. I so hate vendors who..."

"That's great, because whining like a bitch will definitely solve that problem," I interrupted, stepping from the kitchen with a big grin on my face.

Silence fell upon the room. Ed's jaw nearly dropped to the floor in surprise. Mine did likewise at how he was dressed. It wasn't exactly an Armani suit, but since when did he even wear business casual? He stood there in khakis and a button down shirt, a sports blazer slung across one arm, and an actual briefcase in the other. Jesus Christ, I really *had* been gone a long time.

Tom was the one to break the silence. "It's amazing what wanders in if you leave the door open long enough, isn't it?"

Ed dropped the briefcase. Thank goodness, too. Of all the things going on, I think that was potentially the freakiest. "Holy shit, you're back."

"That's what I hear."

"When..."

"A few hours ago."

"You couldn't have called?"

"I didn't get good reception in the dungeon they kept me locked in."

That broke the deadlock. Simultaneously, we both stepped forward and embraced. Holy shit, it was awesome. I mean, Tom had said Ed was fine, but to actually see him in the flesh was...well, I might have gotten choked up a wee bit.

Thankfully, Tom existed to ruin such moments, lest we get used to expressing silly things like our feelings. "Aw, this is just like one of those tampon commercials."

"Fuck you, asshole." I backed up a step. "You have no idea how worried I was, Ed."

"It'll take a lot more than some pussy vampire to keep me down."

"I'm sorry, I..."

"Don't." He held up a hand. "It was a fucked up situation, no matter how you look at it. I got unlucky, is all."

"Yeah, but it was my fault."

"Fuck that shit. I knew what I was getting into."

He'd said that to me before. I guess I didn't want to believe he actually meant it. Regardless, I let it drop so as to avoid getting all weepy again. The bottom line was that he was standing there in front of me, alive. Now wasn't the time to mourn.

"So, when did you sell out and go all corporate?" I asked, eyeing his attire again.

He sighed, as if knowing that had been coming. "Right about the same time that Jim fired your ass."

Oh, shit. That, unfortunately, answered yet another question I should have asked, but hadn't thought to. Once again, it stung, even though it shouldn't have been much of a surprise. It was going to suck majorly come payday, though. "Let me guess. He didn't appreciate my little sabbatical?"

"Something like that."

"So what happened with you? You grow a work ethic while I was gone and get promoted or something?"

"Close. I quit."

"Why?"

"Well...I had another offer."

"Oh, this should be good," Tom muttered as he turned his chair toward us.

I glanced at him sideways, then back toward Ed. Something was definitely up. One didn't need to be a blind seer to see that. "What? Oh, don't tell me you got a job as Sally's gigolo or something like that. Because let me tell you, the severance package is gonna be a real motherfucker once she gets bored with your skinny ass."

"Nothing like that." He tossed his jacket onto a chair, stretched, and then unbuttoned the top two buttons of his dress shirt. It was a casual gesture, but I immediately noticed the nasty burn mark peeking out from underneath. It was in the shape of Sheila's hand. She'd somehow given it to him as she'd attempted to drag him back from the precipice of life and undeath. He'd gotten lucky, but it had been close - so close that none of us had any idea at the time whether she'd been successful.

Ed saw where my gaze was focused. "You're halfway to guessing my sudden career change."

I blinked confusedly in response. What the fuck did that mean? "So...you have a palm print on your neck. What, are you the assistant manager in charge of giving out hand jobs?"

Tom snorted laughter, earning a withering look from Ed.

"No, stupid. It's who gave me the palm print that's important. Before you burn off any brain cells trying to figure it out, allow me to elaborate. You are looking at the acting president of Iconic Efficiencies."

* * *

It's a pity I'd been sipping from my cup at that moment - I immediately doused Ed's nice white shirt with a spray of soda.

I couldn't help it. Iconic Efficiencies had been Sheila's company. She'd left her job as my group's administrative assistant and formed it. It had been part of the change in her attitude that had let her belief in herself blossom - a chain reaction that ultimately changed her into the Icon, dreaded foe of the vampire race.

But how the hell did that lead to Ed taking it over? I mean, the guy was a graphic designer. As far as I knew, he had zero business acumen and even less desire to obtain any. I summed this all up in a nice, succinct manner. "How the fuck did that happen?"

"Can I answer, or do you want to spit on me some more?" He walked into the kitchen and grabbed a few paper towels with which to blot himself dry.

"I repeat, how the fuck did that happen?"

"Sorry. I would have told you after all that shit with Remington was over, but you were missing and I was busy being unconscious."

"But when?"

"Over lunch. Remember that?"

I did and still felt guilty about it. There had been a momentary break in the weather, the first of what was apparently a string of supernatural storms since then.

Ed and Sheila, being the lone occupants who couldn't survive on blood, had left the coven safe house in search of some food. Only Sheila had returned, with the cops hot on her tail following a run-in with some witches.

I nodded, indicating he should continue.

"Well, it's simple really. Before Christy's coven barged in and zapped me, Sheila and I had a good, long talk."

"About what?"

"Lots of things, but we eventually wound up on the subject of her company. Needless to say, she was really bummed that she'd finally gotten something of her own off the ground and then all of this shit had to start."

"I get that, but why *you*?"

"What? You don't trust my impeccable business sense?" he asked in a wounded tone. I raised one eyebrow, waiting for him to continue. "Well, okay, that's basically the same thing I told her."

"Yet here you are."

"She didn't want her company to go under. I guess she sort of saw it as her baby. I mean, I can dig that. At the same time, her eyes were open as to what was going on. She was aware of how the Templar took over things and set that trap for us."

"I think it was mostly for me."

"Yeah, but I got my ass kicked as a consolation prize."

"Not my fault you're a wuss."

"Says the guy who spent the past quarter of a year being Alexander the Great's dungeon bitch," Tom added.

I stopped my verbal sparring long enough to glare at him.

Ed continued. "Anyway, as I was saying, she wanted someone to run the place in case..."

"The worst happened?" I offered, my voice cracking a bit.

Ed put his hand on my shoulder, about as close as he typically came to being comforting. "Listen, Bill..."

I held up a hand. "Let's not right now, okay?" He nodded, understanding showing in his eyes. "So, why you?"

"That's what I was getting to. I mean, I wondered the same thing. We were always friendly when she worked for Jim, but it's not like I was her best bud or anything."

His words from moments earlier rang through my head and I suddenly understood. "You're one of the few people who know the truth."

"Exactly what she said. That, and I guess I was as close to a neutral party as she was going to find. Obviously, I'm not a wizard. I don't work for the Sasquatches, and I'm sure as shit not your thrall - no matter what anyone says. In short, I don't really bring a hidden agenda with me, but know enough to keep my eyes open and make sure her staff stays safe."

"And how are you supposed to do that?"

"Well," he said with a grin, "for starters, I used my very first executive-sized paycheck to pick myself up a nice new Mossberg along with a bunch of shells filled with silver shot."

"It's a start."

"And I hired a few of the surviving Templar as security."

My jaw hit the floor, bounced, and landed there again. I was tempted to question his sanity, but then saw the shit-eating grin he wore from ear to ear.

Asshole.

It was good to be home again.

* * *

The rest of the evening was awesomeness personified. No other vampires, no magic-wielding girlfriends, nothing teleporting in and trying to disintegrate the building - just the three of us, bullshitting and passing around a celebratory bottle of tequila. I brought them both up to speed on what had happened to me - the parts I could remember, that is - being sure to add in a chapter about the hot Freewill groupie who helped me escape, but not before demanding I make furious love to her as payment for her services.

Hey, it's my story, and I'll embellish it as I damn well please.

They likewise filled in the rest of the blanks of what had been my life, which seemed to mostly consist of keeping their noses out of the supernatural world and making up excuses for me. I had to laugh. It had only been little more than a year, but I'd nearly forgotten how so unexciting our lives had been pre-vampire. Take that out of the equation and things apparently went right back to normal.

If it weren't for the impending end of the world, that might have given me pause. Without me around, the forces of the weird and unnatural had no interest in my friends, sans maybe Christy. Sadly, my leaving again would only be a temporary balm for my roommates. There could only be so much normal to be had when the clouds threatened to belch out supernatural death at any moment.

I pushed those thoughts away as the evening went on. Enough guilt already weighed me down. Much more and I wouldn't be able to do anything other than listen to hipster music and write depressing poetry.

Fuck that. If I was gonna save the world, I needed a clean head and any advantage I could get - including being on my home turf.

The phone rang a few times as the night continued, but we ignored it - letting it go to the machine - especially while they got me caught up on a few of the shows I'd missed. Goddamn, I really needed to invest in a DVR with an extra-large hard drive. After updating my resume, I'd need to get my ass to some pirate sites and start downloading. The penalties for copyright infringement weren't so scary compared to all the shit I'd seen.

Tom finally passed out, leaving Ed and me to mock him for a little while. Soon enough, he'd be dragging his ass for completely different reasons. I had no idea what was worse: waking up with a hangover or being dead on your feet from changing shit-filled diapers all night, but I knew which one I'd prefer. I had a feeling Christy wasn't going to tolerate too much of the former. Poor guy. Of all of us, he was the least prepared to grow up.

Of course, that didn't stop us from scrawling "dickless" on his forehead with a Sharpie while he snored away.

Finally, we decided to turn in. Ed looked beat and, despite my vampire stamina, I'd have no problem getting to sleep. Hell, the prospect of doing so in my own bed - and not atop a pile of rotting corpses in a dank cave - had me practically excited.

Ed locked up as I dragged Tom to his room and tossed his unconscious ass onto the bed. I threw a blanket onto him, swiped a micro-USB cable so I could recharge my stolen phone, positioned his Cheetara figure to look like she was going down on Leader 1 from the Gobots, then turned off the lights and stepped out.

I walked toward my bedroom and noticed Ed was listening to the messages on the machine. Most of it was crap - a telemarketer, some charity asking for a donation, and a political message. As I opened my door, Dave's voice caught my ear. He was babbling excitedly about something, but I found myself not really paying attention to the voicemail.

"That one's for you." Ed said, walking past me to disappear into his room.

"*...and shoulders you gave me is turning out to be a goldmine of information. Thanks, man! Oh yeah, and don't forget to show up to the game this week. Give me a call when you get a chance, I want to talk about...*"

Oh, Jesus Christ. The guy couldn't give me a fucking day to relax. I tuned out the rest as I slammed my bedroom door behind me. Whatever he was calling about could wait until the next day.

* * *

Shoulders?!

I sat bolt upright as Dave's words finally sank in. It was dark, but that didn't mean anything to me. I quickly grabbed my glasses and checked out the alarm clock. 10:42, but the display was blinking. Oh yeah, I hadn't bothered to set it before going to sleep.

I grabbed my purloined cell phone, glad to see that it was both charged and hadn't been remotely deactivated. A small part of me wondered whether the vampires had anything to do with that. Maybe they'd found Doughboy's unconscious form in their search for me. If so, a stolen cell phone would be the least of his worries.

I shook my head to clear that thought. There was nothing I could do in that case. That problem was about three thousand miles behind me at that point.

Checking the time, I saw about four hours had elapsed. It had felt like five minutes, no doubt owing to the fact that, even with my supernatural stamina, the events of the past few days were bound to have caught up with me. Hell, I felt like I could have easily used another several hours to charge my batteries, but Dave's message was eating away at the back of my skull.

Hopping out of bed, I walked back into the now empty shared space of my apartment and hit play on the machine, hoping I'd heard Dave wrong.

"*...I can't believe the reaction it's had. If this keeps up, I might not even need to bother you for any more samples. That head and shoulders you gave me is turning out to be a gold...*"

I hit pause, a bad feeling starting to sink in. A small part of me hoped he'd been referring to the dandruff shampoo, but I knew better - especially since that hadn't been what I'd handed him before leaving.

Nah, it couldn't be. That thing was deader than a doorknob.

Then I remembered something I'd been told before. Vampires were tough. Once they were dead, though, you got dust. Anything less than that and you'd be in for a world of hurt once they healed up.

Was it possible?

I had no idea. This was uncharted territory for me. I mean, the thing had sure as shit seemed dead. Then I considered Dave. He wasn't one to just toss it on a shelf somewhere and forget about it.

"You crazy fuck, what have you done?" I muttered, dialing his mobile number. Being a resident and perpetually on call, it was his ass if he didn't answer. It likewise served his players well, as it allowed us to harass him at all hours of the day about our characters.

All I got was his voicemail. After leaving a quick message for him to call me back, I dialed 411. There was always a chance he'd been called in and was on duty. Even he wouldn't blow off a patient to take a personal call, especially if he was currently on the administrative staff's shit list. So, I did the next best thing: I called the hospital where he worked and asked for him to be paged.

That was a dead end. He wasn't on the current roster, and I hung up before the person on the other end could ask if I wanted to be transferred to the resident on duty. Fuck. Twenty-four hours, was that so much to ask? I couldn't even be back for one fucking day before the world decided it needed to shit down my throat the second I opened my mouth to breathe.

Well, okay, this one *was* potentially my fault, but still...

I ran back into my room to get dressed, holding out hope that the only thing I'd find once I got to his place was a sleepy, pissed off DM. That wasn't so bad. I mean, what else could he possibly do to my character?

I stopped that one mid-thought. The answer was a lot. Dave was a master at fucking us over if we ticked him off.

Either way, I had the disturbing feeling that I wouldn't be coming home from this trip unscathed.

A Good DM is a Terrible Thing to Waste

"Where are you going?" Ed's voice stopped me before I was halfway to the door. I turned, not quite knowing what to say. It hadn't been my intention to drag either of my roommates into this mess. So I decided to be clever about it. "Um..."

Yeah, I never did perform well under pressure.

"Well?"

"It's nothing you need to be worried about."

"That means it is," he said, leaning against the door of his room.

"Well, no. I was just jonesing for some...pizza."

"Pizza?"

"It's been a while. Even a fiendish monster of the night gets tired of snacking on nothing but people."

"Don't move," he commanded.

"Why?"

"Because I'm coming with you." He stepped back into his room, leaving the door open. His eyes continually darted back toward me as if he expected me to bolt. It would have been insulting had that not been exactly what I'd planned.

He slipped out of his sweatpants and tossed on a pair of jeans.

"I really didn't need to see that."

"Yeah, well, I really didn't need to be woken up by you clomping around like a fucking herd of elephants," he shot back. "Christ, whatever happened to vampires being all stealthy?" He finished dressing and stepped back out, grabbing his jacket. "Let's go."

"I have a confession to make. I'm not really going out for pizza."

"I kinda figured. You can explain on the way."

"How did you..."

"Because I haven't turned stupid in the past three months, Bill. I know you. You're more than capable of telling people to go fuck themselves if it's something unimportant. The only reason you'd be running out and mumbling like a retard is if some shit were going down. So can we cut the crap and get over to Newark?"

"Wait, you know..."

"Did Dave not call before we went to bed? Duh."

Okay, I guess it was sorta obvious. "Tom?"

"Leave him."

I hesitated at that. Part of the reason Christy's magic had worked to turn him against me had been because I'd been keeping secrets. I wasn't sure I wanted to start off my homecoming the same way I'd left. "Are you sure?"

"He's fucking useless with a hangover and you know it. We'll fill him in when we get back."

"Okay." I shut the door quietly behind us. "It's probably nothing anyway. Just me being paranoid."

"Being sodomized by a greased-up Macedonian conqueror can do that to a person."

"I wasn't sodomized."

"Do you know that for sure?"

"Fuck you."

"Maybe Dr. Death is into all sorts of things your subconscious isn't ready to admit yet."

I could practically feel his grin as I walked down the stairs. "Asshole."

"Happy to be home?"

"You have no idea."

Ed offered to drive. At this time of the morning, he surmised, it would be a shitload faster than relying on the trains. His logic was sound, and being that I wasn't exactly running on full, blood-wise, I wasn't sure I was up for the third option - making a run for it.

We walked a few blocks, parking in Brooklyn being the motherfucking nightmare it always was. Even in the midst of an apocalypse, some things will apparently never change.

Finally, Ed stopped and pulled out a set of keys. He pushed a button and the lights on the car in front of us came on.

"What the hell is this?" I asked, staring at the shiny new Honda Accord.

"What do you think it is?"

"What happened to your car? I mean, last I checked, you were driving that hunk of shit that was pretty much being held together by duct tape."

He smiled as he opened the passenger side door for me. "I may not be making big CEO bucks, but believe me when I say that it's good to be king."

* * *

I was tempted to rue the passing of an era, but then had to remind myself that Ed's old car had been a complete piece of crap. People tended to get too nostalgic for such things, not realizing that there is very limited pride to be had in torturing oneself just for the sake of doing so.

Besides, his new ride had heated seats - nice.

I filled him in on things as we drove. We chanced Staten Island in the hope that this was one of the few times of day that 278 wouldn't be a goddamned parking lot.

We were crossing the Goethals into New Jersey when he asked, "So you just gave him the fucking thing, just like that?"

"How many CDs does this thing hold anyway?"

"Don't change the subject."

"Sorry. It seemed preferable to letting him cut anything else off me."

"And you really thought it would be useful for us otherwise?"

"I don't know," I replied, playing with his dual climate controls. Damn, this thing was pretty sweet. I might have to let him drive me places more often. "I wasn't really thinking too far beyond getting the fuck out of the kingdom of the undead."

"So the vampires own Switzerland. Really?"

"Tell me about it. Fucking crazy."

"Explains a lot, though."

"I can't argue with that."

* * *

We arrived at Dave's apartment complex a short while later.

"Stay here," I said, getting out of the car.

"Fuck you," Ed replied, following. I almost wished Alex were there to see it. Would his faith in his beloved prophecies be so strong if he observed that my leadership prowess didn't even extend toward getting one of my friends to follow a simple request?

"Dave's gonna be mad if there's nothing going on."

"So? I'm not in his game."

He had a point there. We walked over to the door. Light shined through the closed curtains. "I guess he's up."

"Well, then let's stop him before he makes some sort of Franken-vampire or whatever."

That wouldn't be particularly great. Technically speaking, Dave wasn't supposed to be experimenting on vampire blood at all. Hell, *nobody* was. It was considered off-limits - verboten. I wasn't sure why, but probably really didn't need to know. What I needed to care about was that the Draculas were known for coming down hard on anyone caught doing so.

Dave was my friend and I owed him. There was also the off-chance the crazy bastard might one day come up with something useful from his experiments. Even so, I had little doubt we were living dangerously.

I wasn't worried about Ed spilling his guts...even if Sally promised him the mother of all blowjobs. He wasn't that type. Tom was, but I doubted she'd make him that same offer anytime soon. What worried me was Dave getting sloppy. There'd already been an incident with his fucking vampire mice. It was only a matter of time before something happened that we wouldn't be able to cover up so neatly.

I resolved to talk him down from the craziness before it got away from him and ended with both of us taking a permanent dirt nap. If that didn't work, maybe I could convince Sally to compel him to drop it. It wouldn't be ideal for her to have anything else to hold over my head, but she was already in pretty deep. Her involvement in helping me with Sheila was more than enough to bury her. If she could keep her mouth shut about that...

"Are you going to knock, or are you hoping that maybe he'll hear us breathing from inside?"

"Since when are you in such a rush?"

"I have a meeting with some potential investors in the morning."

"I so do not know you." I raised my hand and knocked softly so as to not rouse the neighbors.

"Maybe he's out."

"I don't think so." My ears picked up movement from inside. It wasn't near the door, but there was definitely someone shuffling around inside. I knocked again, a little louder this time. The movement inside ceased as if someone was listening.

"It's too late for this shit," Ed said. "Just open it."

He had a point, but all I could see was a future full of pain for my character if I broke the lock and just strolled in. I shrugged and pushed the doorbell instead.

"You are such a pussy."

I opened my mouth to respond as the chime sounded inside, but the words died in my throat as the noise immediately cut off - replaced by the sound of something being smashed.

I glanced toward Ed, and the look on his face told me all I needed to know. "You heard that?"

He nodded. "Open it."

I mentally kissed Kelvin goodbye and turned the knob until the lock broke with a sharp crack. The door began to swing in, but a chain lock stopped it - fucking useless things. I reached through and gave it a quick yank, clearing our path inside.

We stood there for a moment, waiting. Dave's apartment was quiet again. Whatever had been moving about had stopped. His living room looked as it normally did. It all gave the impression that nothing out of the ordinary was going on. If I heard a toilet flush, followed by him stepping out to greet us, I was gonna feel mighty stupid indeed.

"Dave?" I called out quietly.

"Oh, this is stupid," Ed said from behind me. "Get the fuck inside before someone calls the cops."

Again, he had a point. I did as told and he entered behind me, closing the door as best as he could.

Feeling a bit foolish that my roommate was keeping his shit together better than me, I tried to muster what little pride I had left. "You check the bedroom. I'll check his lab."

"What do you think I'm going to find in there?"

"With any luck, an angry, naked Dave."

He gave me a withering glare in response, but he did as asked - probably realizing that the longer we bantered, the greater chance we had of this operation blowing up in our faces. It was safe to say that neither I nor my friends were cut out for a life of espionage.

I didn't bother to let him know that my vampire ears had picked up enough extra to let me know that whatever had made the sound had originated from the direction of the lab.

Well, okay, "lab" was probably putting it kindly. For anyone else, it would have been an extra bedroom or perhaps used for storage. Dave lived frugally, though, minus maybe his gaming supplies, and he sure as shit didn't have a roommate. I doubted anyone would last long without outright killing him.

I stepped into the back room and that thought caught in my mind. My eyes opened wide at what lay before me.

One didn't need to be a blind seer to occasionally be right in foretelling a dark future.

Showdown in Newark

"Dave!"

He lay there, eyes glazed over - looking at nothing - while what I assumed was the head I'd dropped off earlier sucked on his neck like a leech, taking great pulls as if trying to get the very last drops. I say "assumed" because he was a bit different from last I saw him. Though still desiccated, with pale cracked skin and thin white hair, he'd grown a little.

His head now sat atop a body. It was sickly in appearance - damp and clammy like a wound that had just had a bandage peeled off. He was frail and ancient looking, kind of like that guy at the end of the video for Metallica's *Unforgiven*. Regardless, no matter how pathetic he looked, I knew better - especially as the front of him was covered in blood, at least some of it Dave's, from the look of things.

The room itself was a mess. Tables had been overturned and shelves smashed. Dave's mini-fridge was torn open. The IV bags once contained within littered the floor, sucked dry of all contents. It told a tale of a creature starved for blood. That point was further driven home as the ghoul paid me almost no heed, greedily trying to suck the last of the life from his victim.

That finally snapped me out of it. No fucking way. I hadn't let the forces of darkness take any of my friends to date. I had no intention of breaking that streak.

"Hey, gramps, why don't you chew on this instead?" I stepped forward and kicked his head with everything I had. If only I'd had my vampire powers back in high school, I could've been a star punter instead of having the entire football team give me atomic wedgies. I connected with the fucker's chin with enough force to upend a small car.

The creature's head snapped back and...and that was it. It turned its black eyes toward me, seemingly noticing me in full for the first time.

"Drop my friend, buddy," I ordered, hoping my words carried sufficient menace.

"Bill, what's..."

"Get the fuck out of here, Ed," I said over my shoulder.

The other vampire dropped Dave. He rolled bonelessly to the floor. I wanted to cry out, but there was no helping him so long as I was in a Chinese standoff with Gollum's body double. I needed to get rid of that asshole and then...then, well, I had no fucking idea.

The other vamp tilted his head in confusion, looking like the world's oldest stupid dog, then bared his fangs and stood up. He was naked, sadly giving me full view of his shriveled junk. Why is it always the dudes? Why couldn't someone like that Theodora chick have flashed her goods at me instead?

That, thankfully, wasn't all that caught my eye. Odd markings seemed to cover his body. They weren't much, just darker patches of skin on his chest and shoulders. I could almost make out shapes within them, but that might have just been my brain trying to connect the dots.

He hissed and a gravelly sounding voice emanated from his mouth. It might have been words, but they weren't in any language I knew...meaning it wasn't English.

Fuck it. Among predators, there's a universal language. One must be able to piss with the big dogs, after all.

I darkened my eyes and flashed my own fangs at him, raising a hand and beckoning him on in a manner that would've made Bruce Lee proud.

It was on.

* * *

Or not. To both my dismay and annoyance, Grandpa Munster's face broke into a grin, his dry lips splitting. Something akin to a laugh escaped his lips. That was never a good sign.

I felt what he was about to do a split second before it hit me. Although his words were still alien to my ears, the psychic portion was clear as day.

"ON YOUR KNEES, WHELP!!"

The compulsion hit me like a runaway water buffalo. I flew back through the doorway and slammed into something soft and squishy...Ed. Fuck me. Would it really kill my friends to do as I told them for once?

"Get...the...fuck...off."

"Are you okay?"

"I will be once you're not sitting on my chest."

"Well, then stop whining like a bitch and get the fuck out of here!"

The vamp's words still rang in my head. Whoever he was, he had a lot of firepower behind his compulsion. That wasn't good. Then again, it probably wasn't surprising either. This guy had been Alex's prisoner. It was safe to assume he wasn't some newb who had just forgotten to curtsey at the right moment.

Even so, other than a splitting headache, it had no effect on me. I pulled myself back to my feet, trying not to show any wobbliness. As expected, surprise shown on the other vamp's face. He hadn't been expecting the Freewill.

Just to make sure he got the point, though, I threw one of my own back at him - making sure that he understood it. "*NICE TRY, COCKSUCKER!!*"

I'm not sure what I expected. Anger was a pretty safe bet, and maybe a little fear was even possible at the realization that the legendary warrior of the vampire race stood before him. I mean, shit, Super Saiyans got all sorts of fucking respect in *Dragonball Z*. One of these days, I was bound to meet someone with the good graces to realize that.

It was not that day, alas.

An even wider grin broke out on its face. More laughter poured forth. The creature clapped its hands together in apparent delight and hissed, "*Frater*."

Freighter - what the hell? Was he trying to pronounce...nah it couldn't be. I mean sure, I'd sprung him from that head prison. Maybe this fucker had brain damage and was imprinting upon me like a baby bird. Weird. "Listen, dude, I may be a lot of things, but I sure as shit ain't your father." I backed up a step, risking a glance over my shoulder. Ed was, thankfully, nowhere to be seen. About time he took the fucking hint.

Now I just had to get this delusional asshole out of the way so I could help Dave. I continued to back up and saw that he followed me - obviously unafraid. Wished I could've said the same thing. Being chased by a naked ghoul was a bit unnerving.

Backing up toward the door, I scanned Dave's apartment for something I could use. It was a complete bust. Unlike most gamers I knew, he was just into the rules. He didn't walk the walk: collecting swords, staves, or maces. Sure, most of that shit was for display only, but I certainly wouldn't have turned down an ornamental morning star to beat this fucker's skull in with.

I backed out of the apartment and stepped off the curb. It continued to follow, apparently unfazed by the cold night air against its bare skin. Maybe I'd get lucky and the cops would arrive to arrest him for indecent exposure.

"Frater," it called again. Gah! Why couldn't I meet a hot chick with daddy issues instead?

I kept backing up, leading it away from the apartment. Maybe Ed could get past us while this guy was distracted and tend to Dave.

Speaking of which, where the fuck was Ed? When I told him to run, I hadn't expected him to take it to heart and dash off into the night screaming like a little girl.

A car engine revved from somewhere off to the left.

Ask and ye shall receive.

All right! I didn't need for inspiration to strike. I had something better: a crazy-ass friend and a ton of Japan's automotive finest.

Headlights flicked on, illuminating us. The creature hissed in their direction, raising a hand to shield its eyes. I took the slightly more proactive response of getting the fuck out of the way.

Ed's car slammed into the other vamp at a good thirty miles an hour. A sickening crunch sounded, although whether from the car or the monster, I couldn't tell.

Either way, the vehicle screeched to a halt and the creature went flying, tumbling across the parking lot to come to rest in a heap.

Had I been a complete newb, I might've paused to congratulate my roommate on a job well done. I'd played this game before, though, and knew that celebrating before a vamp was ash would only result in heartache...and probably a massive ass-kicking as well.

Ed looked a bit dazed from the impact, but otherwise okay. I threw him a quick thumbs-up and then ran back inside, noting with some dismay that the lights in the neighboring apartments were starting to come on.

Dave was still where he'd been discarded. His eyes were now closed, but that was all the change there was to him. I picked him up, noticing how cold he felt, and tossed him over my shoulder. All I could do was hope I wasn't too late, but it wasn't much to go on.

I was going to need help. I'd promised myself a full coven-free day before contacting them, but fuck it. Technically, it was *tomorrow* anyway.

I raced back outside with Dave. The entire round trip had taken less than thirty seconds. Sadly, the squeal of metal that reached my ears as I stepped to the curb told me that I'd taken too long.

* * *

The creature was back on his feet, and then some. Raw panic shown on Ed's face as the monster tore the passenger side door clean off. Before I could make a move, it reached in and dragged my roommate out, snapping his seatbelt like tissue paper.

No, not again!

I laid Dave onto the ground as gently as time allowed and put all of my speed and power to bear. The vamp shoved Ed's head to the side, exposing his neck, as I reached his car and dove over it.

Sadly, whatever fatherly thoughts it had couldn't have been all that deep. It backhanded me out of the air as if I were a gnat. I went tumbling and landed on the hood of Ed's car - rolling off onto the pavement and denting the shit out of his front bumper in the process.

I lay there dazed for a moment, realizing it was time I didn't have. The sickening sound of flesh being torn reached my ears. For the second time this day, I'd failed one of my friends - perhaps fatally so.

* * *

I refused to give up. Gathering what wits I could, I pulled myself to my feet just as an ungodly scream pierced the night.

No!

My fangs descended in anger. It wasn't enough to feed off my friend - he had to torture him too? But that's when I noticed the scream hadn't come from Ed. Don't get me wrong, my roommate didn't look so hot - what with an oozing bite wound on the side of his neck, but he wasn't the source of the cry.

The vampire shoved Ed away and doubled over, holding his stomach. I should have used the distraction to my advantage to try and end things right there, but I was at a momentary loss. What the fuck was happening?

Almost as if in answer, the two-legged prune straightened up and threw back his head. He opened his mouth to cry out again and belched a pyre of white flame.

Magic can come in a myriad of pyrotechnic colors. Heck, one needed only look at the sky during one of those storms to see that. As far as I was aware, though, only one thing produced flames of pure white - the power of faith.

Holy shit indeed.

* * *

Of all the things I expected to happen that night, watching a near-mummified vampire puking white fire wasn't even close to making the cut. I might have continued staring like a doofus had movement out of the corner of my eye not caught my attention. Ed dragged himself back to his feet and leaned against the battered car for support.

That snapped me out of it and I remembered Dave lying on the sidewalk like a piece of discarded beef.

"Are you okay?" I asked my roommate.

"Been better," he croaked, but he was able to stand on his own now. The bite on his neck was ugly, but apparently not too deep.

"Can you drive?"

"Away from that thing?" he asked, his voice stronger. "Try and stop me." He steadied himself for a moment and then slid behind the wheel.

I grabbed Dave and made my way over to the passenger side, dumping him into the backseat. "Let's move."

It was only then that I dared look back at the other vamp. He was still clutching his midsection, obviously in agony. Sparks of white flame continued to spew forth from his mouth and nose.

I allowed myself a small smile as Ed peeled out. I wasn't sure what had happened, but if that ass-biter had gotten a stomach full of faith magic, he was thoroughly fucked. By the time the cops arrived, they'd think maybe someone had just emptied out an ashcan in the parking lot. Served the dickhead right.

Unfortunately, that smile wasn't destined to be long-lived. I had two wounded friends, one perhaps fatally. I hated to admit it, but I was in way over my head.

"Are you sure you're okay?"

"Don't worry about me." Ed's voice was steady, but his hands shook a little as he gripped the wheel. "So what do we do? Take him to a hospital?"

"Fucked if I know." I pulled the stolen cell phone out of my jacket pocket and gave it a quick once over - still in one piece, thankfully. I powered it on and waited for it to boot up.

"Who are you calling?"

"Someone who might have a clue."

"Tell her I said hi."

"Polish your knob on your own time," I muttered.

He made a left turn, and I almost lost the phone and myself in the process, thanks to the missing door. "Whoa! You can slow down. That fucker's dead by now."

"Sorry."

I punched in the number for my coven partner's mobile phone, hoping she hadn't changed it since I'd gone rogue. It rang a few times and then I heard the click as it was answered.

"Sally? Is that you?" I couldn't hear a reply from the other end, but that might have been due to the excess wind whipping past my face. "Jesus Christ, where the *fuck* are you? You have no idea the shit I've been through."

I was about to say more when the car jolted violently from behind. I dropped the handset into my lap and turned around.

No fucking way.

Not only was that old vamp not dead, he was actually chasing us. No, scratch that - he was right on our tail. He slashed with his claws and metal screeched as he gouged the shit out of Ed's trunk.

I grabbed the phone again, hoping Sally was listening and that I wasn't currently trying to plead with a wrong number. My eyes locked with those of the creature and nothing but pure unbridled hatred stared back. "I've...sorta...fucked up, just a little bit. I kinda need your help...oh shit!"

The creature swung a fist and connected solidly with the rear of the car - sending us into a dizzying spin. The phone flew out of my hands and clattered to pieces onto the asphalt.

The vampire leaped at us, but just then, we slammed into a guard rail, stopping our sideways momentum. Old-man Logan sailed over the roof to land in a storm drain.

I turned toward Ed, his eyes as wide as mine. "Forget what I said earlier and floor this fucking thing!"

He didn't bother with a witty retort. Sparks flew as we ground against the guardrail for a moment, and then we were free, accelerating as fast as the formerly mint condition car could carry us.

Early Morning Commute

I don't know if it was the early hour, the cops being summoned *en masse* to Newark, or just a little dumb luck. Either way, through some minor miracle, we weren't immediately pulled over. Albeit, by that point, I'd have welcomed a nice, secure jail cell. Still, that wouldn't have solved anything in the long term.

"The office?" Ed asked, blotting his neck with some napkins he'd had in the center console.

"Unless you have a better idea."

He glared at me out of the corner of his eye.

"Sorry. I'm a little on edge right now."

"I have no idea why," he replied.

"Are you sure you're fine?"

"I'm in better shape than my car."

"At least now it matches your old one. Feels like home again."

"Asshole. There's no way my fucking insurance is gonna cover this."

He had a point, but it seemed like a minor worry, all things considered.

"What happened back there?" I asked, now that I finally had a moment to take a breath.

"We got our asses thoroughly kicked."

"I know *that*. I mean with the vamp. He took a suck on you and practically exploded. What, did you give up bathing for Lent or something?"

"I have no fucking idea."

"Anything like that ever happen before?"

He chuckled. "No offense, but I haven't exactly been offering myself up as a vampire buffet since you left."

"Oh?"

"Not for her, either. I haven't even seen Sally in months."

"What came out of his mouth, that was like..." I hesitated to say her name aloud.

"I know."

"But...you and I...we hugged when you got home."

"Thanks for the reminder."

"You know what I mean. There was no reaction. I didn't get blown across the apartment."

"Trust me, I noticed. Oh, and can you kindly not use the word 'blown' to describe something we did?"

"And your eyes," I continued, ignoring his comment, "they're still the same shit brown color they always were."

"I know what you're getting at." The lights of the tunnel flickered over his face as we drove past them. "Trust me. I'm not an Icon."

"But it could..."

"She gave me the keys to her company, not her powers. I don't think it works like that anyway. Besides, faith...well, it's still not really my cup of tea."

"Then what the fuck was that?"

"Let's worry about that later." He hooked a thumb over his shoulder. Oh, fuck. I'd almost forgotten about Dave. "How's he doing?"

I unbuckled and turned to lean into the backseat. I put a finger to Dave's neck to feel for a pulse, but it wasn't exactly the easiest thing to do while driving. It also didn't exactly help that I had no idea what I was doing. I mean, I'm a vampire, not a pre-med student.

Wait. Maybe I wasn't as helpless as I thought.

When in doubt, use what you know. I reached out with my senses - focusing them on his still form.

It was difficult to single out his heartbeat, what with the noise of driving. His smell, though, told me a different story. Vampires and humans have distinct scents, as apparently do all supernatural species. I was still pretty new at the whole bloodhound thing, but I'd gotten enough nose-fulls to begin to have a clue. What I was getting from Dave wasn't encouraging. Even pushing aside the strange odor of the vamp that bit him, I was still getting enough for me to surmise that his days as a human were probably coming to an end. "I think he's turning."

"You think?"

"They don't exactly give us a handbook for these things."

"Can you help him?"

"No idea."

"You guys helped me." Ed was reaching with that one and I had no doubt he knew it.

"Different scenario entirely," I replied softly.

I had the sinking feeling that no battle-angel, alight with the fires of faith, would swoop in and save our asses this time.

* * *

"I gotta say, Bill, this is a new record for you."

"Oh, shut up."

"No, seriously. You've been back for what, maybe twelve hours? That's gotta be some sort of personal best."

I sighed and stepped in something squishy, momentarily losing traction.

"Jeez, watch it." Ed's hand momentarily tightened on my shoulder. In the pitch black of the tunnel, if I went down, he was sure to follow.

My roommate wasn't a happy camper, not that I could really blame him. After exiting the Holland Tunnel, I told him we needed to ditch the car. He really didn't need much convincing, considering we were driving around in a vehicle that would only be considered street legal in the most liberal of definitions. We'd gotten lucky in Jersey, but I had a feeling that luck would run out quickly in the city.

There was also the fact that the sun would be rising soon. The storm from the previous day had passed and left a clear sky above us. I doubted it would last long, but all I needed was a few stray sunbeams for me to turn into a crispy critter. If Dave was indeed turning like I feared, then he, too, would probably soon become increasingly averse to daylight.

Fortunately, New York City was host to an extensive underground, in more ways than one. Thus, we found ourselves tromping through the aromatic sewers, headed toward my coven. With Dave slung over my shoulder, the subway wasn't really an option for me. Ed had declined splitting up and taking it himself - proving that while he might be pissed, he was still a true friend.

We continued onward, slipping and sliding - all while trying not to dump Dave into any random piles of shit.

I didn't exactly know the deepest, darkest recesses of the NYC sewer system like the back of my hand, but I'd been down there enough times to know how to get to the important spots. Fortunately, there wasn't much to sightsee except for maybe the occasional rat of near mutant size - and they, thankfully, gave us a wide berth. It wouldn't do for the legendary warrior of the vampire race to start screaming like a little girl.

Finally, we reached the office's subbasement. Unlike most entrances to coven territory, it was unguarded and unlocked. The office was, true to its name, an honest-to-goodness office building in the SoHo area of Manhattan. We rented a few floors, but so did several other businesses too - at least, that I remembered. Last time I was here, a vampire named Remington had been doing his damnedest to release all of the other tenants from their leases - permanently.

Oh, crap!

I stopped and Ed bumped into me.

"What's the problem?"

"What if the coven isn't here anymore? What if they had to pack up and..."

"You pick really shitty times to think of these things, you know."

"Sorry, but this wasn't exactly the homecoming I was envisioning."

"You were expecting maybe a red carpet?"

I turned to glance at him, despite knowing he couldn't see me in the dark. "That would've been nice."

"In your dreams, maybe."

"In my dreams there were free blowjobs too."

"Oh, I don't know." A grin formed on his face. "I'd say you've been screwed pretty well so far."

"Yeah, well, we're both gonna be if the coven moved and anybody sees us carrying an unconscious body up the stairs."

Yep, that's me...when the shit hits the fan, I'm all rainbows and unicorns.

* * *

Thankfully, the bullshit that the movies feed us about vampires needing to return to their foul coffins during the day is just that - a steaming pile of cow patties. Don't get me wrong. Most vamps still sack out during the daylight hours. We still need to sleep, albeit not as long as most people, and our bodies are pre-conditioned to be nocturnal, but it's more of a guideline than a rule.

I was holding out hope that there might be at least a few vamps still around in the office. Right before I skipped town for my little *vacation*, Village Coven had been decimated. Aside from me and Sally, there had been only three other survivors. I knew Sally, though, and had little doubt she'd probably been itching to rebuild. With me out of the picture to guilt her into doing otherwise, I wouldn't be surprised to learn that she hadn't hesitated to start recruiting.

At least, I hoped that was the case. As much as I had no desire to see others join our ranks, the last thing I wanted right then was an abandoned floor where our coven once stood. Things had turned to shit quickly enough without me also having to learn that a place I considered to be safe - relatively speaking - held no sanctuary for us.

Reaching our floor via the back stairs, I silently prayed to whatever gods compelled Sally to often do the opposite of what I wanted. I could only cross my fingers that she hadn't decided to have a change of heart as of late.

With Dave still over my shoulder, I led the way to the office's entrance. From the outside, it appeared the same. Well, okay, the door was new, but that wasn't anything special. In the time I'd been a part of Village Coven, the damn thing had been destroyed and replaced at least three times. The lives of those in a coven, especially during the middle of an apocalypse, were apparently nothing close to resembling dull.

I didn't give it any further consideration as I turned the knob and opened it.

The problem with being away, though, is if you're gone from someplace long enough, they change the locks.

And even when they don't, sometimes there's a new security system in place.

Back in the Saddle Again

I had no more than stepped through the doorway when hands grabbed hold of my jacket and flung me inside. Losing my grip on Dave, I went tumbling across the floor and landed on my back. The entire scene took no more than a few seconds to play out, but by the time I looked up, several angry vampires had surrounded me. Worse, they were all pointing guns at my face.

"Who sent you?" one snarled, a middle management type wearing a cheap tie. "Was it the Howard Beach Coven?"

"Do I look like a gangbanger, asshole?"

"Freewill?" a heavily accented voice asked. The crowd parted and I found myself staring up at my first familiar undead face, albeit one I wasn't particularly pleased to see.

"Monkhbat?" Oh shit, what the fuck was he doing here?

"This piece of garbage is the Freewill?" the first vamp asked incredulously.

To my surprise, Monkhbat immediately backhanded him, sending Tie Guy flying. The others all backed up a step, uncertain. A few of them, though, were brave enough to point their weapons at Gan's former lackey. This wasn't going to end well.

"That's enough!" a familiar voice said from behind them all. "Monkhbat, how many times have I told you not to..." She paused as she came into view and saw me lying there. "Bill?"

It was Starlight, one of the few survivors of the coven massacre from months back. She was a sight for sore eyes, in more ways than one. A fashion model in life, she had curves that would stop a runaway truck. Sally had been using - or abusing, depending on your point of view - her as her personal secretary, forcing her to dress the part.

This was a new look, though. Starlight was still dressed professionally, but her dark hair was down, cascading over her shoulders. She also had on more jewelry than I had seen her wear during her time as Sally's assistant. The effect was subtle, but powerful. She looked more the boss than the employee and her tone reflected that - a dramatic change in attitude from the vampire I'd known.

What the fuck had happened while I was gone?

"Hey, Star," I said uncertainly.

"Oh my god, Bill!" she screeched, losing all semblance of the authority she seemed to wield just moments earlier. She reached down a hand, which I took. Upon dragging me back to my feet, she threw her arms around me in an embrace. Can't say I minded it much. I loved my roommates like brothers, but I sure as shit would take Starlight pressing up against me over them any day of the week.

She pulled back with a squeal of delight. "Oh my god. Where have you been? When did you get back? Are you okay? Is..." She was starting to babble, reverting back to the Starlight I remembered.

"Uh, can I come in now?"

I turned to find Ed still standing at the doorway.

"Thanks for backing me up, ass..."

"I claim this human as mine if it so pleases you, coven master Alice." The vamp who'd mouthed off to me reappeared, apparently no worse for the wear from Monkhbat's bitch-slap. His eyes blackened and he took a step toward the entranceway.

"Coven master Alice?" I asked.

"That's enough, John," Starlight said.

"But..."

"Now now, John. You heard our *master*," a voice purred from behind Ed, causing him to jump.

Even had he not been surprised by Firebird's sudden appearance, he would have certainly been knocked off-kilter by it, judging from the look on his face. Couldn't really blame him either. Whereas Starlight was dressed for a day at the office, Firebird was ready for a night out on the town...probably followed by a roll in the hay. Her clothes appeared to be spray painted on, and her shoes gave a whole new meaning to the phrase "fuck-me pumps." Whoa.

She stepped past my roommate without a second glance and strolled in. Walking up to the dick I presumed was John, she ran a finger across his chest - oozing sex in a way that made my pants feel uncomfortably tight. Goddamn, I had forgotten how awesome my coven could be. It was almost enough to make me forget...

Oh, fuck.

"Dave!"

That caused everyone in the room to stop and do a double take. I shoved aside a few vamps I didn't recognize and found him lying where I'd dropped him after being so warmly *greeted*.

"I need help." I shoved all of the items off the nearest desk so as to lay Dave on top of it - cringing as I sent a laptop clattering to the floor.

Starlight stepped to my side. "What's wrong?"

"He was bitten." Even as I said it, I realized how stupid it must sound. It was like screaming that someone had just swallowed a carrot in the middle of a vegan convention. Oh well. Some vamps were smart enough to rue becoming what they were. The rest, well, they could go fuck themselves sideways with a rusty engine block.

I glanced around and a bunch of blank stares met mine. It reminded me that most of the vamps present were probably newbs, most likely less than three months turned. They knew even less about their powers than I did. Sadly, the person probably most qualified to make a diagnosis was the one lying on the desk. It was...

"Monkhbat," Starlight said, "please see what you can do."

To my surprise, he gave her a quick bow and walked over to Dave's side. Had I somehow found my way to Bizarro universe? Since when did Starlight command one of Gan's former minions?

That and a million other questions could wait, though. Monkhbat felt Dave's neck, then grabbed his chin and turned his head. He put a hand on my friend's chest, then bent over and began to sniff him. Yeah, vampire examinations were a little weird. Thank goodness they didn't require us to have yearly physicals or anything like that.

After a few seconds, I grew impatient. "Well?"

In response, he shoved my friend off the desk, drew a silvered dagger from his hip, and raised it over his head. Shit!

I grabbed his wrist with both hands, despite knowing he probably possessed enough power to toss me across the room like a tennis ball. "What the fuck do you think you're doing?"

His face swiveled and, for just a moment, annoyance replaced his mask of calm. "He turns."

He said something else, but reverted to his native tongue for the rest - as if that was of any help. Since his arm hadn't dropped, though, the meaning was clear enough for me. Fuck that. Before he could skewer my friend like a shish kabob, I slammed my fist into the side of his head. He barely moved from the impact. I probably hurt my ego far more than his body, but I had a lot more where that...

"Bill, stop!"

I looked over to find Starlight glaring at me. In the past, I'd never heard her say anything that sounded like an order to anyone. As my eyes met hers, I could see a quick flash of her old skittishness pass over her face, but she quickly composed herself and held my gaze. "He's not going to kill your friend. He's trying to help."

"That doesn't look like helping to me. How do you know..."

"That's what he said."

I raised a questioning eyebrow.

"I've been taking an online course in Mandarin," she explained.

"Well, okay, that makes sense then." I sheepishly backed up a step. "Carry on."

She nodded toward Monkhbat. He gently placed Dave's right hand palm down on the floor. I was skeptical that would do much, but what did I know about homeopathic therapies?

He raised the dagger again and plunged it through my friend's hand, pinning it to the floor better than any nail gun could.

What in holy Hell? Maybe I didn't have a doctorate in medicine, but I was pretty sure that wasn't exactly going to help.

* * *

Ed seemed to share my feelings as he threw caution to the wind and came running in to stand by my side.

The vampire called John, apparently letting his hunger override the orders he'd been given, bared his fangs and took a step toward my roommate.

Unfortunately for him, that brought him within my reach.

I might be a piece of shit when it came to fighting vamps like Monkhbat, but John-boy was a different story entirely. Pity he'd caught me on a really bad day.

I grabbed him by the tie and dragged him in, his eyes widening in surprise. I got little enough respect as it was from the vamps who knew me, but these newbs didn't need to know that. Before my disappearance, Sally had done a good job making the others fear me enough to keep their distance. Since she wasn't there, I figured it was up to me this time.

Before John could so much as say, "shit," I buried my fangs into his neck. A collective gasp of surprise went through the crowd as I tore the fucker a new blowhole.

There wasn't much point in taking a long drink. I hardly felt the asshole's blood hitting my system. Yep, like I'd guessed, he was barely out of diapers as far as the vampire world was concerned.

I took one more pull, more for show than anything else - inwardly enjoying his feeble struggles against my attack. I pulled back and gave him a shove, his power added to my own, giving it just enough extra oomph to look impressive.

He landed on his ass - the others making a hole as if afraid to touch him - then quickly scooted back, fear showing on his face. It was about fucking time.

"Anyone else?" It was more warning than question.

The only ones in the room who weren't wearing an "Oh shit!" face were my roommate, Monkhbat, and Starlight. This was all old hat for them. Oh yeah, and Dave wasn't doing much other than lying there with a freaking knife sticking out of his hand.

I turned to Starlight, seeing as how she'd been referred to as coven master. I had a lot of questions about that, but for now, I had more immediate concerns. "So do you want to tell me exactly how that helps?" I pointed accusingly toward the pig-sticker currently bisecting my friend's hand. I felt bad doing so, seeing her flinch slightly. She was a gentle soul - odd for a vampire. I would have never considered her cut out for leadership, but then again, I wouldn't have thought that for myself either. Fate had a way of taking a look at our expectations and wiping its ass with them.

"He turns," Monkhbat repeated, rising from Dave's side. Again, he lapsed into his native tongue.

Starlight listened for a moment, asked one or two stilted questions back - guess that language course was still a work in progress - then turned toward me. "I think what he's trying to say is that your friend is going to turn regardless. I'm so sorry, Bill."

I felt my roommate's hand fall supportively upon my shoulder. It wasn't a real surprise to hear those words - I had suspected as much when I'd given Dave my own once-over - but they still sucked balls nevertheless.

"And the dagger?" Ed helpfully reminded.

Most vamps would have either ignored or just outright killed him for daring to speak in their presence.

Starlight wasn't most vampires, though. "It's to take his mind off the hunger."

"I think I get it."

"You do?" I asked, turning toward Ed. "Care to explain it to me?"

"Remember Mrs. Caven?"

I nodded. How could I forget? Jeff, the vampire who'd turned me, had kidnapped and bitten her as well - stupidly thinking she was my mother. She'd woken up as little more than a feral monster and attacked us without hesitation.

"Well, I'm thinking this is to prevent him from waking up like that. A dagger sticking through his hand is probably going to be pretty hard to ignore. It'll distract him from going on a rampage for blood." He inclined his head toward Starlight. "That sound about right?"

"In a nutshell," she replied. "You're Bill's roommate, right?"

He nodded. "Yep, I'm Ed."

"Sally mentioned you."

"She did?"

Oh, Jesus. We were about to devolve into a high school cafeteria here.

Fortunately, Monkhbat didn't seem to know about that pitfall. He stood up before Ed could ask what Sally had said about him - probably something derogatory yet flattering at the same time - and gave the air around my roomie a sniff.

"You smell wrong," he stated flatly in broken English.

"Well, yeah," I replied. "We've both just spent the past hour refamiliarizing ourselves with the finer aspects of the Manhattan sewer system."

"No," he said more forcefully. "He smells *wrong*."

I had no desire to bring a group of vamps, only one of whom I even remotely trusted, into the loop on what had happened when Grandpa Walton had sunk his fangs into Ed. I didn't know what the fuck was going on with him, but we could discuss that further at a time when we weren't in a position to cause a panic amongst a horde of undead monsters. "Sorry, man," I said to Ed, "but we all wished you used Dial."

A chuckle rippled amongst the assembled and broke the tension for the moment. The good thing about newbs was that they were all up on their pop culture references. I could dig that.

The show over for the time being, Starlight once more took charge - resuming what I assumed we'd interrupted, closing down shop for the day. That was good. It would thin out the ranks and allow us to talk.

More importantly, though, it would allow us to wait. I wasn't sure exactly how long it would take, but in a few short hours, I'd be trying to explain things to one very pissed off formerly human doctor who held the fate of my favorite character in his hands.

Not surprisingly, I found myself wondering if it was too late to catch a plane back to Switzerland.

Chick Fight

After the minions had wrapped things up, Starlight dismissed them for the day. Considering the sun had risen, I figured they'd most likely take the same route we'd used - the sewers - to go back to wherever they'd be sacking out. A few tried to stay behind, no doubt curious to see what was going on, but she shooed them away.

Eventually, it was down to five of us: me, Star, Ed, Dave, Monkhbat, and Firebird. Following the coven's exodus, an uncomfortable silence settled for a while. Starlight didn't seem so pleased with Firebird's presence for some reason. Maybe one had stolen the other's eye shadow or something. Who knows? Personally, I was more worried about Monkhbat. He kept eyeing Ed, the look on his face unreadable.

Any way you looked at it, this sure as shit wasn't the homecoming I'd been expecting. How could things be so familiar yet so strange?

There were plenty of questions on my mind. I wasn't sure I'd like all the answers, but it definitely beat sitting around waiting for Dave to rise from his grave.

"So, coven master Alice, is it?"

I could have sworn Firebird's eyes momentarily flashed at my mention of that, but it was only in my periphery - her other parts being far more interesting.

"It was Sally's suggestion," Starlight replied. "She thought it sounded more intimidating."

"Well, every little bit helps," Firebird snidely commented.

"Don't you have somewhere else to be, *Betty*?"

"Betty?" I asked. Who the hell was...

Firebird stood, her fur obviously ruffled. She pointed one painted fingernail at Starlight. "You don't get to call me that."

To my surprise, Star didn't back down. "I can call you whatever I so please. I'm in charge here."

"Only on paper. That whore may have handed control over to you, but if you think you're my superior in any way, you've got another thing coming."

Well, this was interesting. I turned toward Ed and mouthed, "Chick fight."

His look indicated he'd been thinking the same thing.

Don't get me wrong, I still wanted some answers. Even so, I'd be hard pressed to turn down a good floor show. I mean, we had all day to shoot the shit. If these two wanted to have a knock-down, clothes-tearing brawl in the meantime, then who was I to step in?

Alas, Monkhbat didn't feel the same. Firebird took one step toward Starlight and he rose to his feet, the menace clear in his eyes. She immediately backed off.

I'd never seen her get into a scrap before, and I doubted she wanted to start with a Mongolian assassin.

Oh well, so much for that. "Okay, I'm gonna assume the *whore* in question is Sally. So is it safe to guess that your new position isn't a result of some challenge?"

"Of course not, Bill," Starlight replied, her tone somewhat wounded. "I would never challenge Sally."

"Like a good little lapdog," Firebird spat.

"Like you would?" Star fired back. "I seem to recall her clawing the eyes out of your skull before she left."

Firebird's fangs descended in response, but after a moment, she regained control. "It's late and I'm tired. I'm going to the back for a quick shower and then heading to bed." She turned toward me and inclined her head respectfully. "It is a pleasure to have you back, oh honored Freewill."

I was definitely digging the tone of her voice and found myself sorely tempted to ask if she needed any company. Hell, as coven master, I could just insis...oh wait. I wasn't coven master anymore, was I?

Oh well. I watched her slink out of the room before turning to Starlight and forcing myself to focus again. "So how did this all come about?"

"After you disappeared, Sally had Boston declare her the acting master in your stead. I think James backed her up on that one, so it all happened pretty quickly. Then, a couple of weeks ago, she left on what I thought was just a trip - you know, something to clear her head. A few days later, she called to tell me she was staying.

Turns out she'd somehow taken control of another coven..."

"She did? Where?"

"Pandora Coven in Las Vegas. I hear they run..."

"Wait? Pandora? That wouldn't be Pandora's Box, the strip club, would it?"

"You know about it?"

Hell, yeah, I knew about it. Last time I'd been out there, enjoying a free trip with my parents while they lost a ton of money at the Luxor, one of the casino guards had told me about it - said it was a wild place. Unfortunately, it was also pretty exclusive. I couldn't get in the goddamned door. Albeit, now that I knew it was a vampire den, maybe that wasn't such a bad thing. Who the fuck knew what might have happened...well, aside from several naked strippers grinding their crotches in my face...

"So, you're telling me that Sally left to manage a strip club full of vampires?"

"More or less."

I had to sit down, unsure whether to laugh or be pissed off. After all we'd been through, she'd just up and ditched Village Coven - right at the start of fucking Armageddon, too. On the other hand, there was something amusing about her reverting to type. I briefly wondered if she wasn't both the manager and star attraction. After this shit with Dave was cleared up, maybe I owed it to myself to pay a visit there...with a pocket full of singles, of course.

"The other coven was too far away for her to run both, so she had to give up control of this one. I was as surprised as anyone when she named me as the new master." She lowered her voice to a bare whisper. "Especially since Firebird is older. According to the usual rules..."

"Sally must have had her reasons." The truth was she probably didn't have many other choices. Of our former coven, only Starlight, Firebird, and Sally's hairdresser Alfonso remained. Star at least had the advantage of knowing all the administrative aspects of how things were run. Speaking of the others, though... "Where's Alfonso?"

"Sally flew him out to be with her."

"Of course."

"But she left Monkhbat here with me. He's been a godsend. None of the others want to mess with him."

She threw him a look of gratitude, to which he simply replied, "I humbly serve."

What the fuck was he doing here anyway? That was definitely my next order of business. I figured it wouldn't hurt to be a little respectful first, though. "I'm sorry about your master."

He raised a brow quizzically. Maybe he didn't understand what I was saying.

I made it a point to speak slower. "I am sorry about what happened to Gansetseg."

When I still didn't get any sense of comprehension out of him, I turned to Starlight. "Can you please tell him that I'm sorry that Gan got killed?"

"Oh, Gan isn't dead."

My eyeballs practically shot out of my skull at that revelation. "She isn't?!"

"No. She's the one who left Monkhbat behind to help us rebuild."

Oh shit. Whatever guilt I'd felt over Gan's death was immediately replaced with that basest of emotions...raw fucking fear. "You mean she's fine?"

"Yes."

"Is she here?"

"No. She flew back to her home, but she left him to be her eyes and ears."

That didn't quite ease the sensation of my skin crawling. I turned to Monkhbat and forced a friendly smile. "I don't suppose you could keep my return a secret?"

His response was to match my expression. "The princess will be pleased."

"Need any help reserving the reception hall?" Ed asked.

"Bite me, asshole."

"I think she'll be doing that soon enough."

I faced him, ready to say several rude things about his lineage, when a sharp intake of breath interrupted my train of thought.

It hadn't come from anyone partaking in the conversation. That meant only one thing.

I looked down to see a pair of black eyes staring up at me. Newly grown fangs protruded from the mouth below them.

Dave was awake.

I'm Walking on Sunshine

Dave looked around for a moment, confusion evident on his face, then he hissed at us all. There was no doubt he'd woken up hungry. I worried for a moment that he might do something stupid, but then his expression changed as sparks flew from his skewered hand.

"Holy fucking shit!"

Being stabbed sucks. Trust me, I know. Being stabbed with silver sucks infinitely more when you're a vampire. Something about it reacts badly with our blood, explosively so. It also tends to retard our healing. Thus, I felt safe bending down to wrench it from his hand. The wound would be hard for him to ignore for some time.

I turned to Starlight, ready to bark out an order, but then remembered I was no longer in charge. Oddly enough, it felt pretty damned liberating to be relieved of command. "Star, do you think maybe I could get a towel and a few pints of blood?" My stomach rumbled, reminding me that my sampling of John had been the first real sustenance I'd gotten since returning to the states. I wasn't sure what would happen if I got too hungry, but it was potentially a bad idea to try and find out. "Maybe a few extra for me as well?"

Rather than tell me to go fuck myself as most vamps - Sally included - would probably do, she gave a quick nod and walked toward the back.

"A few Band-Aids while you're at it," Ed yelled after her.

"Goddamn, this hurts."

I turned back to where Dave sat, cradling his hand. The blood from the wound had stained his shirt, but at least it wasn't combusting anymore.

"Doctors make the worst patients," I quipped, handing the dagger back to its owner.

Dave's eyes had returned to normal and recognition flashed in them at the sight of me. "What the hell is going on, Bill? I feel..."

"Sorta off?"

"That's an understatement. Why am I here? And why is my hand bleeding like a stuck pig?"

"Calm down."

"Don't tell me to calm down. What you can do is get me something to clean this wound out with and then start explaining."

"Yeah, about that..."

"What?"

I opened my mouth, not sure where to start.

"I can feel a horrible death heading Kelvin's way, Bill."

Ed chuckled - the dick - but I gritted my teeth and ignored him. "Let's just say you really don't have to worry about infection anymore."

"Why?"

"What do you remember before waking up here?"

"A lot of fucked-up dreams about being picked up and dropped."

"Um...before that."

"Oh, I'd been taking tissue samples from that head you gave me. I was just about to saw it open to get to the brain when the damn thing opened its eyes."

"You were sawing its skull open?" Ed asked.

"Sure, why not?" He turned to my roommate and sniffed the air. "Hey, are you wearing aftershave? Smells...oddly appetizing."

Uh oh. "Let's focus here." I snapped my fingers in front of Dave's eyes. "About the head..."

"Yeah, surprised the shit out of me. But it was awesome, too. Survival post-decapitation. I mean, I knew you guys had some serious recuperative abilities, but that shit was beyond anything I ever expected."

"*Us* guys."

"Huh?"

"Never mind. Go on."

"Anyway, I wasn't sure how extensive it was - he looked in pretty rough shape. So I dumped out my fish tank..."

"You have fish?"

"Not anymore. Anyway, I did the best I could with the materials on hand. I immersed it in a solution of plasma and saline. The reaction was almost instantaneous."

"Reaction?"

"Spontaneous regeneration. The damn thing soaked up that solution like a sponge. I stepped out to use the can and came back to find an extra fifteen inches of spinal cord growing out of its neck, and it didn't stop there."

"I can imagine."

"That's when I called you. I was going out of my mind with the possibilities..."

"And then what happened?" Even though I asked the question, I'd pretty much already filled in the blanks. *What happened* had beaten the shit out of me, my roommate, and his car. What happened had chased us for a mile and ran us down. What happened had put my formerly living friend into his current state.

"I figured I'd refill the tank and hit the hay after sealing things up for the night. When I got my stuff together and looked up, though, I saw it had partially regrown an arm and then..."

Dave trailed off, and reached up to his throat with his uninjured hand. It didn't take a PhD in psychoanalysis to see he was piecing together the rest. He pressed two fingers to his carotid artery to check for a pulse, kept them there for several seconds, then sighed. "Did I at least have a nice funeral?"

"I didn't get a chance to send flowers."

"We were too busy getting our asses kicked," Ed added.

Dave smiled and once more gave my roommate the once over. Where the hell was Star with that blood?

"Is it safe to assume since I'm here that you eventually won?"

"Sorta," I muttered, finding something interesting on the far wall to stare at.

"What happens now?"

"You stay here."

"I have an apartment, you know. A job...good thing I'm on the night shift."

"You can't go back yet."

"Why? Is this some vampire thing?"

"No, it's kind of a police thing...as in they're probably crawling all over the place right now. We may have trashed it a little bit saving you."

* * *

Starlight finally returned with a small cooler full of blood packs, as well as a washcloth and a small medical kit. Ed made good use of the kit - taping some gauze to his neck. Surprisingly, it didn't look all too bad once he'd cleaned it off. Dave wrapped the towel around his still oozing hand, then looked at me questioningly when I popped open the cooler.

"Help yourself."

"This is kinda weird."

"Pretend you're that necromancer you had us hunt down in the mountains of black ice."

"I'm not sure I want to."

I bent down and looked him in the eye. "Yes, you do. I've seen the way you've been eyeing the lone human here. It's either this or I put a leash on you."

He tentatively reached for one of the packs, looking at it for a moment. His fangs descended out of pure instinct and all indecision fled his face. He hungrily tore into the plastic, sucking it dry within moments and making a mess out of things. Watching him reminded me of my own first hours as a vamp, except that I'd been forced to cut my new teeth on a sweaty naked guy.

"Pretty good, eh?"

Lust for more shone in his eyes, but he managed to restrain himself. "It was...okay. I think the donor was a little anemic."

"Show off."

"Is this really how you do it?"

"Nope." I grabbed a pack of my own and picked up a pair of scissors from a nearby desk. Neatly snipping it open, I took a sip. "I'm not a fucking slob."

* * *

Between the two of us, we polished off the cooler. It felt good to be running on a full tank again. Once that was done, Starlight procured some clean clothes for Dave - no doubt appropriated from a previous victim. I told him to go wait in the back so he could shower off once Firebird was done - warning him against sneaking a peek. No fucking way was he getting more of a show on his first day as a vamp than I had in far too long of a time.

The immediate crisis over, the rest of us took a moment to breathe. Monkhbat took up a post near the door. He wasn't much of a conversationalist anyway. Hell, he was probably just waiting for the moment when he could send a carrier pigeon, or whatever, to let Gan know I was back.

Ed had meandered over to the window and looked down on the city below while Starlight and I both grabbed a seat.

"Are there any openings left in Village Coven, Star?"

"A few. Before she left, Sally had brought us pretty close to quota. Since then, Firebird has added a few others too."

"With your blessing?"

Her glare was all the answer I needed. "She's older than me, so she naturally assumed she'd be next in line. That's usually the way it works."

"It didn't work that way with me."

"I know, and Sally was pretty adamant about it - more so, even. In fact, she had a few choice words to say about Firebird."

I shrugged. Sally often had choice words for a lot of people.

"Wonder what's going on down there."

"Huh?"

"Down on the street," Ed said from the window. "I'm seeing a lot of flashing lights."

"It's New York. Something is always burning, being robbed, or getting shot at." I turned back to Starlight. "So anyway, do you think you could take Dave in?"

"Don't you mean *we*?"

I raised my eyebrows, waiting for her to continue. "Oh, come on, Bill. This is your coven. I don't care what Boston says. You were never beaten in fair combat and never stepped down. As far as I'm concerned, we've just been keeping your seat warm."

"Kind of like the Stewards of Gondor?"

Starlight looked confused, but Ed chuckled from where he still stood. "Safe to say, I'd take her over Denethor any day of the week."

"Same here, bro," I replied.

"But you sure as shit ain't no Aragorn."

"Hells, no. I'd have banged Eowyn before heading home to Arwen."

"Like you'd have a chance with either of them."

"Okay," Starlight interrupted, "I have no idea what you two are talking about. Is that a yes or a no?"

I hesitated to reply. Truthfully, I didn't mind being outside of the management hierarchy. Hell, the only thing being Village Coven master had done for me was get my ass kicked several times over. It might have been easier to swallow had I access to all the benefits as well, but Sally had kept a tight rein on things.

Then again, she wasn't around, was she? No, she was off taking her cut from the g-strings of Vegas strippers. Grrrr. The very thought steamed me. How the hell did she somehow wind up with all the cool gigs? Oh well, there were far more pressing questions at that moment. "Do I get the Black Amex?"

Starlight looked as if I'd asked an incredibly stupid question. "Of course. Why wouldn't you?"

"Um...no reason." I took a moment to spare a thought in Sally's direction. *Bitch!* "Well, if you insis..."

The building rumbled slightly and the glass in the windows rattled enough to divert my attention.

"Whoa."

I turned to Ed. "What is it?"

"There's a lot of smoke down below - like something blew up."

"Oh?" I replied, not overly concerned. "Gas main?"

"Maybe. Hard to say from up here."

"Well, let me know if you see a hundred-foot-tall marshmallow man." I turned back toward Starlight. She was a much more pleasant form to hold my attention anyway. "Do you think the others will have any problems with it?"

"Might be some complaining. There are a few jerks in the crowd."

"Asshole vampires? Say it isn't so."

She laughed at that, one of the few vamps who truly understood. "Anyway, there might be a few protests, but Sally did a good job teaching most of them how the food chain works."

"I have no doubt."

"So what do you say? Will the Freewill grace Village Coven with his leadership once more?"

Ed groaned, but I chose to ignore him. Despite my misgivings, it was hard to say no to Starlight and her big brown eyes - not to mention other tasty bits.

I opened my mouth to reply, but whatever answer I might have voiced was lost, thanks to the door picking that exact moment to explode in a shower of splinters.

Hail to the King, Baby

Monkhbat reacted far faster than the rest of us - crouching into a defensive stance, despite the brunt of the debris hitting him. The second a form appeared through the wreckage, he was already moving. Gan had trained her people well.

Sadly, all the training in the world was sometimes meaningless against raw power. He flew toward the door, dagger at the ready. His blade connected, slashing deeply into one heavily muscled arm of the intruder, but he might as well have been attacking with a toothpick. The battle was over a scant second later.

Before he could further respond, Monkhbat was quite literally torn in half. His remains turned to ash before they even hit the floor.

Stunned silence met our visitor's approach as he stepped through the cloud that had been Gan's assassin a moment before. He was a large man, over six and a half feet tall. Rippling muscle covered his bare chest, but at least he had the good graces to have covered up his junk since our last meeting - wearing a kilt made of various torn clothing fragments. I had little doubt they'd come from any new victims he'd managed to claim in the time since our last meeting.

The ensuing hours had been kind to him. He no longer looked like a dried out octogenarian. Hell, he could have just stepped forth from a sword and sorcerer movie.

It was his face that gave him away. I'd seen it before it had withered. The long, black hair and prominent chin - that looked strong enough to shatter a brick wall with just a sneer - were unmistakable.

The dark forms on his body had clarified into tattoos. A moon and a sun sat on opposite shoulders, and a serpent wound across his chest, ending somewhere below his makeshift clothing. What was it with big dudes and ink? Oh well, I was probably just miffed that he pulled it off. What would have been a mural to loserdom on my body looked cool on this asshole.

All things considered, though, discussing bitchin' tats was probably not at the top of anybody's list right at that moment.

* * *

"Starlight," I said, keeping my eyes on the intruder, "take Ed. Go find Dave and Firebird and get the fuck out of here. Get to the safe house down on Fifth."

"But you just told him where..."

"He doesn't speak English. Trust me on this."

"Oh."

"Move it!"

The shaved ape grinned as I spoke. Well, okay, *hopefully* he didn't speak English. The truth was I didn't know shit about this guy. Hell, I didn't even have any idea how he'd tracked us down. We'd come in through the sewer. As sensitive as vamp nostrils were, they tended to be pretty useless when the distinct perfume of shit scented every single breath.

Starlight took a step, but I felt the compulsion a split second before hearing it and immediately realized she wouldn't get very far.

"*ATTEND ME!! KNEEL AND OBEY!!*"

Unlike the last time, this one was sent out in broadcast mode. It washed over me like a tidal wave and knocked me back several paces. Two of the windows in the office blew out from the force of it.

Sirens blared below now that the thick glass was gone. In the back of my head, I wondered if this asshole had been the cause, but immediately dismissed it. It wasn't the clearest day, but there was still enough sunlight to make it impossible for a vamp to walk around without plenty of cover. Considering Conan here was dressed for an outing at muscle beach, that ruled him out.

I had no interest in the cops dragging me away on only my second day back. At the same time, however, I said a quick prayer that someone down below had noticed the debris raining down upon them and were heading up to investigate - hopefully, with lots and lots of guns.

Forcing myself to focus on the task at hand, I quickly glanced back over my shoulder. Sure enough, Starlight was down on her knees. The doors opened in the back and both Dave and Firebird stepped through, their eyes completely glazed over. They joined Star in genuflecting before the powerful vamp who had summoned them. Thankfully, no others appeared. They must have vacated the building when told to. That only left...

"Who the fuck is this guy, Bill?"

My head whipped around. "How are you still standing, Ed?" It probably wasn't the best time to ask such a question, but even so...what the hell?

I had no clue as to how old this vamp was, but his compulsions were at least on the level with Francois's - a seven-hundred-year-old former Nazi asshole of a vamp currently on the front lines up in Canada. He'd once thrown a casual compulsion at my friends and knocked them all for a loop. Yet Ed stood there now with nary a hint of shakiness.

Unfortunately, a detailed analysis would have to wait. Our guest finally noticed my roommate's presence. The big guy's eyes darkened, and a look of pure rage came over his face. "Abominatio," he spat through gritted fangs. Evidently, he was still a wee bit pissed at having his insides scorched. Some people just didn't have a "forgive and forget" outlook on life.

I'd love to say that Ed sprang into action, displaying a whole bevy of awesome new superpowers that he used to kick our foe's ass, but that would be a load of

Sasquatch shit. In actuality, he just stood there, unmoving like a deer in the headlights.

Watching someone else being the target for a change wasn't nearly as satisfying as I'd hoped, but that probably had something to do with my friend being in the crosshairs instead. Regardless, I wasn't about to let this goon have Ed without a fight. "As soon as I have him distracted, get to the fucking elevator."

The vamp turned his head toward me, a look of contempt upon his face. Language barrier or not, it was painfully obvious I was planning something. Oh well, knowing something was a trap wasn't quite as good as knowing what that trap was.

"Don't you mean the stairs?" Ed asked, his eyes firmly trained on the hostile in the room.

"Nope. Take a look at this asshole. Do you think he knows what the fuck an elevator is?"

"Good point. What are you gonna..."

I was already on the move by the time he started the question. I grabbed the nearest desk and flung it at the roidhead, hoping perhaps he expected some drawn out exposition before the inevitable attack.

The mostly particle board construct - fucking cheap-ass Sally - slammed into him and shattered. Office supplies flew in all directions, but the impact didn't even budge him an inch. So much for that strategy.

The vamp merely sighed and shook his head as if judging my battle prowess to be lacking. Everyone's a critic.

I moved over to another desk, hoping that perhaps the owner had stocked it full of lead, but my meaning was hopefully clear. I might be a bug to him, but I could at least be an annoying bug.

I smiled to let him know that.

And then he was right in front of me.

* * *

Goddamn, I hated when older vamps did that. Talk about showing off.

On the other hand, it did distract him from Ed.

"Run!"

To my roommate's credit, he didn't try to pull any stupid heroics. No shout of "Not without you!" No clumsy counterattack that would do nothing more than embarrass us both. He took the hint and got the fuck out of Dodge.

Frankenstein's monster glanced back toward him, which left me with the perfect opening. I may not be able to give Alex a run for his money on the battlefield, but I knew an opening for a cheap shot when I saw one.

I'd learned one very important lesson within the first ten minutes of waking up as a vampire: our nerve endings worked just fine. Some vamps might have a higher tolerance for pain than others, but a good shot to the family jewels was still the great equalizer for anyone with a Y chromosome.

I brought my knee up and felt it solidly connect. I'd hoped to double the motherfucker over, maybe give me an opportunity to slam a stake through his ribcage. He definitely felt it. The roar of rage that escaped his lips was testament to that. His eyes narrowed, and he dropped a hand to cradle his damaged goods, but sadly, that was the extent of my blow's effect.

Oh crap. I metaphorically felt my blood run cold. You know you're up against a tough hombre when the universal calling card for male agony doesn't end the fight.

While I was debating my next move, he made his. He lashed out with his other arm and caught me square in the chest.

Blood sprayed from my mouth as my ribs shattered, and then I was airborne, flying as if I'd just been launched out of a catapult. All the while, the two present members of Village Coven - *my* coven - along with one potential inductee continued kneeling on the ground like a group of sorry sycophants.

Fortunately, I was spared from having to witness anymore by the nice comfy wall I slammed through - pretty much pulverizing the few parts of me uninjured by his initial blow.

I crashed through plaster and slammed into something solid, halting my momentum with a crunch.

As the dust settled, booming laughter reached my ears from the outer room. I may have failed at stopping this truck-on-legs, but at least I'd succeeded in providing amusement. That had to count for something.

Wheezing blood, I grabbed hold of whatever I had hit and dragged my sorry carcass back to my feet...

Your end has come. You shall die screaming the name of the destroyer.

...and subsequently jumped out of my skin. What the fuck was that? I spun and checked the room, coughing up even more blood in the process. I'd have sworn that threat had come from Harry Decker, a wizard who'd made it his life's work to fuck with every aspect of my existence.

But that asshole was dead. During her last visit, Gan had been so kind as to perform impromptu throat surgery on him - extracting needless things from his body, like his windpipe.

Whoa, that monster must've hit me harder than I thought. I shook my head to clear out the cobwebs, and that's when I realized where I was.

It was Sally's office...or former office, anyway. Either way, it was the corner suite from which she'd overseen the coven like some sort of queen bee. She'd spared no expense either, as I could attest having just slammed into the solid as fuck desk that had once been hers.

Wait a second...Sally's office!

Taking a quick look around, it appeared that Starlight hadn't gotten around to redecorating it much. I mean, there was a skull sitting in one corner like the world's most gruesome paperweight. That was new, but not much else had changed. Maybe she was afraid to, not knowing if bitchzilla might return.

That gave me an idea.

What the hell? It was worth a shot...quite literally.

* * *

I stepped back out of the office, still a little wobbly, but infinitely better prepared.

"*...BRING THE ABOMINATION TO ME!!*"

The ass end of the compulsion whispered in my mind. It had obviously been directed elsewhere, probably to my three bewitched comrades. Sure enough, I caught Firebird's tight little rear disappearing just as the stairwell door closed on it.

Considering the similarity to the word spoken earlier, I was forced to conclude that Ed was the abomination in question. Hopefully, he hadn't gotten stuck in a car that was stopping at every floor to pick up some asshole or another. If so, there was a distinct chance I wouldn't reach him in time to do any good.

The fucker who'd made the compulsion faced the doorway where he'd sent his new minions. He slowly turned back toward me, no doubt sensing my reappearance.

That same bemused grin appeared on his face, and he spoke once more. I didn't need to be a linguist to appreciate the mocking tone. Once more, he ended things with that annoying *frater* word.

"Oh yeah? Well, Daddy's here to give you a permanent timeout, asshole." A grin appeared on my own face as I lifted the massive weapon and pointed it straight at him.

I'd gotten lucky. Starlight hadn't really changed much of anything, including the contents of Sally's drawers. One of them had still contained my former partner's favorite response to unwanted pickup lines - a

Desert Eagle loaded with silver-tipped bullets. Oh yeah. Now we were cooking with gas.

I grasped it with both hands, remembering how I'd almost knocked out my own teeth the last time I'd fired it - ending up looking like Dirty Harry's dipshit cousin.

Tarzan the Ape Vamp raised one eyebrow, but continued grinning. A small shiver of fear crept up my spine. Did this guy think he was so tough that a load of high caliber...

Then I remembered he'd spent God knows how long decorating a shelf in Alex's closet. It was quite possible he didn't even know what a gun was.

Well, if that were the case, then it was time to go to school.

I put pressure on the trigger. I'd seen this guy move. If he went to warp nine and appeared in front of me again, I wanted to make sure there was a photon torpedo waiting for him. Fuck that Picard Maneuver bullshit.

He stepped forward and blathered more nonsense. Another idea hit me as he continued yammering. If it worked, then it was surely lights out for Mr. Muscles. The time for taking chances was over. I'd accidentally let this guy out to play, and my friend had paid for it with his life. He was going down, and I was making sure he stayed there this time.

"No habla, hombre," I said, taking a step to my left. *Come on...*

He took a step to mirror my own. Yes! No matter what timeframe you might hail from, the rules of a standoff apparently apply.

"That's right, gruesome," I continued, keeping my voice steady. One of the lessons I'd taken to heart as a vampire was that appearance was everything. Play the role of the bad cop convincingly enough, and people will fall in line to believe it. Show a bit of weakness and the masses will be all over you like hyenas on a rotting corpse. "Be a good little vamp and papa will let you play with his Red Rider BB gun."

We continued to circle in a clockwise manner.

Just a wee bit more.

"*WHY DO YOU STAND AGAINST ME, LITTLE BROTHER?!*"

The compulsion was subtle, with no force to it. It seemed that Ator the Fighting Eagle had likewise come to the conclusion that it was the only way we were going to communicate.

Little brother? What the fuck kind of family issues did this shithead have? I swear, if he called me "Mommy" next, I was outta there.

Finally!

The big dummy took one more step, which put his back to the windows he'd blown out upon his arrival. It was time to pay the piper.

"*I'M NOT YOUR BROTHER, YOUR FATHER, OR YOUR UNCLE BUCK. WHAT I AM IS THE BADDEST MOTHERFUCKER YOU'RE EVER GOING TO MEET. THE NAME IS DR. DEATH...*"

I smiled ever wider. "*AND THIS IS MY BOOMSTICK!!*"

Elevator Music

Yeah, I might have laid it on a little thick. Fortunately, there was nobody around to give me shit about it. That is, nobody who wouldn't shortly be a pile of dust.

I opened fire and - big surprise - the first shot went wide as I re-acclimated to the fact that Sally's gun kicked like a goddamned mule. The look on the other vamp's face turned to one of surprise as the thunderous report sounded in the close quarters. Satisfyingly, it quickly changed to one of pain as my next hit home and blasted a hole in his meaty shoulder. It wasn't a kill shot as I'd hoped, but the douchebag definitely noticed it.

I wasn't about to lose my advantage by gawking, so I steadied my aim and continued to squeeze the trigger.

I'd love to lie and say I blew the fucker to pieces, like Robert Downey Jr. at the end of *Natural Born Killers*, but at least half my shots missed. Oh well, that movie kinda sucked ass anyway.

The ones that hit home did the trick, though. Hunks of gore flew, followed by hot sparks as the silver reacted with his blood. Best yet, each impact drove him steadily backward.

Of course, if the movies have taught me anything, it's that one will *always* run out of bullets right before the bad guy careens to his certain death. Fucking clichés, they always gotta show up and piss on a guy's parade.

Thankfully, I'd anticipated that shit happening. The second the gun clicked dry, I was on the move, racing across the room at top speed and hoping to all hell that my target didn't duck.

Fortunately, he was slightly preoccupied with his missing pounds of body mass. He looked up too late and I delivered a dropkick that would have made any WWE superstar proud.

We connected and my momentum transferred into him - thank goodness. I fell to the floor and he flew backward out the window, catching the express route to the ground floor.

Game over, fucker.

* * *

I may not be the best at anticipating the moves of my enemies. What can I say? I'd once been given the assignment to read *The Art of War* in college and had instead tossed in a few Kung Fu movies - making my best guess when it was time to hand in the report. Got a C on it - not too shabby, if I do say so myself.

Fortunately, I had a lifetime of bad action movies to fall back on. Raising the empty gun in one hand, I stepped to the window and glanced out - ready to club the crap out of Big Brother if he was still somehow holding on.

Amazingly enough, he wasn't there waiting to drag me to my doom. Yes!

I risked a further peek out the window. Sure enough, a tiny, smoldering figure way down below lay atop some poor schmuck's crushed car. At least it wasn't Ed's this time.

Seeing all I needed, I ducked back in. There was just enough sunlight streaming through the clouds to make my day unpleasant otherwise. Also, I didn't want anyone to see me staring at the scene below. I had little doubt that whatever landed would soon be easily vacuumed up, but there were still lots of lights flashing from whatever had blown up earlier. I didn't fancy any confrontations that might end with my ass being hauled downtown for questioning.

I had more important things to attend to.

My hope was that Hercules's hold on my friends would end with his death, but the whole compulsion thing was still a bit fuzzy to me. I couldn't take that chance.

With any luck, Ed had reached the lobby and bolted for the exit. Starlight and the others couldn't follow him there. Even if their orders bade them to do so, the pain of imminent immolation would definitely snap them back to reality. Compulsion was a powerful tool, but strong enough emotions could break its hold.

It was probably also not a grand idea to stay where I was. There had been a lot of commotion, as well as really fucking loud gunfire. Surely one of the other tenants had noticed. It was time to vacate the premises.

* * *

I stepped to the stairwell door just as the elevator dinged open at my floor.

What the hell? There was no way he was still alive. Even if there was, why would he be taking the elevator back up? It was probably Starlight and the others returning now that Muscle-Boy's hold over them was gone.

Still, a little paranoia had served me well in the past. I assumed a defensive stance as the doors opened.

A guy about my age, maybe six inches shorter, stood inside. He was in a bit better shape than me - well, okay, a *lot* better shape. He wore jeans, a jacket, and sported a Phoenix Suns shirt underneath. The irony of showing up to a vampire-owned floor wearing something like that was not lost upon me.

He took a casual step out of the elevator, put his phone back in his pocket, and stopped in his tracks as the scene before him sank in. On any other day, the office looked just like what it was called. Today, it looked like - well, like an ancient vampire had just waged a one-man war in it.

His eyes focused on me and widened. Go figure. I probably looked about as good as I felt. Oh yeah, and I was also still holding Sally's hand cannon. Such a scene might seem just a wee bit suspicious to an outsider.

"Um...I think I got the wrong floor," he muttered as he backpedaled. The doors began to close and his hand immediately went for the pocket where he'd just deposited his phone.

Oh, crap. Like I really needed this shit right now.

* * *

If I'd been smart, I would have just made for the stairs and gotten the fuck out of the building, period.

Instead, I panicked and pointed the gun at him. "Hold the door."

I'd been on the wrong end of the Desert Eagle's barrel and knew it wasn't exactly the least intimidating thing on the planet - even empty as it was.

He hesitated for a bare second - almost giving me reason to put on a burst of speed to reach him in time - but then moved his hand to the button. Apparently, he didn't want to test whether the doors were bulletproof or not.

I stepped in, moved ever so slightly behind him, and placed the oversized gun in my jacket pocket - as much as I could, anyway. It was only then that thoughts of what a stupid fucking plan this was began to register.

"So..." I'd never taken a hostage before, at least not by myself, so I wasn't quite sure where to take this next. It's always so much easier in the movies. "How's it going?"

"Listen, man, it's cool. I didn't see anything. I was just popping by to meet a buddy and grab a bite to eat..."

"Offhand, I'm thinking you got the wrong place."

"No shit." He paused, as if suddenly remembering I was holding a gun with enough power to blow a bowling ball-sized hole in him. "Sorry."

"Apology accepted."

"So, what do we do now?"

Oh. Yeah, I guess we couldn't just stand there like two putzes holding the doors open for the rest of the day. Someone in maintenance was bound to notice that. I was pretty sure the building staff received the occasional bonus to look the other way with regards to weirdness on our floors, but this was the middle of the day - all good vamps should be sleeping.

Ultimately, only one destination made sense. "Hit the button for the basement. If anyone gets in between here and there, play it real natural." I let the implied "or else" hang in the air between us, hoping my words sounded sufficiently threatening. It was all bullshit, of course. I had no idea what to do with this clown, but killing him definitely wasn't on the agenda. Maybe I could lose him in the sewers, let him find his own way out.

"You know, you don't have to do this," he said as the doors finally slid shut. "I won't tell anyone, I swear."

Gah! Talk about cliché. Did that shit ever work with anyone? I mean, who would be stupid enough to...

The elevator stopped between floors and the emergency buzzer rang. A few seconds later, the lights flickered, but remained on.

"What the fuck?"

"It wasn't me, I swear."

Oh, great. I was stuck with a whiner.

I waited for a few moments, hoping the jam was temporary. The buzzing eventually ceased - a good thing for my sensitive ears - but the elevator remained where it was.

Out of curiosity, I tried pushing the buttons for the other floors - nothing.

"You should give up, man. I bet the cops stopped this thing."

I found that unlikely, considering this building didn't even have a security guard at the front desk, one of the few left in Manhattan that didn't - courtesy of the coven pulling a few strings.

"They're probably watching us right now via video camera, like in *Devil*."

"Devil?"

"Yeah, that M. Night Shamalyan movie where a bunch of people..."

"You actually watched that?"

"Not all of it," he replied meekly.

I told my prisoner to pipe the fuck down. If the dude was going to yammer on about movies, at least they could be good ones.

I pushed the service button in the hope that someone in maintenance would pick up. There might not be a guard in the lobby, but there were staff on hand, especially since shit tended to break a lot wherever vampires were concerned.

Several minutes passed with no response. What the hell?

All at once, sounds from outside our little metal prison began to reach our ears. I turned to listen, trying to take it all in. However, one didn't need vampire senses to realize that alarms were going off throughout the building.

Something was going on out there, and I had no idea what...

"Fuck this shit!" The guy I'd been *escorting* slammed into me with his shoulder, sending me off balance. He was a little dude, but had some muscle behind him. Had I been human, he might have very well kicked my ass. That wasn't his objective, though.

He stepped back and I found myself looking down the barrel of Sally's favorite noisemaker.

"Don't move."

"It's not loaded."

"Bullshit. Now stay back; I'm warning you."

"Warn me all the fuck you want."

"I'm serious. Don't make me kill you."

"You're a little late for that."

"Huh?"

"Never mind."

I took a step forward and raised my hand slowly toward the gun. He immediately squeezed the trigger, resulting in a dry click. That surprised me. I figured I would call his bluff. Now I was happy I hadn't been lying about being out of bullets. That would have otherwise been a bit awkward...in an excruciating sort of way.

"It's empty," he said in disbelief.

"That's what I told you, genius."

"Fucking asshole," he spat as he tossed it at me.

"Sorry."

"I almost shit myself."

"Let's be glad you didn't," I said, sitting down in a corner. "Because I've seen enough for one day."

* * *

For probably the hundredth time, I contemplated checking if there really was a top hatch on the elevator car or if that was only an urban legend. Even if there was, I wasn't sure what to do. I had no idea what floor we were stuck at. The display above the doors showed some error message. Trying to shimmy my ass up the cables and prying open random doors sounded like a good way to freak out even more people if I picked the wrong floor.

Instead, I planted myself and waited for someone to come and get us out - hoping that would be sooner rather than later. Despite the alarms, I didn't smell any smoke. That was good. Becoming a cooked turkey as this box slowly turned into an oven wasn't my idea of fun. Chances were, it was just some electrical glitch that was causing all of this crap.

My unwilling companion eventually settled down too, and I gave him some bullshit story about chasing off a would-be burglar when he'd shown up - including how I freaked out and took him hostage by mistake.

Thankfully, he was from out of town and seemed to buy it. He didn't bother asking any of the obvious questions, like why we'd been headed down to the basement. Gotta love tourists.

Fortunately, neither of us had a problem with claustrophobia, saving me the trouble of having to punch him out. So, we did what most people would do in a situation like that - we sat down and bullshitted as we waited for rescue.

Jason Cohen, as he introduced himself, was in town from Arizona visiting some college pals. He'd been looking for a friend working at Vekter Corp and had read the directory in the lobby wrong. Poor schmuck. Two floors lower and he'd probably be enjoying a nice lunch as opposed to being stuck in a six by eight box with a guy who looked like he'd just been punched through a wall.

He seemed nice enough, but I still gave him a fake name. Let's be realistic: I'd still pointed a gun at him, and wasn't quite up to snuff with compelling a human to forget. Starlight or Firebird might've been able to pull it off, but I had no idea where they were or in what shape they were in after the compulsion took hold. I could only hope that they'd all snapped out of their trances before they could hurt anyone, specifically Ed.

The conversation finally turned toward something I had an actual interest in: the weird shit going on in the world recently. Apparently, there were people missing in his town via mysterious circumstances. Jason began to tell me of the crazies who were spreading the word that *ape men* did it - oh boy - when more noises began to reach my enhanced hearing.

They weren't good ones.

The first sounded like something heavy crumbling. The elevator gave the slightest shake, but my companion seemed not to notice as he changed topics to rave about his fantasy football team.

"Hold on," I said, putting up a hand to silence him.

"What is it?"

"I think I heard something."

"You think they're coming to get us out?"

"Uh, sure," I lied, hoping he'd shut up so I could listen to what was really going on beyond our little slice of heaven.

"Awesome." He stood and began to pound on the door. Not quite the reaction I'd been going for. "Hey! Let's go, assholes! I gotta take a piss."

Real classy. Unfortunately, he was also talking over everything else. I was only catching bits and pieces whenever he stopped to take a breath. More crashes, closer. Wait...was that a scream? Shit! I couldn't hear myself think with this fucking rube rambling on. "Do you mind shutting the fu..."

The squeal of metal tearing drowned out the rest. The entire car lurched and nearly knocked us off our feet. What the fuck?

"What the hell is going on?" he asked. "I thought only California had earthquakes."

Before I could correct him that New York had its fair share of minor tremors too, there came another sound just beyond our walls - a snarl of rage.

Oh no.

It couldn't be.

There's no fucking way he could have...

"Get away from..."

My warning came too late.

My ex-hostage had just enough time to turn toward me questioningly when a muscular arm tore through the doors of the elevator, the claws rending the metal like paper.

It grasped blindly for a moment, then fell upon the surprised Jason's head from behind. The clawed fingers slid into his mouth for purchase...ewww.

The arm retracted, pulling its prize toward the hole it had created.

"Shit!"

Before he could be yanked all the way through, I grabbed hold of Jason's legs and tried to pull him back in - putting everything I had into it.

Unfortunately, I didn't take into account the inevitable conclusion when two vampires played tug of war with a human body.

Let's just say it wasn't the best plan I'd ever had.

Tactical Retreat

There was a strangled cry, followed by a snap, and then I finally succeeded in pulling most of Jason back in with me. Sadly for him, that didn't include the part of his head above the jawline.

There came a sickening crunch of bone from outside, leading me to conclude that the poor schmuck wouldn't be getting an open casket funeral anytime soon. Then, the hand reached back in - grasping, clawing, and widening the hole.

Being locked inside a small space with a pissed-off vamp, who I'd just shot full of silver and sent on a hundred-foot freefall to the street below, didn't sound like the ideal situation for us to talk out our problems. That was confirmed when the brute peered into the hole he'd made. The look on his face was most certainly not a happy one. It became even less so once his eyes locked on mine.

There was no way I was getting out of this one with a few amusing one-liners.

"Here's mud in your eye, fuckface."

Okay, so I was wrong. I tightened my grip on Jason's body and squeezed it as hard and fast as I could. The result was not unlike stomping on a tube of toothpaste. A gout of blood streamed out of it and straight into the ugly fucker's mug.

Temporarily blinded, he lunged forward, nearly entering the elevator car and continuing to grasp out before him.

I backed up - nearly terrified out of my mind - but then realized his rage was, quite possibly, my only chance.

Before I could talk myself out of it, I tossed Jason's body into his claws. I felt bad about doing so, not to mention a wee bit grossed out, but it wasn't like the poor guy was going to get killed any worse than he already had.

The other vamp took hold of the corpse, perhaps thinking it was me. That gave me the opportunity to step up and sink my teeth into the meat of his forearm.

It was time to show this asshole what being the Freewill was all about.

* * *

As usual, it didn't take much to get me going. Thank goodness too, because I had a feeling he wasn't going to stand there and let me continue gnawing on him.

A mouthful of blood hit my stomach and went off like a supernova. Holy shit, this guy was older than I'd thought. I had never felt anything like it and wasn't sure I ever wanted to again. There was something *not right* about it. Vampire blood typically tasted as good as human blood - to me, at least - as vile as that might sound, but the shit running through this guy's veins had some kind of weird aftertaste. Ewww, skunked blood.

It didn't matter, though. I got what I needed - just in time for the rest of the wall to give way under his assault. My foe pulled his arm back, tearing the flesh in the process, as I wasn't quite accommodating enough to actually let go.

Speaking of going, it was time to do just that. Unfortunately, I only saw one way out and wasn't looking forward to it. I'd always hated those freefall rides at the amusement part. Sadly, it was either up or down, and I hadn't grown wings the last time I checked.

Putting all of my stolen strength to use, I dropped to one knee and brought both fists down onto the floor of the elevator like a pile driver. The car lurched from the impact. I raised my hands and pounded them down again before that monster could fully force his way in.

There came the pained groan of metal tearing free from its moorings and then, just as I was about to do it once more, the floor gave way and I began to plummet.

A clawed hand scraped against my forehead, momentarily snagging my hair, but thankfully, with all the blood flying around, it was like trying to catch a greased pig. I slipped from Ragnar the Viking's grasp and found myself screaming downward at a breakneck pace.

Now all I had to do was hope the old saying wasn't true: falling isn't bad, but it's the landings that are a killer.

* * *

Amazingly enough, it wasn't that bad - and by that, I mean it was a lot worse. I landed on my side, shattering my arm, ribcage, and probably a whole lot of other body parts I was fond of. Concrete wasn't exactly the softest thing in the world to land on from a swan dive.

I let out a cry of pain, which quickly turned to one of surprise as something thudded down next to me. If he'd followed, I'd be...

Thankfully, it was just Jason's mutilated corpse. Damn, they were gonna need a squeegee to pick all of him up.

Even so, if I didn't get going, the next thing that landed was probably gonna be a shitload less friendly.

I gritted my teeth and prepared for the agony of moving, but amazingly, I was able to stand just fine. In the time it had taken to have the shit scared out of me, the worst of the injuries had healed.

I've said it before, and I'll say it again - being an ancient vampire rocks, at least in regard to having super powers. I just had to live long enough to make it there.

Before I took off running, I risked a quick look up. High above, the light shone through the shattered elevator floor. A moment later, it was blotted out as something peered down at me.

It was most certainly time to make like a tree.

* * *

Fortunately for me, I knew the basement quite well. I took off into the darkness, but had to stop about a dozen steps later. An unexpected coughing fit nearly doubled me over. Weird, but probably just a result of my internal injuries still healing. It passed after a moment and I kept moving.

The lowest level of the building wasn't quite the rat maze of tunnels you often see in a movie, but there were enough side rooms for maintenance, electrical, and storage to hopefully slow down any pursuit.

I hoped the scent of blood from Jason's body, of which there was plenty splattered about, was enough to confuse the big guy's sense of smell as I re-entered the sewers and secured the grate above me.

Even if it wasn't, I was fairly sure my next move would more than make up for it. I launched myself off the walkway, straight into a pungent pile of filth, making sure to roll around for a nice even coating.

Yes, it was absolutely fucking disgusting, but I'd seen it work before. Up in Canada, during the events that had started the world down its current path to damnation, I'd needed to take a dive into a pool of Sasquatch shit. It had been one of the more bizarre - not to mention putrid - experiences in my life, but it had done the job. The Feet, with their highly attuned nostrils, hadn't been able to sniff me out. It was the same general principle here, or at least I hoped so.

Somehow, that asshole had been able to track Ed and me when we arrived, a feat that I'd thought impossible, even for vamps. All I could hope was that this time my extra precautions would prove to be enough.

I stood up, almost losing a shoe as I pulled myself free from the ass-spawned muck of a thousand burrito-loving New Yorkers, and turned in the direction of a place where I could hopefully catch my breath and regroup.

Ready to put my stolen speed to good use, I took all of one step, then fell to my knees as my legs buckled. Spasms racked my body as pain shot up from my midsection.

What in the name of...

That thought needed to be put on hold, though, as my stomach gave a heave and I projectile vomited. A great gout of steaming puke splashed against the wall and hissed down it - quite literally. For a moment, I thought it was just the tears in my eyes causing it, but then I realized whatever I had upchucked was actually sparking.

That was new. Even in the midst of my best college parties, I hadn't seen anything like that - and believe me, I'd tasted the rainbow from both directions during those days.

What the hell? Was it because of all the silver I'd shot that vamp with or something else? I had no idea and really couldn't afford the time to dwell upon it.

My stomach heaved again, filling my mouth with the unpleasant taste of blood-infused bile, but it was more an aftershock than anything else. I waited a moment, well aware that my time might be running short, then tried to stand.

My legs were still a bit shaky, but they held - if just barely. I'd expected to race through the sewers at breakneck speed, losing my opponent in the maze of fetid tunnels. Now, I'd be lucky to manage a brisk walk.

But walk I could.

I might be caught, but it sure as hell wouldn't be from standing still.

I steadied myself and started down the damp tunnel, hoping that whatever luck had abandoned me this day might decide to return to my side.

Calling in the Calvary

Thankfully, I felt mostly normal again by the time I'd gone about a block. Whatever strength I'd stolen from that monster had fled as soon as my stomach decided to ride the vomit comet. Luckily, I didn't need it for something as simple as a trek through the NYC sewer system.

Doubly awesome was that my little ruse of rolling around in stinking shit appeared to have worked. I didn't sense anything pursuing me - aside from maybe the occasional curious rat. I was still cautious, though, and walked in the water whenever I could so as not to leave any obvious footprints.

Goddamn. Had those useless seers told me that treading through piss-water was in my future, I might have just stuck around and been Alex's poster boy for the war effort. Oh well, what was done was done. It had all been worth it too, for the look on his face when I locked him in with Druaga. I had little doubt who'd ended up the bitch in that prison block.

I pushed that amusing thought aside for now, though, having far more important things to worry about - my friends, for starters. I hated flying blind with no insight on anything save that my best efforts to kill a half-naked maniac had failed miserably.

It blew my mind. How the fuck had he survived? The fall itself was easily explainable. It seemed that Gan had apparently survived a much higher drop. The rest, though, was unbelievable - fifty calibers of silver-plated lovin', followed by a nice relaxing nap in the daylight. It just didn't make sense. Of all the vampires that I could have resurrected, I had to somehow pick the last son of Krypton.

Those thoughts continued to haunt me as I reached my destination: the sewer entrance to one of the coven's safe houses. At least, I hoped it was still one of ours. Sally had purchased it with the intent of keeping its location a secret between the two of us until such time as others needed to know. That had lasted all of a day before the place had turned into a veritable flophouse, followed by the prerequisite raid by the police.

Fuck it. It was all I had left. What was the worst that could happen? Well, I guess a shit covered creature of the night emerging into some family's living room was one possibility, but screw it. That would be their problem.

Almost to my surprise, nothing of the sort happened. I had to bust two locks, which caused a loud racket - one that hopefully no vamps were in earshot of. Finally, I ascended from the tunnels to find that not only was the place still seemingly owned by Village Coven - the mystical sigils designed to ward off scrying by mages evident on the walls - but that the security code for the alarm hadn't been changed. Thank goodness. The last thing I needed were bells or whistles going off - or blowing up. I never was quite certain what surprises Sally left behind for uninvited guests.

Unsurprisingly, the place was unoccupied. Covens tended to frown upon members using safe houses for anything outside of emergencies. Considering the events at the office, though, I felt comfortable in assuming that this qualified.

I closed up behind me, rearmed the security system, and dragged the refrigerator out of the kitchen to prop against the sub-basement entrance. None of that would stop an ancient vamp from trying to get in, but it would hopefully give me enough warning to escape through the front door if I needed to.

I'd been angry with Sally for up and ditching the coven just for an opportunity to shake her ass on stage again. Now some of that anger dissipated a bit as I took a look around and realized she'd stocked this place with everything I needed to hole myself up for a while.

More specific for my immediate needs, there was an unopened cell phone in one drawer with a small pile of calling cards next to it. I cracked it open, loaded up the minutes, and dialed Ed.

Thank goodness my roommates had a clue as to how this espionage shit worked. Unfamiliar number or not, the call was answered on the third ring.

"This had better be you, Bill."

"Who the fuck else would call your ugly ass?" I asked, inwardly breathing a sigh of relief at hearing his voice.

"You okay?"

"Sorta. You?"

"As soon as the elevator opened, I hauled ass out onto the street."

"Smart boy."

He put a Southern twang into his voice. "My mama didn't raise her no dipshits."

"That's debatable."

"So what happened? All hell seems like it's breaking loose."

"Seems?"

"For starters, there were cops everywhere. Thought I was gonna get my ass shot off for a moment there. They grabbed me the second I walked out and started grilling me about what was happening inside."

"What'd you tell them?"

"I took a page out of your book."

"Played dumb?"

"Bingo."

I smiled into the receiver. That we could still joke so easily after all we'd seen was near amazing. "So what happened then?"

"You tell me. There was a crash down the block. Sounded like something heavy landed. Your doing?"

"Might have been."

"Whatever it was, it got everyone's attention. They forgot about me and I made it a point to get the fuck out of there."

There came a muffled beep in the background, followed by the hum of an engine. "You in a cab?"

"Car service."

"Heading home?"

"Taking the scenic route. I was hoping you'd call."

"You'd better not be on speaker."

"Don't worry. The privacy glass is closed."

"Privacy glass?"

"One of the perks of my new position."

After muttering a few unkind words about the unfairness of his new job, I turned the discussion back toward what had happened since his departure - minus maybe my roll in shit. He hadn't seen Starlight or any of the others during his escape. I was split on that. It told me nothing of their whereabouts or condition. At the same time, any such run-in wouldn't have been particularly healthy for Ed if they were still under compulsion. He was likewise none too pleased to hear about the massive amounts of damage that our attacker had somehow managed to shake off.

I wasn't overly joyed at that part myself.

* * *

"I want you to get out of town. Maybe head to your stepfather's place. Grab Tom and Christy, if you can, on the way."

"Not happening. I already talked to Tom. I'm swinging by home and then we're heading to where you are."

"Are you fucking insane? Listen I..."

"First off, Bill, my pop's place is in the middle of the fucking woods. We *both* know what's out there. No thank you. Secondly, that motherfucker from earlier was coming after *me*, not you."

I opened my mouth to argue, but he had me there. I'd certainly done my fair share to piss off that freaking ogre, but his focus in the office had initially been on Ed. "Sorry. I'm just so used to everything wanting *me* dead."

"Trust me, it's new for me, too," he replied. "Can't say I really like it, either."

"So you think he could track you down again?"

"He already did once. If he catches us somewhere else..."

He didn't need to finish. Ed might have had something weird going on with his blood, but neither he nor Tom would be able to do much against an ancient vamp intent on tearing them to pieces. Christy might be able to help them out, but she was pregnant - undoubtedly a lot more so than when last I'd seen her. I had no idea what effect that might have on her powers, but even if I did, I wasn't entirely cool with potentially putting her in the line of fire.

Fuck! It could never be easy, could it?

"I get what you're saying," I said at last, "but I don't stand a chance against..."

"Maybe not alone, but at least if we're all together we might."

His words, while potentially suicidal in their stupidity, warmed my non-beating heart nevertheless.

"There's also the fact that Tom and I are pieces of shit as far as the supernatural world is concerned. You, however, the other vamps want alive. If we happen to get saved as a side effect of whatever they can do for you...I'm cool with that."

He'd been reading my mind. That was exactly what I'd been planning. "You remember where this place is?"

"How could I forget?"

"Just get here before dark."

"You don't need to tell me that twice."

* * *

I had an important phone call to make. But first, being that my hidey hole hadn't been invaded as of yet, I chanced a quick shower. In the movies, vampires are always happily covered in filth, either from their graves or their victims. In reality, I liked smelling like shit about as much as the next person with any sense of personal hygiene, which isn't to say very much.

Thank goodness the safe house had a washing machine and dryer too, because the available spare clothing would have only suited me had I been a cross-dresser several sizes smaller. Since I had no plans to walk Forty-Second Street that night looking for Johns, that wasn't going to cut the mustard. I really needed to tell Sally - Starlight, I corrected myself - to stock these places with stuff that would fit me.

Thus, I found myself clad in an ill-fitting pink bathrobe as I sat down about an hour later and dialed the central seat of power for vampires in the Northeastern United States - Boston.

I'll admit to being a bit apprehensive about doing so. Part of the problem was that I'd escaped from Alexander the Great, the guy in charge of the Draculas. Putting myself back on his radar wasn't really something I was looking forward to. Then again, it was probably a moot point anyway. Most of the grunts I'd met in the paranormal world were little more than super-powered dumbasses. The folks in charge, however, weren't exactly stupid.

What had I done upon making a run for it? I'd made a beeline straight back home. Even one of the aforementioned dumbasses would know to check someplace obvious like that first.

The truth was, if I was indeed trying to hide from the upper hierarchy of vampiredom, I was doing a crap job of it. There was no point in pretending to play *Mission Impossible*.

Also, the guy I'd unintentionally released from Alex's personal collection of trophy heads scared the ever-living fuck out of me. That played no small part in my decision.

Bottom line was, member of the Draculas or not, I needed James's help on this one.

Sadly, unlike Sally, I had no idea what his personal cell number was. It just goes to show how unfair things are. Be the chosen one that legends speak of and you'll be lucky to get cab fare out of it. Own a pair of perky tits, though, and the world is your oyster.

That left me having to deal with the equivalent of their 800 number. "Lucky me," I grumbled as I dialed. Vampire bureaucracy was every bit as bad as that in the world of the living. That meant I had best find a charger, because I had a feeling I was gonna be on hold for a while.

* * *

"I'm sorry, but what was your name again?"

"It's Bill Ryder. For the last time, I'm the motherfucking Freewill."

"Sir, the legendary Freewill is listed in our database as 'whereabouts unknown.' I will ask nicely that you disengage from this call or I shall have to report this to my superiors. I need not remind you that prank calls are *severely* frowned upon by the..."

I had to restrain myself, hearing the creak of the cheap phone in my grasp. Much more and I'd crush it in my annoyance. If that happened, I'd just have to start all over again. Finding myself back at the end of the hold queue would probably be the final straw that would cause me to run outside and embrace the sunshine.

I took a deep breath and mentally counted to ten before deciding upon a tactful response. "Fine, report me. Maybe your superiors are less fucking stupid than you are, you fangless cocksucking twat."

I'll admit that might have sounded slightly more respectful in my head.

There was silence for a moment, followed by a terse, "Hold, please." Bland music began to play in the background. Would the world be somewhat less fearful of the coming horrors, I mused, if they knew that vampires utilized elevator music in their day-to-day dealings?

I continued to wait on hold for several minutes longer, prompting me to get up and grab a few pints of blood from the now unplugged fridge before they went bad. Might as well suck down a few while I listened to the instrumental version of *That's What Friends Are For*.

I was just about to conclude that I'd been abandoned, left to the dark Hell of waiting forever or hanging up, when the phone picked up on the other end.

It was about fucking time. Maybe I would finally be allowed to speak to someone who held a position higher on the food chain than drone.

I heard an intake of breath and felt a tickle at the back of my skull. Wait, were they...

"IDENTIFY YOURSELF AND YOUR LOCATION!!"

I dropped the phone with a startled cry as the compulsion rang through my head like a mini-sledgehammer. It wasn't the loudest thing I'd had bounce around in my brain lately, but it had caught me completely by surprise.

Popping out of my chair, I knelt and looked beneath the desk I'd been sitting behind. I grabbed the phone off the floor and was just bringing it back to my ear when it rang out again.

"*IDENTIFY YOURSELF NOW!!*"

"I heard you the fucking first time," I snarled. "I told you already, this is Bill Ryder. I'm the..."

"The Freewill would not have obeyed my compulsion," the person, a female whose voice I didn't recognize, replied.

What kind of chicken and egg bullshit was this? I swear, if it weren't for the fact that the Sasquatches smelled like shit and would probably have us all eating grubs, some days I really wouldn't mind if they overran the vamps. "You'll notice," I said, trying to control the vein that really wanted to pop out of my forehead, "I didn't give my location."

"I will concede that point. However, the fact remains that the Freewill's whereabouts..."

"Are unknown. Yeah, I surmised that already. Who the hell is this, anyway?"

An annoyed sniff came from the other end. Most vampires were not overly appreciative of a little back-sass. What a surprise that I'd get one who fit the stereotype.

"Know, child, that you are speaking to Calibra, acting Prefect of the Northeastern United States, and I am not particularly pleased right now. You have exactly two seconds to convince me not to sentence you to summary execution."

"Wait, Prefect? I thought that was Colin's job."

"One second..."

Oh, for Christ's sake. "Fine. If I'm not who I say I am, then you can kill me to your heart's content. There ain't shit I can do about that. If I am, though, then I have a feeling there might be a few people who'll take offense at executing the one foretold to lead our forces to victory." Ugh, I had to swallow back the bile at reciting that bullshit. "So what does that tell you?"

There was a momentary pause, then this Calibra person replied, "That tells me either you are suicidal or..."

"The Freewill?"

"Perhaps."

Fuck, it was better than nothing.

* * *

Calibra seemed somewhat hesitant to summon James. I couldn't blame her for that one. He was a member of the Draculas, and their reputation preceded them. One didn't bother them frivolously if one wanted to keep living. Of course, I'd always found James to be an exception to that rule. Even so, it was quite possible he kept up appearances for protocol's sake - something he seemed somewhat fond of doing.

While we waited for him to join us, I figured I'd use the time to try and mend the bridges I'd just burnt to ash. "So, Calibra..." - I wasn't sure if her name sounded exotic or stupidly obtuse - "I apologize if we got off on the wrong foot. Congratulations on your posting."

"Assuming you are who you say, I accept your apology and well wishes. Having met briefly, I am familiar with you and your colleague's casual flippancy."

We'd met? Um, okay. I never was good with names, but whatever. This chick seemed to have all the personality of a pile of wet cardboard.

Fuck it. Rather than try to kiss her ass, I decided to satisfy some base curiosity. "Speaking of your new job, is he dead?"

"Is who dead?"

"Colin." The glee in my voice was probably a little too apparent, but I didn't care. This was potentially the best bit of news I'd heard since returning. "That's why you took over, right? Someone finally wised up and staked his smarmy ass."

"I can assure you, Freewill," an oily male voice replied - goddamn, I hated being on speaker, "my *smarmy ass* is quite intact."

So much for good news.

Class Reunion

"Hi, Colin."

"That's Colin, personal attaché to the Wanderer - esteemed member of the First Coven - to you."

Oh, how I despised that guy. "Personal attaché?"

"Yes. I have been tasked with the glorious *privilege* of managing the Wanderer's busy schedule." There was something in his tone that made me think he wasn't all too pleased with his new rank.

Then it hit me. When last I'd heard from him, he'd been freshly promoted to Northeastern Prefect - the smarm practically oozing from his voice. Now, despite the supposed promotion, he was back to being little more than James's assistant again.

Oh, that was rich. A toady to a king was still just little more than a toady.

"Well," I replied, grinning despite myself. "I'm back."

"So I hear." I could practically smell the acid in his remark through the phone. "Perhaps now we can finally get an accurate accounting of what happened to Remington's team."

"Didn't Sally fill you in?"

"Her report left a lot to be desired."

"Oh, well, I'm sure she got the details right." I wasn't about to forget this fucker had been responsible for sending that goon and his hit squad. He'd been responsible for Sheila's...

Once more, I had to mind my grip on the phone's fragile plastic. Smashing it to bits wouldn't do me much good. However, maybe an extra turning of the screw would. "What can I say? Remington did an incompetent job. Whoever picked him for that mission fucked up to the nth degree."

If it were possible for silence to be frosty, I'd say the connection on the other end was entering subarctic temperatures. Now it all made sense. His promotion was in name only. He'd been blamed and subsequently removed from the seat of power he'd so craved. In his new capacity, he couldn't do any more harm than scheduling a bad lunch date. It wasn't quite the punishment I'd have chosen, but it had definitely hurt him. I could dig that.

"I will let the Wanderer know this is not another prank call." Colin's voice registered about as much disgust as one could and still not be gargling sewage. A beep on the other end told me I'd been put on hold yet again.

Waiting as patiently as I could, I noted flashing lights passing by outside. The walls of the safe house were thick and muffled sound fairly well, but even so, the high-pitched whine of multiple sirens came through. That was the third time since I'd locked myself in here. It seemed like Manhattan was going nuts. It couldn't have all been because of that one vamp, could it? Not with the sun still out, it couldn't be.

Plenty of other stuff could be going down. Who knew what the hell those supernatural storms were spitting out? Even outside of that, this was New York. Shit happened here.

There came another low beep on the other end of the line, and all of those thoughts instantly fled as the smooth voice of James, the Wanderer, filled the line.

"We have been eagerly awaiting your return, Dr. Death."

* * *

The mixed feelings I'd had earlier vanished in a second upon hearing him. James represented all of the positive aspects of the vampire nation: intelligence, dignity, honor, and power. Normally, I admired those former virtues, but I had to admit that last one was of interest to me right at that moment. I wasn't sure if he'd get personally involved in this little dilemma of mine, but I had my fingers crossed. I'd seen him in action and knew he was one badass of a vamp.

"There have been a lot of people worried about you, you know."

"So I hear."

"It is good to hear your voice. Now, if you don't mind me dispensing with the small talk, where have you been all this time?"

"Likewise; it's good to hear yours. Listen, James, the whole story of where I've been will have to wait. I have a hell of a problem right now..."

"All in good time, my friend. I'm sure Calibra will be able to help you with..."

"I don't need her, I need *you*." Okay, perhaps that sounded a bit whiny. The startled gasps from the others on the call told me it was probably out of order too.

"Forgive him, Wanderer," that Calibra chick said. Oh great, another suck-up. "I shall make sure he receives *correction* as to the proper ways of speaking with a..."

"It is quite all right, my dear," James replied. "I am well used to Dr. Death's mannerisms."

"Good..." I started, but he wasn't finished.

"At the same time, Freewill or not, he should be well aware that any escalations in priority must first be signed-off by a respective coven master and only then directed to the office of the standing Prefect. Protocol must be maintained, especially in these dire days."

"Coven master?"

"Yes. I take it you were not informed that..."

"I know that Starlight took over, but..."

"Do not interrupt the Wanderer!"

"It's quite fine, really it is, Colin."

Oh God, were we back to *this?* When I saw Sally next, I was gonna make it a point to steal her contacts list. "Starlight handed the keys back to me."

"There have been no records of an abdication from any of my covens," Calibra said.

"That's because she was kidnapped before she could do it." I gritted my teeth and counted to ten. God, this group could be maddening to deal with.

"Be that as it may, Dr. Death," James said, "while I would love to give your return the pomp and circumstance it deserves, please know that the situation is on the verge of escalating and requires my full..."

Oh, Jesus Christ. "Will you listen for just a second?" I pleaded, knowing my interruption would potentially be a painful one. "When I escaped from Switzerland, I may have accidentally..."

"How dare you?" Colin chimed in right on cue. "You pathetic excuse for a..."

"Wait, did you say Switzerland?" James asked.

"Yes."

"But..."

"That will be enough for now, Colin," came the terse reply before I was addressed again. "What were you doing there?"

"Chillin' in the dungeon of Chillon Castle."

There was a brief pause, but before I could lapse into my tale of bodiless vamps sprouting new limbs, James said, "Hold for one moment, please." He put me on mute for a few seconds before he spoke again. "I have sent the others from the room. I want you to start at the beginning. Leave nothing out."

"Yeah, but the most..."

"I *insist*."

* * *

The tone of James's voice was not one to be disobeyed. Even I, purveyor of fine ways of telling folks much stronger than me to go fuck themselves, knew better than to question him. Instead, I lapsed into a quick retelling of where I'd been and what had happened. As I did, my eyes crept over to the clock on the wall.

Where the hell were my friends?

James was silent as I brought him up to speed on my return. Despite his insistence, I omitted some details, like where I found the head and what I did to Alex in order to escape. No point in putting any more of a spotlight on my gross insubordination.

Likewise, I most definitely glossed over Dave's experiments on me. That was strictly on a need-to-cover-my-ass basis. James had partially achieved his current rank by outing another vamp performing similar research. Of course, that asshole had been working for the Nazis at the time, but even so. The last thing I needed was him saving me, only to dole out swift and brutal punishment. So I did what I do best: played dumb and made up some stupid lie about accidentally leaving the errant cranium behind.

Fortunately for me, he was focused on areas other than my untruth.

"So you're saying that Alexander kept you prisoner in your Freewill state all this time?"

"Yep."

"And both Theodora and Yehoshua were aware?"

"Apparently, they weren't the only ones. A whole shitload of vamps saw me, including these blind weirdos sniffing glue fumes in a cave...well, okay, maybe they didn't see me per se, but..."

"This is most disturbing."

"Well yeah, if I had to cut out my eyes every hour I wouldn't be too..."

"Not that. We had all assumed that you'd been lurking in the tri-state area, but all along..."

"I was in vampire central?"

"Evidently."

A small touch of paranoia crept up my spine. "And you didn't know about it?"

"This is the first I've heard of it."

"But you're a member of the Drac...First Coven."

"As I am well aware. I have been stateside during most of your absence and..."

"Most?"

"I visited Chateau Chillon once, two months back, to discuss negotiations with the Jiangshi."

"Who?"

"It is of no real concern to our current discussion. What is, is that I was never given any reason to believe you were close. I spent a good deal of time by Alexander's side. He had more than ample opportunity to tell me."

"Well, I'm sure you two will have plenty to talk about in the coming days, but right now, we have a bigger issue. That vamp I told you about is trashing the fucking place."

"We may have to agree to disagree on what is truly the more important issue. I am aware of the crimes of the decollari kept within the walls of..."

"Deco..."

"The bodiless," he replied dismissively, as if that weren't an entirely creepy-ass thing. "They are mostly a combination of political dissidents and those who have failed the First in endeavors where it was deemed necessary for examples to be made of them."

Ugh, I really didn't need to be reminded. Once, not so long ago, a former member of the Draculas had deemed me in need of being made such an example. That was in the past, though. I had more pressing matters. "Believe me, James, this asshole wasn't waving around anti-abortion signs or anything like that. I sincerely doubt he was a political prisoner."

"That may just be a simple matter of the difference in age between you."

"No. I'm telling you, I emptied a full clip of fifty-caliber silver slugs point blank into this motherfucker and he still kept coming. Fuck, I pushed him out a window in the middle of the day, and the next thing I knew, he was punching a hole in the wall to get to me."

"Are you serious?"

"If I'm lying, I'm dying...hell, if that guy catches up to me, I'm probably doing that anyway."

"I suppose it doesn't hurt to have Colin research this. Can you describe him?"

I was going to do so anyway, but the fact that it was going to cause Colin at least some minor grief made it that much more delicious. Potentially getting some help while pissing off an asshole definitely counted as killing two birds with one stone in my book.

I described my attacker, first in his naked old dude state, and then as he later appeared - doing his impersonation of Lou Ferrigno on crack. A faint scribbling sound in the background told me James was taking notes, either that or drawing caricatures of me with rude captions next to them. My vamp senses were good, but not that good.

"Is that all? Any distinguishing body marks?"

"Not that I...oh yeah, the guy was all tatted up. He had this snake motif sneaking down his chest. Pretty badass. There was also a sun and moon thing going on with his shoulders. As for what he was wearing, now that was kinda..."

"Hold on. Did you say a sun and moon?"

"Yeah."

"Black sun, black moon?"

I snickered at hearing the Conan quote. "Yeah, he tried to sell haga to us too, but a slayer such as me wasn't having any of that shit..."

"I'm serious."

"Oh. Yeah, I guess. They were definitely dark."

James took a deep breath, as if contemplating something. "That is not possible."

"Tell me about it. I mean, I know us vamps regenerate, but how the fuck do tattoos grow back?"

"Can we please *focus* here?" The temperature seemed to go out of the room as he snapped at me. Of course, my current lack of pants probably didn't help either.

"Okay...so what's the big deal with the tattoos?"

"Which symbol was on his right shoulder?"

I forced myself to bite back any more wiseass remarks and simply answered, "Sun."

Again, he said, apparently more to himself than me, "That is simply not possible. They were all wiped out, purged."

"Who?"

"You are to stay where you are. If that is not possible, then I want you to keep a phone on your person at all times. If anything changes at all, you are to inform me immediately." Once more, the tone of his voice had changed from that of a friend to a commander who wasn't about to take any shit from his troops.

I was probably pushing my luck, but I'd been through too much to just nod and smile. "Why?"

"Because I am coming down to you. This must be dealt with posthaste."

"What must be dealt with?"

"You have no idea what you've possibly done, do you? If the cul..." He paused as if censoring himself. "If *they* are allowed to rise again now, we will surely fall before our foes. Now give me your address."

I had no idea what he was talking about. Somehow, though, I wasn't surprised to hear that I'd, once again, screwed the pooch.

If it wasn't for shit luck, I'd have no luck at all.

Top Headlines for the Day

James's words didn't make much sense to me. I mean, as freaky as that vamp had been, I wasn't quite sure how one crazy shirtless guy was going to take down the entire vampire race. Still, if something was serious enough to bother the normally unflappable James, it was probably best not to completely blow it off.

I was busy mulling things over when the downstairs buzzer sounded. Still deep in thought, I opened the door for my friends. Tom stepped inside, looking somewhat paler than usual. "Have you been watching the...dude, why the fuck are you dressed like an escapee from Victoria's Secret?"

I stared blankly at him for a moment before realizing what I was still wearing. "For you, of course. My months of captivity convinced me that we were meant to be together."

Ed smirked from behind as a look of something akin to horror passed through Tom's face. "Really?"

"No, not really, fucktard. My clothes still have five minutes left in the dryer. Now get the hell in here before the wind blows the front of this thing open."

* * *

I retrieved my clean clothing and got dressed, much to all of our relief, then joined them in the living room. "Okay, so what were you babbling about before being consumed by jealousy of my manhood?"

"Yeah, like that's possible. I didn't realize the dungeon they kept you in was airtight."

"Can we stow the bullshit for five minutes, kiddies?" Ed snapped. "I'm thinking we should be concentrating on more important things, like getting the fuck out of here."

"Why? I thought that..."

"Change of plans. Everything is going crazy out there."

"That's what I was trying to say," Tom said. "Have you been checking out the TV?"

"No," I replied. Perhaps I should have paid better attention to all the sirens and flashing lights that had been passing by. "But seriously, how much damage could one vampire do?"

"I don't think it's just one vampire. Turn on the news."

* * *

...The Coast Guard is still searching for survivors after a ferry bound for Staten Island capsized. Witnesses claim it wasn't an accident, describing to police the impossible - a collision with a creature sporting an eight-foot-tall serrated fin...

...resulting in an explosion of green flame that consumed nearly all of Castle Point...

...attacked by a being that is being described as having superhuman strength and speed. This is the second tragedy to befall this building this year. Just three short months ago, it was the scene of a terrorist attack...

...residents in all three boroughs are urged to remain indoors...

* * *

What the fuck? It was like the world picked the past twenty-four hours to go crazy. Almost like...no, that couldn't be. Could I have somehow set this off? Maybe I'd been some sort of catalyst that...

...were saved by what residents are claiming was a glowing blonde warrior, surrounded by what one witness described as an aura of angelic fire...

Tom clicked the television off.

"Wait, what was..."

"Dude, and that's not even half of it." He stepped between me and the boob tube. "I'm pretty sure we saw a fucking pterodactyl flying over the Brooklyn Bridge."

That caught my attention. "A pterodactyl?"

"It wasn't a pterodactyl," Ed said. "It was more like a gargoyle."

"Fuck that. Gargoyles are made of stone. This was..."

"Does is really matter?" I asked. "Seriously, neither of those things should be here. This is like arguing that the Easter Bunny is more real than Santa Claus. Speaking of mystical creatures, where's Christy?"

Tom frowned at that. "She's put on a little weight, but she's not that big yet."

"You know what I mean."

"Oh. She's been putting together a new coven." When he saw the look on my face, he quickly added, "One that's a lot less focused on killing you."

"Good to know."

"Anyway, one of the new recruits is from Connecticut and she was hosting their gathering this week."

"Did you let her know she should stay away from the city?"

"No cell phones allowed in the mystic circle."

"Wonderful. Leave her a message for when she's done...communing, or whatever it is they're doing."

He raised his eyebrows. "Good idea. I hadn't thought of that." Same old Tom.

He walked off into the kitchen to call Christy, leaving Ed and me to converse.

I shifted in my seat, making myself comfortable as I prepared to deliver the news. "I can't leave."

"The hell you can't. We need to get up to Boston and convince them that..."

"That's why I can't leave. Boston is coming down to us."

"Not another assassination squad?"

"I'm pretty sure it's not. James is on the way."

Ed looked impressed. "The big man himself? Awesome. Think he'll be able to take out Hercules?"

"If anyone can, it'll be him."

"What if he can't?"

"Then we probably thank our lucky stars we don't get to live long enough to see the end of the world."

"Good thing I've been neglecting my 401K."

"Corporate douche."

"Unemployed loser."

"Touché."

* * *

After leaving a message for Christy, Tom rejoined us. I filled him in on James's impending arrival. Like Ed, he also refused to heed common sense and get away from the city - preferring to stand by my side.

It was both maddening and touching at the same time, reminding me of how alone I had felt upon awakening in that dungeon. The depths of despair had sent me there to begin with, but I was forced to rethink that in their presence. At the same time, I still wasn't comfortable with it. Both of them had been hurt following me around. Hell, I still wasn't sure that either of them was entirely okay.

Ed, proving to be far more empathic than I would have ever guessed, took a look at my face and promptly smacked me upside the head. "Knock it the fuck off. We're adults, and you're sure as shit not our dad."

Can't argue against logic like that.

That said, all that was left was to kill however many hours it took until James arrived to vastly augment our little group's strength. Thankfully, wasting time was a skill that none of us had lost during my long sojourn.

* * *

"When I go to sleep at night, the last thing I think about is..."

"A good long shit."

"Hitler's dick."

"No contest. Bill takes this round." Tom handed me the token. We were playing some card game I'd found in one of the desk drawers to help pass the time. Everything about it had a perverted bent. I had to admit, it was a shitload more fun than poker.

Darkness had fallen, yet the chaos hadn't subsided. The power had flickered for about an hour and then finally gone out, leaving us without a TV to keep us informed as to what was going on out in the world. The only thing I knew for sure was I could still hear the occasional whine of sirens in the distance.

"What if he can't get in?" Ed took the deck from Tom and reshuffled it in the dim candlelight. "The bridges were crazy enough early on. I gotta imagine they're not going to get any better."

"If shit gets bad enough, the cops might even close them down."

"Do you think any of that will stop James?" I asked.

They both grinned. The answer was obvious.

* * *

My faith in James was rewarded about twenty minutes later when he arrived. I almost shut the door after he stepped in before realizing he wasn't alone. I had thought this'd be a solo mission, but a woman followed him in. Despite wearing heels, she made no noise as she walked - not even enough to set off my vampire senses. The newcomer was tall and thin - big surprise - with her dark hair pulled up in a severe bun. I took a moment to admire her attractive features - throwing a smile at her that wasn't returned - when I realized she looked vaguely familiar.

"Wait a second, didn't..."

"We met once in Boston," she replied in a no-nonsense fashion. "I believe it was your first visit. You and your friend were busy disrupting my department."

The pieces fell into place. She was right. It had been my first trip up there - in an undead capacity, that is. I'd been amazed at the sight of zombies performing office duties and had gotten a little carried away. Sally had been in the middle of bitching me out when this woman had appeared and brow beaten us both. "Are you..."

"Prefect Calibra, although you may address me by my name alone as long as you continue to remember my rank."

"O-kay. Bill Ryder at your service."

There came a snicker from further in the room. Tom, no doubt. The dude really didn't have any control.

Calibra stepped around me and in front of James. "Why are there living unthralled humans in a coven safe house?" Her tone was defensive, bordering on dangerous.

"It is quite all right, my dear," he replied smoothly. "They are the Freewill's friends."

"Friends or not, they are unauthorized to be here. The lawful coven master has not sanctioned it, and the sensitivity of what we are..."

"I can assure you that Dr. Death has already told his friends everything." He cast a sidelong glance at me, to which I grinned guiltily. "I will vouch for their discretion as they were both present at the Woods of Mourning summit. Our secrets are quite safe with them."

Safe was a relative concept. Upon our return from that failed peace conference, I'd had to perform a factory reset on Tom's phone to keep him from uploading pictures of Grulg, one of the Bigfeet, to Facebook.

Seeking to turn the conversation away from my roommates, I locked the door and said, "I'm glad you're here, James. Although I thought you were coming alone. After what you said..." I trailed off, then inclined my head toward Calibra. Her lips had pursed into a thin line. "No offense, Prefect."

"It is simple, really," he replied. "Before I could leave the premises, I was helpfully reminded that the covens of the Northeast are under her protection. Any transgressions against them fall under her jurisdiction."

"Thank you for not taking offense, Wanderer."

"I never take offense at reminders of protocol, my dear," he said before addressing me again. "It is well within her rights to accompany me. Although, due to the potentially sensitive nature of this information, I insisted the rest of the Boston staff remain in the dark for now."

"So no Colin?" I asked hopefully.

"Colin is my personal assistant and confidant. As such, he is aware of the situation, but offered to remain in Boston so as to research this matter further."

"How noble of him."

"Do not dismiss him so quickly. I am well aware of my assistant's strengths and weaknesses. There are few amongst our ranks who possess his ability to traverse our myriad archives with..."

Blah blah blah. I purposely tuned him out and focused instead on the bottom line: the douchebag wasn't here. If he were, I'm sure he'd find some excuse to push me in front of the first bus that came along - metaphorical or not.

Albeit, I considered as once more I heard the whine of a siren as it passed by outside, there was still more than a fair chance of that happening as the night wore on.

Hell, it was more of a question of when than if.

Stake Out

I wasn't sure which hurt more: the solid concrete support pillar that had ever so gently halted my intended trajectory, or the aluminum baseball bat that had sent me flying through the air.

Either way, my body was pounded into a nicely bruised mush. Oh well, it was my own goddamned fault anyway.

First, there had been the bickering at the safe house. James had wanted someone to stay behind so as to keep in contact with Boston and report on the situation from a semi-secured location. The problem was nobody had wanted to do so.

There was no fucking way I wanted another showdown with Brutus Beefcake without James by my side. Calibra had fucking protocol backing her up. Tom or Ed were both obvious candidates, but neither of them wanted the job and I really wasn't big on forcing the issue. If that creep managed to pick up Ed's scent again, it would end badly. Tom...well, who the fuck knows how that would have come back to bite me in the ass? I wouldn't allow them to be compelled either, pulling what little rank as the Freewill that I could. Hell, I wasn't certain it would have even worked on Ed, considering the weirdness from earlier.

The next several hours had turned out to be pointless anyway. New York City was in utter chaos. The site of the first burning building about two blocks away from the safe house and the National Guardsmen nervously blocking off the street told us the underground was a better bet.

We scoured all *officially* known coven properties first. Since Chuck had dominated Starlight and Firebird, we figured it made sense that he might have holed up in one of our hangouts.

That was Tom's idea, by the way - calling that fucker Chuck. He said it was easier than continually referring to our foe as "that badass tattooed vampire who kicked our asses." Also, *Chuck* made him sound a bit less invincible. Never discount the effects of a little positive psychological reinforcement.

I'd first led us to the site of the loft, which had been one of the main gathering points of Village Coven. It had been blown to shit months back, but I figured there was always the chance it had been rebuilt. It hadn't. All that remained was a fenced off crater, the debris having been long removed. The underground larder beneath it remained, but it appeared that it hadn't been used in quite some time.

It was only then that I realized my knowledge of Village Coven was sadly outdated. I honestly had no idea what, if any, new properties had come under our *management*.

Calibra couldn't help much there, either. As Prefect, she had information on all of our official holdings. However, her current insight was no greater than mine. If we had acquired any new digs recently, they might very well be off the grid. I wouldn't have put that past Sally. She always thought two steps ahead of just about everyone else.

I wasn't about to say it in front of my companions, but the truth was I really wished she were there. Together, we'd survived shit that should have easily reduced us to our respective component ashes. Without her, I felt almost...naked.

Once our known locations were scoured and discovered empty - nary a Village vamp to be found - we turned to the safe houses I knew about. Maybe it wasn't such a bad thing Sally hadn't been around. She'd surely have kicked my ass for that part.

At the end of what turned out to be a long, fruitless search, we had only one location left that was still off Boston's radar. And that's where my face was mistaken for a World Series curveball.

* * *

Village Coven shared a safe house near the Brooklyn Naval Yard with the Howard Beach Coven, HBC for short, a rival group of vamps from Queens. Sadly, most of that rivalry stemmed from the fact that they mostly hated my guts. Even so, frosty as our relations were, there hadn't been any open hostilities between us ever since a little altercation that ended with the dusting of their master, Samuel.

We'd approached the structure in the late hours of the night, following a prolonged hike through the subway tunnels. The trains had been suspended, no doubt due to whatever the fuck was going on. All the while, I couldn't help but notice the curious glances James kept giving Ed, albeit he kept whatever he was thinking to himself. I had little doubt that he'd noticed the same thing Monkhbat had - somehow, Ed's scent was off. At least so I'd been told. He still smelled like the same old Ed to me, but then again, I didn't have hundreds of years of gradually heightening powers to fall back on.

Right outside of the safe house, James's phone rang. Colin was on the other end, probably to kiss some ass and blather on about how all of this was my fault.

James and Calibra stepped aside to talk to him, leaving the rest of us to wait for them to finish. Or we would have waited, except that Tom decided we might as well save ourselves the trouble and check things out on our own since every other place had been empty.

Yeah, that was a mistake.

I smelled the presence of other vamps not too long after stepping through the door. They were unfamiliar, though - definitely not the big angry dude we were searching for. HBC, obviously.

Despite the potential danger, none of us had wanted to look like pussies in front of James, so we proceeded with caution. Tom pulled out the magical amulet he'd worn ever since Canada. Christy had made it for him and it somehow channeled faith magic - in his case, the love he'd had for a certain collectible toy. Yeah, he was a bit of a weirdo.

Ed was more practical, armed with a nine-millimeter Glock. I'd found it, along with a few spare magazines of ammo, in the safe house, recognizing it as Sally's backup piece. It didn't hold nearly as big of a bang as her Desert Eagle, lost during my tumble down the elevator shaft, but it was more easily concealed - handy for running around the city in the middle of an emergency.

Even so, I hadn't expected much more than some posturing. The HBC liked to remind my coven that they were going to kick our asses, but it was mostly trash talk.

Or so I had thought.

Upon entering a large room on the second floor, four HBC vamps approached us.

I had just managed to ask, "Which of you guys is in charge, because..." when my face was abruptly chosen for batting practice.

That's the problem with the world today - nobody talks through their problems.

* * *

The blow knocked me for a loop, but I had the express displeasure of experiencing much worse in my short time amongst the undead. Hell, a generic beating by your garden variety vampire goon was practically a vacation in paradise these days - minus the beach, drinks, and topless women sunning themselves.

I pulled myself together in time to duck another swing of the bat. It connected with the pillar behind me with a solid *clunk*, stopping the vamp in his tracks as the vibrations from the impact traveled up his arm.

It was enough of an opening for me. I grabbed him by the jacket, spun, and tossed him into the waiting arms of his buddy, who'd been heading over to help him out - no doubt assessing me as the biggest threat in the room.

That might have been a mistake on their part.

"Yeah, you like that, bitch?"

I turned towards the voice to find Tom hanging off the back of the third vamp, one arm around the guy's neck, the other holding the amulet against his forehead. The vampire's scream drowned out whatever else my roommate had to say as his head caught fire. It was something to behold...reminding me to be wary of the day Tom returned home holding a prize even more valuable than the vintage Optimus Prime toy that had first earned his insane love.

Two shots echoed throughout the room - Ed, no doubt. Unfortunately, I didn't have a chance to check on whether he'd found his mark. The two punks squaring off against me rushed forward and took me down in a double tackle. Fuck. Didn't these guys ever watch kung-fu movies? Everyone knows you're supposed to squander your superior numbers by attacking one at a time. Jeez!

RICK GUALTIERI

I went down with them on top, realizing that I could potentially be in trouble if either of them was armed with something sharp enough to stake me with. Fortunately - sorta - they peppered my face with fists instead.

"What'd you do with them, fucker?" the Major League hopeful screamed at me. "Where are they, you fucking freak?"

What the hell? "I don't know what..."

Another fist slammed into my mouth. "Don't lie to me!"

Okay, this was starting to get old. It was time to get nasty before these guys managed to ugly me up.

Thankfully, one of the hallmarks of those untrained in the fighting arts is to keep making the same mistake over and over again. Trust me, I'm a near expert in that.

"Please, you have to believe me..." Again, the words died in my throat as another punch connected. This time, though, I'd extended my fangs first.

I bit down and crunched the knuckles with my teeth. Oh, gross! When was the last time this asshole had washed his fucking hands?

He let out a scream as he tried to shake me off, but I held fast like an angry junkyard dog, biting down even harder as a dribble of blood began to fill my mouth.

His friend backed off, aghast at the display. Even these days, with vamps knowing what I was, it still freaked some out to see one vampire bite into another. It's always the predators who are the most surprised to find they've become the prey.

Another cry of pain filled the room, one that I recognized. Playtime was over. I crunched down again, then shoved the HBC vamp off me.

Rolling to my feet, I spat out three fingers and turned toward where I'd heard Ed.

The vamp he'd been squaring off against had gotten inside of his defenses and sunk his teeth into the meat of my roommate's bicep - meager as it was. Fuck.

I braced myself for a burst of speed so as to come to my friend's aid, and that's right about when shit got real.

* * *

"END THIS NONSENSE IMMEDIATELY!!"

The compulsion rang out with enough force to instantly erase all of my momentum, maybe even knocking me back a few inches past where I'd started.

James stood at the room's entrance, looking none too pleased. Calibra was by his side, her expression more that of one who'd walked into their children's bedroom to find a minor mess.

The effect was instantaneous. The four HBC vamps ceased what they were doing as their eyes glazed over. They stood still like statues, offering no more threat. Tom was on the floor, staring unblinking at the ceiling. The compulsion had plowed through his defenses like a freight train.

Ed, however, merely stood there clutching his arm and glaring at the vamp who'd bitten him. "Fucking asshole."

"Curious," Calibra said. "How is it you..."

And that's when his attacker burst apart in an explosion of guts and white fire.

Oh boy. When it rains, it sure as shit pours.

White Lies

Even if James's sudden appearance hadn't taken the fight out of the remaining HBC vamps, watching their buddy explore the finer aspects of self-immolation most certainly did. Needless to say, they were suitably freaked out. Not only were they in the presence of the legendary Freewill - albeit that hadn't dissuaded them from trying to kick my ass - but they found themselves confronted by the Northeastern Prefect, a member of the Draculas, and whatever the hell Ed was able to do. All in all, it was probably like walking into a diner and coming face to face with the Pope, the President, and Kim Kardashian all eating a lunch of boiled baby meat together.

James walked forward and gave me the barest of glances out of the corner of his eye. It spoke volumes to the fact that we'd no doubt have some words later on.

When he reached the middle of the room, he released his hold on the compelled vamps. "Tell me why you attacked the Freewill. I am unaware of any open hostilities between Howard Beach and Village Covens. As I need not explain to anyone present, this is an ill time for intra-coven feuds. Such nonsense is intolerable."

It was well known in the vampire community that when a member of the Draculas told you to jump, your feet had better be off the ground before they finished that sentence.

Apparently, *Bat-man* didn't get the memo, though. He stepped forward, eyes wide, and pointed at Ed. "What the fuck is that, man?" Oh well, his funeral.

Calibra raised an eyebrow, but said nothing. Interesting. Colin wouldn't have wasted an opportunity to crawl up James's ass and get nice and comfy.

"Manuel," James replied tolerantly, proving once more than he was cut from a different material than most vampires, "kindly answer my question. I requested information from you. I shan't do so twice."

That got their attention. His two remaining buddies backed up a step as if to distance themselves from the inevitable splatter. The first one, Manuel, I presumed, finally seemed to take the hint. He focused on James as if seeing him for the first time. His face turned a shade paler in the process as he averted his eyes.

"My apologies. Didn't mean no disrespect, man...I mean, sir."

Jeez, how come I never got any brown-nosing like that?

"A couple hours ago," he continued, "these two Village Coven bitches came waltzing into our den like they owned the place."

"Were they alone?"

"No. They was flanking this big dude. Never seen him before. Guy was dressed like some fucking weirdo. Wearing some kind of skirt, but up top, he was sporting a Kevlar vest, like maybe he'd just stolen it from a cop."

Considering what had occurred earlier at the office, I deemed that an entirely likely scenario.

"Anything else about him?"

"He had long hair, like some rock star, and he was sportin' ink."

"Oh?"

"Yeah, a moon and star on his shoulders, and some kind of monster on his chest. Couldn't see it too well with that vest on, though."

"What happened then?"

"I don't know. I walked up and told them they was uninvited - to get the fuck out."

"And..."

Manny seemed hesitant to continue, but one did not try their luck with the Draculas. Finally, he said, "And this big fucker just backhanded me. Next thing I know, my hombres here was smackin' me awake. I got back to my feet and saw that everyone else was gone."

James turned his attention to the two other HBC vamps. "And you didn't witness anything?"

One of them shook his head. "We were out hunting."

"This is worrisome," James said. It was more to himself than anyone, but Manny apparently decided he was being addressed.

"Shit, yeah, it's worrisome." He turned and pointed a finger at me. "What the fuck did you do with my people, asshole?"

"Me?"

"Yeah, that's your group. They don't take a shit unless you tell them to."

Oh, if only that were true. But at least that answered why this guy tried to send my head into the outfield upon seeing me.

"The Freewill is not to blame," James said dismissively as he turned away. Something plainly bothered him, but I figured the present company was most likely not in the need for knowing. "He just recently returned from...First Coven related business."

He turned to me. "Gather your friends. We need to go."

"That's it?" Manny complained, seeming to, once more, forget he was in the presence of one of the thirteen most powerful vampires in the world. Some people just didn't learn. "This fucker kidnaps our people and he just walks?"

Finally, Calibra broke her silence. "As Prefect, your coven's safety falls to me. You will provide me with names and descriptions for all of your missing members, and I will do everything I can to make sure they are accounted for."

"Okay fine, but what about this freak?" He pointed an accusing finger at Ed, who'd moved over to help Tom back to his feet. It was rare to see a vamp push his luck so many times. At the very least, I had to give him credit for having more balls than brains.

James turned back. That couldn't be a good thing. A part of me wished I'd brought a rain slicker because this was going to get messy.

Instead, he simply asked, "You are aware of our war, no?"

"Of course," Manny replied.

"Then know that in any war, new weapons are developed to better fight one's enemies."

"Weapons?"

"Classified weapons. I can tell you no more, but I will stress the importance of discretion. All you need know is that he is on our side and will be of great importance in the coming days."

What the fuck?

James's answer seemed to mollify Manny, though, who nodded knowingly and turned his attention back to Calibra.

Unfortunately, it had the opposite effect on me.

What the fuck did he know about Ed that I didn't?

* * *

Calibra stayed behind, telling us she'd catch up shortly. We'd agreed beforehand to visit all uncompromised Village Coven lairs first, saving one for last in case those didn't pan out. It was risky returning to the office. It was an active crime scene now. There were bound to be cops still there, even with all the weird shit happening in the city.

As if to accentuate this point, a strange cry pierced the night as we made our way back to the subway tunnel entrance.

"What the fuck?" Tom asked, having finally recovered from having his brains scrambled.

"River Naga," James said offhandedly, trudging forward as if that sort of thing were normal. "We can assume one has taken up residence nearby. You may wish to avoid the waterways for the time being. They are not on our side."

"Um, okay," I replied, making a note to grab my Monster Manual the second I got home. "So, what was that stuff about Ed back there?" I glanced back at my roommate, but he raised his hands and waved me off, apparently knowing when to keep his mouth shut.

"Huh?"

"Ed. You said he was a weapon being..."

"Oh, that?" he replied dismissively. "A lie, made up to pacify them. Nothing more. I was hoping perhaps one of you could enlighten me." The weird thing was, his tone suggested otherwise - as if Ed's odd new condition was the furthest thing from his mind. Even so, he had piqued my curiosity.

"Why didn't you just compel them to forget him, then?"

"Did you see their eyes, Dr. Death?" he asked, giving me only the barest of looks. "Fear is a very strong emotion, and they were terrified. Even with my power, it is possible such a compulsion wouldn't hold for long.

Then what? We just barely managed to maintain order during the Icon incident."

Hopefully, he didn't notice me wince. It was far more than a mere incident to me.

"The last thing we need is another panic. If they think your friend is some sort of secret weapon, though, that becomes a completely different story. They will be curious, but that curiosity will be tempered by knowing that one doesn't pry into the affairs of the First."

"And if they blab?" Ed asked.

"Then they shall be doing us a favor - spreading word that we are even more formidable. They will foster confidence instead of chaos."

Holy shit, that was pretty fucking smart. He'd essentially turned their frowns upside down with just a few well-placed spoonfuls of bullshit. It was impressive.

"Do not get me wrong." He stopped and turned to face us, his gaze falling on Ed primarily. "There will be an accounting for this."

That wouldn't be pretty for any of us. I seriously doubted it would shed more light on the situation other than our compounded lies. We'd been ordered to hunt down Sheila and instead allied with her - tried to save her. For me, there was never any other option.

"I do not know what you are other than not fully human. I have sensed as much since I arrived. That was faith magic you somehow employed, yet you are no Icon."

"How do you..."

"Please." James softened his tone a bit. "I observed you all up in Canada. In my many years, I have come to trust in my judgment of others. I can tell you are a loyal friend of Dr. Death's, but a man of even moderate faith? I think not."

I chuckled, despite the seriousness of the situation. It was either laugh or run off screaming into the night.

Fortunately for us all, Tom's lack of tact in situations like these was sometimes a near godsend. "So what has you so spooked?"

That was a double facepalm for Ed and me. There were so many better ways to ask such a question than to insinuate one of the most powerful creatures we'd ever met was shaking in his boots like a preteen in a haunted corn maze. One of these days, I really needed to take out a large life insurance policy on him. The odds of collecting were certainly in my favor.

James, though, proving that he was perhaps as spooked as my friend had implied, merely uttered a sigh as he reached the stairs leading down to the subway. "Many of these myths are from before my time. I had hoped my remembrance of them was wrong, which is partially why I left Colin behind."

"I'm not following," I replied.

"Believe me when I say that I fully understand your feelings toward my assistant." James started downward into the closed station, pausing only to casually rip the locked gate open. "I am well aware that even on his best days, Colin is near insufferable."

"Then why..."

"Because he is good at what he does. He is highly organized and has a near photographic memory. Our archives are not like some sort of...Wikipedia page. They are vast and have been laid down in myriad of tomes across a multitude of languages - some long dead. I doubt even Lord Alexander could retrieve certain bits of lore quickly. Yet Colin has an almost preternatural ability to make sense of them, cross referencing their many secrets. Before leaving, I gave him full authority to access them."

That didn't sound good. Knowledge was power, and James had handed a potential atom bomb to a smarmy dickhead who just so happened to despise me. "Isn't that a bit...risky?"

"Perhaps, but not as risky as what has potentially been unleashed against us."

"Is that what he called about?"

"Yes, and now with the eyewitness accounts by the Howard Beach Coveners to back up your own claims, I fear we are hunting a creature who may be far more than just a vampire with dissenting political leanings."

He turned and faced us again, the dark tunnel looming behind him.

"The Cult of Ib has returned."

The Cult of Ib

"I think I speak for all of us when I ask, what's a Cult of Ib?"

"Yeah," Ed added. "And why was he coming after me earlier? Normally, when things go to shit, Bill is the target."

"Thanks."

"Don't mention it."

Things were unnaturally quiet. I mean, I've been in far more than my fair share of the New York City underground and there's usually something scurrying about. Now it was silent, save for the occasional drip of water. I began to wonder if the rats knew something we didn't.

Luckily for us, James was around to entertain us with a *ghost story* as we continued walking along the exceedingly spooky tunnel.

"We were not always the civilized beings you know us as."

"Civilized?" my roommates and I rang out in unison.

"Comparatively speaking, of course," James added with a chuckle that held no humor.

"So this Ib, is he the guy we're looking for?"

"Of course not," he replied dismissively. "I have no idea who our quarry is yet and nothing to go on but his actions - which are potentially disturbing enough. Ib, however, is a myth."

"So, what, he's like some sort of god or demon?" Tom asked.

"Hardly. According to some of our legends, Ib was the original vampire - the first of us to walk this Earth."

* * *

I couldn't help but feel underwhelmed by his revelation. I mean, what the fuck kind of name was Ib? Dracula, now that's kind of cool. In Marvel Comics, it was some dude named Varnae - not exactly soul-searingly terrifying, but still not too bad. But Ib? That sounded like something an online gamer might name their pet Iguana.

"So what was this *Ib* like?"

"I honestly have no idea. As I said, I believe the tale to be myth or allegory. All cultures have beliefs about creation. Why should ours be any different? The progenitor of our species is unimportant, though. What matters are his zealots and the atrocities they committed in his name."

This was starting to get interesting, albeit disturbing at the same time. I was always fascinated to hear some of our ancient history - at least the shit that involved blood and guts. The political crap could put me to sleep faster than my college philosophy lectures. Considering his tone, though, I had the feeling James's story wasn't going to explore the finer details of robust metaphysical debate.

"You are well aware of our current social hierarchy. The coven system has been in place for millennia. It is structured, orderly, and has allowed us to grow alongside humanity in a symbiotic manner. It may not always be fair, but it is logical in its..."

"Watch out, Bill!"

A hand fell upon my shoulder and dragged me to the left, causing me to stumble.

"What the fuck, man?" I turned to glare at Tom.

"You almost stepped on the third rail." He shined the beam of his flashlight ahead of me - not that I needed it to see.

"Oh...thanks."

"Don't mention it."

Vampire or not, that could have been a somewhat embarrassing fate. It was well known amongst city dwellers that those things delivered a shit-ton of voltage, enough to make me wish I was still being tazed in my dungeon cell. I made it a point to pay better attention to where I was walking.

James continued talking on despite our mishap behind him. Fortunately, he was still just blathering on about covens and the First - explaining things as if I hadn't been dragged kicking and screaming into the world of vampire politics.

"...The Cult, though, couldn't have been more at odds with our modern way of thinking. Their primary beliefs centered on mysticism and portents. The advancements of man held no interest for them."

"Hold on a second. So what about all that prophecy bullshit everyone's been shoving down my throat? That sounds pretty mystic to me. Oh, and those blind psychics in the cave of heavy drugs weren't exactly calling up this shit on their iPhones."

James stopped in his tracks and I nearly bumped into him. "You actually met the elder seers?"

"Yeah. Alex took me on a field trip to see them. I told you earlier."

"Interesting," he mused. "They and the prophecies are hold overs - the last remnants of the old ways. Magic is most obviously real, so we would be fools to ignore it entirely. However, for the most part, we do not let it govern our day-to-day lives. As for the seers, rumor has it their order is actually descended from the Cult."

"Oh?"

"I have heard it said, although none have ever confirmed it to me, that the blinding ritual is only partially to attune their senses. Some say it was originally instituted as punishment, so that they would never forget their place in this world."

"Is it me," Ed asked, "or does none of this make much fucking sense so far?"

"Indeed it does not," James replied. "As I said, much of this was thought to be just rumor or myth -

anecdotes to keep the younger vampires amused. Now I begin to fear it may be more than that."

"So what if it is?" I asked. "Seriously, what harm is a bunch of mystics right now? What are they gonna do, sit around and get stoned while everyone else is off fighting Bigfoot?" Truth be told, that didn't sound so bad to me. Hell, if that were the case, I'd consider signing up.

James spun around to face me. "It is very simple." He raised a hand and poked my chest for effect - a small token effort on his part, but it packed enough power behind it to make me wince in pain. "This group of stoned mystics, as you so flippantly put it, nearly destroyed us all twelve hundred years ago."

Oh, well, when he put it that way...

* * *

As we made our way slowly back to Manhattan, James continued to explain things. I'd known a bit about our war with the Feet and how the vampires had sided with mankind to fight them off - resulting in the Humbaba Accord, a treaty that had held the peace for about five thousand years...that is, until yours truly came along.

According to him, the Cult of Ib rose to prominence shortly after the treaty was signed - long before we were organized into covens and the formation of the Draculas. At first, they served as a priesthood of sorts for the vampire world, but as their power grew, they assumed partial influence over the warrior caste as well.

The problem? These guys were fucking psychos. They were the role models such kindly folks as the Assyrians and Aztecs based their cultures on. We're talking blood sacrifices, genocidal culling, the works.

Their shit eventually started to seriously tick off the more progressive-minded members of the vampire community - not to mention the humans who were busy forming their own empires.

If you're thinking this powder keg eventually ignited into a bloody-ass civil war, give yourself a cigar. What a surprise - super-powered beings eventually decided to kick each other's asses rather than talk through their problems. Sounds like comic book material to me.

"Okay, so it was vamps killing vamps." Tom said, wheezing a bit. The long walk had started to catch up to him.

Thankfully, the five of us were nearing our destination - Calibra had caught up with us at some point around Canal Street.

"It was far more than that," James explained. "It was a very different world in those days. Freewills mercilessly led the charge on either side. Wholesale slaughter became commonplace. Come the sunrise, it is said ash covered whole battlefields. What we had all fought so hard to avoid at the hands of the Feet..."

Tom and I dissolved into laughter at that.

Calibra bared her fangs, no doubt to remind us of how fucking disrespectful we were being, but James waved her off.

"I am well used to it by now," he said with just a touch of sarcasm before continuing. "The chaos we had fought so hard to avoid was now in danger of consuming us wholly. The Cult was relentless. They used everything they had to their advantage and nearly succeeded."

"So what happened?" I asked.

"Humans. Seeing that the Cult of Ib would not stop until the entire world had bled out for them, the few vestiges of humanity who still remembered the days of the Humbaba Accord rallied to our side. They entered the fray just as our defenses were about to crumble. Magi and Icons alike bolstered their forces. The tide turned until, eventually, the Cult was crushed and their leadership scattered."

"I've heard it said that Alexander was rewarded with a promotion to the ranks of the First for his bravery during that final battle," Calibra said, drawing our attention.

"Oh?" James replied. "I did not know that."

"It's just rumor, of course."

"Of course," he said. "Regardless, the Cult was hunted down over the next hundred years - destroyed to the last man."

"Apparently not," Tom rightfully mused.

"Evidently, and that is what disturbs me most. The archives make mention that none of the Cult were to be spared, not even as the decollari."

"Let me guess," I said. "It's because they were afraid of what's happening right now?"

James stiffened as he walked, giving me his answer before he voiced it. "Precisely."

Some days, I really hated being right.

Sunset is Never Far Away

The sewer entrance for the office was sealed tight. Usually, nobody paid any attention to it. Nobody human, that is. Now, however, the manhole cover leading up to the subbasement wouldn't budge. That was probably my fault as well, seeing as how I'd fallen to the bottom of the elevator shaft with a mutilated corpse in tow - a mess I certainly hadn't time to clean up.

"Allow me."

James put his back into it and there came a loud squeal of metal - echoing for some time down in the tunnels. Once the heavy duty locks snapped, I was near certain that we'd ascend to find a small arsenal of riot guns pointed at us.

Instead, nothing but darkness and quiet greeted us, like it would any other night. However, this was definitely unlike any other night I remembered. In the space of less than forty-eight hours, the world had apparently lost its fucking mind.

"Notice anything?" Ed asked.

"Yeah, it's a basement," I replied.

"Not you, jackass."

"Difficult to say," James said. "The smell of blood is heavy down here, but there are too many other scents to be more specific: old wiring, mildew, greased electronics, a cot belonging to a maintenance employee who doesn't believe in washing his hands after masturbating." He gestured toward what I thought to be a janitor's closet. Note to self: don't touch anything in there *ever*.

"Vampires?" I asked, not smelling nearly as much as he did - and quite thankful of it for once.

"Their passage, yes. Recent, too, but it unfortunately doesn't give me insight into whether any are still here."

"Only one way to find out," Tom said.

He had a point, although I'd be lying my ass off if I claimed to be looking forward to a rematch with Chuck. That being said, I felt a shitload better knowing who had my back. "Let's use the stairs. Elevators are out...trust me on this one. Everyone set?"

"Not all of us," James said.

"Oh?" Tom replied defensively. He must have expected to be told this was vampire business. Fucking twit. He didn't seem to realize that if James didn't want him there, he wouldn't be there. He'd already had his brains scrambled by one compulsion this night. Guess that wasn't enough for him.

"Indeed," James replied, turning to Calibra. "Please go and wait for us in the safe house, the one in which we met Dr. Death and his companions."

"Wanderer?" she asked questioningly.

"I know your conviction to your duties. Believe me, I do not doubt them. The situation, however, has changed. What was a disturbing hunch has now become a frightening reality. I need someone in authority to coordinate a response should our search here prove fruitful."

Wait...fruitful? Was James basically telling her what I thought he was - that even he wasn't sure he'd make it out of this alive? So much for feeling better about things.

Calibra put up a mild argument, but she was too ingrained in the vampire hierarchy to do much more. When one of the Draculas started handing out orders, the only ones who questioned them were the insane or the stupid.

Considering my habit of doing such, that left me wondering which of the two that made me.

* * *

James told Calibra to give us until sunrise before calling in the troops. That gave us a little under two hours. Considering the safe house wasn't too far away, we'd have plenty of time to search the office and discover it empty - or get pummeled into tiny bits of goo if it wasn't. For the record, despite the worry I felt for Dave, Starlight, and even Firebird, I still hoped for that former scenario.

The stairwell was empty and dark. Perhaps this building was experiencing a similar outage as we'd seen at the safe house. It seemed a likely explanation.

We made it up only a few flights before James declared, "A lot of humans died here today...some very recently." That didn't exactly fill me with warm fuzzies. "Gunfire, too."

"Police?"

"I can smell nine-millimeter discharge, so that is distinctly possible."

"You can tell that?" Ed asked.

"I can tell a great many things," he replied with a wry grin, "including that you used exactly one spritz of Drakkar Noir to freshen up your clothing yesterday and your friend here last showered with Axe body wash, but used Dove ladies' deodorant afterwards."

I stopped in my ascent to peer at Tom.

"What? Christy left it in the bathroom."

"I hope she didn't leave any douche behind too," Ed muttered.

"I'd say we already know the answer to that one," I replied before turning to James. "The people that were killed, were they..."

"Some. They're likely to be feral, so be on your guard."

He didn't need to tell me that twice.

* * *

The door to the office's main floor had been locked and sealed, unsurprisingly, with police tape - *had* being the operative word. Whatever had broken in before our arrival had done so with supernatural strength, using the old vampire trick of turning the knob until the tumblers snapped.

A soft thud from the next landing alerted me a split second before James said, "Movement above."

"We rent that floor, too, for storage. Occasionally, some of the group will sack out there. Maybe..."

"I concur. It bears investigation."

"Human or vamp?"

"It is difficult to tell. A great deal of vampire scent is lingering on this floor, most of it recent. There's much more, though: blood, smoke mixed with fresh air, and the trace of an ashing as well." He no doubt sniffed Monkhbat's last stand. "This was the epicenter of whatever occurred here."

Hell, I could've told him that. "Should we go up?"

"I am reluctant to give up the high ground before we've secured this floor."

That sounded like a good strategy...similar to what Obi Wan warned Anakin about right before he made the whiney little fucker two feet shorter.

"Shouldn't someone guard the door?" Ed asked.

"When's the last time you watched a horror movie, genius? You *never* split up."

"Actually, your friend's advice is sound," James corrected, earning me a victory smirk from my douche of a roommate.

"It would be wise to have warning should an attack be imminent."

"Tom or Ed?"

"Neither. No offense, but if one of our kind decides that hostilities are in order, they would both most likely die before they could even cry out an alarm."

I was kind of doubtful on that front. My friends had faced off against vamps or worse. They'd certainly get a chance to scream their heads off before being horribly killed.

Still, I got what James had implied. A lookout who could both fight off a potential attack and, if not, at least have a chance in hell of outrunning their assailant was preferable. "I guess I'm on guard duty."

"Have fun," Tom said as he and Ed turned to follow James.

"You're both ditching me?"

"Sorry, man, but we stuck with you in Brooklyn and almost got our asses kicked. Time to mix it up a bit."

Dickheads. However, they had a point. They were my best friends, but James could fell a bull elephant with a punch. I'd have chosen him too.

Fortunately, it's not like they'd be going far. Hell, it's not like there was even a door to obscure the view inside anymore. "Okay, guys. I've got..."

The prophecy is a lie. One of your own shall be the downfall of your filthy race.

Once more, the voice of Harry Decker carried through the air. I didn't know what the fuck it meant, but it sure as shit got our attention.

* * *

I abandoned my post without a second thought and the four of us raced into the office. The main section was as I'd left it...a fucking mess. They hadn't even boarded up the windows that'd been smashed. Cold air blew in freely, bringing with it the scent of smoke that James had mentioned.

But that was it. There was nothing in the room save for a bunch of office furniture, a good deal of it smashed to all hell.

"The back offices," I said, leading the way. That's where I'd heard his voice last time - more specifically, the main corner suite. I thought maybe I'd gone loopy the first time, having just gotten pummeled by Chuck. Now, though, I had to think differently. The others had heard it too. Shit, it had been loud enough to wake the dead. Almost as if it'd been broadcast in my head...

That thought just barely had time to coalesce when three things happened in short order. First, I reached the corner office by way of the hole I'd been thrown through earlier, then James cried out a warning to wait just as a very familiar scent reached my nostrils.

Oh, did I say three things? I meant four. Right as I crossed the threshold, a well-manicured fist shot out from the side, sending me flying.

Before I'd even landed, I knew the owner of said office had returned to claim it.

I found myself on the floor, looking up as Sally stepped out and stood over me, looking none too pleased.

"What the fuck have you done to my coven?"

A Bird in the Hand is Worth Two in the Ambush

A mix of emotions ran through my head, as well as a good chunk of pain as I waited for my jaw to reset itself. Before I could say anything, though, Sally hauled me to my feet and threw her arms around me.

"Don't you *ever* run off again, asshole."

Stunned as I was, I hugged her back. Goddamn, I hadn't realized how much I'd missed her. It was like having my arm chopped off, only to find it regrown - a not entirely impossible occurrence when you're undead.

Sadly, this probably wasn't the time for us to get too sappy with each other. "This would be a lot nicer if you weren't wearing that shir...OOF!"

Her knee came up so fast it was almost like she'd expected me to say something like that. Note to self: next time, back up a step before opening my mouth.

I crumpled to the floor, the moment obviously over.

"Welcome back," Ed said as he stepped forward, ignoring my obvious trauma. The whole band of brothers thing went right out the window when a piece of ass was up for grabs. "I missed...I mean, *we've* missed you."

She looked around and took in the destruction. "It's good to be back...sorta."

Not quite getting the memo that now was probably a poor time to flirt, he tried again. "You didn't say goodbye."

"I also didn't snap your neck before leaving. Not every guy can make that claim."

"Fascinating, I'm sure." James stepped in between them. "While I am not entirely surprised to find you here, I had thought us clear on the importance of your current post."

"Don't worry. Steve has things covered back at Pandora."

"Who's Steve?" I croaked, slowly pulling myself to my feet.

"A more competent vampire than you," she said offhandedly, falling right back into it as if we'd last talked just a few hours ago.

"Be that as it may," James replied, "I was under the impression that..."

"I'd do the right thing?" she questioned, not breaking eye contact with him. What the hell were they talking about? "I was thinking that over and came to the conclusion that the right choice was where I could do the most good. Sure, I was helping people out there in Vegas, but realized I could potentially help them a lot more by coming back."

"Wait, *you* were helping people?" Tom asked. "How?"

"By relieving them of all their troubles. Care for a demonstration, meatbag?"

"That's quite all right," he replied, backing up slowly.

James appeared to consider things. I wasn't sure what was going on, but it seemed painfully obvious he'd been aware of Sally's relocation. What that meant, though, I had no idea.

"Under different circumstances, I would be concerned over what could be construed as negligence toward upholding one's assigned duties. The situation has changed, however. You may very well be right in your assumption."

"Tell me about it," she replied. "I'm surprised my plane landed in one piece. I don't know what the fuck was circling around JFK, but they sure as shit weren't seagulls."

"I was referring to what's been going on here. Speaking of which..." He tilted his head as if listening. "I dare say we forgot to guard the stairwell."

* * *

Something hissed from near the doorway a split second after James's warning. All our heads turned to find about a dozen vampires piling in, their eyes blackened and no trace of humanity showing on their faces.

"Yours?" he asked.

"None that I've met."

"They aren't my recruits, either," Sally added.

My roommates wisely moved to a position behind the rest of us as James said, "They must be freshly risen, then - quite possibly within the past hour."

Sure enough, the dress of the vamps seemed to reinforce this. Half were in business suits, but there was a janitor and several uniformed cops amongst their number. The only question regarding that latter group, though, was whether they'd been victims of the original attack or had been left behind to watch over the premises and pulled the most unlucky guard duty shift ever.

I raised my fists. I wasn't too worried about the vamps individually, but wasn't a big fan of being dog-piled, either.

"*STAND DOWN!!*" James commanded. "*CEASE ALL HOSTILITIES!!*"

Oh...I had completely forgotten about compulsion. Duh! Yeah, I guess that would probably be a bit less messy than fighting them.

Or maybe not.

His compulsion was powerful as all fuck. While it couldn't control me, it could most certainly make me feel as if somebody had set off a hand grenade in my skull.

The vampires before us barely shrugged, though. Additionally, whatever hostile actions they had planned sure as shit didn't cease.

"What the fuck?"

"An apt question indeed, Dr. Death," James replied, confusion evident in his voice.

Your end has come, dismembered by the claws of destiny.

My roommates and I all spun around. Even James turned his head as Harry Decker's voice once more cried out from nowhere.

Only Sally seemed unfazed. "Oh, will you shut the fuck up already?"

What the...?

Unfortunately, the feral vamps converging upon us picked that moment to charge forward.

* * *

The battle was brief, but brutal - helped in part because they all ignored us and went straight after Ed. It wasn't until we got in their way that they engaged us.

I doubted a dozen newly risen vamps would have been a match for James were he alone, but he wasn't. Sally and I were there to back him up, while my roommates made sure we weren't flanked. There was no strategy to the attack. The vamps in question acted like little more than rabid animals. Hell, a few of them even tried to bite me and James, seemingly not caring that doing so would reduce them to quivering balls of puke.

Had they their wits about them, they might have realized that was the kinder fate. Sally snapped off a desk leg and dusted two of them. I managed to take down one. James, though, provided a perfect reminder of why he was on my "do not fuck with" list. He'd barely extended his claws before four plumes of ash exploded where there had been vamps a moment prior. The remainder leapt upon him en masse...for all of two seconds.

"That was most disturbing," he said a moment later, dusting himself off.

"You ain't shitting us, dude," Tom replied, wide-eyed. "You fucked them up before they even knew they were being fucked."

"I wasn't speaking of that, sadly."

"You mean how they ignored your compulsion?" Sally asked, echoing what the rest of us were probably thinking.

"That in of itself is worrisome. But it is how they were able to do so that disturbs me most."

"Why?" I asked, curious.

"As I mentioned earlier, these vampires were freshly risen. The blood upon them, their own, had barely dried. I wouldn't hesitate to guess they were still turning as we entered the building."

"Okay, so they woke up hungry."

"No," Sally said flatly. "They woke up compelled."

* * *

"What do you mean, woke up compelled? I'm not following."

"Good to see you haven't changed..." She stopped and gave me the once over. "Did you lose some weight?"

"Well, I'm not one to brag, but..."

"Children!" James snapped. "What is it with you two? The problem, if I may be allowed to address it, is that whoever compelled them did so before they were fully turned - quite possibly as they were being attacked."

He turned toward my roommate. "They came to this floor specifically, it would seem, to attack you. May I ask a question? Were you, perhaps, bitten earlier by the cultist we are searching for?"

"Wait, what cultist?" Sally asked.

"All in good time, my dear. Please answer the question."

"Yeah," Ed replied. "He tried to take a chunk out of me...back when he was still looking like Skeletor. It definitely hurt him, but obviously not as much as that HBC vamp."

Sally raised a curious eyebrow. Obviously, I was in for a long night of bringing her up to speed - amongst a million other things.

James waved her off for now, though, his expression becoming more serious by the moment. "This is all painting a very grim picture. The art of compelling a victim before they have fully turned is both subtle and powerful. In the past, vampire lords were known to do so in order to plant assassins amongst their enemies. That I couldn't easily undo the compulsion speaks to that power."

"So why me?" Ed asked.

James appeared to mull this over. "My knowledge of the Cult of Ib is limited. The purge of their existence was quite thorough. Only members of the First and their closest advisors are allowed access to those archives, and I must admit to being a bit distracted since ascending to their ranks to continue my studies of ancient history. That I suspected them at all is pure luck, gained through whispers heard when I was in service to the Khan. All that being said, I believe his motivation could be quite simple. To him, you are an aberration."

"I'll try not to be offended."

"Don't be. The Cult of Ib were said to be purists of the highest order. I dare say, had they survived, they would have found the standards of Hitler's Aryan Nation to be, how do you say it, wishy washy."

"So they were racist assholes?"

"Something of the sort. Within our kind, they acknowledged only two variants: normal vampires and Freewills. Dr. Death, do you remember when I mentioned compiling a list of extraordinary vampires for the war effort?"

"Yeah. Gan was on that list for being a creepy little psycho or something like that."

"Close enough," he acknowledged. "Well, I believe the Cult would have allowed no such thing. Had they been in power, she would not have made it out of her formative years."

"Yeah, but *I'm* not a vamp," Ed pointed out.

"I would not be so certain if I were you." James leaned in for a sniff. "I do detect the faintest hint of our taint upon your person."

Ed turned to me. "Remind me to never hug you again."

I reached up to scratch my head with my middle finger. "Remind me to keep my door locked so you don't go touching my taint again."

"Yet there is something about you that channels faith magic," James continued, ignoring us. "In accepting Freewills, it seems logical that the Cult may have likewise acknowledged Icons as honored enemies. Such things are not unheard of. You are neither, though. To them, you would be..."

"An abomination?" I offered, remembering the word Chuck had spoken earlier.

James didn't reply. His look said it all. The shit pile we stood in was getting deeper by the minute, and I had a feeling the bottom would soon drop out beneath us.

Headquarters is Where the Heart is

James spent the next hour combing through the wreckage of the office - including the elevator as he surveyed the damage done when I'd been trapped with the unluckiest tourist ever. A few more newbs came searching for us during that time, all intent on tearing Ed a new asshole, but Sally and I took care of them fairly quickly.

All the while, I brought her up to speed - making sure to give an edited version of my tale, at least for now while James was in earshot.

"So you really can't turn into that thing anymore?"

"Not right now anyway."

"Pity. It was kind of cute."

"Really?" I asked, my interest most definitely piqued.

She held a straight face for about two seconds and then cracked up laughing. Bitch!

Damn, it was good to have her back.

Sadly, she wasn't quite as forthcoming as to what she'd been up to, insisting she'd just grown tired of waiting for me and needed a change of venue. I might not be the most clued-in fellow walking the planet, but I could smell bullshit when it was being spoon fed to me.

She kept glancing sidelong toward my roommates while telling her tale, which was likewise a bit odd. I could understand it with Ed - sorta - but she kept looking at Tom as if expecting him to say something. What, had she gotten into a drunken threesome with him and Christy while I was gone?

I was busy mulling that over, considering the concept from all angles - especially the ones requiring a great deal of flexibility - when James rejoined us.

"I believe I have a solid lock on our quarry's scent."

"That's great," I said. It was the first real break we'd gotten all night. A vampire like me could perform reasonably well as a tracker. One as old as James, though, would be like a shark sniffing for blood in the water. Hell, Gan was half his age and she seemed to have the infuriating ability to track me down from miles away, like some kind of micro-chipped pet.

"Perhaps not." He stepped toward the broken windows and breathed in the early morning air. It was still saturated with the smell of smoke. I'd been so focused on our task that I'd forgotten about the outside world. Sirens still echoed through the corridors of this vast concrete jungle: a mix of police, fire, and ambulance alike.

How many people were in the hospital right now? Hell, how many weren't even that lucky?

And what was *I* doing? I was on a snipe hunt for some crazy-ass vamp. Sure, the guy was dangerous, but he was just one small threat in a world that seemed to be rapidly filling with hostile monsters.

"What's happening out there?"

"Is it not obvious?" he replied, still staring out. "It has begun."

"So this is it?"

"This is nothing. A few advance scouts causing chaos for the sake of chaos. Soon, the brunt of the attacks will begin - small skirmishes will level towns and major battles will leave behind a wake of destruction not seen since the last World War. Our forces will meet those of the enemy and..."

"Speaking of our forces," Sally interrupted, "why is this clown compelling the shit out of my coven and those HBC assholes?"

"Your coven?" I asked.

"There's only one vamp here right now who's a coven master, and it ain't you."

"There's also only one tramp here who's a..."

"I am not sure," James replied, cutting off our banter. "All I do know is that if he is here, he has hidden himself quite well."

"Oh?"

"Yes. I couldn't be certain earlier, but now that I have isolated his scent, I realize only lingering amounts have been present in the places we've been tonight. Whoever our friend may be, I would venture to guess he's vacated this city. Wherever he has gone, it is entirely likely he may have brought your compelled coven with him."

"But what about those vamps that ambushed us?"

"Those were nothing. Cannon fodder left behind as an afterthought, if I had to guess. The recently turned know nothing of us or our ways. Most of our kind would sacrifice them without a second thought."

"Go ahead and eat one. We'll make more," I commented under my breath.

"More or less, true."

"Well, let me grab a few things and then let's get going," Sally said. "We need to find this asshole and get our people back."

"Oh, is that caring I hear creeping into your voice?"

She shot me a glare, but to my amazement, it softened as she replied, "Starlight's the best admin I ever had. Would be a shame to let some other employer have her without at least making a counteroffer."

I decided to keep any asshole remarks to myself for once. Her tone betrayed her words and I understood what she meant. There were also Dave and Firebird to worry about. Hell, even the HBC vamps probably deserved...

While you idle like fools, your seat of power shall burn around you.

My roommates and I jumped again at the disembodied outburst. Damn, that was getting annoying.

"And *that's* one of the things I need to grab," Sally blithely said as she stepped back toward her office.

"Yeah, about that," I called after her. "Any chance you care to explain why I keep hearing Harry Decker's fucking voice reverberating around in my head? It's starting to creep me out."

James turned away from the windows, his eyebrows raised. "That was the Magi we temporarily aligned with, was it not?"

"Also the one who blew the shit out of most of my coven," I helpfully reminded him.

"The one and the same," Sally said over her shoulder. "He was one of the *unfortunate* casualties of that little adventure." Her tone conveyed that she found his passing to be about as sad as I did. "Once the dust settled and our alliance dissolved, I figured nobody would mind if I made an ashtray out of his noggin."

That was surprising enough for me, but it definitely caught Tom's full attention. "Oh, shit, Christy's gonna fucking flip when she hears that."

"Well then, make sure she doesn't find out. Loose lips sink dipshits."

James stepped forward, his look thoughtful. "Are you saying you have the skull of an Arch-Magi?"

"Sounds like it," I said. "Pretty fucked-up. Although I can't say I'm not tempted to put out a cigar in that dickhead's eye socket."

"No," he replied, following Sally toward the back. The rest of us joined him, intrigued as to where this was going. "These outbursts, have they happened before?"

"Been happening on and off since I got him," Sally said, stuffing items from her former desk into a shoulder bag. "Used to really freak the others out."

She picked up the skull I'd seen earlier and packed it away. Harry Decker, former VP of marketing at my old job, I presume. I was half-tempted to steal it and mail it to the CEO of Hopskotchgames. Let it serve as warning to all overpaid, but nigh useless, executives.

James, however, seemed to have a more practical use in mind. "I think we may be able to deduce where our friend is going."

"How so?" I asked. "For all we know, he just got freaked out by all the technology around him and decided to head for someplace simpler - maybe hole himself up in a barn or some shit."

"I don't think so," he replied. "My sire once told me a tale of how his father used the bones of a sorcerer to help plot out his campaigns, learning his enemies' weak points so as to strike them down more efficiently. We have not been at odds with the Magi in centuries, so I have not seen it personally, but I have no reason to believe he was lying."

"Really? How?"

"The Magi are able to tap their own essences into extra-planar forces. It is said an experienced mage's entire being will become infused with that magic the more they utilize it. It is why witches were often burnt at the stake - to ensure no part of them remained viable. It is why it was once customary for chieftains to devour the hearts of any captured shamans so as to absorb their power."

"So you're saying this thing has residual magic in it?"

Sally stopped what she was doing to roll her eyes. "Well, duh. How many other screaming skulls have you come across? When most people put Grandpa's urn up the mantle, they don't expect it to keep yelling at them to get off the lawn."

"She has a point," Ed needlessly replied, no doubt trying to work his own form of magic on her. And yet they dared call me pathetic.

"A short while ago, the skull declared that we'd be attacked. That came to pass," James said, refusing to allow the rest of us to sidetrack him. He began to pace, his brow furrowed in thought. "Earlier, it told us our downfall would be by one of our own. Perhaps it was picking up what we were beginning to suspect about the danger of this cultist."

"Didn't it say something about the prophecy being bullshit?" Tom asked.

"Yes, but alas, we are already aware of that. The Icon's death has proven the future is malleable in ways..."

"It said something to me earlier, too," I interrupted, hoping to steer the conversation elsewhere. "Pretty much told me I'd get my ass kicked, and then voila...I got my ass kicked by this guy."

"It happened to me, too," Sally said, her eyes wide. "A couple of weeks ago, it said something about drowning in filth. I just never made the connection."

"What happened?" I asked.

"Let's just say the Las Vegas sewer system isn't a great place to be when a flash flood hits."

"Ewww."

"You have no idea."

"Okay, so this thing can somehow see things...sometimes before they happen," Ed surmised.

"Yeah, but why is it only bad things? I mean, it hasn't spit out any winning lottery numbers, has it?"

"I wish," Sally muttered with a sigh.

"Perhaps it has become an oracle of doom," James said. "Or, more likely, some part of its owner's spirit remains."

"And said spirit pretty much couldn't stand any of us," I pointed out. "The only thing the asshole seemed to like better than trying to kill me was gloating about it. Sounds like a logical theory to me."

"So, going with that," Ed said, "any time it speaks up, we'd do well to listen because shit is probably going to get real."

James nodded solemnly, his gears obviously spinning.

"Where's my gun?" Sally asked, still going through the drawers.

"Err...I think that guy stole it," I replied, earning a dirty glare from her. She no doubt saw through my lie. "Um, let's not worry about that for now. What was that thing Decker was just talking about?"

"Something about a seat of power being burnt to the ground," Tom said.

"Yeah, but that already happened. That asshole took down this place hours ago, unless there's some other super-secret coven hangout I don't know about." I looked toward Sally for that last part.

"Nope. I've been concentrating on recruiting, not real estate, these past few months."

"Maybe its City Hall," Tom stated, looking smug, as if he'd just solved a Rubik's Cube in record time. "He's gonna declare himself Duke of New York."

I narrowed my eyes at him, wondering how he came up with this shit. "This guy's been stuck in a jar for God knows how long. I'm pretty sure his first order of business upon kidnapping our coven wasn't to sit down with them and watch *Escape from New York*."

"Dr. Death is right," James said flatly as he looked at all of us. "In fact, New York isn't even in the equation any longer. He's gotten what he needed here."

"Two covens' worth of vampires?"

"Yes, vampires, some of whom are knowledgeable about our power structure. Coven Master Alice, the one you call Starlight, she's familiar with the layout, the staff..." He trailed off, looking almost ill. I really didn't like seeing him like this. Somehow, in the space of a second, it managed to erase all the hope I'd felt when he'd first arrived to help us out.

"You don't mean...?" Sally asked, leaving the question hanging.

"Sadly, I do. Our seat of power in this region. The stronghold from whence we have been coordinating all war efforts in the Northeast."

"Oh shit," I said, realization sinking in. "He's going after Boston."

It Sure Beats Driving

The first rays of sunlight had started to peek over the buildings of downtown Manhattan when we arrived back at the safe house. Due to the late hour and the chaos in the streets, we'd been forced to use the tunnels to make the return journey. Sadly, that rendered cell service unusable - something that in our rush we didn't bother to remember until we were well under way.

Calibra was in the living room, watching the news, when we walked through the front door. She barely even flinched when we entered. Obviously, she wasn't immune to the general arrogance any vampire over a century old seemed to be inflicted with.

"Wanderer," she said, rising. "Your timing is impeccable. Another few minutes and I would have carried out your orders. I trust the hunt was successful."

"Anything but," he replied, clearly agitated. "We will need to follow through, regardless. I just wish I had the foresight to have done so sooner."

"Wanderer?"

James ignored her, though. He already had his cell out and was dialing a number.

Calibra looked toward the rest of us, her eyes briefly settling upon Sally as if to size her up. "I know you."

Recognition flashed in Sally's eyes after a moment. "Aren't you that bitch who..."

"Prefect," she corrected, her tone dangerous. "I am Calibra, Prefect of the Northeastern Covens. Now would you care to reword that question?"

"About you being a bitch? Not at all. I'm outside of your jurisdiction. Sally," she said, holding out her hand, "master of Pandora Coven, Las Vegas."

"Please," James hissed, "we do not have time for games."

"Oh yeah," I said, trying to ward off any potential conflict. "Listen, Calibra, you need to get on the horn with Boston now."

"I don't take orders from..."

"Don't argue! Just do it because if we're right, then they're about to receive some very unpleasant company."

She narrowed her eyes at my insolence, but stopped short of kicking my ass in front of company. "I was speaking to my staff manager just an hour ago, going over invoices from the past quarter. There was nothing amiss to..."

"There will be," James said as he hung up from his call. "I regret the breach in protocol, but I have put Colin temporarily in charge of the Boston office until such time as we are able to relieve him personally."

Calibra looked ever so slightly miffed, her ego probably superseding the urgency she should have noticed in his voice. Or it could have just been about Colin. I'd have blanched, too, if someone told me they'd handed over my job to that shit-burger.

She composed herself quickly, though, no doubt remembering that she was speaking to one of the Draculas. Their word was law. If they ordered you to jam a pogo stick up your ass and like it, you'd best start bouncing around with a smile on your face. "How bad is it?"

"Unknown," James replied, "but we can ill afford any disruption at this time. Our troops are mobilized around the globe. They are counting on us to provide them with guidance and intelligence. If one of our seats of power falters this early in the conflict, it could very well have a domino effect."

She nodded, finally getting the hint. "I'll put our people on high alert."

"Already done."

"The strike teams?"

"Taking up defensive positions."

"Strike teams?" I asked. "Where..."

"Trust me, Dr. Death," he said. "You have seen but the very tip of the iceberg of our operations up north. Believe me when I say our facilities house far more than just offices."

"What kind of chance do they have if this guy shows up?" Ed asked.

Calibra visibly bristled, displeased as what amounted to a walking juice box voiced an opinion. "That is none of your concern, human."

I stepped up next to my friend. "Fine, what about me asking, then?"

"I have placed the entire facility on high alert," James replied. "They will be able to repulse a sizable force now that they are aware of the threat."

"But what about this other vamp?" Ed pressed. "You said it yourself - only someone really powerful could do what he did. Couldn't he just compel them all to surrender and join him?"

Calibra chuckled in response, as if my roommate had told a clever knock-knock joke. "Believe me, human, unlike the covens of this city, our facility is not staffed by children. They have been conditioned against all such contingencies."

"Conditioned?" Tom and I asked in unison.

"Via compulsion," Sally said. "Not unlike how thralls are made, if I'm not mistaken."

"As usual, my dear, you are quite insightful," James replied fondly. "Yes. All of the staff at regional facilities are given several deep compulsions over time, subtly reinforcing their subconscious minds and creating a barrier of sorts."

"So you're insulating them," she replied. "Kind of like what you did to me with Jeff..."

"Similar, but far more complex. A more powerful vampire can undo a simple compulsion under normal circumstances. There is simply no way to fully insulate another from that. What we can do, though, is provide protection against specific directives. Loyalty to their station and the First are continually compelled within them by multiple levels of management, each weaving their own strands of the thread. Where one rope may snap under pressure, a finely woven net will hold strong. Do you understand?"

She nodded, as did me and Ed. Tom, unsurprisingly, had a blank look on his face. "So you...put a net in their heads?"

"Yeah, everyone wears a psychic hairnet, Einstein," I said, then turned back to James. "So everything is good, then?"

"Perhaps. But the same cannot be said of the covens along the way. If he were to raise a sizable enough force..."

"They'd be decimated by our tactical teams," Calibra said smugly. "No offense intended, Wanderer, but Boston is equipped to repel an extended assault from the Grendel themselves, even if aided by up to a class six entity. I very much doubt..."

"Grendel?" Tom asked.

"Class six entity?" I echoed, voicing my own confusion.

"The Feet," Sally explained, at least answering my roommate's question.

"Yes, of course," Calibra corrected herself. "The Feet."

"Regardless of our preparations, I believe it is time for us to return," James stated. "The others of the First must be made aware of this."

I was tempted to ask about that class six thing again, but decided to let it drop for now. There was every reason to believe I'd probably learn what that was eventually - most likely because one would be trying to eat my face off. Besides, his mention of the First was the more pressing concern to me at the moment.

"Do we really need to do that?" I asked. "I mean, if Boston can repulse this clown like a gnat, then there really isn't a problem." I left unsaid that I really preferred not to wake up tomorrow to find a pissed off Alex standing over me.

The look James gave told me he wasn't entirely unsympathetic to my cause. "This has escalated beyond your coven. Were times different, I might be persuaded to keep this matter as an internal affair. Now, though, any distraction could prove misfortunate to our cause. At minimum, the others must be briefed."

"At minimum?"

"As a group, we shall decide the best course of action."

That wasn't good. I really didn't fancy learning what that course of action would be. I had a feeling it wouldn't end in my favor.

"You're not going back, so stop worrying about that," Tom said. "We won't let it happen."

"Yep," Ed added. "We'll figure out...something." By his tone, it was obvious he understood that promise was easier said than done, but I appreciated the solidarity, regardless.

I looked toward Sally, expecting her to say something both insulting and supportive at the same time, but she just said, "I need to pack some things."

"Why?"

She turned toward one of the other rooms. "I don't know when I'm going to be back here again."

"You're leaving *now*?"

She stopped to stare condescendingly at me. "Yep."

"But..."

"Oh, stop being so fucking dense, Bill. You are too."

"That will not be necessary," Calibra said. "You would be best served staying here and..."

"And what? Watching this city crumble around us? Going back to Vegas and defending a bunch of casinos against the fucking Jahabich, while the rest of the world goes to Hell?"

The Jaha...? Oh well, one more thing in a long list of items I'd apparently missed. Whatever they were, it wasn't important. Sally was trying to clue me in as to what was, and I think I understood the hint. "Want to go get our coven back?"

She smiled in return. "I'd say it was a date, but you'd get the wrong idea."

* * *

My roommates, bless their insane hearts, both agreed with that course of action, despite lacking any vested interest in my coven. Friends to the end, as far as they were concerned.

Calibra had different plans, though.

"Absolutely not. I will allow the Freewill to accompany us, as this involves him. I suppose his hanger-on," she glanced sideways at Sally, "will follow regardless of what I say. But this affair is not for human eyes."

My friends opened their mouths to protest, but James held up a hand. "I am forced to concur. The situation is potentially volatile and I cannot guarantee your safety while..."

"Wait," Ed interrupted. "We've already established that I'm somehow not quite human." Tom tried to comment, but Ed cut him off. "Say it and I'll cock-punch you into next week." Once he was sure Tom wasn't going to reply with something asinine, he continued. "You don't need to worry about anyone trying to snack on me. Not to mention, I really don't want that asshole sneaking up behind me when I'm alone, just in case everyone here is wrong about Boston."

"He's got a point, James," I said. "Worst case is he just stands around being useless."

"Thanks, Bill."

"My pleasure."

"He can be bait," Sally added.

"What?"

"You heard me. If this asshole is really after you, then there's a chance we can use you to draw him out."

Ed raised an eyebrow, to which she replied with a saucy little smile. Sally was one of the few women I knew who considered flirting to be more fun when it was potentially lethal.

To my surprise, Calibra agreed. "There is logic in your words. Very well..."

Tom raised his hand to high five me.

"This human may come with us."

Tom's hand paused in midair. "What about me?"

"Unless you have a similar purpose, then I expressly forbid it."

Tom turned to James, but there was no dissent to be found there.

"I am truly sorry, but Boston is under the Prefect's jurisdiction. I have already ignored enough protocol for one day. Her ruling stands." As if to accentuate that the matter was closed, he turned away and pulled his phone out again.

Sally walked out of the room, probably to grab whatever it was she wanted. I had little doubt, though, that it was also partially to escape the whining that was sure to follow.

"Bill, you need..."

"No," I said, feeling like a complete dick. "Ed's a part of this, but that thing doesn't know about you."

"Not cool, man."

"I know, but it's for the best. You have a girlfriend, a kid on the way. It's a stupid risk. Besides, if anything happened to you...well, I sure as shit don't want another coven of witches out for my blood."

Tom visibly deflated, but offered no argument against my words. I put a hand on his shoulder and smiled. "We need someone to guard the homestead. Can't have any pterodactyls breaking in and stealing our shit, can we?"

Tom didn't look pleased, but he threw me back a small grin in return. "Says the twat-waffle who hasn't paid rent in three months."

* * *

Ed and I walked Tom down to the front door and opened it just enough to see his ride waiting outside. We had called for car service and, amazingly, they had responded. The past day had been weird, but apparently not weird enough to make people risk giving up a paycheck. With the sun up, the chances of him getting home safely were hopefully better than they would be otherwise, even if he needed to take the long route.

We said a few words, and I left off with the warning that if things got too freaky, he and Christy needed to get themselves gone. Thankfully, I wasn't too worried about that part. Pregnant or not, having a girlfriend who could apparate basically anywhere she wanted to go was handy. I wouldn't mind getting me one of those someday.

That thought brought Sheila to mind. Rather than let myself get depressed about it, though, I took some comfort. I'd made a vow to do whatever I could to take her place against the coming darkness. Sure, my current course of action would sorta help the vampire cause, but I considered Chuck to be the greater evil - cutting a swath of destruction through the office and God knows what else. That fucker was a loose cannon, one that needed to be put down. After that, I could figure out how to keep the world from sliding even further into the pit of crap it currently dangled over.

Our goodbyes exchanged, Ed and I closed the door behind us. James and Calibra waited in the living room in deep discussion - probably going over items of great importance to the vampire world that a low level doofus like me wouldn't appreciate. After a few moments, Sally stepped out to join them, a large duffle bag in hand.

"Let me guess: some trashy dresses, a thong, and a few pairs of six-inch heels that you can't live without?"

"A girl has to have her priorities," she replied, reaching into the bag and withdrawing a massive handgun identical to the one she'd kept at the office. "You lost Mark, but fortunately for me, he has a twin brother."

"You named your gun Mark?"

"Yep. Got a problem with that?"

I was tempted to comment, but Ed spoke up first. "I don't suppose you have something in there for me?"

Sally grinned devilishly and looked to have a reply, but thankfully, James spared us any disturbing double *entendres*. "When we get to Boston, you may feel free to peruse our arsenal. I have little doubt you'll find something there to your liking."

That seemed to mollify my roommate, although he did look a little crestfallen that he wouldn't get to finish his game of flirtation pong. That gave me pause to wonder if Sally really understood what he could do. If not, then the next time she tried to give him a little love bite was gonna be a doozy.

Such things could wait, though. As it looked like we were all ready to head out, I addressed the ranking vamps in the room. "I guess that's it. I hope your car has a big back seat and tinted windows."

James slyly smiled back. "I believe I can do one better."

"Oh?"

"Yes, although we shall need to journey to One Police Plaza first."

"Police escort?" Ed asked.

"Something of the sort."

That was interesting, but not entirely surprising. The upper echelons of human authority knew of our existence. Certain wheels were kept well-greased, ensuring eyes were properly turned away from the worst of our activities. I had a feeling that whole deal would come crumbling down soon enough, but apparently things hadn't yet escalated that far.

"Sure they're going to be able to spare anyone?" I asked. "I can still hear sirens out there. I wouldn't be surprised if martial law was declared by tonight."

"Nor would I," he replied. "Do not fret. They are merely providing us with the most efficient waypoint back - a means to an end."

Why didn't that instill much confidence in me? It probably had to do with the fact that for vamps, the shortest distance between points A and B was often through whatever warm bodies stood in the way.

There was also Sally to consider, currently carrying a gun big enough to set off metal detectors a block away.

I was sure James had some plan, but I still couldn't help but wonder how we were going to do this without reenacting a scene from *The Matrix*.

* * *

Another problem with our plan was the time of day. It was partly cloudy out, which meant enough sunshine to ensure things wouldn't be easy on us vamps. We could take the tunnels most of the way, but there was a vast difference between surfacing in the basement of a coven property and doing so in a building full of armed cops - ones who were likely to be a bit on edge from the events of the past twenty-four hours.

Thankfully, Sally kept the safe house stocked for nearly all contingencies - including trips outside. That meant hooded jackets and a couple of industrial-sized tubes of high SPF sunscreen.

Ironically enough, this left most of us looking like exactly the sort who would get stopped right at the door of a police station.

I helpfully pointed this out, but seemed to be the only one overly concerned. James was anxious to get a move on, while Sally was busy trying not to laugh at Calibra's discomfort with the bright pink hoodie she'd been given to wear. So glad to see everyone had their priorities in order.

One quick jaunt through the sewers later found us a few short blocks away from our destination - far enough so as not to arouse suspicion when we surfaced. Shaded by the tall buildings on either side of the street, it was smooth sailing from there out.

Or maybe not.

The place was mobbed with a crowd spanning out nearly a block in every direction. I couldn't really blame them. New Yorkers were a tough bunch, but the shit that'd been happening was enough to unnerve anyone.

The people were frightened and angry. Worst of all, it looked like a lot of the cops that should have been out doing stuff to help the situation were stuck here in crowd control - barely keeping the nervous mob from swarming the doors.

There was no fucking way we were getting through this shit.

Or so I thought.

James led the way, subtly using his enhanced strength to push through the crowd, allowing us to follow, but not hurting anyone or drawing undue attention to us.

As we approached one of the cops on duty, I had a moment to muse that, in addition to being greasy and dressed like creeps, we now smelled like an unholy mix of aloe and garbage.

"There's no fucking way we're not getting tossed in the drunk tank," I whispered to Ed as we got near.

"Who's this *we* you're talking about? Shit goes down and I'll just claim you fuckers kidnapped me."

"At least victim is a step up from bait."

"Good point."

Our banter petered out as James waved down the officer. I held my breath to see what would happen next. There was something about being at a police station that suggested silence would be the best course of action - as if just our proximity to it would cause every person in uniform to point their fingers and cry, "Guilty!"

"Oh, for Christ's sake," Sally said as she stepped near us. "Will you two stand up straight? You both look like you're about to turn yourselves in."

"Well excuse me," I replied. "I'm sure when you've been booked for soliciting Johns enough times this becomes old hat. Some of us, though, have a healthy respect for the law."

She cocked her fist back as if to clock me one, but stopped when she saw my grin - no doubt realizing that committing assault right in front of Cop Central was a dumb move, even for a vampire.

James and Calibra spoke to the officer while ignoring our antics. Their body language suggested authority at odds with their dress. I tensed as the eyes of the other cops close by narrowed on them, ready to hit the deck if lead or body parts started flying. That didn't happen, though.

Instead, the tiniest of tremors passed through me, almost imperceptible - as if a subway had passed by far beneath. Ed appeared not to have noticed, but Sally's eyes met mine.

"Was that..."

"I'm not sure," she replied, "but I think that may have been the subtlest human compulsion I've ever seen."

"I didn't even catch what he said."

"I know. I guess that's why he's one of the Draculas and we're not."

"Freaky."

"Kinda hot, too." She noticed my sidelong glance. "What? It is."

I was about to comment, but Calibra turned and waved us on.

To my surprise, we were escorted past the crowd, their angry taunts momentarily directed at us. They probably wondered why we were such VIPs.

We were led through the front doors and, amazingly enough, ushered past any security checkpoints that would have otherwise revealed some of us were packing some serious heat. James directed us to the main desk, where we were all handed visitor passes.

"Have a good day, sir," the clerk said respectfully.

That caught me by surprise. My run-ins with the police during my college days were more likely to end in *punk* than *sir*. I looked down at my pass and saw why. A fake name stared back, identifying me as a fed. Hot damn.

As James led us toward a bank of elevators, I had to ask, "NSA?"

"Yes. I find they are the organization least likely to be met with any silly territorial posturing."

"You do realize that impersonating a federal agent is a pretty major crime."

"Of course. Just as I realize that with the onset of hostilities, the majority of said agencies will most likely be rendered moot in the coming months."

"Oh."

An elevator opened and a white-haired, uniformed man stepped out. I wasn't entirely up on my rank insignias, but I was pretty sure he was a captain. He stepped up to James, giving me momentary pause to consider that perhaps the jig was up.

"Your ride's waiting for you."

Or maybe not.

"Excellent," James replied. "Please lead the way."

We stepped into the elevator. I expected us to head down, perhaps to a subbasement garage. To my surprise, though, we ascended.

"Anything you can tell me about all the shit going on?" the captain asked.

He must've seen my eyes pop open wide, because he said, "Yeah, I know all about bloodsuckers."

"That's such a crude term," James said conversationally.

"I was referring to your friends in high places. Goddamned politicians."

"On that we can agree."

A few minutes later, we were escorted out onto the roof. The daylight momentarily blinded me, but I could plainly hear the sound of rotors engaging.

"Not the least conspicuous bird we've ever had here," the cop said.

James stepped forward and clapped him on the shoulder amicably. "I dare say, Captain Valente, the days of subtlety may very well be over. Please take care of yourself."

I looked past them and took in our ride for the first time. Yeah, subtle definitely wasn't the right word. A sleek chopper awaited us - black with no markings. Fuck me if it didn't look like the helicopter from that old show *Airwolf*...complete with the weaponry to back it up.

"So what do you think?" James asked, turning back toward me.

"What do *I* think?" I repeated, grinning. "I think I'm calling shotgun."

A Slight Detour

James overruled me, thus showing that - amongst myriad other offenses - the Draculas didn't respect the universal rules for calling dibs. Oh well, at least Ed didn't get the hot seat either - albeit he didn't exactly appear to be suffering with his consolation prize: a seat next to Sally.

Calibra sat up front next to the pilot, who was no doubt also a vampire, judging by his full body jumpsuit, including helmet. The rest of us took the rear compartment, which was far more comfortable than the aggressive exterior of the chopper suggested.

The windows were heavily tinted, allowing us to ditch some of our coverings once the doors were shut. That was at least a minor plus, albeit we all still smelled like the losers in a Coppertone battle royale.

Even so, it was a lot better than my last trip in a copter - when Alex's men flew me back home from the Woods of Mourning. Sally and I had sat in uncomfortable silence then, afraid to say much. Now, despite the fact that we were potentially flying into - as opposed to away from - the frying pan, I found the company much more agreeable.

"This sure as hell beats driving," Ed said.

"Especially in your car."

"I got rid of that piece of shit."

"I meant your new one," I replied, ducking out of his reach.

"This is okay, I guess," Sally commented. "Not quite one of our chartered jets, though."

"True enough," James replied. "There's no champagne service, but at least it allows us to bypass check-in."

"Speaking of which," I asked, "how long to Boston?"

"We should be touching down in roughly an hour and a half."

That definitely kicked the shit out of driving, especially since a good chunk of the trip usually entailed rotting in traffic. Sure, there were rest stops, but the daylight ensured I would be a veritable prisoner in the car. That wasn't particularly cool when one was in need to take an epic piss. Also, last time we made the trip, Tom fucked up my order for lunch - purposely, too. The dickhead knows I don't like onions on my burger.

Sadly, burgers weren't on the menu for us that day. However, a stopover most certainly was - I just didn't know it yet.

* * *

James spent the next twenty minutes compelling Sally...sadly, not for anything fun. As the potential weak link in our group - which she helpfully planted a heel into my shin upon my pointing out - she sat there as James attempted to fortify her own mental barriers against compulsion. That seemed like one motherfucker of a smart idea to me, considering how easily Chuck had snared Starlight and Firebird. James wasn't entirely sure of the other vamp's age or power, but he was confident in his own abilities to temporarily erect enough walls in her mind to fend off anything but a direct attack.

His compulsions couldn't affect me, but they still reverberated in my skull - especially in those close quarters. It wasn't long before a headache set in.

I tried to tune him out by attempting to figure out how long the traffic jam below was - no doubt made up of those trying to flee the craziness going on in the city. I stopped doing so after a while, though, and just estimated it to be really fucking long. The intermittent police lights likely made it worse. The officers were probably dealing with the accidents that tended to occur whenever one introduced a little bit of panic to the unwashed masses. By the look of things, if we'd traveled by car, our ETA to Boston would be roughly sometime next month.

After finishing his compulsion reinforcements, James sat back and appeared to retreat into his thoughts. That left Sally, Ed and me to banter about mostly meaningless bullshit - with a lot of pathetic flirting on Ed's part thrown in to add a little nausea to the mix.

Finally, about forty-five minutes into the trip, I grew tired of it and figured I'd see what the skinny was on our new Prefect - especially since she was up front with the pilot and out of earshot...hopefully. "So, tell me about this Calibra chick."

"Calibra chick?" James repeated as he raised an eyebrow.

"You know what I mean. How'd she get Colin's job?"

"Calibra has been with the Boston office since before I was transferred there. She's an exemplary employee and a top-notch manager. The truth is, she was overdue for a promotion. She tried to turn it down, in fact, but I insisted."

"Interesting," I lied. "So..."

"So what's up with her name?" Ed asked, interrupting me. "Don't think I ever heard anyone called that." He stifled a yawn as he finished. I could commiserate. We'd been on the go for over twenty-four hours. Even with my vampire physiology, I was starting to feel my concentration waver.

"That one is easy. She was named for the Calabria region of Southern Italy, where she was born. It's a lovely place - highly recommended to visit."

"Yeah, but what can you *really* tell us about her?" I asked, trying to learn something useful. I mean, if she was going to be the one bossing us around, I wanted to know what kind of person she was. The last thing I needed was someone worse than Colin breathing down my neck every time I stepped out of line.

Sadly, just as James began to speak, the radio came to life.

"I beg your pardon, Wanderer," Calibra said over the speaker. I had to wonder whether her ears had been burning.

He pressed the button to respond and held up his other hand to shush the rest of us. "Go ahead."

"We're receiving an encoded S.O.S. - it's one of ours."

"The source?"

"Norfolk Coven."

"Have you been able to make contact?"

"Negative. I haven't been able to hail them, either via radio or cell."

James took his finger off the button and rubbed his jaw, his face serious.

"Could be a malfunction," I offered.

"Possible, although I highly doubt it." He depressed the button again. "What was their previous status?"

"Before we left for New York," she replied, "I ordered all covens under my command be put on high alert - although I left the reasons purposefully vague, considering the past forty-eight hours."

"Is that all?"

"Affirmative."

"I don't believe in coincidences," James replied after a few moments.

"Neither do I, Wanderer."

"Boston?"

"I spoke to them a few minutes ago. They gave the all clear. Requesting permission to investigate."

"We still need to secure our main..."

"With all due respect, Norfolk is under my jurisdiction. I would be remiss in my duties were I to ignore them."

James smiled. "Indeed you would."

"Also, I needn't point out there is a good possibility our quarry might be responsible. We may be able to head him off before Boston."

His grin widened. "Your logic is sound, my dear. Permission granted."

James took his finger off the button. He had all the appearance of a proud teacher watching his student succeed.

"As I said, she was long overdue for a promotion."

* * *

From James's description, Norfolk Coven sounded like a bunch of yokels - small town, less than fifteen thousand humans, mostly rural. The only way it could have been more in contrast to Village Coven was if it were located in some pygmy village deep in the Amazon. I wouldn't have doubted that half the coven was married to their sisters and went line dancing every Friday night.

"What do we do if we find him?" Ed asked.

Sally smiled in response. "Did you see those big noisemakers attached to this bird? I'm thinking that's what."

"A distinct possibility," James said. "But if it's all the same to you, I'd prefer we make certain before we level the entire town."

"You take all the fun out of a manhunt," she replied with a mock pout.

The joking done, he once more grew serious. "We shall circle the area and take stock of the situation. Assuming we see no hostiles, we'll land and reconnoiter on foot."

"On foot?" I asked, glancing out the window.

"We will use the daylight to our advantage. If our target is indeed here, he will not be expecting that."

"Works for me," Sally said, pulling out her weapon and checking to make sure it was loaded.

"I don't suppose you'd let me borrow that?" Ed asked.

"Never ask to touch a girl's piece until at least the third date."

"Or unless you have a five-dollar...is that a falcon?" I quickly changed the subject as she leveled her weapon toward me.

"Fret not," James said. "Underneath your seat is a weapons locker. It contains everything we'll need."

Ed's eyes shined. As the lone human amongst us, I knew he would feel a shitload better if he was holding something that went bang. Fuck it, so would I. Sadly, I doubted even a howitzer would erase the chill currently running down my spine.

A part of my mind insisted that I'd seen things incorrectly the day before...that I couldn't have emptied an entire clip of fifty-caliber silver bullets into Chuck...that I hadn't sent him out of a window directly into the sunlight...that something had played out differently than I remembered it. It had to. These were all things that ended a fight as far as vampires were concerned. Yet all it had done was piss him off.

Still, even if that were the case, things were different now. I had people a lot stronger and who could shoot a lot straighter than me. Elder vampires might be tough as cast-iron balls, but they weren't invulnerable. I just had to keep reminding myself that. Enough times and maybe I'd even believe it.

Just then, the radio buzzed to life again. "Sir?" a voice, the pilot's I assumed, asked.

"What is our current ETA?" James asked.

"That's part of the problem, sir. I'm not sure." The nervousness in his voice was evident. I could only guess that the very worst job in the vampire world - aside maybe from sitting bodiless in a fish tank day in and day out - was the poor schmuck whose job it was to report bad news to the Draculas. I couldn't imagine the applicant pool for that position was particularly overflowing.

"Elaborate," James replied calmly.

"We've arrived, sir, but I can't find a place to land. I can't find...anything."

* * *

I wasn't sure what to expect of Norfolk - maybe a one-horse town with a bunch of old timers sitting out on their porches wearing flannel and chewing tobacco. What I saw was...well, not much of anything.

Trees stretched for miles in every direction. Some ways off in the distance, I could see a road, but it appeared to run directly into the forest.

"This can't be right," I muttered.

James hit the button on the radio. "Are you absolutely certain of our location?"

"Global positioning confirms it, sir," the pilot replied, sounding like he'd much sooner dive out and try his hand at freefall than relay the news.

"There!" Sally pointed a well-manicured finger. I followed her gaze and saw something white sticking out amongst the trees.

"What the?"

"Looks like the steeple of a church," James said.

"Why would they build a church in the middle of the freaking woods?"

"They didn't," he replied. "If I'm not mistaken, the entire town is down there - completely reclaimed by the forest."

"Not completely," Sally said, pointing again. "What's that?"

It was a small clearing, but not a natural one. Trees were broken off, lying about as if something big had plowed through them. From this height, even I had to strain my vampire-enhanced eyes, but I could see that the ground within was stained a dirty brown color.

There was something else too. A body, perhaps, lying partially concealed amongst the destruction. I couldn't see it too well, but I could make out enough to tell it was very large and probably not human.

James's gaze hardened and he scooted over to survey the other side. "Down there, about a half mile away."

It was a small field, possibly belonging to a farm, but only partially overrun with vegetation - as if whatever had claimed the town had grown tired and given up.

He clicked the radio and instructed the pilot where to set down, before turning back toward the rest of us.

"Stay if you will or come with me, but this is now officially a rescue mission."

Forewarned is Four Armed

"Our guy didn't do this, did he?" I asked, donning one of the ski-masks that had been stored in the chopper's lockers. It was completely close-faced, with mirrored Mylar lenses covering the eyes. That would make our daytime jaunt a bit easier.

"Just figuring that out, are you?" Sally replied, her voice slightly muffled behind her mask - albeit not enough.

"I will warn you," James said, confirming my fears. "This will not be like Canada. We are no longer under protection of truce." He hefted an assault rifle and checked the magazine.

Ed barked out a laugh, his face the only uncovered one amongst ours. "You mean like all the good that truce did when Turd was busy kicking our asses?"

I couldn't help but chuckle at the mention of the unfortunately named Sasquatch chieftain. As big and mean as he was, his dopey moniker had gone a long way toward unraveling whatever menace I felt at the sight of him.

"This is no laughing matter," Calibra warned, donning a belt containing a nasty-looking handgun.

"Of course not," James said soothingly. "Believe me, they take this seriously. This is just their...nature."

I couldn't see Calibra's face, but her body posture told me she probably wore a sour expression underneath her mask. Oh well, she could go fuck herself with it.

The insane thing was, I felt a bit better. We were walking into potentially hostile territory, but it was against a foe I knew and had bested...if just barely. Also, I mused as I tested the weight of the sawed-off shotgun in my hands, I was slightly better prepared than last time. The weapon might not put one of the Feet down permanently, but I was fairly confident it would do a good job of blowing one's kneecaps off - hopefully.

I turned toward Ed, the manic look on his face mirroring my own. "Just like playing paintball."

"Except for the part where they rip our arms off."

Gotta love the optimism.

* * *

James once more offered to let us remain with the chopper while he and Calibra went and investigated, but we all turned him down. I wasn't certain about Sally's motivation, but I was fairly sure that in my and Ed's case it was because neither of us wanted to be called out as a pussy first. There were some things worse than death.

The pilot took off. James instructed him to shadow us from the sky, staying low enough to fill anything in our path with a friendly burst of thirty-millimeter greetings.

Once inside the tree line, the shadows were deep enough that I felt comfortable removing my mask.

"What are you doing?" Sally asked.

"My glasses are getting steamed up in that thing. I can't see shit."

"Fascinating, I'm sure," James said through what sounded like gritted teeth. I could feel his glare through the mirrored eyepieces he wore. "Thank the darkness this isn't a stealth mission."

He had that right. With the bird overhead, there was little chance whatever was out there wasn't aware of our presence. That was just as well. I had about as much chance of pulling off a Mission Impossible-style raid as I did of giving birth. I'd never been much into stealth games anyway. I mean, I almost always seemed to end up hacking my way out of bad situations in *Assassin's Creed*.

It didn't help that the forest was unnaturally quiet. Every step I took sounded like a marching band in the silent woods. At least we made good time. Although we were surrounded by densely packed trees, the undergrowth was minimal. In fact, in some places, it was almost like finely cut grass. Whatever had caused this odd growth of foliage seemed to be restricted to the trees only - maybe a limitation of whatever power they had. Who knows? I certainly didn't have a clue...except for maybe...

I stopped for a moment to look at a branch, specifically the leaves.

"Yep," Ed said from beside me. "Maple."

"I bet somewhere Francois is shitting a syrup-flavored brick."

Even Sally let loose a hiccup of laughter, causing Calibra to quickly turn back and shush us. Jeez, sorry, *Mom.*

"There," James said, his voice low enough that I'm pretty sure only the vamp ears amongst us heard him. A building, a house from the looks of it, stood before us. We'd reached the Norfolk city limits.

* * *

"The coven's central nest is beneath the courthouse," Calibra said, motioning us forward. We were obviously in the main stretch of town. Empty shops - some destroyed, others nearly whole - stared back through the trees on either side of us. Beneath our feet were the remains of an asphalt street - torn up, no doubt, thanks to the abrupt growth of forest.

What we didn't see or hear were any signs of life. I raised my head to sniff the air.

"I wouldn't," Sally warned.

"Why wouldn...oh fuck!" I nearly gagged as a ripe stench filled my nostrils. It was the smell of decay, of rot, of unwashed ass. I'd smelled it before, right as I was about to take a nosedive into a pool of Sasquatch shit. "We're not alone," I said once I'd finally stopped coughing.

"Obviously," Calibra replied derisively. "Up ahead. I see the courthouse." She quickened her pace, darting in and out behind the trees to the point where I nearly lost track of her.

"Bring up our rear, but remain outside," James said. "Form a defensive perimeter at the entrance."

I was about to question at what point he'd forgotten that I was a computer programmer from Brooklyn and not an Army Ranger, but he'd already sped up to match Calibra's pace. Just wonderful.

"Okay," I muttered to myself. "This isn't so bad." Ed had spent time in the backwoods of Pennsylvania where his stepdad lived. Also, Sally had once confessed to being a former Girl Scout. That all had to account for something, right? And, hey, they didn't call New York "the urban jungle" for nothing. One had to develop some survival skills. I mean, if one could make it there, they could make it anywhere. It...

It was all a load of bullshit, sadly.

A slight crunch of leaves sounded behind me, which wasn't particularly good since Ed and Sally were both a step ahead.

A moment later, a foul breath acrid enough to bring tears to my eyes wafted down the back of my neck. A growl followed along with a word I had really been hoping never to hear again.

"*Tlunta!*"

Oh, fuck.

* * *

I turned and raised my weapon only to have a meaty fist the size of a basketball pluck it from my grasp. Another hand, equally as large, grabbed hold of the stock and bent the gun neatly in half. Then a third took it and tossed it casually over the beast's shoulder.

I had to blink to make sure I was seeing what I just saw. Maybe the events from the past few days had driven me over the edge.

A Sasquatch stood in front of me...I think. It was both familiar yet entirely unlike any of the ugly fuckers I'd seen. It was over eight feet tall and covered in shit-stained fur. That much was expected. From there, though, the differences were enough to make me consider staining my own pants.

Bony protrusions covered its shoulders, chest, elbows, and knees, looking more solid than any concrete I'd been unlucky enough to be thrown through. The freakiest part, though, were the arms - all four of them. That was new. There was the usual set, as big and disturbingly muscular as expected - scary enough, as far as I was concerned. Add to that a second set, sticking out from its sides right below the first, and you had a perfect formula for freaking me the fuck out.

I had a scant second to remember back to my youth, playing video games in my bedroom. I'd always liked *Mortal Kombat*, but never the higher levels - mainly because Goro always used to kick my ass mercilessly. Standing before the monstrous ape, I got the distinct impression that history was about to repeat itself.

I looked up into the creature's slobbering face and was taken aback; not so much by how ugly it was, but by all the blood. A large gash ran down the side of its face, bleeding freely. Something had taken a chunk out of this thing. Heh, maybe Johnny Cage had recently been in town.

It raised its arms to pummel me into the dirt just as a thunderous report sounded nearby. A section of the bony armor covering one arm exploded in shards. The creature reared back its head and let out a roar of pain.

"Get down, shit-for-brains!" Sally shouted from behind me.

That was enough to spur me out of my shock. Someone had managed to fight back against this monster. Now, it was time for us to finish the job.

"Here's a message for Turd from yours truly!" I cried, pulling back my fist and driving it home into the beast's crotch.

The scream that rang out must have echoed through the woods for miles around. Sadly, it was from me as I cradled my freshly broken hand.

The beast let out a chuckle, like someone gargling on metal shavings, then reached down with its two lower arms to part the fur between its legs, showing the bony plate beneath. Well, that was unexpected.

Luckily for me, the creature decided I needed a broken jaw to match. It clubbed me like a baby seal with one of its massive paws, which sent me to my knees in a daze.

I could hear my friends coming to back me up, as much good as that would do against the tank version of the creatures that pretty much kicked all of our asses several months earlier. A moment later, I got a good look at them closing in as the mutant Sasquatch lifted me over its head like this was a goddamned wrestling match.

Thankfully, my friends' version of the classic steel chair cheap shot was to pepper this thing's midsection with bullets. As they blasted the shit out of it, I briefly prayed it didn't decide to use me as a shield against them. I could probably count on Ed to stop shooting if that happened. Sally...well...

And then, I was airborne as the beast flung me toward my former coven partner, she the far better shot of the two.

Proving herself to be a team player, she caught me mid-throw and gently lowered me to the ground without further injury.

Oh, wait...that's what I was *hoping* would happen.

In reality, Sally stepped nimbly to the side and a fucking smirk lit up her face as I flew past - bitch - allowing me to gently slam face first into a tree trunk.

Ouch.

Next time, I was gonna go investigate the abandoned building and James could stay outside to trade blows with King Kong.

A deafening barrage of gunfire erupted as I slowly peeled myself off the tree. I checked to see if any of my teeth were lodged in the bark, then turned back to the fight.

To my amazement, the big goon was down on one knee. His torso contained enough bullet holes that I was sure he'd set off the metal detectors at airports a hundred miles away.

Ed was reloading, but Sally approached with her gun held out - apparently with a few shots left to spare.

The creature raised its head. Hatred shone in its eyes, but that was the extent of the fight it had left - thank God. It was good to know that something could stop these fucking freight trains on legs.

"What did you do to the people who lived here?" I asked, partially to test whether I could still speak following the beating I'd just received.

It raised its lips in an ugly imitation of a sneer and growled, *"Muff kill them. Muff eat them. Muff eat you all."*

Muff? Its name was Muff?! Jesus fucking Christ! How in hell did these things expect us to take them seriously when...

I nearly jumped out of my skin as Sally pulled the trigger, splitting Muff's head with one of the mini-torpedoes from her heavy gun.

"Muff ate the people," Ed commented, once the echo of the shot had died down. "Normally, it's the other way around."

"Too easy, dude."

"Sorry, couldn't pass up the opportunity."

"Sally," I asked, likewise unable to resist, "tap any good Muff lately?"

"I still have one bullet left."

"Shutting up now."

Giant Furry People Eaters

U nfortunately for us, where there was one Muff, there were more...sorta. An angry howl rose up in the distance, followed by another. I had no way of knowing how far away, but I'd seen these things move. In the open, they couldn't match a vampire's speed, but they had some sort of freaky affinity with the trees - able to use them to sneak up on creatures that would otherwise smell them coming a mile off.

"How much ammo do we have left?" I asked, hoping for a good answer.

"Probably not enough," came the unsurprising reply.

Just then, the high-pitched whine of a military-grade machine gun filled the air.

Ed and I instinctively ducked before the realization hit that it wasn't us being fired upon.

"Looks like our backup has arrived," Sally nonchalantly commented, rolling her eyes in my direction.

A moment later, the black form of our chopper roared past overhead, its guns still spitting death.

"It's about fucking time!" I screamed to the heavens.

"One should have clear targets before one opens fire unless one has a grudge against treetops," a voice said from right behind me. I nearly jumped out of my skin again as I spun to find James and Calibra had rejoined us, their stealth nearly matching that of the apes.

Momentarily forgetting myself, I asked, "Where the fuck were you while Konga was busy testing out what would shatter first, my face or its...urk!"

I finished my accusation with a croak as I suddenly found my throat being crushed by Calibra. "Freewill or not, your insolence is growing tiresome."

I expected - and hoped - that James would come to my rescue, telling her that he was well used to my eccentricities. Much to my surprise, though, it was Sally who responded first - by pointing her gun right at the Prefect's face.

Shit had just gotten real.

* * *

"And what do you intend to do with that, child?" Calibra asked scornfully.

"Oh, I don't know," Sally replied, careful to stay out of the older vampire's reach. "Maybe celebrate my homecoming with some fireworks."

"I order you to cease this nonsense or I will..."

"Get to experience the unique sensation of your fucking skull being blown apart? Like I said, I don't answer to you."

"Yes, but you answer to me," James bluntly said, then turned to Calibra. "You as well. I understand tensions are high, but now is not the time."

For a second, neither of them budged. "Do not make me say it twice." The tone of his voice sent icicles down my spine.

Sally quickly lowered her gun. Calibra released my throat a scant second later.

"Thank you," he said frostily. "Now, in answer to your question, Dr. Death, I was doing exactly as I said. We were searching Norfolk Coven's nest for survivors - trusting that you could handle yourselves, which you did."

"Oh...well, did you find any?"

"No, but we did find clues as to what occurred here."

"Awesome. Like what?"

"Let us get back into the air first. There is nothing more for us here."

Sadly, that order was easier said than done.

* * *

James led us to the clearing with downed trees we'd seen earlier. The chopper couldn't land there, but the space was wide enough for it to descend for a pickup.

Being at ground level afforded us a much more sobering view of the scale of what had occurred. Trees, many snapped off at the trunk level, were strewn about haphazardly as if a tornado had touched down. The body we'd spied from above was only the tip of the iceberg. Over a dozen of those hairy, four-armed, whatever-the-fucks lay crushed beneath the debris as if they were no more than ants that had run afoul of a really big boot.

"Okay, anyone want to explain what the hell these things are?" Ed asked.

"The Alma, obviously," James replied.

"I kind of figured that," I said. "But what kind? They sure as shit don't look like the fun bunch we met up north. Are these like Mega-Sasquatches or something?"

"Hardly. The Alma are forest spirits. Their tangible forms are malleable. What you saw up in Canada was how they choose to manifest themselves during times of peace."

"As ten-foot fanged gorillas? That doesn't exactly scream happy little pixies to me."

"Be that as it may," he continued, "when they go to war, their appearance is decisively less friendly."

"I'd hate to see them really pissed off."

"As usual, Bill, you're missing the real point," Sally added, raising her voice to compensate for the whine of the descending chopper.

"Care to enlighten me, Miss Marple?"

"With pleasure. Who cares what the fuck they look like?" She nudged one of the hairy bodies with her foot. "What you should be asking yourself is why they're dead."

There was just one little problem with her theory: they weren't...at least, not all of them.

The attack came without warning. Though we were all on our guard, weapons at the ready, the creatures still somehow got the drop on us. I could see why they used the trees. Out in the open, it was pretty hard to miss something that looked like Mighty Joe Young's pissed off cousin. In the forest, though, these things were like the fucking Predator - minus, thankfully, the laser blaster.

One reared up behind James, but its element of surprise was short-lived. He'd fought these creatures before and had survived an attack that had claimed even his sire.

Its club-like arms were still descending when he spun. A blade appeared in his hand from seemingly nowhere. In less time than it took to blink, he'd buried the knife hilt-deep in the creature's unarmored stomach.

Calibra was nearly as fast, leaping upon the Sasquatch's back before the rest of us could even raise our weapons. I was now glad James had interceded earlier. Seeing her move, I wasn't entirely convinced Sally could have fired before this chick would have disarmed her and finished off both of us.

With a sharp crack, she broke the beast's neck, nearly twisting its head around one hundred and eighty degrees. The battle was over before it had even begun.

Or so I thought.

It had just been a diversion - a desperate gambit that drew our attention long enough for our enemies to figuratively fuck us in the ass. Gee, and they didn't even treat us to dinner first.

A roar of rage turned all of our eyes skyward. Two of Muff's buddies - hopefully not named Twat and Pubes - leapt from the trees, their target the chopper.

One of the pair underestimated the descent rate of the helicopter and went high. This brought him into direct contact with the spinning blades. The Sasquatch exploded into a shower of blood and guts that rained down upon us like we were standing in Hell's shower stall.

Sadly, the helicopter's rotor didn't fare much better in the exchange. With a shriek of rent metal, what had been a controlled descent now became an imminent crash landing. The second Sasquatch hung halfway in the cabin, clawing at the pilot, as the aircraft spun wildly out of control.

I'm not exactly what one might call a trained soldier, but even I know not to stand there gawking like a dipshit when a ton of whirling metallic death is headed my way. Thankfully, I had vampire reflexes at my disposal.

Ed had taken the brunt of the Sasquatch shower and was suitably distracted by what must have been twenty pounds of entrails landing smack dab on his head. Fortunately, he had an awesome friend like me by his side to save his ass.

Make that *friends*, as Sally apparently had the same idea. We both grabbed hold of him and dove for safety - fortunately, not in separate directions. That would have been pretty fucking awkward. I trusted James and Calibra were both doing the same. Tough as they were, a shank of twisted metal through the heart would fuck up any vamp's day.

We sought cover behind the trunks of the trees. Whatever magic had caused their unnatural growth had thankfully been thorough. Although they couldn't have been more than a few days old, they had all the thickness and strength of trees that had stood tall for a hundred years. The Feet might have worse hygiene than a cracked out hobo with a case of cheap wine, but they didn't fuck around when it came to whatever plant magic they employed.

The ground shook as the chopper slammed into it, accompanied by the sound of metal folding in on itself and the tortured engine blowing out.

After a few seconds, when I was fairly sure no flying chunks of helicopter blade would decapitate me, I dared a peek. The chopper was pretty much trashed - definitely not in any condition to fly us back to Boston anytime soon. Even so, a flash of light from inside the cockpit told me it was in better shape than the pilot.

The Sasquatch tore loose from the wreckage, bleeding freely from several wounds, but otherwise very much alive. It held up the now empty helmet of our former pilot and screeched triumphantly.

For about one second anyway.

James's knife buried itself hilt deep into the creature's neck with barely a sound of its passage. The Sasquatch's right eye then exploded in a spray of blood a scant moment before the roar of a gunshot reached my ears.

Without further ado, the ugly fucker - arms still raised in victory - fell backward to land with a meaty thud, one more body to add to the pile.

I shared a quick glance with Ed, who merely inclined his head and shrugged. It was close to embarrassing how quickly the older vamps could take down creatures that were capable of breaking me in half like the wishbone of a Thanksgiving turkey.

James stepped out of the tree line, followed by Calibra, and retrieved his knife. He wiped the blood off on his pants leg before returning the blade to its sheath. Damn. Not only was he a badass, but he looked cool doing it too.

Of course, cool or not, he was equally as fucked as the rest of us.

We joined him in the clearing and wordlessly began to search through the wreckage for anything salvageable. We looked for weapons and ammo mostly, although Sally made it a point to retrieve her duffle bag, too.

"Really?" I asked. "Thinking we might run into a floating rave out here in the woods?"

"If so, then things wouldn't be any different than they are in New York. I'd get in and you wouldn't."

I shot her a glare. "We should probably get out of here before the rest of those things find us."

"I agree we should get moving," James said, "but for different reasons."

"Oh?"

"Is it not obvious, Freewill?" Calibra gestured at the corpses lying about. "The *rest* are all around us."

"There could be others," I sheepishly pointed out.

"Not in the immediate area," James replied. "The few who attacked us were merely the remnants of their force."

"This is odd." Sally bent over and examined one of the Sasquatch bodies. After a few moments, she moved on and did the same to another. "No bullet holes on these - just lots of broken bones. I'm thinking this wasn't done by humans."

"The Norfolk Coven, then?" Ed asked. "Maybe they were able to fight back."

Calibra exchanged a glance with James, who gave her the barest of nods.

"Unlikely, human," she replied. "The master of Norfolk was a vampire named Sarah Porter. She was only one hundred and thirteen years old. The majority of her brood were far weaker - not a true warrior among them. I very much doubt they could have routed such an attack so utterly."

"Maybe the townsfolk helped them."

"Excuse me?"

"The people," I replied, remembering the briefing Alex had given to Sally and me before sending us up to the Woods of Mourning. "Way back during the first war with the Feet, vamps and humans fought alongside each other, right? Well, who's to say history didn't repeat itself? Maybe together they..."

"Do you smell any humans in the vicinity?" James asked.

That was a good question. The only thing I'd really smelled since arriving here had been the ass-like stink of Bigfoot fur. I took a deep breath through my nostrils, trying to filter past their lingering stench. I was fairly sure my nose hairs would catch fire long before that happened. After a few fruitless seconds of trying, I shook my head.

Sally raised an eyebrow and sighed derisively. A couple of moments later, though, a look of confusion came across her face. "Bill's right. There aren't any people here. Hell, I can't even smell their bodies. How many..."

"Nearly twelve thousand."

"Where'd they all go?" I asked. "That first fucker said he ate them, but that..."

"An empty boast meant to unnerve you, in all likelihood. The Alma may be omnivorous, but they are not known for eating people. Besides which, it would take an army of them to devour a town of this size."

"So where..."

"Is it not obvious, Freewill?" Calibra asked again. That was twice. Once more and I wasn't sure I'd be able to restrain myself from taking a swing at her. She was getting really fucking annoying.

"Pretend I'm a moron."

"Very well. They never left. They are all still here, standing around us."

The Long Walk Home

I blinked stupidly for a few seconds. "So, what? Are they ghosts?"

"No fucking way," Sally gasped.

"Holy shit. They can actually do that?" Ed asked.

"Do *what?*" It was exasperating, always being the last person to get the freaking memo.

"The trees, Bill," he replied. "They didn't grow them. Somehow, they turned the people *into* them."

I opened my eyes wide. That was shit straight out of a bad horror movie. "They can do that?"

"Thankfully, not en masse," Calibra replied

"Twelve thousand people isn't en masse?"

"Not comparatively. Be thankful. Otherwise, our original war with them may well have ended quite differently."

"It's powerful magic," James explained as casually as if he were discussing last night's baseball game. "Requires a lot of effort and they must destroy as much as they create - something the Alma are often loathe to do. I wouldn't doubt that somewhere amongst this carnage is the body of one of their shamans. Likewise, if we were still capable of flight, I would expect to find a similarly sized patch of forest no more than a few miles away - dried up and devoid of all life."

"That doesn't explain the Norfolk Coven," Sally pointed out. "Were they also..."

"No. This type of magic wouldn't work upon us. Our life force isn't compatible."

I briefly glanced at Ed and gave him the once over. "I'll let you know if you start to sprout roots."

"Bite me, asshole."

"I'm sure Tom would be happy to help me fertilize you as often as needed."

"If you two are done sucking each other's balls, maybe we can get back to the topic at hand," Sally said before turning back toward James. "You think our guy killed these furry fuckers, don't you?"

James turned away from us and clasped his hands behind his back. "The remnants of his scent linger in the courthouse. There is also no denying these Alma were killed by something with considerable power."

"So what about the coven?"

"Gone. No ashes. Just gone." Once more, his voice carried a worried tone. He'd barely blinked when fighting off the Sasquatch. In fact, the entire war effort appeared to barely faze him. Something about this vampire, though, had him on edge. There was little doubt he was hiding something.

Being that I hadn't learned my lesson on impudence from earlier, I figured I'd just come right out and ask. "What is it you're not telling us?"

I took a deep breath, anticipating Calibra cutting off my air again, but she barely glanced in my direction. When James began to walk away from us, she fell in step with him almost instantly.

"The only thing I think any of us need to know right now, Dr. Death," he said from over his shoulder, "is that we must get back to Boston and still have a very long walk ahead of us."

* * *

James wanted to waste no time, but then again, he hadn't gotten his ass beaten down and then had to expend the energy to heal from it. We convinced him to give us fifteen minutes to get ready. He wasn't happy about it, but was forced to acknowledge we all weren't as invincible as he.

Thankfully, with the town devoid of any other life of the non-plant variety, we didn't need to be overly careful. Sally and I made a quick circuit of the courthouse sub-basement to look for any bottled blood, while Ed raided a nearby convenience store. The end spoils were very different, but the purpose was the same: making sure we weren't running on empty before setting off on a twenty-five-mile hike.

Unfortunately, any caravan is only as quick as its slowest member. We were hampered by two issues: it was still daylight and we had Ed with us. It most certainly didn't help that he was starting to smell pretty goddamned ripe. Our pit stop hadn't included time to find any shower facilities, so he was forced to live with the stench. With us in our daylight terrorist gear and him smelling like the inside of a jungle latrine, that pretty much ensured we wouldn't be hitching a ride once we'd found our way to a main road.

That wasn't in the cards anyway. It didn't take a genius to realize that a missing town wasn't exactly something that would go unnoticed. We hadn't gone far when we heard the first helicopter. I looked up through the trees, thinking maybe a rescue mission had been sent for us, but it was pretty clear that it was just a news copter. Soon, others flew by overhead, more media and some police choppers as well.

It was a fair bet that emerging from the woods onto a main thoroughfare would only put a massive spotlight on us from any rescue vehicles and curious onlookers wondering what the fuck had happened. James voiced as much and made us stick to the woods for several miles longer than was probably necessary, slowing us down even more.

Hours later, the sun had finally begun its descent in the sky when Calibra stated, "Boston still reports all clear," before putting her phone back into her pocket.

"Yeah, I was meaning to ask about that," I said, catching up to the two elder vamps at our vanguard. "Why haven't either of you called for a pickup? Wouldn't this be a shitload faster if they even sent a car for us?"

James's reply was a curt, "Keep walking, please."

I fell back to where the others were keeping pace - Sally attempting to stay slightly upwind of Ed. She shrugged, just as confused as I was. Ed's look, however, conveyed an unspoken question I'd been expecting. But due to the overly sensitive ears just a few dozen steps ahead of us, it was better not to say anything. I merely gave my head a single shake. It was premature for that option anyway. Perhaps James had been wrong. Maybe Chuck was smart enough to ask the vamps he'd kidnapped about the situation and realized he didn't have a snowball's chance in hell of taking on the Boston facility with anything short of an army.

Don't get me wrong. I'd seen what this ass-cheese could do. He was one tough fucker, but he was still just one vamp, out of his own time and the last member of some radical sect that had been burnt to the ground. Conversely, who knew how many towns across the world had been instantly swallowed up like Norfolk? Who had any idea how many freaky-ass monsters were now loose, swimming in rivers like the Hudson or flying high above the buildings? Wasn't all of that ultimately the bigger threat?

As we continued walking, mostly in silence, save for the occasional snarky remark as to Ed's odor, I realized I had far more questions than answers.

Previously, things had been pretty black and white. I now realized that, in addition to being an uphill battle, the whole saving the human race concept was perhaps not as cut and dried as I thought it would be.

Jeez, maybe I should've just stayed in my dungeon cell after all.

The Office Park of
Ultimate Doom

The sun had set by the time we made it to the outskirts of Boston. Ed was wheezing pretty heavily from the extended hike, but otherwise, we were in fine condition.

We were able to discard our coverings, which went a long way toward making us not look like a pack of roving weirdos. Any weapons that couldn't be hidden on our persons Sally stuffed into her bag. I'm sure that didn't exactly render it light, but she continued carrying it with no apparent discomfort. She even rolled her eyes when I tried to be a gentleman and offered to lug it for her. Chivalry is such a dead concept.

With only a few miles left to go, James led us to a parking lot that didn't appear to have a lot of foot traffic in it. Hell, come to think of it, I hadn't seen a lot of traffic *period* since we'd emerged from the woods. For the suburbs of a major city, it was eerily quiet.

He singled out a large SUV, a Nissan Armada, and put his hand on the door handle. I saw his muscles tense for a moment, but then he paused and turned toward the rest of us. "Sally, if you would kindly work your magic."

"My pleasure," she replied with a smile.

A few minutes later, we were cruising along in the stolen vehicle sans any visible damage. Calibra drove with James riding shotgun. The rest of us were in back with the windows rolled down to help dissipate Ed's reek, a prospect that was only partially successful. I almost felt bad for the poor guy. I'd been on the receiving end of Sasquatch stink before and the only thing that had washed it off had been a prolonged soak in a raging river.

Oh well. In a few minutes, we'd be locked up safe in the undead nerve center for this section of the country. I didn't even have to worry about keeping an eye on my roommate. Anyone taking a nip from him would get the mother of all nasty surprises.

Once there, we could maybe catch some shuteye and then figure out what the hell to do next. At the very least, I could amuse myself by gawking at all the zombies that were employed as clerical help in...

The car swerved, knocking me into Ed - ugh, nasty - and the brakes squealed as we skidded to a halt. Thank goodness I was used to driving in my roommate's old shit-bucket. It had taught me to appreciate wearing a seatbelt. "What the fuck?"

"Zombie," Sally said, turning around in her seat.

"How'd you know I was thinking about..."

"No, stupid. Back there."

I craned my neck to look out the back window. There were two figures in the middle of the road, both human in appearance. The only problem was that one was busy chewing on the other - ripping off hunks of flesh and stuffing them greedily into its mouth.

"I repeat, what the fuck?"

"Proceed, please." James said evenly.

"But, Wanderer, if that is one of..."

"Proceed."

Calibra didn't need to be told twice.

Hell, I was tempted to get out and push.

* * *

We finally pulled into the car wash that served as the aboveground façade of the Boston compound. Although we'd only been driving for a short while, it felt like a lot longer than we'd been hiking. I tried to wrap my head around the zombie we'd seen. Aside from when one had bitten Tom's hand - and let's face facts, he'd deserved it - I'd never seen the slightest bit of aggression from any of the walking corpses in the employ of the vampire nation. Hell, if anything, I'd considered asking whether we could requisition a few for Village Coven, as they seemed pretty damned efficient.

My mind raced back to Switzerland. Hadn't Alexander proclaimed Druaga one of the lords of the dead? I had no idea what that really meant, but supposed it was possible he'd been pissed at my escape and decided we could go fuck ourselves. I couldn't see why a death god wouldn't be able to command...

Gah, I had no idea. It was like I'd emerged from my hole in the ground to find a world similar to the one I remembered, yet topsy-turvy at the same time. I'd barely had a moment to myself long enough to take a shit, much less make sense of anything.

Oh well, hopefully, once we were parked and nestled inside of Boston's massive complex, we'd have a moment to think things through properly.

Calibra rolled down her window for the attendant present - the only soul we'd seen out and about since the zombie. He simply nodded and pushed a button. Within seconds, we were diverted from the main track and into an underground garage - parking, I noted, in a much better spot than whenever I'd visited as a guest. Once more, I was forced to consider, with no small amount of amusement, how much Hollywood got wrong. On the big screen, the world of the undead was a dark place full of mysticism and terror. In reality, there was a disturbing amount of the mundane that anyone who'd spent any stint whatsoever within corporate America would instantly recognize.

At least this time, we had the benefit of being with the main man himself. No having to sit around in waiting rooms dealing with Colin's smarminess while he debated whether or not we were worthy of an audience. With any luck, James would transfer his foul mood toward his lackey. It was a petty hope, but fuck it. What good was being immortal if I didn't allow myself the occasional dickish indulgence?

As we entered an elevator leading - where else - down, I was forced to wonder whether entrances were this low key for all of the Draculas. Alexander certainly seemed to like his pomp and circumstance. James was different, though. Hell, he hadn't even wanted to bother his people for a pick-up in the woods. The dude was as salt of the Earth as vamps got.

The door dinged open and we stepped out. I tensed up, wondering what we'd find, but everything seemed to be business as usual. Vampires, most of them in typical corporate dress, scurried about performing what looked to be mundane tasks.

A small part of me cringed as I watched them. While getting my ass kicked on a semi-regular basis wasn't exactly a walk in the park, it was at least more interesting than being conscripted into middle management for all of eternity. I had liked my job at Hopskotchgames, but trust me, I wasn't exactly ready to curl up and weep into my stew at losing it. A short vacation while I got my resume out there again didn't seem like the worst thing in the world. Sure, I might need to bum some cash off my folks, but...oh, shit.

I still needed to call them when I got five minutes to myself and make sure they were okay. Thankfully, I was fairly sure Scotch Plains, New Jersey was pretty damn low on the list of tactical targets in this war.

James still looked tense as we walked through the halls, but I was relieved to see Calibra relax a bit. Various minions respectfully approached her for a signature or permission to do some bit of business or other. She waved most of them away, but took a moment to take care of a few quick inquiries.

I glanced at Sally and Ed and they both shrugged. The feeling was mutual...much ado about nothing, I suppose.

"So what's the plan?" I asked, stepping forward to catch up with James.

"The plan," he said, "is for me to touch base with Colin and then convene a conclave of the First to discuss this issue. Beyond that, I cannot say more."

"Let me guess...need to know?"

"Precisely." He turned to address Calibra. "Kindly make sure our guests are comfortable, my dear. I will be heading to the lower levels. Please see that I am not disturbed. I will send for you once I am finished."

If she was curious - like I sure as shit was - she didn't show it. She simply nodded, then turned to face the rest of us, blocking the path. Beyond her, James kept walking, barely acknowledging any of the vamps who scurried out of his path.

"I take it we're not invited," Sally said.

"The Wanderer shall be speaking with the rest of our masters. Such proceedings are not for the eyes of children."

"So we're not allowed to watch whatever mystical ritual he uses to summon them?" Ed asked half-jokingly.

"Hardly, human, unless you consider an encrypted video conference via our transatlantic fiber cables to be mystical."

"Wait, you have..."

"Of course," she said offhandedly, her look one of barely concealed impatience. "We have a multi-gigabit connection. This is the twenty-first century, after all."

"Uh, yeah," I replied, a little dumbfounded. "So what do we do until then?"

"I have business of my own to attend to." She stopped and pointed toward her left. "There is a lounge down the hall. Please feel free to help yourself to any refreshments or," she threw Ed a quick look of disgust, "freshen up a bit. When you are finished, you may make yourself comfortable in my waiting area. I believe you know the way."

She turned and walked away with no further fanfare, her pace brisk and business-like. After about ten paces, though, she stopped and once more faced us. "I will, of course, stress that you are not to do anything that would disrupt this place of business."

"Wouldn't dream of it," the three of us replied in unison.

* * *

"This is some good shit," Ed replied as he sipped a cup of steaming coffee. "Nice to see they don't cheap out on everything."

I offered him my cup. "You should try it with some blood."

"Pass."

"You don't know what you're missing." I turned, waiting to see if Sally had some snarky comment of her own to make, but she just sat in a chair, her own cup untouched in front of her.

I stepped over and took a seat opposite her. "What's the matter? You switch to decaf in my absence?"

"Not this century," she replied with a quick grin before turning serious again. "Something about this whole thing isn't right."

I opened my eyes wide in mock surprise. "Really? You're just catching on to this now? What parts aren't right: the uber vamp who kidnapped our coven, the fact that the Feet should now be called the Arms, or maybe all the fucking monsters running about and making themselves at home?"

Ed chimed in. "Me having anti-vampire blood, the fact that Bill managed to wreck my new car within twelve hours of returning home, that sk..."

"Never gonna let me forget that, are you?"

"Not as long as you live."

"No. It's not about any of that shit." Sally slammed her cup down, spilling all of the awesome coffee goodness inside. Some things should really be a crime. "James isn't himself. I've never seen him act like this before. And this place..." She waved her hands about. "There's something off."

"I haven't noticed it."

"Same here," Ed added. "Seems pretty much to be running like the last time I was here - vampires performing menial office..."

"Vampires," Sally said, cutting him off. "That's exactly the problem. Where are the fucking zombies?

They should be out there in droves, pushing papers and shit."

She stood up. "I have a bad feeling the one we saw out on the streets wasn't some aberration or stray."

"You think it was one of ours?"

"Could be. Why else would James have told that bitch to floor it instead of investigating? Something is wrong, and he's well aware of it."

The sound of movement caught our attention and we turned to the entrance of the lounge. My jaw nearly hit the floor as I spied the source.

Firebird was standing there.

Her clothes were torn and her eyes appeared a bit glazed, but she otherwise appeared hale and hearty.

"You always were a smart one, Lu. Pity you're a day late and a dollar short this time."

The Gauntlet

Sally snarled and launched herself forward. She reared back her arm, claws extended, and was about to erase Firebird's vacant stare - along with the rest of her face - when I caught her by the wrist. Even so, she nearly tossed me over her shoulder with the effort. It was all I could do to stand my ground and hold her at bay.

"Down, girl!"

She spun toward me, eyes blackened and fangs fully extended. Whoa, she looked massively pissed - and believe me, I've seen Sally pretty goddamned angry before. I almost released her before catching myself.

"That's enough."

"Let go of me, Bill," she snapped. "I owe this bitch. She's been ratting us out to Marlene this whole time and nearly got me kill..."

"Who the fuck is Marlene?" I had no idea what had her in such a lather, but I wasn't about to let her do as she wished. "Oh, and what's with the Lu stuff again? You ever gonna tell me what that means?"

My second question caught her off guard, which was what I was hoping to do - mostly, at least. This was the second time someone had let that slip. The first being Colin way back when...

"Yeah, calm down," Ed said, stepping up to us, albeit staying slightly out of her reach. "The whole point of all this bullshit was to find her."

"No," Sally corrected. "The point was to find Starlight and the rest of our coven. This fucking whore is collateral damage as far as I'm concerned."

"Stow it," I said, my own frustration starting to boil over. "Look at her, she's obviously been compelled."

"Yeah, and if she's here, then maybe so are the others," Ed pointed out.

"Fine," she replied, taking a deep breath. "When this is over and everyone is back to their normal selves, though, she and I are having words."

"Fair enough." I let her go - ready to pounce should she decide to go postal again. Jeez, chicks could be so goddamned catty when they wanted to be.

I asked Firebird, "Are the others here?"

"No," she replied with a hollow voice. "I don't know where they are. The master did not allow it."

"The master?" Ed asked.

I turned toward Sally with a smug grin. "See, I told you...compelled." I then addressed Firebird again. "Where is this master?"

"Not here. He's gone elsewhere to seek his army. He fears he is not yet strong enough to take this facility. He released me first, though, to deliver a message."

"What message?"

"A message for the ears of the First.".

"We need to go find James," I said.

Sally just sighed and replied, "No shit, Sherlock."

* * *

Sally led the way and I followed, making it a point to stay between her and Firebird. We decided it was safer to seek out Calibra first rather than disturb James. Also, neither of us had any idea where his chambers were located in the complex.

"You could have left that in the lounge," I said, indicating the duffle bag which seemed to have become a permanent fixture on Sally's arm.

"All of our party favors are in it."

"I seriously doubt we're going to need to shoot James."

"It's not James I'm worried about."

I was about to respond when Ed nudged me from behind. I turned to find we'd attracted an entourage. Several of the office drones had dropped what they were doing and were following us.

"How..." I started, but Sally shushed me.

"I have a feeling we're about to find out."

The double doors leading toward the Prefect's wing were just ahead of us. This was the one area of the place I'd seen that lived up to its reputation - the office motif giving way to an obsidian cavern. It housed a waiting area, as well as the office of the vampire in charge of the Northeast - Calibra, at the moment.

Sally turned toward me just a split second before I caught the scents in the air - a lot of them. In this crowded den of the undead, it was nearly impossible for me to tell who they belonged to by smell alone - especially with Ed hovering so near. Sadly, the lounge hadn't included shower facilities, just a couple of packs of wet wipes.

"You're smelling it, too?" I asked her.

"Uh huh. Either Calibra is hosting a really large staff meeting, or we're about to be royally fucked."

* * *

The first thing that caught my eye upon pushing open the doors was the flash of light at the far end. I was familiar with it, having seen it more times than I cared to - a vampire had just gotten dusted.

The second thing I noticed was all the semi-familiar faces in the room. I didn't know them personally, but I'd met some briefly in the office - the new recruits from Village Coven.

They weren't the only ones, either. Judging by the street dress of some in attendance, we'd found the missing HBC vamps as well. More disturbing, though, were the vampires standing guard at the periphery. Many of them were dressed in what looked to be riot gear, silver stakes at the ready. I hadn't seen any of them before, but if I had to guess, I'd say that they were part of the strike teams James had mentioned.

I continued scanning the crowd and realized something else: those in attendance displayed a mix of expressions - some clear-eyed, while others were glazed and vacant. Many were apparently still under compulsion, but there were a good deal that appeared to be there of their own volition.

"What the hell's happening?" I asked nobody in particular.

"I'd say *that's* what's happening." Sally pointed straight ahead. "Is that the guy who has everyone so frazzled?"

It was. Chuck sat at the far end - lounging in an office chair, but making it seem like some sort of throne. His back was against the doors leading into Calibra's office. He'd once more changed outfits. Gone was the mismatched kilt, and in its place was a pair of black tactical pants matching that of the guards - no doubt appropriated from some unlucky vamp. He was still shirtless, though, his tattoos standing out in stark contrast to his bronzed skin. A part of me couldn't blame him. If I had a physique like that, I'd probably toss all my shirts into the wastebasket as well.

He gave us no notice as we entered. Instead, he casually motioned with one hand and two of the compelled vampires stepped forward to stand in front of him.

I saw the barest furrow of his brow and the two vamps staggered for a moment, shaking their heads as if coming out of a daze. They'd been set free.

The big goon addressed them in whatever gibberish Latin he spoke. I didn't understand the words, but it was obviously a question. Maybe he was wondering what they thought of his bitchin tats.

Rather than answer, the two vamps looked around, as if seeking help - their eyes landing upon us.

"Freewill?" one of them asked, obviously recognizing me. "Save us!"

Unfortunately, that wasn't to be. The big guy made a disgusted "Feh!" sound. At this, four of the armored vamps stepped from the sidelines and staked them both without warning. Two brief flashes later, and they were nothing but ashes on the ground - joining what I now realized were several other piles lying about.

I needed to do something, but was rooted to the spot, with no clue how to proceed. Where the hell was James or Calibra? Without them, there wasn't any...

I let out a sigh, realizing I was a fool to expect anything else.

Without them there, I was pretty much on my own.

What a surprise.

* * *

Well, not entirely on my own. I had my friends with me, but forgive my pessimism for not believing they were exactly going to tip the odds in our favor. Then I remembered that part of this crowd was made up of Village Coven vamps. Most of them were newbs, but there was the old proverb about safety in numbers.

I quickly scanned the crowd as our host finally seemed to notice us for the first time. He made a come-hither gesture, to which I was about to reply with my own one-fingered salute, but his motion wasn't directed at me.

Firebird stepped past us and began walking forward.

I hoped this guy couldn't understand English yet. "Firebird," I hissed, "if you're still in there, just do what he wants. Save yourself and we'll figure out..."

She stopped mid-step and glanced over her shoulder at me. Gone was the vacant look that had been on her face. Her eyes were clear and the smile on her face predatory.

"I already did," she purred. "He released me hours ago."

"He did?"

"Told you! You should've let me kill her," Sally grumbled.

Firebird continued on her way. She reached the shirtless vamp and knelt by his side, wrapping one arm around his leg. The way he stroked her hair as she did so suddenly spoke volumes about the disheveled state of her clothes. Oh crap.

"You should have listened to little Lucinda, Bill," she said, leaning her head down upon his knee like some sort of rock star groupie on a bad eighties hair band cover.

Wait just a second...

I turned toward Sally and opened my mouth, but she cut me off. "Really? You want to do this *now*?"

"Yeah, good point...*Lucinda*." I couldn't help but let out a small chuckle, earning a glare of death from her. Sadly, my grin wasn't long lived.

Sally took a step forward, her posture saying she was rapidly falling out of the mood to talk. "Where's Starlight, bitch?"

"Poor little Alice. The master released us both at the same time. Alas, she chose poorly."

"Poorly?"

Firebird stretched one hand forward and waved at the various heaps of ash on the floor.

Oh no!

The implication hit me like a freight train. Starlight had been a gentle soul amongst vamps - almost a mother hen. She'd paid for it by being constantly used by the more manipulative elements of the vampire world. Yet in the end, she'd managed to do all right by herself - having achieved mastery of Village Coven.

And now this was her reward? I couldn't believe it.

Neither could Sally, apparently. A look of utter shock appeared on her face and I finally realized that, for all of the times she'd coerced Star into being her personal secretary, she nevertheless considered her a friend.

The thing with friends is that if you have one like Sally, you can be sure as shit they're gonna take exception to others mistreating you. And if, God forbid, something happens to you - you *will* be avenged.

With a blur of movement, Sally reached into her duffle bag and produced her Desert Eagle.

The time for talking was over.

Meet the New Boss

O ne of the problems in dealing with vampires is that the older they get, the more powerful they are. This includes strength, healing, and speed. Sally, for all of her attitude, was still relatively young. To me, it looked as if she had reacted like lightning. To an elder, though, it would barely be slow motion.

Before she could even aim the massive weapon, two of the riot crew had converged upon her - one forcing the barrel of the gun down and the other striking her in the side of the head.

That was enough for me. First, there was the anger at knowing this asshole had casually dusted one of the few vampires who'd somehow managed to retain her human heart. Now, it was watching Sally struck down by creatures that were supposed to be on our side.

Within moments, I was seeing red, and when that happened, I tended to forget my own limitations and dive into the fray.

"Bill?" Ed asked from my side, but I ignored him.

These fuckers were going to learn that you didn't mess with the Freewill's friends.

"Enough!"

Authority and gravitas resonated in the voice, so much that nearly all action in the room, my own included, ceased as our attention turned toward its source.

Ed and I spun to find James. He'd entered through the double doors, flanked on either side by more of those strike-team vamps. Unfortunately, they were all pointing their weapons at him. He was their prisoner, although from the tone of his voice, he hadn't come to that conclusion yet.

"This ends now." He blinked and his eyes turned black as onyx.

"*Primoris*," a deep voice chuckled from the opposite end. I looked over my shoulder to find that Chuck had risen, a grin upon his face.

Oh, boy. It was the irresistible force on one side and the immovable object on the other...and looky here, me and my friends right smack dab in between them. Not quite where I wanted to be.

"I take it you didn't get to make your call."

"Not now, Dr. Death," James warned, never taking his eyes off the cultist.

All of the other vamps in the room had cleared the aisle, including the assholes who'd cold-cocked Sally. I used the opening to step forward and help her to her feet, praying that the Mexican standoff didn't break before we got a chance to move out of the way.

"You okay?"

"I'm fine," she replied, brushing me off. "That guy hits like a pussy."

"Yeah, well, we're standing between two badass mofos who I'm pretty sure hit like freight trains, so I'd suggest you move your tight little ass."

I half dragged her to the side with me, briefly looking to make sure any vamps still under Chuck's spell weren't about to shank us in the rear.

I was about to turn back toward the main event when my eyes settled upon a familiar face. "Dave!"

My former, and hopefully future, DM stood there, eyes completely glazed. Apparently, he hadn't yet been called up for whatever *test* the Glenn Danzig lookalike had put the other vamps through.

Remembering my experience with compulsions from when I was first turned, I figured it wouldn't hurt to see if things still worked the same when a much older vamp was the one putting the whammy on another.

So as all eyes were turned, some voluntarily while others not so much, toward the two big dogs in the arena, I hauled off and backhanded my friend across the mouth. The blow made a resounding *crack* loud enough to put the spotlight back on me, which was exactly what I was hoping to avoid.

One moment, James and Chuck were about to throw down, the fate of all vamps in the Northeast on the line. The next, they were all looking directly at me.

"Uh...I suppose you're wondering why I asked you all here today."

A voice behind me muttered a muffled curse. "Goddamnit, Bill. You broke my fucking mouth."

Hey, at least it worked. "Ixnay on the uckingfay outhmay, Dave," I whispered through clenched teeth.

A deep chuckle issued forth from Chuck's barrel chest. He once more spoke some of his gobbledygook. Whatever profound observation he made was lost in the translation. I did happen to catch that father word again, though. Oh, Jesus Christ, were we back to that bullshit?

"For the last time, you fucking retard, I'm not your father!" If I didn't have the room's attention before, I sure as shit did now.

"What the hell are you talking about?" Sally asked.

"This dipshit keeps calling me his dad."

"No, he didn't."

"Yeah. He keeps saying it like he's some kind of goddamned lost puppy who..."

"You do realize," Dave said from behind me, "that frater is Latin for *brother*, right?"

"It is?"

"Yeah."

"Even I know that," Ed added.

"Oh." The looks from those around me, the non-glazed eyes at least, were a mix of humor and pity. Jeez. I took two years of remedial Spanish in high school, the bare minimum to graduate. It's not like I was some sort of cunning linguist.

"Fine, but last time I checked, I was an only child. Unless Mom was off banging a Swiss bodybuilder when I..."

"Move *now*!"

It was James. As the entire room focused on me and my language deficiencies, he'd made good use of the distraction.

He spun like a miniature tornado. Within the space of a second, several flashes of light erupted as all of the vampires guarding him were reduced to piles of ash. The look on his face when he was finished told a pained story - he did what needed to be done, but hadn't liked it. Who could blame him? All of the vamps present were supposed to be both loyal to the Draculas and impervious to control. From the look of things, both concepts had been proven to be complete fantasy.

All of that could wait, though.

For now, we had a room full of confused monsters and an open path toward the exit.

"You thinking what I'm thinking?" Ed asked.

"Yep. The bus is about to leave. Let's be on it."

* * *

Ed, Sally, and I had been through the shit-wringer enough times to know that when an opportunity presented itself, you didn't spend time gawking. Dave, being fairly new to the game and having just awoken from having his brain scrambled, was likely not to take the hint.

When I ran for it, I made a point to drag him along for the ride. Sure, he was a bit of a loose cannon, had nearly negligible ethics, and was more often than not an asshole, but he was also my buddy and one of the best game masters I'd ever known. I'd already lost one friend this day. I wasn't about to leave another behind to be judged like cattle.

The five of us made it out the doors before any of the vamps inside could react - albeit Chuck hadn't seemed in all that big of a hurry. James slammed them shut behind us and fumbled with a section of the wall.

Forgetting all sense of rank or respect, I spun and asked, "What are you doing? Those assholes are gonna be right on our..."

He pried away the wall panel, revealing a hidden keyboard beneath. A lightning fast press of buttons later, and a steel wall slid down from the ceiling, barring the doors to the Prefect's lair. Okay, that was kinda cool.

James continued pressing keys. Red emergency bulbs replaced the dim interior lighting. Klaxons began to sound throughout the floor we were on and seemingly beyond.

"What the?"

"Emergency lockdown," he replied grimly. "Let's move. We have thirty seconds before the entire facility is sealed tight enough to withstand a missile assault."

Whoa.

James wasn't fucking around, either. He must have realized who our weak link was because next, he grabbed Ed and flung him over his shoulder, much to my roommate's protests. I spared him maybe half a second of smirk before I turned to Dave.

"Don't ask questions. Just think of this as a real life game of Paranoia and the computer just told us to bug the fuck out now." I didn't know Latin for shit, but I could sure as fuck speak gamer.

That was good because those were all the words I could spare. James and Sally were already at the far end of the hall.

It was time for us to put all of our vampire speed to bear and hope it was enough.

Title Fight

We made it outside with plenty of time to spare, and by plenty, I mean Dave and I dove through the front entrance of the car wash just as a blast door rose up from the ground to seal it shut. Another half second and he would have gotten a really good primer in vampire healing as we'd both have had to wait for our legs to grow back.

Once out, James lowered Ed to the ground, then turned to Sally and me. "Calibra, did you see her?"

"No," I replied, catching my breath. I hadn't realized the main office complex was so deep underground. "But considering where Funboy there was seated, it's safe to say they were already waiting for her by the time she got there."

"Do you think they killed her?" Sally asked.

"That I cannot say," James replied. "The truth, though, is that it would be in our best interest if they had."

"Really?" I was a bit surprised at that. He'd seemed somewhat fond of her. To dismiss her as casually as...

"There is a similar panel on the other side of that door," he explained. "Calibra is one of the few others in the facility who can singlehandedly deactivate those security measures I put into place."

"Oh...well, in that case, I hope they shanked her too."

"I do not understand how he was able to take control of the facility like that," he continued, ignoring my assholish comment. "But the fact remains that he did. As Prefect, Calibra's mind is stronger than the others, her training more complete. Even so, if that creature is able to breach those defenses as he somehow did the others, then I fear many of our secrets will be laid bare. He will have intelligence at his disposal far beyond what even our ancient foes, the Alma, will have ascertained."

"Were you able to get in touch with the First?" Sally asked as I stepped over to Ed to make sure he was okay. "Maybe they can nuke this place from orbit."

"It's the only way to be sure!" Ed, Dave, and I replied in unison. Neither she nor James saw the humor in what we said. What can I say? It was either laugh or cry.

"Don't mind them. Stress tends to make them stupid."

"So I see," James replied dryly. "Sadly, no. My chambers had already been compromised and ransacked. Thankfully, most of the damage was to my material possessions - nothing critical. My personal files are all heavily encrypted. The one advantage we seem to still have," he said with a ghost of a smile, "is that our foe is likely not adept when it comes to technology."

"Hulk smash!" I chuckled, then left them to discuss things. I turned to Ed. "Now would be a good time."

"Fuck that. Twenty minutes ago would have been a good time."

"Twenty minutes ago, everything seemed hunky dory. Now, are we gonna argue about this?"

He gave his head a quick shake and began fishing around in his pocket.

"Now's probably not the time to play with yourself," Dave said.

Ed raised his other hand in an obscene gesture, then cried out, "Fuck!"

"What?"

"It's gone. I must've lost it when Ozymandias over there was playing sack of potatoes with me," he replied, referring to James by the moniker we'd first known him under.

"Goddamn it."

"What about yours?"

"Didn't survive me getting thrown into that tree back in Norfolk."

"What are you fucking idiots whining about now?" Sally spun to face us. "Did you forget to tape the latest episode of *Star Trek*? Because I swear, if it's something stupid like..."

Her voice trailed off as the hum of machinery filled the night air, followed by the scrape of metal against metal.

We turned to find the blast doors lowering back into the earth.

Oh shit. I guess that answered the question as to the fate of our missing Prefect.

* * *

I half expected a strike force to come pouring out of the opening, guns at the ready. That would have been bad. Instead, the doors lowered to reveal Chuck's lone form.

That was worse.

His stance spoke of a confidence that said we were little more than bugs to him - gnats to be swatted.

The thing about gnats, though, is they bite.

"Think fast!" It was Sally. She'd popped open that duffle bag of hers, the one she infuriatingly refused to put down, and pulled out the guns we'd stored inside. Okay, so maybe her newfound OCD wasn't entirely a bad thing.

Chuck raised an unconcerned eyebrow as she distributed the weapons. He'd seen what they could do and had come to the apparent conclusion that they weren't any more than an annoyance...either that or he was a fucking dumbass. I found myself hoping for the latter, but wasn't quite ready to put my life savings down on that bet.

Even so, the last time had just been me alone - albeit with a very high-powered handgun. The thing being, I'm an admitted suck shot. Nothing had changed in that regard except for the fact that my friends now joined me, some of whom happened to have a knack for hitting whatever they aimed at. I was fairly certain that smug grin would be erased in the few seconds between now and when his head got properly ventilated.

"Stand down," James said quietly.

Dave was still fiddling with his weapon, some sort of Uzi variant. "Bill, if you don't mind me asking - who the fuck is this guy and why is he batshit crazy?"

"Um..." I stepped between them. "Don't mind him, James. He's new. Hasn't watched the orientation video yet." I spun back to my DM. "Trust me, you really want to shut the fuck up now."

James ignored us, though. The cultist had stepped forward, his muscles rippling in the night air. Once more, these two powerhouses sized each other up. I had a feeling there would be no distractions this time. They aimed to settle this. The past versus the present with the fate of...well, actually, I had no idea what was on the line. As Sally had said, the Draculas could probably just converge on this place with all the power at their disposal and reduce it to rubble.

Of course, that assumed the Draculas knew what was going on.

But they had to. As much as I might've thought myself clever, I had little doubt Alex would eventually figure out a trophy from his head collection was missing. It wouldn't exactly take a master sleuth to deduce it had gone AWOL at the same time as me.

Of course, that brought other questions to mind, especially, what this guy was doing in Alex's boudoir to begin with. James seemed to be of the mindset that fuckers like Chuck had been toasted long ago and weren't a part of the general head prison populace.

"Whoever this guy is," Sally said, sidling up alongside me, "you may want to ask him about his workout."

"Really?"

"What? Just because he's an evil psychopath doesn't mean I can't look."

"Maybe I'll table the questions about his Pilates routine, if it's all the same to you." I lowered my voice to a bare whisper. "What's the plan?"

"The plan is to do as you are told," James said. "Do *not* interfere." He and the other vamp began to circle one another as the rest of us grouped up, weapons at the ready despite the warning.

At last, James spoke to the brute, but of course it was in fucking Latin again. Goddamnit. I caught a few words I'd heard used before, but nothing that gave me much of a clue.

"Any chance of a blow by blow, Sally?" I asked.

"Pretty safe to say that you can count me out of anything that has to do with you and the word blow."

"Not helping."

"I'll see what I can do, but I'm used to taking my sweet time with this stuff. I have a feeling these guys aren't going to talk slowly just for us."

In that, though, she was wrong.

The push of a compulsion tickled against my mind a split second before I heard it. As usual, the cultist's words were meaningless to me, but the psychic aspect instantly translated them.

"*SO THE FIRST SEND A MERE SUCKLING AGAINST ME?!*"

There was no real force behind it. This was confirmed when neither Sally nor Dave were bowled over. The asshole was actually doing it for our benefit. He wanted an audience.

I was actually impressed by the burn. I'd figured maybe this guy had been born in the days before trash talk had been invented. Guess the more things changed, the more they stayed the same.

James, sadly, wasn't interested in playing that game. His response was more of the same in that dead language that I was pretty sure nobody but priests and vamps spoke anymore.

"He's telling Muscles over there that if he surrenders now, the First might be merciful," Sally said. "Or as near as I can tell."

"Thanks."

"Don't mention it."

"I thought the First didn't have mercy," Ed said.

"I'm pretty sure it's the swift death kind of mercy," she replied.

"Oh."

"Who are the First?" Dave asked.

"Shhhhh!"

Based on the confidence the cultist showed, I was almost willing to bet that he wouldn't blink.

Thus, I was completely caught by surprise when he was the one who made the first mistake.

* * *

The two continued circling, trading more barbs - some of which we caught and some we didn't. Chuck almost certainly kept compelling for our benefit, no doubt thinking that James was an easy mark and that he'd send us on our way with a warning for the rest - your basic super villain bullshit. Jeez, you'd think folks would be able to come up with some new material after a millennium or so.

At one point in their posturing, the ox circled close to our position - his back to us. Sally's finger twitched on her gun. It seemed she was tempted to plug this guy in the most unsportsmanlike manner possible - probably a little payback for Starlight. Can't say I would have dissuaded her. However, she stayed her hand, no doubt because of James's insistence this be a solo duel.

I looked around to check out the rest of the parking lot and saw the telltale red glow of security cameras. They were tracking the two combatants. Now it made sense. James was well aware that the others could have swarmed us, but no doubt their new master had forbid it. This was some sort of stupid honor thing going on between them - may the best man win. Well, fuck that. If these guys thought I wasn't above a cheap shot to save my own ass, they were...

Just then, Chuck glanced over his shoulder at us. His eyes landed upon me and narrowed. Apparently, my previously scheduled ass beating was unfinished, as far as he was concerned. He glossed over Dave and Sally, but then his gaze lingered on Ed. For a moment, there was no recognition on his face, but that was replaced with a look of confusion. He actually turned and lifted his head to sniff the air.

How could he not...but then I realized that his attention had first been focused on me and then James at this place. He'd barely given Ed a second glance, when earlier he'd seemed focused on squashing him into paste. The reason was now obvious: Ed smelled less like himself and more like a pile of rotting Sasquatch guts.

Now, the facade was falling apart. The cultist narrowed his eyes once more. Oh, shit.

"Sally, give Ed your cell phone," I said without moving my lips - trying not to provoke our foe, as if he were some sort of stray dog.

"Why?"

"Just do..."

The words died in my throat as James became a blur of motion. Vampires have an interesting interpretation of fair duels - a very liberal one, if you will. Taking a swing at your foe when he was dumb enough to turn his back on you was considered fair game.

All things considered, I could dig that.

* * *

James wasn't dicking around either. In the split second it took to reach the cultist, his fangs and claws were bared for battle. Once more, I found myself glad not to be on the receiving end of his bad mood. The guy moved like the Flash with all the skill of Batman thrown in. Hell, if we all lived through this whole Sasquatch Apocalypse, he was my bet for vamp most likely to end up with his own comic book.

For all the musclehead's power, he was seemingly not all that when it came to actual battle. James swept his feet out from under him before he was even aware of it. He followed up with a massive elbow to the asshole's sternum, which bounced him off the pavement like a fucking basketball.

The big douche landed on his back with a heavy thud, the wind knocked out of him. It was a fatal mistake when fighting against a seasoned foe. Pity for him James was practically a ninja master - for real, maybe. I mean, the guy had spent a lot of time in Asia. Who knew what kind of badass fighting skills he'd honed over the centuries?

Judging by how things were going, we weren't going to find out in this fight. Claws at the ready, James slashed at Chuck's throat - intent on once more separating this goon's head from his freshly grown body. Hopefully, he had some of that special poison handy that kept a vamp's severed parts from instantly ashing. I for one wouldn't have minded playing a quick game of soccer with this asshole's noggin once it was all over and done with.

James's claws dug deep into the cultist's neck, drawing blood. Triumph shown in his eyes as he was about to...

Without even realizing he'd moved, I saw Chuck's hand close upon James's wrist and yank his fingers from the wound he'd created. To my surprise, the bastard was actually smiling despite half his throat being ripped open.

His arm gave the barest of twitches, followed by the sickening snap of bone. Judging from the grin he still wore, it wasn't one of his.

James gritted his teeth in pain and prepared to strike with his free hand, but it was the other vampire's turn to show off. With a quick movement of his legs, he performed a kip-up and drove his fist into his opponent's head as he rose.

It appeared to be a casual blow, but James went flying across the parking lot as if he'd been shot from a catapult.

The brute stretched, his joints cracking as if he'd just finished warming up. Before our eyes, the wounds on his throat closed until it was as if they'd never been made.

Thankfully, James was no slouch in that department either. Standing and dusting himself off, he straightened out his broken wrist and tested the fingers. Their exchange would have left me sobbing for my mom, but both of the combatants now stood facing each other whole, as if their first clash hadn't occurred at all.

"Kinda like watching Wolverine fight Deadpool," Ed muttered.

"Sabretooth," Dave corrected. "Definitely Sabretooth."

"I gotta concur," I said.

Sally eyeballed the three of us for a moment, pity in her eyes. "Goddamn, there's another one of you dorks?"

"We are legion," I replied with a smirk before turning my full attention back to where it should've been.

To my surprise, and immense relief, James's face was calm - betraying not a hint of fear.

"Tough guy," Dave commented.

"You have no idea," Sally replied.

"He will not cry, so I cry for him," I added. Raising my voice, I called out, "You okay?" Both combatants turned toward me. "Not you, asshole!"

"Way to live dangerously, Bill," Sally said, taking a step away from me.

"I am quite fine, Dr. Death," James replied curtly. "Now if you would kindly allow me to concentrate."

"Oh, sorry."

Thankfully, Chuck seemed content with letting us finish our little discourse. He didn't seem to be in a hurry - a fact that wasn't particularly reassuring.

He and James began to circle again, closer this time. My experience with actual combat training was limited, but I'd seen enough kung fu movies to conclude that their first clash had been little more than them feeling each other out - getting a sense of their opponent's power.

Considering the care with which both of them now moved, almost synchronized, I got the impression the main event was about to begin.

"Place your wagers," I muttered to nobody but myself.

All of your hope fades as the Destroyer rises.

"What the fuck was that?" Dave asked, looking around.

"Isn't there any way you can shut him up?"

Sally shrugged and gave her bag a small kick. "Sorry, haven't found the off switch yet."

I refocused on the fight. James and the Chuckster were now starting to tussle. It was like watching a sparring match. Each of the combatants threw a couple of quick blows, then feinted - no doubt in the hope of finding a weak spot.

Punches and kicks were thrown only to be blocked again and again. It was almost choreographed in its elegance. As it continued, I began to wonder whether either of the two would make a mistake on which the other could capitalize.

As it turns out, one of them did.

Unfortunately for us, this time it was James who made it.

* * *

It wasn't much, just a misstep, but Chuck's next parry sent James ever so slightly off balance. My breath caught as I hoped he would recover quickly enough.

The larger vamp stepped in and found an opening, throwing a blow to James's midsection that nearly doubled him over. He followed up with his claws, raking my friend's back and drawing blood.

Oh, crap.

James cried out in agony as his foe fell upon him, doing his best to block the attacks, but being slowly driven back.

Despite his warning to stay out of the fight, I raised the weapon I held in my hands - a submachine gun, not unlike what Kurt Russell used in *Big Trouble in Little China*. "You were not brought upon this world to get it," escaped my lips as I took aim.

"Put it down."

"What?"

"Lower it, dipshit," Sally warned.

"But..."

"James is fine."

"No, he's not, he's..."

But she was right.

It was all an act. As the one-man brute squad stepped in to deliver a haymaker, James spun and responded with a crushing kick to the side of his knee. The crunch reverberated in the night air. Ouch.

Before Chuck could hit the pavement, James grabbed his arm and tossed him over his shoulder in some kind of super-powered judo throw, cracking the pavement with his opponent's body. Double ouch.

Just like that, the tables had turned and we...

"Um, Bill..."

"Yeah?" I replied, not really paying much attention to my roommate.

"James might be fine, but I'm not so sure we are."

"What the hell are you..." And that's when I noticed the shapes shambling in our direction from out of the darkness. "You've gotta be fucking kidding me."

Dead Office Drones Walking

I will admit a small part of me was disappointed. Every single zombie movie I've ever seen has had one thing in common: when the decaying hordes of the undead attack, they do so in massive numbers. I mean, outside of the stupid trend in the past couple of years of sprinting zombies, the whole concept is that they swarm you like fire ants. Otherwise, you could easily avoid them with a brisk walk.

The three that lurched toward us weren't exactly sending chills of terror down my spine. The only thing creepy about them was their silence. No moans or growls - just step after step.

As they got closer, I could see the tattered remains of office wear. I had little doubt they were amongst the missing zombies from the Boston complex. The main question was still why were they out here feeding upon the denizens of Boston? I'd never seen them eat any...

Well, okay, I really didn't have any idea what the vamps fed them, if at all. I didn't know much about them other than they had a knack for paperwork.

"Who invited the stiffs?"

"Don't look at me," I replied to Ed. "My dance card's full."

The mystery of what these decaying assholes were doing would have to wait. We really didn't need this distraction at the moment, what with James duking it out with Paul Bunyan over there.

I strode toward the rotting assholes, intent on doing my part to keep this mess somewhat contained. "I got this."

Three shots rang out in the night, practically causing me to shit myself. Less than a second later, the zombies fell dead, or deader, to the ground - large chunks of their heads missing.

I spun back to see Sally lowering her weapon. She made a dismissive noise and turned back to the fight.

I trudged back over to where she stood. "I said I had this."

"Sorry, I needed to shoot something."

"Dude," Dave whispered, nudging me. "Your friend is..."

"Out of your league," she finished for him.

On that I couldn't disagree.

The whole exchange had taken maybe a minute, perhaps less. In that time, the battle had continued in much the same manner. James continued to frustrate Chuck with a combination of blocks and throws, each one hitting home with bone-jarring intensity. The craters littering the parking lot were testament to the power being displayed.

Both opponents were bloodied, although superficially from the looks of things - like some kind of ultra-extreme version of *Fight Club*.

Unfortunately, despite being on the receiving end of the worst of it, the big guy kept getting up - seemingly no worse for the wear.

And that's when it hit me. "He's toying with James."

"What?" Ed asked.

"The cameras. I doubt the fucking Neanderthal understands what they are, but he knows the others are inside watching. He's purposely making a show of this."

"But why? If he could win that easily, then what rea..."

Sally's head turned toward us, understanding in her eyes. "Because he's trying to send a message. He knows James is one of the First. They are the baddest of the bad. Cross them, and they will erase you without a second fucking thought."

"Thanks, we know all of that."

"Yeah, and what would you do if you came across a vamp who not only stood up to them, but took their best shots like they were nothing?"

"Oh, shit."

"'Oh, shit' is right. James needs to end this, because with each punch he throws, he's losing more and more."

The one thing he wasn't losing, though, was his hearing. I had little doubt he was following us because, just then, he upped the ante on his attacks. Claws replaced fists, one of them cutting a deep furrow into the side of his foe.

I finally began to understand what he'd been so worried about earlier, as well as maybe why some of the vamps inside were no longer compelled. Vampires were a disloyal bunch at heart. They only jumped when some bigger dog said so. This fucker was giving them a choice. Some of them were obviously taking him up on it.

That still didn't explain how he'd gotten through Boston's defenses so easily, but it did speak to the threat he represented. If even a portion of our forces decided to throw their lot in with this asshole, it could be catastrophic to us in the current war effort.

Don't get me wrong, I didn't want to see Alexander win, but I sure as shit didn't want the world overrun by Sasquatches either. I wanted...well, okay, I didn't know exactly what I wanted other than maybe D - *none of the above*.

Back on the battlefield/parking lot, James pressed the attack. He managed to get inside of his foe's defenses and sink his claws into his midsection.

All right; go, James! Show this cock-muffin that he can't fuck with...

Chuck responded by driving his head forward into his opponent's face. The crunch of the blow resounded around us. Blood sprayed from James's shattered nose and split lips. It looked like his head had almost caved in from the impact. He fell to his knees and withdrew his claws from the wound they'd opened - a wound which began to mend itself back together almost instantly.

"You both thinking what I'm thinking?" I asked, raising my weapon.

Sally flashed me a predatory smile that was both beautiful and terrifying. "Do you even need to ask, partner?"

"Let's ventilate us some asshole," Ed added.

"Do...not..." James sputtered at us, spitting out teeth.

Sally ignored him and continued to take aim. "Fuck that noise."

* * *

I was tempted to warn her about not hitting James, but that was more of an issue for me than her. How embarrassing would that be? Thankfully, she was one step ahead of me there.

"Hold your fire unless he comes at us...then feel free to blow as many holes in him as you like."

Whatever reply I may have had was drowned out by the roar of her massive handgun.

Her first shot hit the goon in the back, right in the kidneys - opening a nasty-looking hole. To my surprise, though, he barely flinched.

"Tough guy, eh?" she said and squeezed off another. This one clipped his shoulder and sent bone chips flying, resulting in at least a grunt of pain from our adversary. Meanwhile, the silver of the first bullet was working its magic. The wound cauterized from the inside out as sparks replaced the blood spraying from it.

Chuck finally turned his head toward us, his eyes black with anger. We'd gotten his attention.

"That's right, smile for mama..."

A mass of lumbering arms and legs tackled her from behind before she could finish either the quip or the shot. I jumped back, surprised as all shit since my attention had been firmly directed ahead.

There were three of them - disgusting, putrid...err, headless creatures wearing business casual. The zombies? What the fuck?!

The three of them had her face down, via their superior leverage, and were using their hands to club at her. Unfortunately, I didn't have time to process the hows and whys of this latest development. A quick glance out of the corner of my eye confirmed the cultist had bitch-slapped James to the side and was headed in our direction.

Oh, crap. I wasn't particularly looking forward to a rematch with this freak, but I didn't exactly have much choice. I stepped in front of Sally and put myself between her and Chuck. "A little help here, if you don't mind."

Ed, the crazy motherfucker that he was, didn't hesitate for a second. Dave, on the other hand, still wasn't quite with the program. Sadly for him, I didn't have time to bring him up to speed.

Fuck it.

"*HELP HER!!*"

I won't lie and say it didn't give me at least some slight amusement. I mean, hell, the guy had gleefully tortured my characters for years. Even so, I didn't want to make it a habit. Too many vamps used compulsion to impose their will upon others. I had no intention of becoming one of those dickheads.

Considering the angry moose headed my way, though, that wasn't my biggest issue right then and there.

I'd be lucky to live long enough to become a dickhead.

Applying for Dismembership

James was an honorable fellow. He no doubt wanted the vamps inside, the ones holding Calibra hostage, to see his victory as reassurance of the strength of the Draculas - a company man to the end. I didn't have any such noble aspirations. My main driving force was to continue living in the absolute least painful manner possible.

So as I faced off against an asshole who would give most superheroes cause to hesitate, I did the sensible thing: I raised my gun and emptied it point blank into him.

The weapon lacked the punch of Sally's hand cannon, but made up for it by having a magazine with a shitload more bullets - bullets that I gleefully fired at my target until I was out.

Sadly, the end result was not his immediate incineration. I was forced to conclude that either the gun didn't have enough power to punch through this asshole or I couldn't hit the side of a barn to save my life.

At least I'd staggered the meathead a little, which gave me an opening. Calling upon all the speed at my disposal, I raced forward, noting the mini geysers of sparks that began to spurt from the holes I'd riddled him with. Not being one to admire my own handiwork - much - I cocked my arm back and used the gun as makeshift brass knuckles, augmenting my blow and slamming it against his jaw.

Much to my surprise, it worked - sending the economy-sized prick flying to land on his back dazed...hopefully.

Acting quickly, lest I think better of my plan, I leapt and elongated my claws at the same time. My plan was simple: finish what James had started.

Sadly, Chuck had different plans. He got one leg beneath me as I landed and kicked out with it. I'd jumped about ten feet and flew back more than thirty, hurtling as if I were auditioning for a role as a cruise missile. I snuck a quick glance at my friends - still busy dismembering the zombies - as I flew by and then my momentum was halted by something nice and solid.

I initially thought the loud crack that sounded was my spine shattering, but then saw my friends scramble out of the way as a telephone pole came crashing down, electrical wires snapping in the process.

One of them landed on the now armless torso of one of the zombies and ignited it. The air filled with a stench that almost made Ed seem like a summer breeze by comparison.

Unfortunately, I didn't have time for further gawking. Chuck was back on his feet again. The fucker actually had the nerve to hold up his hand and gesture me onward - mocking my Bruce Lee move from the day before. What a prick.

Fine. If this asshole wanted to rumble, I was...actually, I had no idea what the fuck I was going to do. He had me outclassed in just about every single aspect, minus maybe mastery of the English language. Sadly, I didn't think a lively debate about the finer points of dangling participles would win the day.

Screw that, I wasn't sure *anything* would win the day. The entire affair had gone tits up. We needed to cut our losses and fast. James was probably going to kick my ass for doing so, but it was time to put my contingency plan into play.

I dragged myself back to my feet, feeling my body, probably now one big bruise, protest. Oh well, in several hundred years I could look forward to one of those ultra-fast healing factors. For now, though, I needed to suck it up, pretend to look unhurt, and stop wasting time on stupid distractions.

Sally was still busy stomping one of the zombies into paste. I couldn't blame her. Who'd have thought they'd pull a mind-fuck and keep moving after their brains had been splattered? Jeez, didn't any of these assholes watch *The Walking Dead*?

Ed and Dave were busy grappling with the remaining one. My newly undead friend was failing to grasp that he now had super strength - and they dared call me clueless. Oh well, he'd figure it out eventually.

I raced forward and leapt over wires so as to not end the day like a deep-fried Twinkie. "Any time you get a free moment," I shouted to my roommate, hooking a thumb toward Sally.

Nearing my foe, I took a running jump, hoping to take him high. Unfortunately for me, James had recovered and decided to take him low. The two went down in a tangle of arms and legs as I sailed over them and landed flat on my face against the cold, unforgiving asphalt. That's okay, I really didn't need pesky things like skin.

"I told you, this is my fig....oof!"

Chuck broke the hold James had upon him and brought up a knee into his stomach, doubling him over. A casual backhand sent James crashing to the ground.

It appeared that the gloves were off now. If I had to guess, I'd say the Chuckster had been toying with James, making him feel like he had a fighting chance. That in of itself scared the ever living shit out of me. Since being turned into a vamp, James had been a cornerstone, a pillar of power to be respected. To see him manhandled like that was sobering. It was like getting into a fight with some drunk at the bar, only to watch him pull open his shirt and display the S insignia underneath.

Chuck delivered another kick to James's midsection, audibly pulverizing his ribs and putting him down for the count. Then the fucker turned back toward me.

He raised his fists, threw back his head, and screamed a victory cry, doubtlessly signaling his utter triumph to the eyeballs watching. I was half expecting him to ask if we smelled what he was cooking.

He wasn't finished yet, though. His eyes settled upon me. Uh oh.

Just then, a surprised cry came from the direction of my friends. "What the fuck are you doing?"

It was Sally. Although turning my head for even an instant could be an immediate death sentence, I looked over nevertheless.

Ed, finally heeding my advice, had one hand in her pants pocket, presumably digging for her phone - while she stood there with a look somewhere between surprise and amusement.

"I didn't say to enjoy it, asshole," I shouted at him, certain that I was going to die surrounded by idiots.

Perhaps not, though.

Rather than throttling me into paste, the big goon had his hand outstretched, palm up. "*JOIN ME, BROTHER!!*"

The compulsion, like the others, had no force behind it. He was merely projecting it so that I would understand. Even so, what the fuck?

That's when it hit me. He'd obviously figured out I was the Freewill during our first meeting when his compulsion fell flat. Now here he was, triumphant. Over one of the Draculas, no less. Could there be any more complete of a victory for him? Well, aside from taking down the rest of that fun bunch - there was me.

Defeating the Freewill would be good, but cowing me would be even better.

The very thought repulsed me, but I sadly realized I probably didn't have much choice. This guy could crush me within seconds, if not less. He'd then finish off my friends at his leisure. Even Ed's faith-imbued blood wouldn't do him much good if it was smeared all over the street.

Goddamn, how I hated times like this - faced with my own personal *Kobayashi Maru*. It seemed to be far too common of an occurrence in my life as of late.

Stepping forward slowly, I gritted my teeth and sucked it up. It was the only way to buy my friends some time - damning myself to save them.

I reached the big goon and looked up at him, half expecting him to lunge forward at any moment and skin me alive. But he just stood there, arm outstretched, giving me a chance to join him.

I lifted my hand to his, knowing one thing was certain...

If given the choice between the smart thing to do and pissing off some asshole, I will *always* choose the latter.

* * *

"Psych!" I cried, lifting my hand just as they were about to touch.

His brow furrowed in annoyance, to which I added, "You got something on your face."

That something was a bullet from Sally's gun. It struck him high in the temple and snapped his head to the side. Bone fragments went flying. Even as that happened, the sound from the massive gun's report reached my ears.

As I'd approached, I'd seen Ed retrieve Sally's phone then quickly back up to let her take aim - and probably keep from getting decked. Bad luck Chuck might have power beyond anything I'd ever faced before, but I had friends - good ones I could count on.

"Yeah, asshole, how do you like..."

The words died in my throat as he turned back to me. The bullet had dug a deep furrow in his forehead. The cracked bone gleamed white in the night but, somehow, it hadn't penetrated.

Goddamn, what did it take to put this guy down for good?

My eyes went wide as I realized what that something was. Chuck stared at me, rage in his eyes. His canines elongated until they were nearly daggers. However, my full attention was on who was standing right behind him.

I had mentioned earlier that the kid gloves were off, and James had seemingly drawn the same conclusion. He appeared behind the monster, his silver combat knife - the one he'd used on the Sasquatch - raised. I smiled as he brought it down with hopefully enough momentum to filet this motherfucker.

Amazingly, the blade stopped less than an inch from its intended target.

Chuck had moved faster than I could comprehend. One moment, his hand was still outstretched toward me, and the next he'd spun to catch James by the wrist.

Before any of us could react, he yanked back - his true strength finally on display - and ripped James's arm out at the socket.

I barely even had time to register my horror at this act when the brute swung around and used the arm as a makeshift club on me. He contemptuously batted me away, then discarded it atop my prone form as he turned back, no doubt to finish this fight once and for all.

* * *

I lay there with the severed limb atop me, trying to shake the cobwebs from my head. As I regained my senses, a pained scream rent the night. It was nearly impossible to believe, but that tortured sound was coming from James.

Chuck held him up with one arm, positioning him so that he was an inhuman shield - ruining any shot Sally had. His other hand was wrist deep in James's stomach. His fingers flexed beneath the skin as he slowly tore my friend apart from the inside. Anger filled me at hearing the anguish of the man who had saved me on the night I was turned and had always treated me fairly when others had not.

First Dave, then Starlight, and now James. If I didn't stop him, Sally and Ed would surely follow. How much more would this asshole take from me before he was through?

No. I wouldn't allow it.

I gritted my teeth and forced myself to confront the impending reality of their deaths. It was too much and I began to see red.

Yes, that was it. I willed the rage to take me away. It was the only way to stop this motherfucker once and for all. He would know the true power that lurked inside of me. In the past, I had been frightened of the beast waiting to be released, certain he would kill my friends if let loose. I still wasn't entirely sure Dr. Death wouldn't, but they would certainly die without him. It was a chance I was willing - no, *had* to take.

I said a silent goodbye to the world, then gave myself wholly to the rage - closing my eyes to let it carry me away on a tidal wave of bloodlust.

A moment passed.

Then another.

Then yet another.

Nothing fucking happened, except me continuing to lie there, feeling really pissed off, with a severed limb bleeding out on me.

What the fuck?

I may have just imagined it, but it seemed my inner voice replied, *Which part about me being on vacation did you not understand?*

Fucking asshole!

Goddamnit! This shit never happened in the comic books. Wasn't the hero supposed to come to some sort of bullshit truce with his inner demons during the climactic battle?

Fuck me. Lying there and having an inner monologue with myself wouldn't do jack shit to help James.

Unfortunately, that was my trump card. I had nothing left...except...

I glanced at the arm lying atop me. Oh, the things I was willing to do to help my friends.

Grasping it, I upended the ragged end toward my mouth and used it like the most gruesome beer stein ever. I gave it a squeeze and was rewarded with a small trickle of blood, which I wasted no time in swallowing. It wasn't much, but it didn't need to be.

It hit my stomach and I immediately felt the effect, powering up to several times my normal level. I rose to my feet, feeling nearly invincible, but didn't allow myself to be fooled. I'd seen more than I needed to know that James's power wouldn't be nearly enough. But maybe that wasn't all I had at my disposal.

I just had to hope Chuck's body had expelled enough of the silver...and that he also didn't kill my ass before I got a chance to sink my teeth in. The odds certainly weren't in my favor, but were they really ever?

Launching myself at his back, I grabbed him in a choke hold with one arm. The asshole barely budged, but that was okay. He could stay where he was if that floated his boat. All I needed to do was bare my fangs and...

Be tossed over his shoulder?

Chuck dropped James's broken form and peeled me from his back like an old coat. Thankfully for me, I wasn't exactly running at my normal levels. I spun, a blur of motion, and smacked him in the face with James's severed arm - which I still clung to like it was some sort of freaky-ass talisman. It hit with a meaty thud, but aside from smearing the goon's face with gore, it didn't do much more than cause him to raise a bemused eyebrow.

Fortunately for me, I had two arms - well, two that were mine anyway. I followed up with my other, this one cocked into a fist.

I hit home with enough force to shatter cement, but all I did was turn his head a few degrees. Goddamn, this guy had a jaw built like the bulkhead of a battleship.

Okay, I had a couple of legs at my disposal, too...more specifically, a knee. I had James's strength to back me up this time - more than enough force to make this guy taste his own testicles in the back of his throat.

I kicked out with everything I had...and immediately felt the scream bubble up in my throat as my leg met his claws. My own momentum sunk them in nearly to the knuckle.

A fist to the stomach took the rest of the fight out of me, pulverizing several of my favorite organs in the process. I puked blood, not all of it James's, from the force of it and would have doubled over had his powerful hand not grasped my shoulder - forcing me to stay upright.

I was spun around and dragged roughly backward until I could feel Chuck's muscular chest pressed against me.

Uh oh. I really hoped that he wasn't about to try compelling me to squeal like a pig.

To my surprise, though, he roughly pushed my head to the side.

What the...?

Searing pain erupted from where my shoulder met my neck as sharp teeth tore apart my skin.

So that was what it felt like. I could understand why other vamps weren't too appreciative of me doing that to them.

Oh yeah, also...*Fuck!*

My only solace was in knowing this asshole would end the day curled up in a fetal ball, as if he'd just eaten a plateful of spoiled enchiladas. I was the only vampire alive who could drink another's blood and not projectile vomit his guts out.

That's when I realized what he was doing. He'd beaten James, one of the Draculas, at his own game - outfighting and overpowering him. Kicking my ass, too, wasn't much of a stretch under normal circumstances for an older vamp, but if he put me down by laying the bite on me, his victory would be complete. He'd have bested me with my own trick - even at the cost of suffering for it himself.

I tried to pry him off with my free hand, but it was no use. As strong as James's blood made me, this guy was a metric fuck-ton stronger and I was getting weaker by the moment.

In fact, it wasn't long before I began to feel woozy from loss of blood.

"Bill, get down!"

Get down? I didn't hear any music playing. Fucking raves and their drugged up teenyboppers - but not drugged up enough to want to dance with me...

"Bill!"

Wait. I gave my head a quick shake, momentarily clearing it. That was Sally. Maybe she was hoping to plug this fucker with another bullet. That'd be nice.

Sadly, I was right in the line of fire.

Oh, screw it. What was that line from *Speed* about taking the hostage out of the equation?

I couldn't believe I was doing this, but I needed her to shoot through me in the hopes of getting this asshole. I opened my mouth to tell her such, but only a choked, blood-filled gurgle escaped.

There had to be some way to signal her to go ahead and open fire. I began to wave my arms...in turn waving James's arm, which, for some reason, I was still hanging onto...

Hold on a second.

James's hand was clenched in a death grip, still holding the knife he'd tried to bisect this fucker with earlier.

It wasn't exactly a gift horse, but I wasn't about to look it in the mouth either.

As Chuck continued sucking the lifeblood out of me, I pried the cold, dead fingers open and grabbed hold of the heavy Bowie knife, silver coated for those times when one was in the mood to slice and dice the undead.

I couldn't afford the time to line up the perfect shot. He'd just block me anyway. So I raised the weapon and blindly brought it down with everything I had left.

Suck on this, dickhead.

The weapon was razor sharp and I slammed it straight into Chuck's kneecap with whatever strength I had left. Tough as he was, even he couldn't ignore that.

He released me as he threw back his head to howl in pain.

Booyah, motherfucker!

Knowing that my partner was no doubt developing an itchy trigger finger, I immediately threw myself to the ground and was rewarded by the sound of her massive handgun - the bullets splitting the air above me.

Sparing a quick look over my shoulder, I was pleased to see King Kong had multiple high caliber holes in his torso, each starting to spurt sparks.

I knew better than to lie there gawking, hoping for a shower of dust, so I slapped myself across the face to clear out the cobwebs - *ouch*. Clambering to my feet, I slowly made my way to where James lay unmoving. He was a mess, pale and bloody, but at least the ragged stump of his shoulder had scabbed over. As long as there was a body, there was still hope - however small it might be.

Thankfully, I still had enough left in me to hoist him over my shoulder, hoping that the Chuckster would at least be slowed down by the pig-sticker currently turning his leg into a Roman candle.

I lurched as fast as I could to where my friends waited, leaping over the downed wires again lest that prove to be a somewhat embarrassing end to this adventure.

Dave was the first to greet me. "Dude, that was fucking hardcore, even for Kelvin."

"Stow it," I replied, stepping past him. I laid James upon the ground and dared a look back. Chuck was still staggered, but the flames shooting from his body had started to die down. He'd be on our asses within a few seconds at most.

"James?" Sally asked, but rather than come over to us, she began rooting through her duffle bag.

"He's still alive...or undead...or whatever the fuck," I said. "Is now really the time to go searching for your comfortable shoes?"

"Don't be a dipshit your entire life," she spat back. "Bullets aren't cutting it with Superman over there. We need to bring out the big guns..."

"Ed," I snapped, ignoring her. "What's the what?"

"What are you two...?"

"They should be here any second now," he replied, Sally's phone still in his hand.

He wasn't just whistling *Dixie* out of his asshole either. Almost as if on cue, multiple flashes of light appeared from nowhere - eight in all, forming a circle of sorts around us.

"About fucking time," I muttered, only to see that Sally had stopped what she was doing to lift her gun again - prompting me to dive over and shove the barrel aside. "No!"

The lights coalesced and folded in on themselves, dying down to reveal people...no, more than people - witches.

Oh, and Tom, too.

He stood there, grinning, next to Christy. I had never been so glad to see him and the girl who'd once had a mad-on for killing me.

"The cavalry has arrived," he declared.

Christy, a bit larger than I remembered, ran forward and threw her arms around me. "Good to see you," she whispered.

"A *lot* better to see you."

"Guys," Sally warned, still a bit dumbfounded. "I think the reunion can wait."

I released Christy and turned to look, expecting the worst.

I wasn't disappointed.

A squad of vampires, all dressed in riot gear and armed to the teeth, raced out from the entrance of the car wash. For a split second, I held hope they were there to properly ventilate Chuck, but no such luck. They formed a line on either side of him and took aim at us.

"Time for the cavalry to get us the fuck out of here," I cried.

"Way ahead of you. Sisters, if you will," Christy said as she closed her eyes. The others followed suit. Light began to emanate once more from them.

With my enhanced senses, I could see the muscles on the vampire A-team's arms tense as they squeezed their triggers.

This was gonna be close.

Just then, I felt the barest of twinges in my frontal lobe. Chuck was throwing a compulsion at us...a big one. Oh, shit.

"*ACCEPT YOUR FATE AND BOW BEFORE VEH...*"

His voice, powerful as it was, receded into nothingness as the light became nearly blinding in its intensity, erasing the world around us - sights, sounds, and all.

The Aftermath of an Ass-Kicking

"How's he doing?"

"Still out, but he seems to be just resting for now. His arm is already grown back almost to the elbow."

"Amazing what a little blood will do."

"Yeah, a little blood and six hundred years' worth of enhanced healing," Sally replied, closing the door and joining me on the rooftop of my apartment building.

It had the advantage of being one of the taller structures in the neighborhood. I couldn't see Manhattan from my vantage point - just parts of Staten Island and I doubted too many people gave a fuck about that place. I could, however, see the smoke rising over the horizon, presumably originating from the heart of the city. The smell of it permeated the air, at least to one with super sensitive nostrils like mine.

We'd only been gone a day, but things had gotten worse in that time. The bits and pieces Christy's coven had shared, along with the few newscasts we had managed to pick up, painted a bleak picture.

Battle had erupted in midtown between glowing beings made of light. An entire city block downtown had collapsed in on itself and sank into the Earth. No survivors had been recovered.

And that was just Manhattan. Up in Albany, they were supposedly debating declaring a state of emergency and there were even rumors of martial law being enforced. All in all, it was a grade-A clusterfuck.

Thankfully, I'd learned that suburbia hadn't been too hard hit as of yet, being of general strategic unimportance to pretty much everyone. My parents were safe and sound for now, confirmed by a quick call after we'd arrived - in which they hadn't even questioned not hearing my voice for the last three months. Gotta love parents.

I'd managed to convince them to at least pack an emergency bag just in case, but for the time being, it sounded like they were content to watch the world fall apart via their TV.

Sally moved to stand by my side. "James is going to be pissed at us when he wakes up."

I glanced over at her, taking comfort in her presence, as well as the generous cleavage her low cut top showed. I'd missed both.

"One doesn't need to be a dismembered wizard skull to foresee that. The only question is what will tick him off most - us interfering, me eating his arm, or calling in a coven of witches to save our asses?"

"If I were a betting girl, I'd say a smidgeon of all three."

"What about you?"

"I'm a little annoyed you didn't tell me you'd invited Christy to the party. I almost blew the poor girl's head off."

I was a bit surprised to hear her voice any sort of worry at almost causing collateral damage. Something had definitely changed about her...even if just slightly. "Sorry about that. Tom, Ed, and I planned the whole thing out before you showed up. Afterwards, there were too many sensitive ears hanging around to spill the beans. Even if James didn't object..."

"Which he would have," she pointed out. "If not, though, then that Calibra bitch would have certainly had a few words to say about it."

"No doubt. So are we good?"

"I'll let it slide...this time."

"You're too generous."

"I am, aren't I?"

I smiled, letting her get the last word on the subject. She'd earned that much.

Things had been a bit hectic since our return several hours earlier. James was badly injured and Dave was completely freaked out, as were Christy's coven. Apparently, neither she nor Tom had mentioned the possibility of a vampire strike team shooting at them.

Christy and her new sisters had stuck around for a short while, helping Sally to bring some order to the general uselessness the rest of us offered. They managed to turn our apartment into a supernatural triage unit. Being that we weren't sure how James would react upon awakening, though, they'd thought it best to leave before then. They'd departed as a group - safety in numbers and all of that - with Christy reassuring us she'd be back later to help out.

As for Dave, well, Sally knocked him out cold with a compulsion. He was currently snoozing away in Ed's bedroom, at least until such time as we all had our heads on straight and could think again.

Things were far from great, but we'd at least managed to dodge a few bullets. That was better than nothing. Speaking of which...

"I forgot to ask earlier, what were you talking about back in Boston - big guns or some shit like that? Don't tell me you packed a fucking bazooka."

"Not a bazooka," she said, "but close with regards to vampire slaying."

"Holy hand grenade of Antioch?"

"I have no idea what the fuck that is."

"It's..."

"Um, Bill?" a voice called from the door. It was Tom.

"Yeah?"

"I hate to interrupt, but you guys might want to get your asses down here."

"Is something wrong with James?"

"Not quite." He ducked back in, obviously expecting us to follow.

"What's that about?"

"Who knows? Your moron of a roommate probably just forgot how to unzip his pants to take a piss."

"Thanks for the imagery."

"No problem. Don't expect me to remind him how, though."

* * *

The odor of other vampires hit me as soon as I reentered the building. Sally and I shared a glance, more curious than alarmed. That Tom had appeared on the roof in one piece went a long way toward telling us a hit squad hadn't burst in and shot up the place.

Right before I could relax, though, Sally's expression turned sour. A moment later, I realized why. I recognized the owner of one of the scents - someone I wasn't particularly fond to see, much less so in my own building.

Tom waited by the door to our apartment. Seeing us approach, he made an *after you* gesture - earning him a dirty look from Sally.

The scene awaiting us was...interesting.

"Colin," I said, entering.

"Freewill," he replied contemptuously. "Always a pleasure, my dear Sally."

He was standing in our living room, flanked by three large vamps decked out in trench coats over what looked to be body armor. Colin himself was wearing his typical expensive suit, as usual doing little to mask what a greasy fucking weasel he was. He and the vamps had adopted casual, almost bored, stances. That was in stark contrast to Ed, who stood with shotgun raised in front of my bedroom door where James lay.

"You okay, man?" I asked my roommate.

"Right as rain. This guy here, though, said he was here for James."

Sally tensed up beside me at that. I couldn't blame her. And here I'd been hoping we'd paid our last renter's insurance hike.

"Kindly call off your pet," Colin said, sniffing the air, "whatever he may be. I assure you, we're not here to fight."

"Bullshit," I replied. "Did your new master tell you to say that?"

"New master? Has your extended vacation damaged what little sense you had? I serve the same masters I always have, the glorious First Coven."

"Oh really?" Sally crossed her arms across her ample chest. "That cultist asshole took control of the entire Boston complex and everyone in it."

"By the way, what *are* you doing back on the East Coast?" Colin asked, ignoring our accusations. "I had thought you'd returned to your roots - your true calling, so to speak."

I quickly stepped in front of Sally, blocking her lest she decide to launch herself at the smarmy prick - no matter how much I might've enjoyed watching that. "Don't try to dodge the question. We know you were placed in charge right before everything went down."

"I need not dodge anything thrown by you, child. The answer is quite simple. Upon receiving back my rightful authority, I immediately assessed the situation and decided the most prudent course of action was to set up a mobile command center."

"Mobile command center?"

"Yes. I was miles away by the time I realized security had been compromised."

"So you ran like a pussy?"

"Quite the contrary. I simply proved myself smarter than any of the others tasked with the position - my successor included."

If that were really the case, I had little doubt he'd been crowing about it to anyone in a position of authority who would listen. It probably wasn't the time to bring that up, though. There were more important matters at hand. "Do you know what's happened to Calibra and the rest?"

"No. Nor does anyone else. Boston has gone dark, as have..."

"As have what?" Sally asked.

"My apologies. I forgot for one moment who I was speaking to. You need not fret about matters best left in the hands of your betters. I'm sure you understand. Speaking of which, as I informed your house pets upon my arrival, I am here for the Wanderer."

"Why?" I stepped to block the front door and crossed my arms.

The three goons reached into their coats, no doubt ready to produce a few nasty surprises at my implied threat. Ed, in response, pulled his shotgun's pump, chambering a round.

We were probably about a second away from reenacting the finale from *Blade Trinity* when Colin shook his head slightly. "Enough with this foolishness. They are no threat."

Sally opened her mouth to reply, but he held up a hand. "Before you say anything to make yourself look even more inept than usual, allow me to elaborate. You are no threat compared to that which you have unleashed."

"What do you know about Chuck?" I asked. A confused look came across his face. "I mean, the cultist."

"Under normal circumstances, I would inform you that such information was not for the ears of children with delusions of grandeur."

"But?"

He smiled broadly - a look that didn't give me a good feeling inside. "*But* the level of your incompetence this time goes beyond anything I have ever encountered before. Even I have to admit to being impressed." He pulled a sealed envelope from an inside pocket and laid it on our kitchen counter next to the phone.

"What's that?"

"A little present from me to you, so that you might understand exactly how deep of a hole you have dug yourself - how badly you have utterly botched everything for all of us."

"If I've fucked up so badly, then why are you still smiling?"

"Because whatever fate awaits me and those I serve shall be nothing compared to what you bring upon yourself." He let the statement hang in the air for a moment. The smugness emanating from him was nearly suffocating in its thickness. "Now, if you'll excuse me, I do have a timetable to maintain. Kindly produce the Wanderer."

"If you think we're gonna let you hurt him, you..."

"Hurt him?" Colin actually looked insulted for a brief moment before his eyes grew cold again. "Whatever you may think of me, Freewill - not that I care - never question my loyalty to the First. If you must know, I am here to escort the Wanderer to a secure location so he may report to his peers. More, I shall not say to the likes of you."

I shared a quick glance with my friends. Aside from Tom, who shrugged confusedly, the rest were with me. "If you think for one moment we're going to let you..."

"You are not required to *let* them do anything." The door behind Ed opened. James looked like a walking pile of shit, but he'd borrowed one of my jackets to cover up the worst of it. "I am more than capable of making my own decisions, thank you."

He took a step, stumbled, and used his remaining hand to steady himself against the wall. "It is good to see you, Colin."

The little toady immediately snapped to attention. "All glory to the First, Wanderer."

"Yes," James replied doubtfully. "All glory, indeed."

"Wanderer?"

"Uh, James," I said carefully, "you're really not in any shape to go anywhere."

GODDAMNED FREAKY MONSTERS

Despite the condition of his body, there was steel in his voice. "I will not be derelict in my duties any longer than is necessary, Dr. Death. There is much to do and much to atone for."

"What does that mean?" Sally asked, concern in her voice.

James turned to his lackey instead. "Colin, would you be so kind as to wait downstairs for me? I shan't tarry but a minute or so."

"As you wish." Colin nodded toward his goon squad, and they immediately headed for the door. He followed them, stopping just before stepping out. "We are fighting the daylight. Sunrise is imminent."

"I am well aware."

"All glory to the First," he said, then left, his footsteps heading down. I'd love to say I was sorry to see him go, but let's not kid ourselves.

After a few moments, James addressed us. "My thanks to you all. The battle was lost and I should have fallen before my foe, but even I must admit a part of me is glad of your infuriating inability to follow orders."

"It's what we do best," I replied.

"Do not push your luck."

"What now?" Sally asked before I could shove my foot further into my mouth.

James was quiet for a moment, almost as if he, for once, didn't have the answer. "I wish I knew. Due to my failings, much damage has been done - perhaps irrevocably so."

"It sucks what happened in Boston, but it's not the end of the..."

"The world, Dr. Death? It may very well be. More eyes than theirs were watching us. Have no doubt that what the cameras captured was shared as widely as possible. With Calibra under his control, the one you so disturbingly refer to as *Chuck* could easily have ordered her to broadcast our fight to every Prefecture in the western hemisphere."

Oh. I hadn't considered that. Despite knowing better, I had this nasty tendency to assume the vampire nation were a bunch of luddites - more prone to sacrificing goats to primal gods than surfing the web. What can I say? I'm a product of the pop culture that's been shoved down my throat since birth.

"I should have told you before we reached Boston," he continued. "Alas, I did not want my trepidation to show in front of those under my charge. I fear I may have also overestimated myself. Such is my hubris. My failings were twofold this day. We are a predatory species - that much you know. Weakness is neither respected nor tolerated. For a member of the First, the rock upon which our society is planted, to be humbled so is a blow to the confidence of those loyal to us."

"Dude, even Rocky lost a few," Tom added, unhelpful to the very end.

"Indeed he did." The ghost of a smile crossed James's face. "But things are not so simple. The loyal may waver, but the disloyal are those I truly fear right now."

"I'm not following," I said.

"There are many among us who are not happy with Alexander's leadership."

Sally and I shared a sidelong glance at each other, but otherwise kept our fucking mouths shut. No way were we opening *that* can of worms.

"It is not spoken of openly, but many despise the institution of the First and the coven system. They serve only out of fear - the knowledge that retribution shall be swift and brutal - not understanding that order is necessary to our continued prosperity."

"How does this cult play into that?" Sally asked.

"They represent change. That is all any vampire tired of being compelled into their duty will care about. Soon, that which was buried in our past will become known again. It is inevitable. The Cult of Ib were cruel in their tactics and narrow-minded in their acceptance of those falling outside their ideals, but their methods involved choice - freedom for us to be the monsters we were perhaps meant to be. It was their downfall in their struggle against us, their inability to work as a cohesive unit. Now, though, the lessons of the past are forgotten."

"So you're afraid vampires are going to ditch the Draculas in droves for this asshole?" Ed asked.

"I wish it were only fear." James started toward the door. I'd never seen him look so...defeated before. It was as if, in his mind, the war was already lost.

He stopped in the doorway and turned toward us. "Stay safe, my friends. These are dangerous times, more so by the minute. Dr. Death, I have no doubt the First shall call upon you soon."

He left before I could ask whether that last part was a threat or a warning.

A part of me was sure that was on purpose.

* * *

"What are you thinking?" Sally asked me once we'd shut and locked the door.

"I'm thinking I need to clean up my mess."

"At least when you make a mess, it's a spectacular one."

"Bill is a master of extreme fuck-uppery," Tom said, drawing a grin from me. I couldn't exactly deny that one. When I stepped in shit, it was often up to my neck or deeper.

Sally walked over to the corner where she'd dropped off her bag upon our arrival and retrieved it. Carrying it over to our coffee table, she unzipped it. "Well then, I guess it's time to discuss those big guns I mentioned."

"Going to lap dance Chuck to death?"

She raised an eyebrow at me as she reached into the bag. "If you fuck this one up, that may be the only option we have left." Wincing briefly, she stopped whatever she was doing long enough to extract a pair of leather gloves and put them on. "Almost forgot."

Tom, not being smart enough to keep his mouth shut, chuckled. "What, are you going to throw some nasty, crusted underwear at him?"

"Here's an idea," she replied. "Why don't you go stand way over there and I won't kill you."

The look on her face stopped his grin dead in its tracks and he immediately backed up toward our kitchen nook.

"Much better." She resumed digging through the bag, finally pulling out something long wrapped in a blanket. My eyes nearly popped out of my head as it was unfurled. She was smart to wear gloves. The three crosses on the hilt gave it away, but I would have otherwise known it anywhere.

"Is that Sheila's sword?"

"The sword of Joan of Arc," Sally said, holding it aloft. "The Icon's weapon."

"Is it..."

"Yep," she replied. "Touch it with your bare hands and get used to the idea of scratching your ass with hooks."

I stared raptly at the deadly blade. "How did you..."

"I retrieved it after the battle. Didn't seem right to let the cops just stuff it into some evidence locker."

Multiple emotions ran through me at once: sorrow, grief, regret...but I was amazed to find the one that stood out amongst them all was hope.

Upon my return, I'd pledged to take up the mantle of humanity's last defender. Now that position was needed more than ever. I'd unleashed a great evil upon the world, one that I couldn't put back in its jar. But now...

"Let me go get a pair of gloves. I need to start training with that thing right away."

"That's not what I had in..."

Ed, who had been uncharacteristically quiet since James's departure, interrupted her. "We don't have time for that, Bill. Besides, it's not yours."

"I know that, but we don't have a..."

"It belongs to Sheila. We need to give it back to her."

Silence fell upon the room. A part of me wondered whether the pressure had finally gotten to Ed and had caused him to snap.

I gritted my teeth for a moment, not wanting to say the words aloud, but it seemed nobody else was speaking up. "Sheila is dead."

"No," he said. "She's not."

The Earth-Shattering Epilogue

"You know that?" Sally asked.

I quickly turned toward her.

"I mean...how do you know that? We...uh, saw her die..."

"Are you okay?" I asked.

"Never better," she snapped. "Don't change the subject."

"Uh, yeah, what Sally said. We saw her die."

"No, you didn't." Ed walked over and took a seat on the couch. "She survived."

"But..."

"Her powers saved her," he said, refusing to meet my eyes. "All she got was the equivalent of a really hard kick to the face. She was bruised to all hell, probably had a concussion too, but she lived." He chuckled a little. "Scared the shit out of the ambulance driver, too, when she woke up."

"Whoa whoa whoa, hold on." I noticed Tom's eyes were nearly as large as mine. He had a stake in this game as well, but I waved him off for the moment. "How the fuck do you know that?"

"Because she told me."

"What?! When?"

"Maybe a week and a half after you disappeared. Thought I was seeing a ghost, that maybe whatever she'd done to me when I got bitten had turned me into that kid from the *Sixth Sense*."

"That's a fuckload better than becoming Anakin Skywalker," I mumbled, barely even aware I was doing so.

"Honestly, I'm surprised you didn't figure it out, Bill."

"How the fuck was I supposed to do that?"

"Seriously? How do you think I got my new position? People don't just walk in the door of a company and proclaim themselves the new president. There's paperwork to be filled out."

"He does have a point."

"Not helping, Sally," I growled. "I can't believe you didn't tell me, man."

"*You*?" Tom asked, jumping into the fray. "At least you were off being a dungeon bitch for the past three months. I've been here this entire time. Christy is going to fucking *freak*."

"Why do you think I didn't say anything?" Ed replied defensively. "The last time this happened, she wigged out and flash-fried your brainpan."

That gave Tom pause to consider, allowing me to resume my line of questioning. "That still doesn't answer why you didn't tell me the second I got back."

He stood up and faced me. "She asked me not to."

"What?"

"She was confused. Can you blame her? The whole thing with Remington went to complete shit in the end. She felt guilty as all fuck about what happened to you, me, Tom, Gan...even those Templar assholes."

"Gan survived, by the way," Sally said.

I turned to her. "You knew about that?"

"Of course. How else did you think I wound up with Monkhbat?"

"The bottom line is," Ed said, ignoring her, "she thought that teaming up with us had resulted in more harm than good. She wanted to disappear for a while, let the world - especially the vampires - think she was dead. That way, she could fight the good fight anonymously."

I glared at him, sure that my eyes had turned black. "Us? You mean *me*, don't you?"

"I was trying to be nice. I think she might've also been a bit freaked out by how you finished off Remington and then disappeared."

"You told her that?"

"She asked."

"Thanks," I replied sarcastically, slumping down in a chair.

"You're missing the point here, Bill," Sally said.

"Oh? And what do you know about this?"

"Um...nothing," she replied quickly. "I just swiped the sword - that's all. You and your roommates can hash this shit out amongst yourselves. I just want to point out one very important tidbit."

"What?"

"She's alive, stupid."

"I know, but..."

That's when it really hit me. Holy shit, what a fucking moron I was. I was busy arguing bullshit better left in a bad sitcom when the reality was there was only one item of importance: everything I'd blamed myself for was a load of crap. We'd set out to save Sheila from the vampire nation. For the past three months, I was certain I'd failed miserably - becoming a monster in the process. Now I was learning that I was wrong. Amazingly, we'd somehow pulled it off. She was safe. She was alive.

"She's alive," I repeated out loud - softly at first, waiting for it to sink in. And sink in it did. I bounced to my feet. A big, stupid grin covered my face despite everything. "Did you hear that? She's alive!" I threw my arms around Sally and hugged her hard, holding her tight.

"I'm the one who gave you the news," Ed complained.

"Yeah, but she's a lot softe...argh!"

Sally reached up, grabbed hold of my ear, and pried me off. "Moment's over, jackass. Besides, I wouldn't celebrate quite yet."

"Why?"

"Think about it, genius."

"What's to think about? She's fine and..."

"She's still the Icon."

"Yeah, so? And I'm still the Freewill..." Oh, fuck. "The prophecy?"

"The prophecy," she echoed.

Well, wasn't that just a wonderful bucket of ice water with which to douse my excitement.

"Uh, guys," Tom interrupted, "we might have bigger problems to worry about."

"Oh?"

"Yeah. I'm not sure even she's going to be able to put that musclehead down for good."

"What are you blathering about?" I turned to find him standing near the kitchen - leafing through several sheets of paper. Colin's envelope, all but forgotten by me in light of recent news, lay open on the counter.

"What is it?"

"It's some kind of file...like a dossier," he said.

"Holy shit. Colin ID'd him? You're telling me he figured out who Chuck is?"

"Not Chuck," Tom replied, looking over the top of the pages. "Says here, this guy's name is Vehron...known more commonly as the Destroyer."

"Vehron the Destroyer?"

"Yep...also known as Vehron the Render, Vehron the Hater of All Life, Vehron the Sun Strider, Vehron the..."

"Sun Strider?"

"It doesn't elaborate."

"Dude has a lot of aliases," Ed remarked.

"Tell me about it. Why don't I have any cool nicknames like that?"

"Oh, remember Johnny Collins from fifth grade?" Tom, asked looking up from the file.

"No."

"He used to call you Rytard. I thought that was pretty cool."

"Give me that!" Sally stomped over and yanked the pages out of his grasp. She flashed her fangs, as if daring him to object, then began reading. "It's definitely our guy. There's a crude drawing of him here, but the tattoos seem to match."

"What else does it say?"

"Oh, shit."

"What?"

"Oh, shit."

"We've already established that. Is there anything in there that we can use against this asshole?"

To my surprise, her face appeared to have turned a shade paler.

"What is it?"

"This guy has a rap sheet a mile long, Bill. Born in Germania about twenty-two hundred years ago..."

"Whoa."

"That's not the half of it. After being turned, this guy rose in rank to become one of our best generals, and not the armchair variety, either. There are battles listed here I've never even heard of, against foes I can barely pronounce."

"That's not promising."

"Oh no..."

"What now?"

"He's credited with killing at least three members of whatever passed for the Draculas back then."

"How did they..."

"It says they were all honorable duels, but who the fuck knows what that means? It gets worse, though. Before disappearing..."

"Disappearing?"

"Yeah. About fourteen hundred years ago. All records of him just ceased. It's as if he fell off the planet."

"Or into someone's closet," I mumbled.

"What was that?"

"Never mind," I replied, waving it off - feeling a chill creep down my spine.

"Anyway," she continued, "according to this section, even more honor and glory were draped upon his shoulders after..."

"After what?"

She looked up and held my gaze. "After he killed two Icons."

Now it was my turn to blanch. "Oh my God."

Silence descended once more as we digested this.

"Good job, Bill." Tom sat down next to me and clapped me on the shoulder. "Only you."

"Huh? What do you mean by that?"

"Think about it. Someone else might have grabbed any other head there: Burko the Lover of Puppies, Silas the Grower of Flowers, but not you. You somehow walked out of there carrying a guy called *the Destroyer*."

"He does have a point," Ed agreed.

"Jeez, you guys are all acting like this is somehow *my* fault." Two sets of incredulous eyes stared back. "Okay, I will admit, perhaps I have a slight responsibility here. But come on, how the fuck was I supposed to know?"

"I don't think you had a choice," Sally said flatly, her nose buried in the pages again.

"How so?"

"Fate."

"What are you blathering about?"

"The prophecy."

"What about it?"

She looked up from the papers. "I'm not sure it applies to you."

"What are you..."

"Vehron. He's not just some cultist asshole with a penchant for killing everyone. There's one last fact about him here."

She looked at us one by one, finally meeting my eyes.

"He's a Freewill."

* * *

To say Sally's revelation made my head swim was an understatement.

"Bill, are you okay?"

"I'm gonna need a moment." I leaned back and stared at the ceiling. Such an interesting pattern of swirls up there. It helped me think non-horrifying thoughts as the pieces started falling into place one by one.

That certainly explained the whole brother thing he'd been yammering about, as well as why he'd so casually put the bite on me. Chuck...err, Vehron had realized it from the start, but I didn't have a clue, having never met another of my kind before. Albeit, now that I had, I wasn't sure I ever wanted to meet one again.

Sadly, that didn't seem to be in the cards. This guy still needed to be stopped. "It's going to be harder than ever now."

"What is?" Ed asked.

"I doubt he's talking about his dick," Tom said, snapping me out of my funk.

"No, shit-for-brains. It's even worse than James thought. He was worried about this cult of assholes gaining a foothold again. But think about it. How much has been heaped on my plate because of this whole Freewill crap - even when I haven't really done anything?"

"This guy is the real deal, though," Sally rightfully, if unhelpfully, pointed out.

"Yep."

Ed's eyes opened wide as he realized what we were saying. "The vamps are going to flock to him like sheep."

"Again, yep."

"Do you think he can do everything you can?" Tom asked.

"No idea," I replied, remembering that I was currently one power short of a full set. "All I know is that he took everything we threw at him and laughed it off."

"I'm not laughing," Sally said.

"Neither am I."

"There is one good thing," Tom said offhandedly.

"What?"

"That thing Sally said about the prophecy not applying to you."

"Oh yeah, great. The Freewill shall lead our troops to victory against our enemies. Well, they wanted a leader; now they've got one." I stood up and began to pace, my mind reeling.

"Not that part."

"What are you getting at, meatsack?" Sally asked him.

"Yeah, care to clue the rest of us in?" Ed asked.

"I mean the end of it," he explained. "Doesn't it talk about Sheila kicking Bill's ass in their final battle?"

I raised an eyebrow at his somewhat liberal interpretation. "I don't think it's quite phrased that way."

"Yeah," Sally added. "The outcome is hazy, or some bullshit like that."

A grin lit up my roommate's face. "I forgot about the hazy part, but whatever the fuck. The main thing is, what if it's not *your* ass she's supposed to kick?"

For a second, my brain refused to process what he'd just said. I was used to his words often being the opposite of insightful. "You mean I might not be the one who's supposed to fight her?"

It wasn't just me, either. Sally's jaw nearly dropped to the floor as comprehension dawned in her eyes. "I hate to admit it, but shithead here actually seems to be making sense."

"It might be even better than that," Tom continued, no doubt enjoying the spotlight. "If this prophecy is so fucking noncommittal on the outcome, I'd be willing to bet it's also pretty goddamned vague, too, on whether she has any help in that final battle. Am I right?"

I turned to Sally. She knew the actual texts better than any of us, having done her homework while I'd been fucking off. She shrugged in the affirmative, even though I knew it killed her to agree with Tom on anything.

That was enough for me. It was a shitload better than sitting around feeling sorry for myself. "You may want to record this, because I doubt I'll ever say it again, but Tom, you are a fucking genius."

"This is all well and good," Ed pointed out. "But what are we going to do with it?"

"It's simple. This Vehron guy is tough, but he can't defend from all directions at once. So what say we stack the odds in her favor?"

"She hits him high, we hit him low? Could work, although it's still dangerous."

"Near suicidal," I agreed.

"Count me in. Heck, maybe I can make some water balloons out of my blood to peg this fucker with."

"Gross, but possibly effective," I replied. "That's one. Tom, it's your brainstorm."

"Fuck yeah, I'm there. I can probably get Christy's sisters to help, too, but..." A familiar look of worry settled upon his face as his own words began to sink in. Sheila was also foretold to destroy the Magi - of which Christy was a member.

"I know. Believe me when I say, I will do everything possible to make sure Decker's prophecy is total bullshit. I think Sheila will, too."

"How do you know?"

"Because..." I paused as I dredged up the memory. It was one of the few moments we'd had alone while Remington's vamps hunted us. "She didn't want to hurt anyone. In fact, she made me promise I would stop her if it ever came to that."

"Stop her?"

I drew my finger across my throat to get the point across - keeping to myself that I wasn't sure whether I could follow through with it.

Tom was quiet for a moment, probably thinking things through. "That'll have to be good enough. Besides, I don't think I'll get the same assurances from Chuck."

"Doubt it. How about you, Sally? Are you willing to throw in with a covenless loser?"

"Nope," she replied.

"*No?*"

"That's what I said. I might, however, be willing to help my second in command. That is, if you think you could handle being *my* silent partner for a change. Pandora could use some fresh blood."

"Do I get free lap dances?"

"Don't make me hurt you."

Shit. "Well, do you think they'd be willing to at least help us, then?"

"Oh, they'll help, or they'll die trying." She flashed her fangs at me, making me wonder what kind of hell she'd put her people through without me there to temper her. Oh well, that was an issue for another day.

"Deal...coven master Sally." Ugh, no way was I going to live that one down. "Now, what else do we have in our corner?"

"Maybe James, but probably not the Draculas. They're going to be gung ho to kill this Vehron guy, but not at the cost of working with the Icon. They might also be just a little peeved to learn we lied about all that crap from months ago."

"Maybe not. I met a few of the other Draculas, and they weren't too big on Alex either..." I paused as I said his name. The final piece of the puzzle teetered on the edge of falling into place.

"What is it, Bill?"

"I didn't exactly tell James the truth about where I'd found that guy's head."

"You mean it wasn't in some vampire prison?"

"Yes and no. It wasn't an official holding cell or anything like that. I found him in Alex's private quarters - his bedroom, to be exact."

"His bedroom?"

I held up a hand toward Tom. "Stop, don't even go there. He was in a locked closet...kind of a trophy case."

"Weird."

"That's not the weird part. There were others, a lot of them." I paused as I tried to digest what my subconscious was trying to tell me. "Son of a bitch!"

"What?"

Was it even possible? "I got this strange feeling looking at them all. At the time, I figured it was nothing more than being weirded out by a bunch of decapitated craniums staring back at me, but now I'm thinking..."

"Yeah?"

"What if they were all like me?"

"Doofuses?"

Sally's comment caused my roommates to chuckle, breaking the tension a bit, but I could tell she knew what I was getting at.

"Freewills," I said. "They all disappeared hundreds of years ago - just like that. Nobody seems to know why, and if anyone is asking, I haven't heard about it. But I might have a sneaking suspicion where at least some of them went."

"Alex?"

"Yep."

"How...*why* would he do that?" Ed asked.

"Who the fuck knows?"

"Power, probably," Sally said. "Remember what he told us up North, how he'd played the game, eliminated those who stood in his way? Well, who would be the biggest threat to even an ancient vampire like him?"

The answer was painfully obvious. "Someone he couldn't control."

"More like an army of super-powered someones."

"And one of them is loose now."

"Yes, and now we know where he came from. More importantly, Bill, *you* know."

"Yeah," Ed said. "And you're kind of high profile."

"Meaning?"

"Meaning, Tom or I talk and we might as well have mouthfuls of shit. We're humans...nothing to them. Sally..." He trailed off, probably not wanting to get slapped.

"I get the picture," she replied. "But our people know you, Bill. They'll listen to you, whether or not they should."

"Oh, crap," I said, sitting down. "I've just become a liability."

"Just become?" Tom was no doubt hoping for a chuckle, but he got silence instead.

All I'd wanted to do was come home and live what little of my life I could until the world tore itself apart around us. Instead, I found myself making enemies out of two of the most powerful creatures on the planet. They were going to try destroying each other, and I was smack dab in the middle.

How the hell did I find myself in these situations?

A hand on my shoulder pulled me from my funk. Sally looked down at me, smiling softly - displaying no sign of her customary snark. Her face said it all - she understood. More than that, though. We were in deep shit, but she was there for me in spite of it all.

Ed joined her, his look echoing that sentiment.

A moment later, Tom did likewise.

They didn't say anything, but maybe they didn't need to.

Goddamn, I could be such a freaking idiot.

I now realized that whatever happened, however big the odds stacked against me, they'd be there by my side. They weren't alone, either. I had allies - friends, people I loved. I'd been a fool to discount them and run off in my grief. The truth was I didn't deserve them, but they were there for me regardless of how imperfect I might be.

In the face of everything I'd seen, it was impossibly awesome to have friends like them.

I knew then, from the bottom of my unbeating heart, that I wouldn't let them down.

We had a world to save, and by God, we were gonna do our damnedest to save it - even if the odds made winning the Powerball look like a sure thing in comparison. It was both insane and near impossible, but we were going to try.

Looking at them standing there, I couldn't help but smile too.

"Are we gonna start singing Kumbaya now?" Tom asked after a moment.

"Fuck you, asshole," I replied cracking up. The others soon joined in.

The world was going to Hell around us, but we dared to laugh despite that.

THE END

Bill Ryder will return in:

Half a Prayer
(The Tome of Bill, part 6)

Can't wait for more Bill? Follow his ongoing misadventures on Facebook at
www.facebook.com/BilltheVampire

Author's Note

Welcome, dear reader, to the beginning of the end. With this installment we have marked our entry into the second half of *The Tome of Bill*. The world is rapidly going to Hell and Bill Ryder must figure out whether he wants to stop it or enjoy the rollercoaster ride for as long as it lasts. Which will he choose? Well, that would be telling.

I find myself with mixed feelings in this regards. On the one hand, I can see the end on the horizon. It's still quite distant, at least a few books away, but it's there nevertheless and I find that a bit sad. On the flip side, much like a child playing with wooden blocks, there is the fun of knocking down what I have worked so hard to build. Yeah, I'm easily amused that way.

We're probably getting ahead of ourselves, though. Let us not bury the patient before he has indeed passed on. There's still plenty of story left to tell and it's only going to get wilder from here.

Likewise there's still plenty of challenges left for me: that fine balance of being a tour guide through a deadly apocalypse - one in which there are most certainly repercussions - while still ensuring that Bill and Sally never lose that spark that keeps them trading quips.

Regardless of how things play out, the journey has been and continues to be incredibly enjoyable for me. I sincerely hope you feel the same way.

Until next time...

Rick G.

About the Author

Rick Gualtieri lives alone in central New Jersey with only his wife, three kids, and countless pets to both keep him company and constantly plot against him. When he's not busy monkey-clicking out words, he can typically be found jealously guarding his collection of vintage Transformers from all who would seek to defile them.

Defilers beware!

Rick Gualtieri is the author of:

Bill The Vampire (The Tome of Bill - 1)
Scary Dead Things (The Tome of Bill - 2)
The Mourning Woods (The Tome of Bill - 3)
Holier Than Thou (The Tome of Bill - 4)
Sunset Strip: A Tale From The Tome Of Bill
Goddamned Freaky Monsters (The Tome of Bill - 5)
Half A Prayer (The Tome of Bill - 6)
Bigfoot Hunters
The Poptart Manifesto
Meeting Misty
Necromantic

To contact Rick (with either undying praise or rude comments) please visit:

Rick's Website:
www.rickgualtieri.com

Facebook Page:
facebook.com/RickGualtieriAuthor

Twitter:
twitter.com/RickGualtieri

Bonus Chapter

Half a Prayer
The Tome of Bill, Part 6

The flimsy plywood gave way as my body slammed through it - the force of the blow more than enough to send me flying. It wasn't the hardest I'd ever been hit, but had been perfectly placed - catching me straight on the jaw. I probably could have either blocked it or stepped out of reach before it had connected, but alas I'd been too busy enjoying the expression on my soon-to-be assailant's face. What can I say? Some things just never stopped being funny.

Of course, humor was a relative concept when one found themselves in an uncontrolled thirty-foot freefall. On the upside, at least I didn't have to worry about hurting anyone other than myself. The squatters had figured out weeks ago that the main stage was best left clear of people and possessions.

There was likewise no need to fret about interrupting any dancers in the middle of a set. Tragically, it had been over a month since the last pair of tits had been flashed there to the beat of trashy music. That's when the main power had gone out for good and the denizens of Vegas had been forced to stop pretending that everything was just fine and dandy - that the weirdness of the outside world would just pass them by.

Those were thoughts for another time, though. The condition of the world as a whole wasn't my main concern right at that moment.

I landed hard on the formally mirror-polished surface - now marred by scratches, scrapes, and a body-sized crater which marked the landing place of most who dared test Sally's wrath.

Oh well, at least the ballistic glass that once covered the window looking down upon the club hadn't been replaced. That shit kinda hurt to be flung through. Thankfully custom-made, bulletproof, one-way mirrors were in short supply these days.

Even so, damn! Marlene, the previous owner of this fine establishment, had certainly constructed this place to exceed specs. When your VIP clientele were vampires, some of them centuries old and with the strength to back it up, it paid to make sure the place could withstand a beating. Whether by coincidence or design, the bomb-shelter grade durability had proven to be highly convenient as the world plunged headfirst into chaos.

"You know she doesn't like to be called that."

I pulled myself back to a sitting position and turned to find Kara's grinning face staring back at me. Tom's younger sister was cute in all the ways her brother wasn't. Unfortunately for her, he made up for that by still living in all the ways she was no longer capable of. She'd been turned into one of the undead at some point in the recent past, under circumstances that I still wasn't entirely clear on. The only part of which there was no doubt was that I sure as shit wasn't going to be the one to break it to my oldest friend that his sibling was now Sally's bloodsucking sorority sister.

"I think you'll find," I replied, stretching and feeling my vertebrae snap back into place, "that I have no problem calling our illustrious leader whatever the hell I please."

"Your funeral."

"Smart girl," Sally's voice carried down to us from the now open portal above. "Now kindly get the fuck back to work."

Kara muttered something under her breath before scampering away. It was probably a petulant dig at being ordered about. She tended to do that a lot, but Sally mostly pretended not to hear - oddly displaying an extra dollop of tolerance for her antics. Of course maybe that was just relative to what she afforded me.

"Care to rephrase your earlier statement?" Sally asked, her grinning blonde countenance peering down at me. I was so *glad* to see that clonking me seemed to help improve her mood.

A momentary temptation to nod respectfully passed through my mind, but fuck that shit. Our roles might've been reversed from back in our Village Coven days, but all that meant to me was I could give her a dose of her own medicine. "Yeah, I was thinking maybe we should just quit with the foreplay and move right on to the sex. Sound like a plan, *Lu?*"

Her eyes flashed black with annoyance. "How's this for an answer?" She ducked back in and I heard the sound of wood scraping against wood.

Maybe it was the punch or the fall, but it took me an extra second to put two and two together. By the time I did, her desk was already crashing through the remainder of the plywood and headed my way.

I rolled to the right and fell off the stage just as it landed where I'd been sitting a moment earlier - shattering into pieces and greatly widening the crater in the middle of the stage.

Some people just had no sense of humor.

* * *

I was still dusting myself off when Sally came downstairs. While there was little doubt she'd probably put on a show for all the eyeballs present, I could also tell whatever real annoyance she'd felt had already burned itself out. Had she been serious about chewing me a new asshole, she'd have just taken the express route from above - probably landing far more gracefully than I had. Instead, minutes had passed and I saw that she was taking the time to acknowledge some of the refugees as she walked by them.

As much as I wanted to make a douchey comment about that, I couldn't. Despite her iron-bitch exterior, she'd continually surprised me by showing what appeared to be genuine concern toward the welfare of most of the humans here.

Most being the operative word. It certainly didn't go unnoticed by me that some had just up and disappeared - there one day, gone the next. Usually it was troublemakers, people that the others wouldn't be sad to see leave. I wasn't quite so naïve to believe they had conveniently moved on, though. At the end of the day this was still a coven and there were vampires that needed to be fed.

Sally sure as shit hadn't reformed to the point of becoming Mother Theresa. It was just something to keep in mind.

She walked up to me and put her hands on her shapely hips. Despite the rapidly deteriorating state of the world, she somehow still managed to appear both kempt and fashionable - no doubt thanks to her personal stylist and fellow Village Coven refugee, Alfonso. Sally was only willing to go so far when it came to suffering for the cause. "Shall I assume my point has been made?"

She'd asked her question loud enough to get the attention of the room. It wasn't surprising. Since joining her in Pandora Coven, she'd continually reinforced upon me that showing any weakness wasn't an option for her. I could respect that, but it still didn't mean I cared to lie down and play dead at her whimsy.

No matter what title she held, she was still Sally to me. Thus I was opening my mouth to reply with something guaranteed to piss her off when we were saved by the proverbial bell.

"We have visitors," a voice called out. "They look official."

We both turned toward the source, Steve - her other lieutenant in the coven. He was tall, thin, and pretty much all business - definitely a yes man, but I couldn't deny he tended to get results. Needless to say, I had to listen to Sally constantly crowing about him. It would have become grating quickly had I not been certain that was exactly the reaction she was going for.

"Check them out," she called back to him.

Much like an obedient dog, he turned back toward the entrance of the club and disappeared - nary a comment being made. There's always gotta be one kiss-ass in the crowd.

I raised an eyebrow. "Vamps?"

"Or shape-shifters," she replied tersely, our little spat apparently over for now.

In the weeks prior, the few visitors we'd had could mostly be compartmentalized into two camps: things trying to kill us and those seeking protection from the things trying to kill us. The former were usually not overly subtle, but there had been a couple of near disasters - enough to make everyone a bit paranoid. The ugly rock monsters that inhabited the storm drains beneath the city - I never could remember what the fuck they were called - made for pretty good doppelgangers when they wanted to. They'd tried more than once to gain entrance that way, but had failed mainly because we weren't complete fucking idiots. No matter how human something looked, if it smelled like a pile of shit-encrusted granite, chances were it was getting blasted to hell. Pretty simple rules to live by all in all.

After a few minutes passed, and we noticed no gunfire or other such pleasantries being exchanged, we made our way to the entrance hall. Steve was just reentering the building followed by five others. Two were ours, guards. They stood flanking our guests. Even with so-called friendlies one couldn't be too safe.

I didn't need to catch their scent to conclude that the three newcomers were vamps. Most humans who came looking for sanctuary were in pretty dire straits, usually lugging the tattered remains of their belongings with them. These guys didn't look nearly that desperate, though. Decked out in their black suits and trench coats, it almost seemed they hadn't noticed the world going to Hell around them. Judging by their bored expressions, they found Armageddon about as interesting as watching moths fly into a bug zapper.

We'd gotten official visits before. The Prefect of the West Coast, a vampire named Yvonne, was known to send her representatives every so often. Sometimes they came with orders. Occasionally they came to check on how we were holding up. Rarely did they come with supplies, though.

That's what caught my eye. The two in the rear were carrying a large cargo container between them - roughly seven feet long by about three feet wide and deep. "Is it Christmas time already?"

"Could be," Sally commented by my side.

The lead vamp, sporting an overdone mustache and goatee combo that made me wonder if he was going to start bartering for our souls, stepped forward. "Coven Master Sally, I presume."

"You presume correct."

His eyes strayed in my direction for a moment, looking as if he wanted to say something, but then turned back toward her. I seemed to be getting a lot of that lately. "We have been ordered to provide safe passage to your newest charge."

"My newest charge?"

"Yes. We are delivering an assignee to your coven."

I glanced toward Sally and her eyes met mine. They asked the same question I was thinking, *what the fuck was this joker talking about?*

"I didn't realize Yvonne was in the habit of pre-stocking her covens," Sally said. "If I'd known, I'd have baked a cake."

"We are not from the Santa Clara complex."

"Oh?"

"Orders from the First Coven," he replied. "For security and safety reasons, the designee has been placed under your command."

"Security and safety?" I asked. "Whose?"

"They didn't elaborate." He produced a thick sheet of papers from his jacket and held them out. Ye gods, even in the middle of the freaking apocalypse the rulers of the vampire world loved their goddamned paperwork.

Almost as if sensing my disdain, Sally took the bundle from our visitor and passed it over to me. "My assistant will see that these are properly filed."

I took hold and promptly tossed them over my shoulder. "Filed. Can we open our present now?"

The look on the other vamp's face was priceless. Typically that sort of thing would be an instant beating at the hands of an elder, but I had little doubt these clowns knew who I was. Maybe I wasn't the prophesized flavor of the month anymore, but I still had enough of a reputation that most vamps wouldn't start shit with me if they didn't have to.

Sally, for her part, was wearing an expression that was halfway between exasperation and amusement. She liked the official bullshit about as much as I did, but still had an image to maintain. Concealing the barest of grins, she addressed the lead vamp. "Do you have anything else for me?" He shook his head. "Okay, then. Steve, kindly provide our guests with some refreshments and then show them the fuck out."

Needless to say, her skills as a hostess had been somewhat strained these past several weeks.

Steve, being a far better subordinate than me, nodded for our guests to follow him inside - most likely to the bar. There was no point in ticking off the Draculas over something as silly as not offering their lackeys a little hospitality.

The two holding the crate let go unceremoniously and it landed with a heavy thud. A muffled curse sounded from within.

My eyebrows shot up at the seemingly familiar cadence. Nah, it couldn't be.

I held my tongue until the undead delivery boys left the room, leaving Sally and me alone with the package. "Did that sound like..."

"Only one way to find out." She stepped up to the crate, extended her claws, and shoved them under the lid. Being a vampire meant never needing to keep a crowbar handy. One quick heave later and the nails holding the top shut squealed against the wood as they gave way to her strength.

The cover clattered to the floor and we found a very familiar face staring angrily back at us from within.

"It's about fucking time. I couldn't breathe in this thing."

Smiling broadly, I offered a hand to help our newest *recruit* out. My eyes glanced toward Sally and I asked, "So what do you think? Return to sender?"

"Nah," she replied, a wicked grin forming on her face. "I think this one has possibilities."

* * *

Half a Prayer

Coming Soon

17919505R00303

Made in the USA
Middletown, DE
15 February 2015